postcards
from no man's land

Aidan Chambers

Definitions

ALL WRITING IS MEMORY

Also by Aidan Chambers

The Dance Sequence

BREAKTIME

DANCE ON MY GRAVE

NOW I KNOW

THE TOLL BRIDGE

POSTCARDS FROM NO MAN'S LAND

THIS IS ALL: THE PILLOW BOOK OF CORDELIA KENN

POSTCARDS FROM NO MAN'S LAND
A DEFINITIONS BOOK 9781862307766

First published in Great Britain by The Bodley Head Children's Books,
an imprint of Random House Children's Books

The Bodley Head edition published 1999
Red Fox edition published 2001
Definitions edition with Afterword published 2007

Copyright © Aidan Chambers, 1999, 2007

The right of Aidan Chambers to be identified as the author of this work has been
asserted in accordance with the Copyright, Designs and Patents Act 1988.

Definitions are published by Random House Children's Books,
61–63 Uxbridge Road, London W5 5SA,
A Random House Group Company

Addresses for companies within The Random House Group Limited
can be found at: www.randomhouse.co.uk/offices.htm

THE RANDOM HOUSE GROUP Limited Reg. No. 954009
www.kidsatrandomhouse.co.uk
www.aidanchambers.co.uk

A CIP catalogue record for this book is available from the British Library.

Printed and bound in Great Britain by Cox and Wyman Ltd, Reading, Berkshire

POSTCARD
Amsterdam is an old city
occupied by the young.
Sarah Todd

Not knowing his way around, he set off back the way he had
come. But changed his mind about picking up a tram to the
railway station, not yet ready to return to Haarlem, and
kept on walking along the canal, the Prinsengracht, still too
jangled by what he had just seen to notice where he was and
too preoccupied to wonder where he was going.

Ten minutes or so later he came to when a tram clanged
across his path. Suddenly he wanted to be in a crowd,
wanted to feel the push and press of people, wanted noise
and bustle and distraction, wanted to be taken out of
himself—the past twenty-four hours had been a ruffle—
wanted something to drink, wanted to sit and drink it at a
touristy on-street table while watching the goings-on of
passers-by. And, though he could not admit it to himself at
the time, wanted an adventure.

His skin prickled and he shivered, not knowing why, for
though the day was overcast with a threat of rain, the mid-
September temperature was mild and he was sweating
slightly in his anorak, which he wished he hadn't worn, but
its ample pockets were useful for carrying money and
addresses, phrase book, street map, and such stuff as he
needed or might pick up on a day out on his own in a
foreign country.

Choosing to turn right across the bridge over the canal,
he soon found himself in a bulge of open space, dominated

1

by the bulky frontage of a theatre, in to which many streets and tramways flowed. Leidseplein. To one side of the theatre, facing in to the rest of the plein like an auditorium facing a stage, was a mini-square crammed with tables served by waiters who fluttered in and out of canopied cafés like birds from nesting boxes.

He chose a table on the edge nearest the theatre, three rows in, and sat and waited.

And waited. But no one came. What should he do? You're the bloody customer, their job to serve you, don't be such a wimp, assert yourself. His father talking. Shyness, his strangulating shyness, kept him quiet. So he did nothing, but didn't mind, there being plenty to look at. Accompanied by incidental music from a trio in the middle of the plein, two butch boys about his own age, one white on fiddle, one Afro black on tin whistle, and a plump girl, eye-catching centrepiece squatting on an upturned litterbin, going rampant with a pair of bongos, long blonde hair flying, eyes closed, tanned arms deliciously bare, rapping hands a blur, roly-poly breasts alive in tight black tank-top, white Lycra'd heavy-duty thighs gripping the little battered drums he suddenly envisioned as the willing cheeks of someone's bum. His own perhaps. Hello, where did that come from? Never a hint before, not of himself anyway.

He shifted in his seat and smiled secretly. The pleasure of self-discovery.

I wait for a waiter but no waiter waits for me, he dittied under his breath to the rhythm of the bongos. Until a slim leather-clad arm obtruded a languid finger across his view. A girl's face smiling down at him, questioning, more stunning than she of the cheeky drums. Cottoning on that she was indicating the unoccupied seat beside him, he scrunched up to allow her to squeeze deliciously by, trailing the tantalising smell of worn leather and warm jeans.

She sat, easing her proportionately long legs (for she was not tall) under the cramped little table, where they grazed

2

his on the way to arranging themselves. More, more, his inner voice pleaded. Ruffled black short-cut hair gave her a boyish look; pale complexion without make-up; loose black leather half-jacket over white T-shirt; trim black jeans.

She smiled a thank-you. 'British?'

'English.'

'I understand. I like it that I'm Dutch.'

He shrugged an excuse for his pedantic affliction that some (his father and his sister Penelope aka Poppy) denounced as the tic of a literal-minded bore, and added, 'Just meant I'm not Welsh or Irish or Scottish.'

'And I'm glad I'm not Frisian or Flemish. Not that I'm against them, only . . .' A glance at the table. 'Served yet?'

'No.'

She looked behind them, this way, that. Raised a lazy long-fingered hand, the sensuousness of which to a hand fancier like him was enough to induce sexual trauma. Her ease daunted his shaky confidence but notched up his desire. There was also something puzzling about her, a difference from the usual he couldn't quite locate.

'On holidays?' she asked, holidays sounded as holid*aysh*. Impediment or something imported from her Dutch? Whichever, he liked it.

'Sort of,' he lied, not wanting to go in to the whole complicated story.

'Okay to talk?'

There was a deep note in her voice that added enticement.

'Sure. Fine.'

A waiter arrived to whom she spoke Dutch.

Then the waiter to him: '*Meneer?*'

'Just a cola, thanks.'

'Not a beer?' she said. 'Try a good Dutch beer.'

He avoided it usually, but when in Rome. 'Okay, a beer.'

'Trappist?' he thought the waiter said, but supposed that couldn't be right.

3

She nodded and off the waiter went.

Suddenly he felt like a nerd sitting there beside her, coddled in his anorak, so stood up, took it off, draped it over the back of his chair. And now his leg nudged hers as he settled himself again. Dare he? Would she? Picking up girls wasn't his style. Not for want of wanting to, but from fear of rejection. And dislike of what he thought of as the sex-hunt, a blood sport the brutishness of which, when he observed others at it in full-blown lust, offended him. A fastidiousness his father scorned as further evidence of his wimpishness.

He so much wanted to look at her that, nervous of giving anything away, he forced himself to stare across the plein— the bongo trio were packing up—at the modern ads and familiar international icons, Burger King, Pepsi, Heineken, that adorned/polluted the old high-peaked Dutch facades.

She rescued him by asking, 'First time in Holland?', which allowed him to turn his gaze on to her again.

'Yes. Arrived yesterday.'

'You like it here? Holland, I mean, not *here*,' she dismissed the plein with a nod. 'A tourist trap, to tell the truth.'

'You're not a tourist.'

A wincing smile. 'No. Just—what's the English?— passing over?—and wanted a drink.'

'Passing by. Passing over would mean that you're dying.'

Now a deep ironic chuckle. 'Not yet, I hope.'

'Look alive enough to me.'

She pantomimed relief. 'Thank god!' And held out a hand. 'I'm Ton, by the way.'

'Jack,' he said, enjoying the brief contact, not at all an English shake: quicker, no grip, a kiss of hands rather than a hug.

'Jacques?'

'If you want.'

'I like Jacques.'

4

The waiter returned and unloaded two big mammary glasses of chestnut-brown beer. Jacob twisted in his seat to get money from his anorak, but by the time he'd managed to unzip the safety pocket, extract his wallet, and fish out a note, Ton had paid and the waiter was gone.

'Look, I can't let you do that,' he protested with no great conviction, because he rather liked it that she was paying and because it meant he owed her one (he ignored the pun) and the meeting would be prolonged by his buying another.

'Your first time here. Be my guest.'

'But . . .'

'Your turn next time.'

So there'd be a next time. 'Well . . .' He slipped his wallet back in to its pocket and held up his glass. 'Thanks.'

'*Proost.*'

'Prost,' he mimicked.

They drank.

'Like it?'

'Pretty strong! Is it really called Trappist?'

'Sure. Made by monks. Got to be pure, eh?'

They laughed.

'You're here with someone?'

'On my own.'

'And staying in a hotel?'

'No. With some people near Haarlem.'

'Nice for you,' Ton said, 'perhaps?'

'Yes,' Jacob lied and, not wanting to go in to the subject, took another slurp of the thick beer he was finding even less to his taste than any he'd tried before. Already he could feel it curdling his stomach. Ton was downing hers in long swallows.

She said, 'You know your way around Amsterdam?'

'No. Haven't a clue where I am now, to be honest.'

'You've a map?'

'Sure.'

'I'll show you.'

5

For the next few minutes Ton orientated him, tried to explain the tram system, marked with Jacob's pen the location of places she thought he might like to see.

'Think of the old town as half a spider's web, with the railway station at the centre,' she said, 'the canals being the half circles, you see, and the streets across them the—strings?—'

'Threads?'

'Threads that connect them.'

'Looks more like a maze to me.'

'Yes, perhaps that too.'

'Easy to get trapped in one and lost in the other.'

Studying the map had brought them head to head, bodies touching shoulder to shoulder. Ton gave him a gentle nudge and, her teasing smile only a fist away, said, 'You're a pessimist, Jacques.'

He smiled back, held by her green eyes, and very much wanting to kiss her wide mouth, but only said, 'Typically female to think of a spider's web and typically male to think of a maze, wouldn't you say?'

'Oh! You—' She lowered her face to the map again.

'What?'

'Nothing.'

He waited for her to go on, puzzled by her reaction.

'Must go soon,' she said, shifting away.

'Really? Sorry about that.'

She drained the remains of her beer. 'No, I must.'

He said, all in a rush, 'Could we meet again? I mean—would you like to?'

Looking at him deadpan, she said, 'Are you sure?'

'I'm sure. What about you?'

She smiled again, but the corners of her mouth turned down. 'I'll give you my phone number. Call if you still want to sometime.' She searched in a pocket, brought out a book of matches and took up his pen from the table. While she wrote he folded the map—why is it always such a test to

6

refold a new street map the way it's meant to be?—and stuffed it in to the anorak's marsupial pouch.

As he turned back, Ton took his hand and, holding it firmly under the table, said, her face square and close, 'I'd like to see you again. Show you some places tourists never go. I mean this. But you know—such a brief meeting. You might decide you made a mistake.'

'No, I—'

Two simultaneous actions silenced him. Ton's lips placing fleetingly on his the ghost of a kiss. And her hand pressing his hand deep in to her crotch, where he felt the swell of a compact set of penis and balls.

In the ensuing daze he was aware of Ton standing up, saying 'My tram', of himself standing up to allow her (him) to squeeze by, of her (him) saying what sounded like '*Good thingsh*', and of her (him) slipping away through the crowd and climbing in to a tram, and of her (him) waving through a window as the tram door closed, its bell tringalinged, and it moved off. Only then did he find his voice again and as he raised an impotent hand heard himself call out, 'Hey, you took my pen!'

You took my pen? He looked down at the table and saw that indeed she (he) had. But lying beside her (his) empty glass was a book of matches. His actions still running ahead of his thoughts, he picked up the book, turned it over, front, back. Nothing. Was about to lift the flap when the edge of his chair rammed in to the back of his knees and he collapsed on to his seat. Turning instinctively, he saw his anorak flying past his face, clutched in the hand of a scrawny youth, the bright red of whose reversed baseball cap mapped his path like a beacon as he dodged through the crowd.

Letting out a yell, 'Hey, that's mine! Come back!', he struggled to his feet, stumbled away from the table, sending beer glasses shattering to the ground as he set off after the thief. Who, pausing in the middle of the plein, stood on the

7

upturned litterbin earlier occupied by the bongo player, where he remained, with a blatant grinning cheek that inflamed Jacob's rage, for long enough to be sure that his victim had spotted him. It was as if he wanted to be chased. 'Stop him!' Jacob shouted, pointing as he careered through the crowd, but people only gave him startled glances and did what they could to get out of his way.

As soon as Jacob was three or four metres from him, the thief was off again, this time making for a corner of the plein that led in to a narrow street full of bars and cafés and touristy shops. So fleet was Red Cap and so obviously practised that he easily put distance between himself and Jacob, who was only a few strides down the street when his quarry swerved left. Arriving there, Jacob saw him standing twenty metres away at the other end of an alley, holding up the anorak, leaving no doubt he was waiting for Jacob to catch up, before setting off again, along another narrow street parallel with the first.

And so the chase continued: right at the end of this second street, where it joined a canal, up to the top of the canal, left across a bridge and half-left down a narrow street of houses, left and right again, and then left in to a busy wide shopping street with trams running down the middle. On went Red Cap, agile as a whippet, Jacob now hampered by a stitch and beginning to lose breath. At a bridge over a major canal Red Cap sprinted across the road and along one more block before swinging right in to another narrow street, this one mostly of houses with here and there a small shop or art gallery, a longish stretch with few people or vehicles to inhibit Jacob's progress. Feeling there wasn't much left in him, he put on a desperate last-try sprint, almost catching his quarry by the time they reached the end of the street. But Red Cap bobbed to the right along yet another canal and with dispiriting ease accelerated away.

Out of puff and out of heart, Jacob couldn't help himself, but clung to a canalside tree, while catching his breath and watching in tear-jerking anger as Red Cap paused long enough on a humpback bridge a hundred metres away to look back and wave a perky farewell before disappearing down, oh god yes, another canal that intersected this one by which Jacob was panting. Red Cap had certainly all along been leading him a fool's dance. But why? It made no sense.

Sour beer rose in his gullet and emptied itself in to the canal. He thanked heaven there was no one about to witness his humiliation. The canal was deserted. But no one to ask where he was, either.

Rain now began to fall in a limp and dreary fashion. He welcomed it as a face douche and mouth wash. Then realised that, dressed only in sweat-shirt and jeans, he would be soaked before long. Nor could he see anywhere to shelter except for a strange-looking wooden building, the Kort, a restaurant?, in a large open space on the other side of the water, and he could guess how he would be received there without money and in his present gungy condition.

What to do? Not having a clue where he was, he didn't know which way to turn.

His stomach clenched in a fit of minor panic.

His nature, when caught in a fix, being to do something rather than nothing, and to go on not back, he took a deep breath, swallowed hard, belched and trudged off to the intersecting canal. Which, to judge by its width compared with the one he had just left and the larger imposing houses on both sides, must be one of the main waterways. He looked for a sign and found it on the corner building between the first and second floors: Prinsengracht.

Yes!

In the whole of Holland, never mind Amsterdam, there was only one address he knew by heart: 263 Prinsengracht. The house where Anne Frank and her family hid from the Nazis in the secret annexe during the Second World War, the house where she wrote her famous *Diary*, one of his favourite books, the house which was no longer a house but a museum, and the house from which earlier that morning he had fled in distress at what he had found there.

Even in his fuddled state he knew that if he walked the right way along the canal he would reach 263, where perhaps the staff would help him. Or a visitor. There had been plenty while he was there, mostly back-packing youths about his own age and English-speaking. He had had to wait in a long queue before he could get in.

His stomach unclenched.

The corner house was unnumbered, the next was 1045, the one along from that 1043. The right direction. He walked on at a brisk pace. But the rain was seriously wet now, he'd be drenched before reaching 263. Maybe it wouldn't last long, and he could do with a rest, if only there was somewhere to shelter. He could find nowhere that would do till quite soon he reached a house, the entrance of which was in a portico, a steep flight of six stone steps leading up to a hefty wooden door. At least he could sit there protected from the rain.

Having turned round on the top step a couple of times, like a Jurassic dog inspecting his bolt-hole, and seated himself, and dried his hair with his handkerchief to stop water draining down his neck, and draped it on the door-handle to dry, he wondered whether anything else was in his jeans pockets that might prove useful. No money for sure; all he'd had was in the anorak. A comb in his back pocket, as usual. He gave his hair a going-through before returning it. Nothing right front, where his hanky had been. Left front: the book of matches. Quite forgotten. Couldn't even remember putting it there.

He examined it again. Nothing on the outside. Flipped the flap. Inside, not the expected parade of cardboard matches, but a circle of crumpled pink plastic poking from a pocket where the matches would have been. He had slipped the object from its pouch before he realised he was holding

10

a condom. Only then did he also take in what Ton had scrawled in a spidery hand on the inside flap: a row of telephone figures under which were the words:

BE READY
NIETS IN
AMSTERDAM
IS WAT
HET LIJKT

GEERTRUI

Parachutes falling like confetti from a clear blue sky. My most vivid memory of his arrival.

Sunday 17 September 1944.

'Good flying weather,' Father had said. 'We must expect more raids.'

All week British aeroplanes had bombed nearby. The railway line at Arnhem had been sabotaged by the Resistance and on Saturday the German authorities announced that if the culprits did not give themselves up by twelve o'clock on Sunday a number of our people would be shot. Everyone was very tense, now hopeful, now despondent. We knew the Allies had reached the Dutch border. Surely, people said, they will be here soon. But German soldiers were on the move all the time and more of them than ever were billeted in our village.

'Are you ready to sacrifice everything for the sake of your freedom?' *De Zwarte Omroep*, our underground news-paper, had asked and told us: 'Keep a bag ready with some underwear, some food, and your valuables.' Mother had sewn money into our clothes. Father had instructed me in what to do if the worst came to the worst and we were separated. He meant, of course, what to do if he was killed.

I had just had my nineteenth bithday, and that Sunday morning should have been at church with my parents. But my brother Henk and his friend Dirk Wesseling were in hiding in the country with Dirk's family on their farm because they did not want to be sent to the German labour camps, where many of our young men had been forced to

12

go. I was anxious about him. So early that morning took the risk, despite Father's warning, and bicycled to Dirk's farm from our home in Oosterbeek.

I was on my way back when I heard the planes and saw the parachutes. 'Oh look!' I called out, though there was nobody to hear me. 'Look! How beautiful!' And then I raced for home, saying to myself over and over again, 'The Tommies have come! The Tommies have come! Liberation! Liberation!'

Father had been right. There had been more bombing while I was away. This time on the railway line near home. Windows were shattered in the houses near the railway dyke. And a Spitfire had strafed the German anti-aircraft guns in the meadow, killing some of the soldiers and wounding others. By the time I reached our street, the Germans were lined up waiting to leave. Trucks were already taking some of them away as I arrived at our house, where Father was fretting for me, sure I must have been killed. Mama, calm as ever, was busy carrying food into the cellar. But I knew she was not as calm as she appeared because between each trip she paused at the top of the cellar stairs and vigorously cleaned her spectacles. She always did that when she was excited. I stopped by her on my way down with an armful of blankets, and gave her a kiss. 'Four years,' she said, 'four years I have waited for this day.' I admired my mother and loved her dearly, and never more than at that moment, which, as things turned out, was the last quiet time we had together until it was all over many weeks later.

I was coming up from the cellar two or three trips after that when I heard a German soldier running by, shouting, *'Die Engländer, die Engländer!'* I wanted to go out and see but Papa said no, frightened soldiers were the most dangerous of all, we must wait inside. We huddled together in the hall behind the front door, the three of us, Mama, Father and myself, but did not have long to wait before we heard

13

men going by in the direction of Arnhem and the sound of voices that were neither German nor Dutch. So many times we had sat round the radio, secretly listening to the news on the BBC. Papa and I had even practised our English on each other to be sure we would understand as much as possible when the liberators finally arrived. Yet now suddenly to hear English spoken right outside our own front door was a shock. Not that we could make out what was being said. But we knew from the sound, so different from German and Dutch. Papa whispered to me in English, 'Music to my ears!'—one of a list of 'familiar sayings' we had used in our practice. We giggled together like small children before a long-awaited party. 'You two!' said Mother. 'Behave yourselves!' Mother had been a school teacher and was always very proper, even when we were on our own. But it was also a game; she liked to pretend Papa and I were naughty children.

At that moment there was a burst of gunfire, a thud against our door as if a couple of sacks of potatoes had been thrown against it, and then silence. We three clung to each other. Nothing happened for an age. Then we heard a man's voice. What he said was such a shock, I still remember his words exactly. 'By Christ, Jacko, I can't hardly spit for thirst.' He was so close up against our door that we all jumped. It took a moment or two for the words to sink in, but when they did, I ran to the kitchen, drew a jug of water, grabbed a glass, and ran back to the door. 'Be careful, be careful,' Mother was muttering. Papa held me back, and himself cautiously opened the door a crack and peered through. When he saw that two English soldiers were standing there, he threw the door wide open and held out his arms in welcome. But instead of saying anything, we three found ourselves tongue-tied. The soldiers were as startled by our door opening as we were by their arrival. They swung round, guns at the ready. But when they saw Father with his arms held out, Mother behind us with her stern but smiling face, and me grinning stupidly, with a jug of water in one hand and a glass in the other, the one who had spoken before said, 'Blimey, that's what I call service!'

At which, Father found his voice and said in his very best English, 'Welcome to Holland. Welcome to Oosterbeek. Welcome to our home.'

We laughed and there was hand-shaking all round, except for me, with my hands full. So I filled the glass and when the formalities were over, gave it to the soldier who had not yet spoken, who now said, 'Thanks, miss, you're an angel of mercy.' He had eyes that made me melt. While they drank we exchanged names. Theirs were Max Cordwell and Jacob Todd.

By this time doors had opened all along the street and people had come outside, bearing flowers and food and drink, and waving orange ribbons, and even some with Dutch flags, which were strictly *verboten* by the Germans. There was kissing and hugging too.

When they had drunk, the soldiers asked how far it was to Arnhem. 'Five kilometres,' Father told them. As he spoke a Jeep drew up, and an officer stood up and shouted an order. 'Sorry, got to go, sir,' said Max. '*Veel succes*,' said Father, forgetting his English. '*Succes!*' Mother repeated. 'Goodbye, miss,' said Jacob. 'Thanks for the water.'

As they turned to leave us, a member of our air-raid precaution volunteers came striding down the street, shouting, 'Go inside, everybody! Go inside! It is still dangerous.'

The soldiers moved off. Father closed our door. Mother started polishing her spectacles more vigorously than I had ever seen her polish them before. And I realised only then that I had not uttered a word. 'Oh Papa,' I said, not knowing whether to laugh or cry; 'I didn't even say *hallo*!' Father and Mother looked at me as if I had gone mad. Then Father broke into gales of laughter, and Mother put her arms around us, and swirled us round and round, saying, '*Vrij, vrij, vrij,* free, free, free!', till we were too giddy to stand. I don't think I have ever felt so light-headed, before or since.

All this I remember with such perfect clarity, it makes my eyes water even now.

The next day, Monday, many more British soldiers arrived by parachute and glider. We watched the aeroplanes as they flew over Wolfheze. And as the day before, red, white, brown, green and blue parachutes filled the sky. A thrilling sight.

But by then some of the soldiers who had passed by on Sunday had come back, tired and dirty, and placed artillery guns in the meadow near the church, which they were firing all the time towards Arnhem. Mother made sandwiches, which we took to them, because they had so little food. They were very happy to see what they called 'the second wave' bringing in fresh comrades and supplies. 'We'll be okay now,' they said, 'soon have the Hun on the run!' They explained that their orders were to capture the bridge at Arnhem so that the main army, which was coming up from Nijmegen, could cross the river and cut off the German army occupying Holland. It would help to end the war very soon, they said. They were cheerful and made jokes, teasing each other, and me too, and flirted after the sandwiches. So different from the Germans. But of course we were glad to see them, and that makes a difference. It was such a relief, no one minded that our electricity and gas had been cut off and that our lovely old village was being battered by bombs and shells. 'The price of freedom,' said Papa. He was restless, wanting to help but not knowing how. The air-raid precaution volunteers kept warning us to be careful and stay inside. It was too soon yet to be sure we were safe. German soldiers were in the countryside north of the village, where some fighting was going on. And the Resistance reported heavy fighting round the Arnhem bridge.

In the evening a neighbour told us that the Hotel Schoonoord on the Utrechtseweg, at the corner of the main crossroad in the village—one of our best hotels until the Germans commandeered it for themselves—was being prepared as a hospital for wounded British soldiers, and volunteers were needed to help. Already casualties were arriving. I wanted to go, but Papa said no. Nowadays, I suppose, I would not have asked, but then life was different. A girl in her teens did as she was told by her parents, and though I pleaded, Papa flatly refused. Since the night before he had not been as optimistic as Mama and me.

'Why have the soldiers returned?' he asked now. 'Why have they set up guns in the meadow? Why are they firing them all the time? And why do they need to turn a hotel into a hospital, if the army will be here from the south tomorrow, as the gunners say? Why is all this happening if everything is going well?'

'You know a battle is not a nice neat game you can plan down to the last detail,' Mama told him. 'It's a messy business and unpredictable, it ebbs and flows, and people get hurt.'

'That may be so,' said Father, 'but until we know who is ebbing and who is flowing and which part of the beach our house is on, our daughter is staying with us at home.'

Wasn't it bad enough, he went on, that their son was out there somewhere, alive or dead no one knew, without allowing their only daughter to risk her life also? Did Mother want them to have a childless old age? Who would look after them then?

When Father was in such a determined and pessimistic mood Mother knew better than to oppose him. So at home I stayed with only Sooji, my childhood teddybear, to nurse while I watched the soldiers from my bedroom window. Every time one of their guns went off, the blast shook our house, rattling the windows and making the dust fly.

That night, for the second time, we slept with our

clothes on—or tried to sleep. The sound of fighting seemed to be all around us. And after a while more troops, along with jeeps and even trucks with caterpillar tracks, went by the bottom of our street.

By six o'clock on Tuesday morning there was a lot of noise. Soldiers from the guns came for water, and warned us that the Germans would probably start firing back, so we should be careful. They were right. Shells started exploding in the meadow and even near us soon afterwards. For the first time we sheltered in the cellar. The attack did not last long, but it dampened even Mama's confidence a little.

But we had no time to brood. Almost as soon as the shelling stopped we heard a commotion upstairs. When we got there we found two soldiers in our front room holding a third man between them who was bleeding badly from a wound in his side. It was a shock to see these three men, who seemed to fill the room, in their dirt-covered battle-dress and bulky packs of equipment and clattering weapons, standing in their big muddy boots among our best furniture, and one of them dripping blood everywhere.

Somehow, I suppose, till that moment, the war, the fighting, had been outside, separate from us. Now suddenly it was happening right inside our home. Papa and I stared at them from the doorway as if turned to stone by the sight. But not Mother. She was always good in a crisis. It brought out the best in her. I once saw her round on a German officer who was inspecting our house to see if it was suitable as a billet for himself, and give him such a fierce dressing down, as if he were a naughty schoolboy, for daring to cross our threshold without cleaning his boots and removing his cap, that he decided not to honour us with his presence, but sent his corporal instead, who soon ended up living in our garden shed, saying he was more comfortable there rather than having to face Mother's disdain every day. Now she did not hesitate one second.

18

'Geertrui,' she said, 'bring warm water and disinfectant.' And to Father, 'Barend, bring the first-aid box.' As she spoke she was arranging the cushions on the sofa and, as she had very little English, was saying *'Komen, komen,'* and motioning to the soldiers to lay their comrade down.

When I returned with the water, they had removed all the gear and outer clothing from the wounded man, who was lying on the sofa, grimacing in great pain. Mother was kneeling by his side, inspecting the wound. Father had brought the first-aid box and was busy removing the man's boots. The poor boy was no older than my brother Henk, his face was smudged with dirt and sweat, but even so I could see he looked deathly pale. His friends were talking quietly to him, trying to be cheerful, telling him he'd be fine now. One of them lit a cigarette, and held it to his mouth so he could smoke it without using his hands. He was trying to smile, but there was fear in his eyes, and he kept flinching as Mother tended him. The wound was terrible.

In the four years of our occupation, I had seen wounded soldiers only after the recent air raids, and then always at a distance. This was the first time close to. And what was more, close to in our own home, our reception room, where until now there had only ever been polite guests in their best clothes, and parties for St Nicholas and our birthdays and our parents' wedding anniversaries. Happy times. Family times. Celebrations. Now, here was this heart-breakingly young man, his blood draining onto our sofa, his pain silently filling the room, along with the smell of sweat and grime, and the unfamiliar sweet odour of English cigarettes. I felt so sorry for him, lying there quite helpless, and wanted to hold him, and somehow to magic his pain away and give him back his body whole and lively, as it must have been hardly an hour ago. It was at that moment, too, that the awfulness of what was happening, and what had been happening to us for all those dreadful years, became clear to me properly for the first time.

Mother stood up and said to me, 'Ask one of the others to come with us.' I chose the one who looked oldest and told him in my best English that Mother would like to speak to him. He, Father and I followed Mother into the kitchen. She wanted me to explain that the wound was so bad she could not do anything to help, and that though she was not a doctor, she felt sure the poor man would die if he did not receive proper attention very soon. When I translated this, the soldier nodded. Now that he did not have to appear cheerful for the sake of his comrade, he looked weary and dispirited. His wounded friend was called Geordie, he said, the other one Norman, and he was Ron. They had been ordered to come to our house and ask to use it as an observation post, because our upstairs rooms had good views of the meadow and along our street. They feared the Germans might come this way. But they had been caught in the shelling, and Geordie had been hit by a piece of shrapnel. They must stay at their post. The only thing he could do was get a message back to their unit and ask for a medical orderly to be sent.

Patching up the wound would not be enough, Mother said. It needed surgery. Father agreed. 'We hear a hotel in the village has been converted to a hospital,' he said. 'You must get him there.' Ron did not know where the hotel was, so I explained: up the hill in to the centre of the village, less than a kilometre.

'It would take both Norm and me to carry him that far,' said Ron. 'We can't both leave our post, not even for a badly wounded man.'

'Then the boy will die,' said Mother when I translated. 'It must be possible to do something.'

'We could take him,' I said, 'Papa and me. We could push him there on the garden trolley.'

'No,' said Papa instantly. 'It would be too dangerous.'

I said, 'The shelling has stopped. And anyway they're aiming for the guns. We would be going away from them.

We'll be safe, Papa.'

'No,' he said, 'I'll go on my own. You must stay with your mother.'

'Mama, speak to him, please.'

Mother looked firmly at Father and said, 'Geertrui is right. It would take two. If you won't have her with you, I'll come.'

'No, no,' said Father, agitated now. 'We can't leave her alone with the soldiers. It isn't right. It isn't safe. I won't allow it.'

Mother took Father's hands in hers and said gently to him, 'Think, my dear. We owe it to these people. They've come to help us. We must do what we can to help them. And think of our daughter. Isn't it natural she wants to play her part? When this horror is over, what would you have her say, that she had to stand by and watch while others took all the risks? That when the moment came, she wasn't allowed to help. And it is right, isn't it, that we get this poor boy to hospital? Think if he were Henk.'

Just as Mother could never resist Father when he was hotly determined, so Father could never resist Mother when she was lovingly logical. He used to say he would have been nothing without her. They were so devoted to each other that I do not think they could ever have parted. Papa's greatest fear always was that he would somehow lose Mama. Throughout the years of occupation he had been undaunted. But now that freedom was in sight (or so we thought at that moment) his nerve suddenly seemed to falter. It surprised me at the time, I even thought how weak he was. But now I am old in my turn, and have been through so much more than I had then, I think I understand. It is when success seems to be almost in your grasp that you become aware of how fragile is human existence, and of the unending possibility, almost the inevitability, of failure. And this makes you hesitate.

Father was silent for a while, then breathed a sigh.

21

'You're right,' he said, and, cupping Mother's face in his hands, kissed her delicately and with such privacy that I turned away. And heard Papa say quietly, 'These years have been possible only because of you. I couldn't survive without you.' And Mother murmur in reply, 'It won't come to that, my dear.'

Then the bustle began. The trolley was prepared with blankets and cushions to make Geordie's journey as comfortable as we could. Ron and Norman lifted him in. Goodbyes were said with our best attempts at cheeriness. And Papa and I set off towards Utrechtseweg and the Schoonoord.

On the way we met friends who were carrying a few possessions in bags. They had heard that the battle was not going well for the British at the bridge, so they were leaving their house because they were sure there would be fighting in the village and thought their cellar wasn't sound enough to protect them. Further on we met a group of people loaded with baggage, all of them from Klingelbeekseweg, on the other side of the railway, not far from Arnhem. They told us that everyone who lived there had been ordered to leave by the Germans. But where should they go? they asked. They had also heard that people in Benedendorpsweg, which was on our side of the railway, were being cleared out too. Papa looked anxiously at me. We both knew without saying it that this news was all bad, for it meant the Germans must be pushing the British back from the town towards us. 'We must hurry,' said Papa, 'and get back to Mother.'

As we approached Utrechtseweg the noise of guns was much louder, coming from the other side of the railway to the north of the village, about a kilometre away, as well as from the direction of Arnhem to the east. We were both breathless and sweating, as much from fear and excitement as from the exertion of pushing the trolley. Geordie was being bounced about, poor boy, because of us going so fast over the cobbles. But he was unconscious, I think, for his eyes were closed and he made no sound.

The Schoonoord was an awful sight. The veranda where we had often sat for coffee was full of wounded men lying on stretchers, waiting to be attended. I was surprised to see a few German soldiers among the British. How could the British lie beside them so calmly, I wondered. One was even handing a German a cigarette. I was appalled! Inside, every room was packed with men lying on stretchers and mattresses and even on the bare floor. Because there were so many the hotel across the road had also been taken over. The smell of blood and dirt and sweat was almost overpowering. It turned my stomach. Women and even boys from the village were helping as best they could. I saw Meik and Joti, two friends from schooldays, washing wounded men, Meik as always in a hurry and Joti putting on her most cheerful face. The soldiers were amazingly calm and patient, even though some must have been in terrible pain. One young man, he could not have been older than I, had five open bullet wounds in his arms. While Hendrika, the daughter of the hotel owner and a school-teacher in normal times, was washing the poor boy, they came to take him to the operating room. She dried him off and tried to stiffen him with hope before they carried him away.

I took Hendrika outside to where Papa was waiting with Geordie. She saw at once that he urgently needed treatment and called out a couple of the boys. They lifted Geordie on to a stretcher and took him inside. It was the last we saw of him. After the war we learned that he had died later that day.

I longed to stay and help but Father said no, we had promised Mother we would return straightaway. How I resented him just then! And I think I would have defied him had Hendrika not said they had plenty of help, except for trained nurses, which I was not of course. I have always thought she only said that to make it easier for me to leave without feeling bad. So off we went, trundling our empty trolley as fast as we could back down the hill, the noise of fighting already louder than on our way up. I remember the bitter-tasting hot smell of gunfire, which seemed to singe the air.

At home, Mother had cooked potatoes with cold pork and apple-sauce for Ron and Norman, who were keeping watch upstairs. Father and I ate some while we told Mother what we had seen and heard. During the afternoon, soldiers came streaming back from the direction of Arnhem, looking worn out. An officer visited, checking on Ron and Norman. They talked in the front bedroom for a few minutes. When the officer left, Ron looked unhappy but would not say very much, only that things were not going as well as they had hoped. Other soldiers came for drinking water and asked if they could wash. We helped them of course. And afterwards in the cold dusk we stood outside looking south towards Nijmegen, where we could see in the sky the glow of flames and hear the crump of large guns firing again and again. Ron said that was the main army fighting its way to us. He and Norman were so tired by now, not having slept for three nights, that Father suggested that he and I keep watch while they got some sleep. But Ron said they would be 'for it' if they were both caught sleeping on duty. So Father suggested I watched with Ron, while Norman slept, then Father and Norman would take over while Ron slept. Norman persuaded him that this would be okay. So for the first half of the night, I sat with Mother watching from the back windows, while Ron kept watch at the front.

On Wednesday the worst time began. Till then it had been the battle of Arnhem. Now it became the battle of Oosterbeek. We did not know it at the time, but only a small group of about one thousand men had reached the bridge at

Arnhem and were holding it against overwhelming odds. The Germans had cut off the rest of the British troops, about eight thousand men, and were surrounding them at Oosterbeek, in a rectangle bounded by the western part of our village and the woodland beyond, with the railway as the boundary to the north and the river to the south.

The Germans started an artillery barrage in the morning, and this time we were not spared in our part of the village. All our windows were blown in, one of our chimneys received a direct hit, shells burst against our walls and fell all around. We sheltered in the cellar whenever this was happening. And were soon joined by soldiers who had been instructed to form a defensive line along our part of the village. In the intervals between bombardments they dug trenches in our back garden, but they asked permission to come in to our cellar as soon as the shelling started because they said they preferred our company to a lonely hole in the ground with no protection from a direct hit or from flying shrapnel.

In the evening German tanks were spotted coming our way and everyone was ordered in to the cellar, taking food and water and whatever else we thought would help in case of a siege. I counted twenty-seven of us crammed together, leaving no space for anyone to lie down flat, while up above it sounded as if the world were falling on our heads. We had no light, except candles, of which there were plenty, because the soldiers had been issued with one each as part of their equipment. But the worst of our hardships was that we had no proper lavatory, only a bucket in the cellar's coal hole. I hated using it and tried not to drink so that I would not need to go. But fear and anxiety are great makers of urine. Next day Father searched out a large metal container with a lid which he had stowed away in our shed. He cleared a space for it in the coal hole and nailed up a blanket to provide a little privacy. When we had used the bucket, we poured the contents into the container and that made life a little more bearable.

Men who were seriously injured were carried off to a dressing station, which by now had been set up not far away. The men with only slight injuries stayed with us and Mother and I helped clean and bandage their wounds. So after all I became a nurse. At first I was squeamish, but I discovered then how quickly you learn to cope with terrible things if you have no choice. And luckily I inherit from my mother a practical view of life. While we worked, the soldiers told us about their homes and families, their friends and girlfriends, and showed us photos. Mostly they were very young, nineteen and twenty, and I think wanted more than anything to be mothered.

All the time the noise around us from every direction was endless and nerve-wracking. At first I had been afraid. Not now. I think this was because of the cheerfulness of the soldiers and so many of them being about my own age. For a protected and well-brought-up girl like me, sitting squashed up against these young men from another country, talking about our lives, eating and sleeping beside them, and performing our most private functions together was like a liberation in itself. One after another, my inhibitions were stripped away. Never mind the stench and the noise and the dust flying and plaster falling from the walls, covering us with a pall of pink powder whenever a shell burst, I felt as if my future was with us in our crowded embattled cellar.

From time to time the barrage stopped for a while—'Jerry's having some schnapps to keep his courage up!' the men would say, and Norman would mimic Hitler, which he was very good and funny at doing. Then we would stumble out into the garden to stretch our creaking limbs and breathe some fresh air, though to call what we smelt 'fresh' is perhaps not the right word. Some of the houses along our street were burning and others were so damaged they looked like ruins in the process of being torn down. The

26

roof and walls of our house were full of holes, the chimneys had gone, and the top corner at the front had been shot away, leaving a ragged gap staring into my parents' bedroom at their wrecked bed with its torn bedclothes flapping in the wind. I felt embarrassed, as if my parents had suddenly appeared in public wearing only tattered underwear.

'Now we know what war means,' said Mother.

I tried not to, but could not help shedding a few tears at the sight of our battered home. Ron, who was with us, said nothing, only put his arm round my shoulders and gave me a comforting hug.

POSTCARD
I can shake off everything if I write;
my sorrows disappear,
my courage is reborn.
Anne Frank

He was beginning to hate this place.

His arrival yesterday had been embarrassing. His visit to the Anne Frank house, the event he'd been looking forward to the most, had been upsetting. His confusion of boy for girl had unnerved him. The mugging had left him duff. The muggin's run had left him bushed. It and the rain, still piddling down, had left him humectant. And now this: a phoney book of matches, a condom, and a message.

The book was not a book and didn't have matches, for all he knew the condom was defective, and the message was in a language he couldn't read. Well, mostly. The figures were probably a phone number—but was it Ton's or another con? *Niets* probably meant no. Was *in* in Dutch the same as 'in' in English? Amsterdam he knew, and what he knew of it so far he could do without. Was *is* the same as 'is' in English? Too much to hope for, surely? *Wat het lijkt?* Oh, to hell with it! Who cares!

Why did he always react to things when it was too late? Why was it that he never knew whether he liked something till it was over, never quite knew what he thought till it didn't matter any more? Take yesterday. As soon as he found out there were problems he should have said thanks but no thanks and flitted back home straightaway. But it wasn't until he was in bed that he felt—really *felt*—just how

28

embarrassed he was. And, for heaven's sake, how could he *not* have realised that Ton was a boy? Thinking about it now, he knew he'd known all the time. Had sensed it. But he'd wanted Ton to be a girl, had wanted it very much, and wouldn't let himself *see* that he wasn't. The truth was he'd deceived himself. And then when he was made to see that Ton was not what he wanted him to be, he'd not known how to react, not known what to say or do, but had just stood there like a dummy.

Maybe his father was right and he really was a congenital wimp.

For the next few minutes he indulged in a bout of self-loathing, his mood encouraged by the rain. Hamlet was dead right. How weary, stale, flat and unprofitable were all the uses of this world. How sullied he was himself. And how maybe he should shuffle off this mortal coil. Not with a bare bodkin of course but in a more appropriately modern fashion. By ODing on E perhaps or smoking the pipe of a car exhaust—his father's, naturally.

After a while of such musing he told himself what a disgusting contortion of unadulterated crap he was (adding many other luscious deprecations selected from his extensive thesaurus). But such thoughts only served to prove that he was indeed a wimp, a jerk, a nerd, and therefore that he had very good reason to be suicidally mopey about himself. And so the circle was closed and his melancholia, feeding on itself, became self-sustaining.

At home, when such a mood possessed him, two people usually helped him break out of the vicious circle. One was Anne Frank. Reading her *Diary* always revived him, but he didn't have his copy to help him now, which was just as well, as it would have been stolen too, and he was sure he couldn't have borne that loss. The other was his grandmother. Sarah had persuaded him that these attacks of what she called his mouse moods were not his fault, not a failure in himself for which he should feel guilty, as he always did when the bouts were over, but that they were simply growing pains, an adolescent affliction, like being short-sighted or allergic to house dust, something people suffered as an accident of birth or of everyday life that you learn to control or deal with.

He sat staring out from his refuge feeling like the mouse looking out from its bolt hole in the episode he wished he did not remember, the one that gave Sarah the name for his fits. That memory went along with a recurrent dream which he had had again last night, so he should have expected an attack of mouse mood today. Apart from its role as a herald of gloom the dream also upset him because he sensed that it was telling him something vital he needed to understand about himself but could never quite grasp. Even when he was in good spirits, cheerful, light-hearted, the memory of the dream would for no apparent reason invade his mind and occupy his thoughts with its riddle.

As it did again while he waited for the rain to stop.

One evening soon after he came to live with his beloved grandmother, Jacob spotted a mouse scuttling along the floor right up against the wainscot. Sarah screamed and jack-knifed her feet on to her chair. Though not the slightest prissy, she had an unbearable phobia about mice, associating them from childhood with dirt and disease, dreading their quick unpredictable movements, and, being fastidious, unable to abide the thought of touching them or, worse, of them touching her. Nor could Jacob, being in this respect as in others very like his grandmother. His knee-jerk reaction was to jump up and chase after the wee sleeket timorous cowerin' beastie, yelling imprecations and waving at it the book he had been reading. (What ridiculous stereo-typical reactions, Sarah had said afterwards, the female closing her legs and trying to climb out of danger, the male shouting violent curses and rushing off in counter-threat to hunt the enemy down.)

As startled by them as they had been by it, the mouse turned tail and skittered in to the first, as it hoped, safe hiding place it could find, which happened to be a very narrow space between the bottom of a bookcase and the wall it didn't quite abut.

Silence. What's it doing? Sarah wanted to know. From a safe distance Jacob bent down and tried to peer in. Too dark to see. Fetch a torch, Sarah suggested.

Using the torch and pressing his cheek hard against the floor so that he could squint in to the gap, Jacob saw the small grey-brown mouse snugged in to the back corner, facing out, big ears almost transparent, large black baby eyes, hairless paws as pink and handlike as a miniature monkey's. Sitting there on its haunches, panting (oh what a panic's in thy breastie), cleaning its whiskers, and staring out at him.

Only a fieldmouse, he said. I don't care what sort it is, Sarah said, I don't want it here, and if it's a fieldmouse, it's in the wrong place anyway. We'll have to get rid of it or I'll never sleep. Maybe, Jacob said, if I get a stick I could winkle it out and chuck a towel over it and take it outside.

The only suitable prod he could quickly find was a fluffy brush with a thin bamboo handle which was flexible enough to lever into the awkward gap. Even then it would only enter at floor level and move in and out like a piston.

Jacob never liked to think of what happened next. Instead of winkling the mouse out, he poked too hard. His hand could feel the fatal skewering thrust for days afterwards.

The dream occurred for the first time a few nights later. He was not unhappy at the time, nor was it a dream on its own but only the end of a longer one, the rest of which he couldn't ever remember until a moment when:

He is talking, he doesn't know who to or what about, though quite cheerfully. He is in an ill-lit confined space, maybe a large cupboard: there are no windows. As he talks

31

he sees out of the corner of his eye towards his right on a wide empty wooden shelf at chest height a small dark-brown lumpy bundle hardly bigger than a man's fist. He turns his head to look directly at it, then gives it a poke with a short thin iron rod with a flange on its end shaped like an upper lip that he finds he is holding in his right hand. As soon as he touches it the bundle falls apart, turning into two large mice about the size of rabbits. One flops on to its back, legs splayed wide like a dog wanting its tummy scratched, the pink of its belly sparsely covered in soft light-grey fur. His attention, however, is taken by the other mouse, which has rolled on to its side and is curled in a foetal position, head tucked in to paws. It is lying very still. Is it alive? He pokes it with the lip of his metal probe. Nothing. He taps it lightly on the side of its head. Now at once it is a mouse no longer but a human child, with a large, much too large head, and a face that disturbs him. He taps it again, harder and on the temple this time. The child whimpers but does not open its eyes. He hits it again, and again, each time with deliberate increasingly powerful force that he feels in his hand and along his arm and into his bicep. Between each blow he carefully observes the child's reaction. After each hit the boy moans in pain and distress and has also grown larger and is closer to Jacob. It is as if the child is coming closer without either of them moving. Like a film, each shot in bigger close-up than the one before. After the fourth or fifth assault a wound appears on the child's temple and blood oozes out, thick bright red blood, but not in great quantity. It doesn't flood out or run down his face but congeals into a shiny lozenge on the boy's temple. Excited by the blood, Jacob strikes him harder still. And harder. But now he is thinking to himself between each blow: *What am I doing? I shouldn't be doing this! Why am I doing this? I don't want to do this!* But goes on hitting him again and again till the child is in such big close-up the only part of him Jacob can see is his injured bleeding head. And the little whimpering cries the child lets out after each blow are more and more upsetting, more terrible than if he were screaming. Yet all the time the child's eyes are closed, as if he is asleep.

Then the eyes open, and Jacob sees that the child is himself.

POSTCARD

Old and young,
we are all on our last cruise.

R. L. Stevenson

'*Is er iets? Kan ik je helpen?*'

An old woman addressing him from the foot of the steps. Round face with kind eyes, shapeless long green coat, sky blue umbrella protecting from the rain her crinkly grey hair tied back in a bun, empty linen shopping bag dangling from her other hand.

'*Voel je je niet goed?*'

'Sorry?'

'English?'

He nodded.

'Are you all right?'

He nodded again, shrugged, then, thinking she meant he shouldn't be there, stood up. 'I'm in your way?'

'No, no.'

'Sheltering from the rain.'

'You looked unhappy.'

'I'm okay. It's, well . . . Been mugged.'

'Och! Were you hurt?'

'No. Just upset. Angry mostly.'

'What did they take?'

'Anorak. Money. Everything, to be honest.'

'Oh dear!'

He started down the steps, but stopped two from the bottom when the woman said, 'Can I help?'

He thought of what he'd intended to ask at the Anne

34

Frank house and said, 'If you have a phone book . . . ?'

'Yes.'

'The people I'm staying with live in Haarlem, but my rail ticket was in my anorak so—Well, they gave me the address and phone number of their son, who lives in Amsterdam. That was in my anorak as well—But he should be in the phone book . . .'

'I'll have a look. What is the name?'

'Van Riet. Daan van Riet. I think he lives near the railway station.'

'Van Riet. Near the station. I'll have a look.'

'Thanks.'

'Wait there, please.'

Instead of coming past him up to the door, as he had expected, she turned and, seemingly, set off down the street. Wondering where she was going, Jacob stepped on to the footpath, only to see her round rear end disappearing in to the tendrils of overhanging ivy and rambling roses, which, along with numerous pots of red and white flowered plants, luxuriantly wreathed the basement windows. She was climbing down into the basement through one of the pair of windows he now saw was also a door which had a protective iron grille in front of it that opened out in to the street. It was, he thought, like the entrance to a gated cave or an enchanted grotto.

Very soon the old woman reappeared, looking out from just above pavement level.

'*Hallo!*' she called. Then, seeing Jacob peering at her through the encroaching foliage: 'There you are!' She held up the open phone book. 'Many Van Riets. But one with the beginning letter D near the station in Oudezijds Kolk.' To Jacob the name sounded like chewed vowels and sloshed consonants. 'I'll try it,' she went on. 'Wait on the steps. You're getting wet.'

Which was true, though the rain had eased off and the sky was brightening. He was curious to see more of her subterranean home, but did as he was told and returned to the porch.

While he waited a sleek white glass-roofed tourist boat with the word Lovers in large letters on the side ghosted by on the canal, half full of gaping sightseers sitting in fours at little tables, some with cameras or camcorders raised to their faces like snuffling snouts. Camhogs, he thought, on the scavenge. Sitting alone at the back, a beautiful black dreadlocked girl of about his own age, hand propping up head, stared dully at him until the boat was almost past, when she gave a sudden radiant smile and a little wave. He raised a hand in reply and instantly felt more cheerful.

The rain stopped.

A leggy young man, very tanned, in tight white showoff mini-shorts and flapping pink T-shirt cycled by, a small pugdog sitting in a basket attached to the handlebars, ears back, grinning, head-to-wind.

A red Alfa Romeo drove fast along the opposite side, its arrogant noise echoing across the canal.

At last the woman reappeared at the foot of the steps, empty linen bag dangling from one hand again but without her umbrella.

'No answer. I tried three times.'

'Thanks.'

'I've written the address and phone number.' She handed him a piece of paper.

'You've been very kind.'

He looked away, not knowing what to say next, wanting help but not wanting to ask for more. There was the kind of awkward silence that comes between strangers when one has tried to help the other and has not succeeded, leaving both feeling guilty and irritated.

He decided he would go on to Anne Frank's house.

But before he could move, the old woman said, 'It isn't good you should stay there. I'm going for coffee before shopping. Would you like to join me? We can try again from the café in a while.'

He could not prevent himself from accepting.

'What is your name?'

'Jacob. Jacob Todd.'

'Please call me Alma.'

He nodded, smiling.

They were seated either side of a table on the mezzanine floor of Café Panini on a broad street with trams in the middle that Jacob recognised as the one he'd run down when chasing Red Cap. Coffee and hot croissants were brought by a robust young waitress, henna dyed hair cut very short, whitened face, lips painted purple, white singlet hugging braless small breasts, black leather mini-skirt, black stockings, Doc Marten boots. Obvious from the way she and Alma gabbed that they knew each other and were talking about him. As she left she gave Jacob a wicked smile that brightened his spirits even more than the girl waving from the boat.

'A student,' Alma said, enjoying the exchange, 'she works here to pay for her studies. Now, I suggest we enjoy our coffee, then I'll try Van Riet again. If he's there, I'll show you how to get to him. If not . . . well, we'll cross that bridge when we come to it. You agree?'

'I agree,' Jacob said, matching her sunny tone.

He eased his shoulders inside his clammy sweatshirt and tucked in to his croissant with an over-eager appetite. Then, aware of Alma delicately sipping her coffee and observing him closely, gave her his best appreciative smile, politely tasted his comfortingly hot coffee and said, 'Thanks for this. It's very good.'

'I come here every morning. For coffee, to read the newspapers, and to talk to anyone I know. A good place for meeting interesting people. Very popular with writers, actors, musicians. When you're old and live alone, as I do, it's important to keep in touch.'

37

Jacob looked around. Only a couple of blubbery middle-aged men sitting on their own, smoking cigarettes and reading newspapers. Formica-topped tables, in tasty shades of blue, green, yellow and orange. Black metal seats. Thick beams in the ceiling painted yellow. Original art on cream walls: etchings, brush drawings of horses. The wall at his side was top to bottom a mirror reflecting himself and Alma and the tables on his other side. Italian designer version of a working-men's caff? Making a point, or a pretence anyway, of being anti-bourgeois unposh?

'And what about you?' Alma asked. 'Are you on holiday?'

'Kind of. My grandfather was wounded in the Battle of Arnhem. Some local people looked after him. But he died. I'm going to visit his grave at the battle cemetery.'

'You've been to Holland before?'

'No. Well, I was brought once by my parents when I was a baby, but I don't remember that.'

'And the people you're staying with in Haarlem?'

'The family of the woman who looked after my grand-father. She and my grandmother have kept in touch. Really, it was my grandmother who was supposed to come now but she couldn't. She fell and broke her hip.'

'I'm sorry. You'll attend the commemoration of the battle next Sunday?'

'My grandmother thought I should see it.' He shrugged. 'I'm named Jacob after my grandfather.'

Remembering home he suddenly became inward and didn't want to say any more about all that. He dabbed flakes of croissant on to a finger-end and licked them away.

'Have mine,' Alma said, passing her plate, 'I'm not hungry', and waited while he had made the usual polite noises before asking, 'And how did you get mugged?'

'I was having a drink in the . . . Leidseplein?'

She said it, he repeated it, she chuckled. 'Better!'

'Well, there, anyway!' They laughed together at his

incompetence. 'I'd put my coat over the back of my chair. Suddenly it went flying past me! I chased after the guy who took it. Just a kid, really. Well, my age, roughly. Had a red baseball cap on. Backwards, naturally!'

'Naturally!'

'He ran this way and that way, and up this canal and down that one, along one street, across another till I was completely lost. Chased him down this street, as a matter of fact. I remember the bridge just outside.'

'Vijzelgracht.'

'If you say so!'

Alma smiled indulgently. 'You must try.'

'I will, I will. Promise!' Maybe it was the coffee that was making him cheeky, or more likely the relief he was feeling. But he could see Alma was enjoying it too. 'Couldn't catch him. I'm not a great runner and he was wickedly fast. But the odd thing is, I'm sure he wanted me to chase him.'

'What made you think so?'

'He'd wait sometimes till I'd nearly caught up and then off he'd go again. Why would he do that? You'd think he'd want to get away as quick as possible so he couldn't be recognised later.'

'Perhaps for fun.'

'Fun?'

'He sounds to me like a regular thief, not just someone doing it because he's desperate for money to get drugs, which is the reason for most of the muggings in Amsterdam, of which there are a lot, I'm sorry to say. In cities everywhere these days, so I'm told. But if you mug people as a job, let's say, perhaps it becomes . . . *vervelend* . . . tedious?'

'Boring?'

'Exactly. Boring. Every job has its boring times. For a thief too. Making a good chase out of it, making it a chance that he might get caught, adds some spice. And perhaps he liked the look of you. Thought you a worthy challenge. You should feel complimented.'

'Oh, thanks! Some compliment, to steal everything I've got.'

'And then give you a run for your money.'

He laughed. 'Your English is very good.'

'You English! Always impressed by anyone who can speak more than their own language.'

'About all I can manage is holiday French.'

'People learn what they have to. The English can always get by because your language is international. We Dutch have a minority language surrounded by countries with major languages. And historically we are traders. We have to speak other people's languages to survive.'

'Still, I wish . . .'

'It's only a matter of application. If you lived in the country for a while, it would be easier for you.'

'Maybe I will. I want to do something between school and whatever I do next.'

'You don't know?'

'What I want to do? Not yet.'

Alma took a sip of her coffee. 'I'm still thinking about your thief. Perhaps in his mind, he wasn't stealing.'

'What, then?'

'He made it into a game, a competition. He gave you a chance. He won. So he took the prize.'

'Hey, whose side are you on!' Though meaning a joke, there was an edge in his voice.

'Yours, I think, wouldn't you say?'

He felt a hint of rebuke.

'Sorry. Wasn't being ungrateful.'

'I understand. It's a shock, something like that. I only mean, you aren't hurt. You've lost a little money, a few unimportant other things. Your pride is bruised, but is pride so precious? I'll see you get back to your friends, then all will be well again, and soon what has happened will be just a good story to tell. But the boy who stole your things, what about him? What kind of life does he live? And who looks after him?'

'Sounds like you'd have helped him just as much as you're helping me, if he'd been the one you'd found on the steps.'

'I imagine he's a street boy who lives on his wits. You had something worth stealing, he probably has nothing. Why should I help you and not him?'

'You're like my grandmother. She always puts the other side.'

'Is that such a bad thing?'

'No. Just a bit galling when you're on the receiving end, that's all.'

'I don't mean to lecture you. A failing of the old.'

'You're not. I'd agree if we were talking about someone else.'

'Always easy to be wise when you're only an onlooker. Would you like another coffee?'

When he hesitated she added, 'I usually have two.'

After she had ordered she said, 'I remember the war, you see, the occupation. Especially the last winter before the liberation. We call it *de hongerwinter*. It was terrible. Food was desperately scarce. And fuel for the fires. People burned their furniture, even the wood in their houses—doors, panelling, floors even. There was nothing. Even the German soldiers were hungry. So they behaved badly sometimes. They hadn't until then. In the first years of the occupation, at least where I lived here in Amsterdam, I could walk about on my own and not fear them. I was a young woman, only eighteen, nineteen, but I wasn't afraid. I didn't like them. Hated them, in fact. But they were very strict about behaving properly to us. People forget that now. Unless you were a Jew of course. For them, it was always dreadful. What was done to them . . .' She raised a hand from the table and let it fall again. 'Unforgivable.'

She was silent for a moment, collecting herself.

41

'But what I wanted to tell you is that though it was awful at the end, we were all in it together. Now it isn't like that. Most of us in your country and mine are well off and comfortable compared with those days, yet we allow it to happen that great numbers of our young people are homeless. Abandoned to live on the streets. Even here in Holland, where we pride ourselves on looking after our children, it's happening more and more. I see them begging and sitting in doorways looking like bags of old rubbish. We are told not to give them money, that they are dangerous and it only encourages them and they spend it on drugs. But I don't care. If I can, I give something. Not to all of them, there are too many. To ones I think might benefit.'

'But which ones? How can you know?'

'I guess. Use my intuition.'

Moved, and a little embarrassed too, by the passion roused in her, the flush that tinted her pale face, the hint of tears in her bleached-blue eyes, the quiver of anger in her voice, Jacob was sure she would have said more, but the coffee arrived, Alma sighed, took possession of herself and drank, and became again the calm assured person she had so far been. But he knew he had glimpsed the feisty young woman she once was, and thought how much he would have liked her then. And did now.

Thinking of what she might have been when young and what she was now, he said, 'I know a bit about Amsterdam in the war because of *The Diary of Anne Frank*. Which is just about my favourite book. Well—*is* my favourite book, really.'

'Then you'll want to see the secret annexe where they hid and where she wrote her diary. It isn't far from here.'

'Yes, I know.' He didn't want to tell her about his visit that morning. 'In the diary, Anne says that youth is lonelier than old age. D'you think that's true?'

'I haven't thought about it. Do you think it is?'

'How would I know? Haven't been old yet.'

42

'Nor had Anne, so how could she know?'

He smiled. 'I've wondered that too. But she says all sorts of things that make me wonder how she could know them.'

'Do you feel lonely?'

He hesitated, not liking where the conversation might go, but took a chance and said, 'Yes.'

'I read the book a long time ago and forget. Does she say why she thinks youth is lonelier than old age?'

'I know what she says by heart. It's one of my orange passages. Would you like to hear it?'

'One of your orange passages?'

'Every time I read it I highlight any passage I really like in orange. Sounds silly, I suppose.'

'Not at all. I'm much less colourful. When I mark passages in my books I only underline in pencil. And you use orange—?'

'Because that's—'

'The Dutch national colour.'

'Yes!'

'Of course!'

They laughed together again.

'You're a reader, then?' Alma said.

'A lot. From living with my grandmother.'

'The one who should have been here now?'

'Yes. Sarah. She reads all the time. Infected me with the bug.'

'You're fortunate. So, recite the passage about old age. After all, I've a vested interest in it.'

Jacob paused a moment to check his memory before saying, 'Okay. It goes: "'For in its innermost depths youth is lonelier than old age.' I read this saying in some book and I've always remembered it, and found it to be true. Is it true then that grown-ups have a more difficult time here than we do? No. I know it isn't. Older people have formed their opinions about everything, and don't waver before they act. It's twice as hard for us young ones to hold our ground, and maintain our opinions, in a time when all ideals are being shattered and destroyed, when people are showing their worst side, and do not know whether to believe in truth and right and God."'

Alma had listened with her head down over her cup, almost as if she were listening to a prayer, and was silent for a moment before saying quietly, 'She was writing during the war when everything was terrible.'

'I know.' Jacob leaned forward, elbows on the table, and spoke so that only she would hear. 'I know it isn't so awful now. But surely in some ways it isn't any better, is it? I mean, Bosnia, parts of Africa, Cambodia, other places, nuclear pollution, drugs, Aids, the kids on the street. And that's just for starters.'

'It upsets me too.'

'And there's racial prejudice still, isn't there? Everywhere. There are still plenty of Nazis about, it seems to me. People showing their worst side.'

'Every day, the news is full of it.'

'I mean, Anne talks about ideals. But what ideals are there to believe in? And who knows what the truth is any more?'

Alma glanced up, assessing him, before saying with a bleak firmness, 'You have to know your own truth and stick to it. And never despair. Never give up. There's always hope.' Then, as if aware of how stern she must sound, she smiled and shrugged and added, 'This I learned during the war.'

Jacob nodded. 'She's right, then, Anne?'

'I'm not sure. You do have more to go on when you're old. More experience. It helps.'

Before he could stop himself, Jacob said, 'And less time to live.'

She gave him a hard look. 'True. But don't for a second think that makes it any easier.' She finished her coffee. 'Even so, in my opinion people are mostly good.'

At once he remembered, '"In spite of everything I still believe that people are good at heart. I can feel the suffering of millions and yet, I think that it will all come right, that this cruelty too will end."'

'Anne Frank again?'

He nodded.

'You do love that book, don't you.'

'To tell the truth, I think I'm in love with Anne herself.'

Surprised by his unintended confession, he sat back, drained his coffee, rubbed his thighs, was aware of his toes tapping a rapid tattoo on the floor and his face blushing. Laughing to cover his confusion he said, 'I do feel as if I know her better than anyone else. I mean, better than any of my family or friends.'

'And what do you love so much about her, I wonder?'

'All sorts. For a start, she's funny. Very witty. And she's serious about things.'

'But what do you like most of all?'

He pondered the question, pushing back in his chair till he was balancing on its two back legs, before saying, 'Her honesty. About herself. About everybody. She wants to know about everything. And she sees through everything. She's a thinker. She was fifteen when . . . they took her.' He always had trouble with his emotions when he thought of Anne being dragged away and of her tortured life and her ugly death in the hell of the camps. He returned his seat to its four legs, his eyes fixed on his hands clasped on the table in front of him. 'Only fifteen, but she already understood more about herself and more about other people and more about life than I do, and I'm seventeen. Even though she was shut away in those—' he couldn't think of the appropriate word for what he had felt that morning '—those rooms.' He rapped the table with the edge of his clasped hands. 'She had such courage. And she really knew what she wanted out of life. I wish I had her courage. And I wish I knew myself that well.'

He paused, thinking hard before he went on, 'I don't know how to put this, but—. It isn't what she talks about that matters so much. It's the way she thinks that I like. And it's not just thinking, not just her thoughts. It's more than that. I always feel more myself, always feel better in myself I mean, when I'm with her . . . When I'm reading her . . . I know I'm not *really* with her. I know she's only words in a book.'

He gave Alma an anxious glance.

'Never told anyone that before.'

'You're away from home in a foreign country, you have just had a shock, I am a sympathetic stranger. It's not unusual.'

'But you must think I'm mad, falling for a girl who's only words in a book.'

'Some people say falling in love is a kind of madness whenever it happens. If that's so, all I can say is I would rather be mad than sane.'

They laughed with the warmth of friends who share a secret.

'*Nog koffie?*' asked the waitress as she passed their table. The place was busier now.

'*Nee, dank je,*' Alma replied, pushing herself to her feet; and to Jacob, 'I should telephone again.'

'*Gelukt!*' she said when she returned. 'He was there and will wait for you. Now I'll put you on a tram to the railway station. You can have my *strippenkaart* to pay for the journey. It has only two journeys left on it so you see I'm not being so generous. You know the station from your arrival this morning. The tram terminates there. When you get out, look across the plein in front, to the left. You'll see a large church standing above the rooftops. Go towards that, across the road by the water, and down the small street behind the church. There's a narrow canal between the street and the church. You have the address on the paper I

46

gave you, and here are five guilders to use should you need to telephone again. But you'll be quite all right now, I think.'

'You've been very very kind.'

'I've enjoyed meeting you. You've earned your keep!'

He held up the coins. 'I'll return the money.'

'No, no. Think of yourself as one of my street kids.'

Putting the money in his pocket he found the book of matches. He showed it to her.

'Someone gave me this just before my stuff was stolen. Look inside.'

Alma gave a loud guffaw, and exclaimed, '*Dat kun je in Amsterdam verwachten!*'

'The words he wrote, what do they mean?'

'"Be ready", you understand of course. Perhaps "be prepared" would be better English. *Niets in Amsterdam is wat het lijkt.* "Be prepared. Nothing in Amsterdam is what it appears to be."'

'I see.' Jacob pocketed the book again, thinking how in Ton's case that was certainly true.

'Now we must go.'

'Have I time to use the toilet?'

'Of course. I'll pay the *rekening*.'

As the yellow tram came bowling up to them, a caterpillar on roller blades, Alma said, 'Not to be outdone, I've written something for you too.' And she gave Jacob one of the café's paper napkins folded into a small neat square. 'Now, *dag hoor*, goodbye. I hope the rest of your stay in Holland is happy and mug free.'

She held out her hand, which Jacob took with such a sudden rush of grateful affection that he couldn't stop himself from giving Alma a brief kiss on her cheek. She let out a little breath of pleasure, brushed her cheek with her hand, and smiled broadly. Flustered by his impulsive action, he stumbled up the steps of the waiting tram, the doors hissed shut, the bell tringalinged and the tram jerked into motion. By the time he had located the yellow box which automatically stamped his ticket and had found a seat by the rear window, they had crossed the bridge over the Prinsengracht and Alma was already lost to view.

While he calmed himself, he stared, half-seeing, at the procession of small shops and larger office buildings and the bustle of people along the way. But by the time the tram swung round a sharp busy corner in to a wide street, Rokin, a canal to his right packed with waiting tourist boats, he began to relax. Only then did he think to unfold the napkin still clutched in his hand. On it were the carefully written words:

> WAAR EEN WIL IS,
> IS EEN WEG

GEERTRUI

It was late on Wednesday evening when Jacob returned. Or I should say, when he was brought to us. There had been another bombardment. After it, a wounded man was found unconscious in our garden and was carried in to the cellar. We laid him on a mattress and inspected his wounds. None of us recognised him because his face was completely black, covered with what looked like a cake of soot and mud, as were his hands, and his legs from which the trousers seemed to have been torn away. He was bleeding from a deep cut in the temple, and from a bad injury in the calf of his right leg.

One of the soldiers went searching for a medical orderly. While he was gone, Mother and I prepared a bowl of water and clean cloths, and carefully removed the wounded man's equipment and loosened his battledress. We were afraid to do more in case he had other injuries and we made them worse.

It took about half an hour before the medical orderly reached us. He himself looked exhausted. He said he had seen many like this man, he knew what must have happened. A shell had exploded near him, knocking him unconscious and covering him in mud and burnt explosive, and injuring him with flying shrapnel. He quickly did an examination, said there were no internal injuries he could identify, and began cleaning and dressing the wounded leg. 'He's lucky to have got off so lightly,' the orderly said.

While he worked he told us that the blackened skin would have to be cleaned with disinfected water, but that we must be very careful because there would probably be many painful scratches on the skin under the dirt caused by tiny splinters of shell. There might also be little pieces still stuck in the dirt, which would cause more damage if we rubbed too hard or quickly. Cleaning would take much time. The troops in this sector were suffering a lot of casualties and so he was needed everywhere. Did we think we could clean up the wounded man and bandage his head wound? I translated for Mother, who said we would do our best, asking how long the man would remain unconscious and what we should do when he came round. The orderly said it was difficult to tell. He had seen cases like this come round in a few minutes, but others had remained unconscious for days. Nor could he be sure how the man would behave when he came to; some were all right, but others were so badly shaken they were, as he put it, 'basket cases'. Do whatever seems best, he told us. Shouldn't he be taken to the hospital? Mother wanted to know. The fighting and shelling between here and the nearest dressing station, said the orderly, were so bad that the poor chap would probably be killed before he arrived. At least here in our cellar he was as safe as he could be and would be well attended 'by two devoted nurses'. He gave us some ointment for the wounds and some painkillers, said he would return when he could to see how we were getting on, checked the injuries of the other wounded men in the cellar, and scurried off in to the night. Such courage. We never saw him again. I have often wondered if he survived the battle.

By now most of the soldiers were upstairs, taking what rest they could during the lull in the shelling. As well as the container for the lavatory, Father had managed to find an old paraffin lamp packed away in the garden shed along with some fuel. He got it going and by its light Mother began cleaning the wounded man's face and I his hands. Father made it his business to keep us supplied with fresh warm water (not easy to do by this time) and to rinse out the cloths, which had to be done often because they soon became soiled from the thick grime we were slowly removing from the poor man's encrusted skin. Meanwhile, he took off the man's boots and cut away what was left of his trousers and covered him with a blanket.

We had been working for about half an hour when Mother said, 'Look, Geertrui, look who he is!' She had cleaned his brow, his closed eyes, his nose and mouth, so that his face looked like a white mask on his still blackened head, with tiny blood-red scratches all over it. 'Isn't he one of the soldiers on Sunday?'

Father said, 'He is. The one called Jacob.'

'The one you gave a glass of water,' said Mother when I did not answer.

But I had seen at once who she meant. I was thinking: the one with the melting eyes. But I said, 'He called me an angel of mercy.'

'More of a prophet than he knew,' said Mother.

After his face and hands we began on his legs and lower body. All was in a dreadful state. Then we came to his private parts. This was a shock to me, the first time I had seen a mature man's penis, let alone been expected to handle it. I was fascinated, seeing so closely this secret of maleness, and felt a twinge of fear too. How innocent we young people were in those days. How little informed about such things. An embarrassing shyness came over me. I turned my eyes away. Though I did so, I think, more because I felt this was expected of me, rather than because I wanted to. On the contrary, I wanted to look and look.

Mother touched my arm and said with a sad smile, 'This week, I think you finally leave your childhood behind.' And with that she got on with the job, and I too.

For fear of hurting him, I'm sure we went far more slowly than we needed to. It was nearly two hours before we were finished.

During the next four days the fighting worsened. At times I

51

thought our house was being demolished brick by brick. More and more wounded soldiers were brought in to our cellar, and Mother, Father and I had our hands full tending them. They bore their pain with great fortitude. Except for one poor boy called Sam, who was suffering from what was then called shell shock. One of the medical orderly's 'basket cases'. His nerves had completely gone. He crouched in a corner, suffering from terrible bouts of shivering, would sometimes suddenly cry out or burst in to tears with his head held in his hands, but would say nothing and would not allow anyone to comfort him.

'You wanted to be a nurse at the Schoonoord,' Father teased. 'Well, you've got your wish, only here at home.' And then he said in English one of the 'familiar sayings' we had used for practice in those days before the parachutes fell from the sky, which already seemed a century ago: 'All things come to he who waits.'

The soldier I was tending at that moment, hearing this, said, 'But he who hesitates is lost.'

To which Father replied, 'Because time and tide wait for no man.'

Not to be left out, I said, 'But a stitch in time saves nine.'

At which: 'Come what, come may,' called out another soldier, 'time and the hour runs through the roughest day.'

And another, '"The time has come," the Walrus said, "to talk of many things—"'

'"Of shoes and ships and sealing-wax—",' another butted in.

At which several voices shouted together, '"Of cabbages and kings."'

Everyone was laughing by now.

'You can fool all the people some of the time,' someone sang out in a comic voice, 'you can even fool some of the people all of the time—' and the others shouted back, 'But you can't fool all of the people all of the time.'

We were just recovering from the fresh burst of laughter this caused, when someone, flapping a piece of paper in the air, said in a high squeaky voice, 'Peace in our time!', which reduced them to such uncontrollable gusts of laughter that some soldiers upstairs heard the noise and came down to see what was going on. So the joke had to be repeated, which caused further gales of merriment. Even though I did not understand why it was so funny, not knowing about Mr Chamberlain and his pact with Hitler at Munich, their laughter infected Papa and me and soon we were holding our sides too.

'What is it, what is it?' Mother kept asking. 'What are they saying?' But neither of us could find the breath to tell her.

Then, just as we were calming down and blowing our noses and wiping our eyes, a mock-cheerful voice said, 'Well lads, for sure, life is a bowl of cherries.' There was a second's pause before another voice muttered with exaggerated sorrow, 'But someone's eaten all mine.' And this set everyone off in aching laughter again.

As we were recovering from this I saw poor Sam laughing with us—or I should say that is what I thought he was doing. It was only when he suddenly stared unblinking at me with blazing raw eyes, tears streaming down his cheeks, the skin of his face stretched tight and white over the bones of his skull, that I knew he was not laughing at all but—well, I think wailing would be the right word. Everyone else seemed to become aware of him at the same moment. I was about to go to him when the soldier next to me laid a hand on my arm and shook his head. And then Sam spoke for the first time since he was brought to us, saying in a clear high sing-song voice, 'I have desired to go where springs not fail, to fields where flies no sharp and sided hail and a few lilies blow. And I have asked to be where no storms come, where the green swell is in the havens dumb, and out of the swing of the sea.'

How must I know such things, from so long ago and in a language not my own? The old often say they remember their youth more clearly than the day before yesterday. But this is not it. I know these things because those few days and the few weeks that followed them were such an intensity of living, so much more than any other time of my life, that they are unforgettable. And I have gone over and over them ever since. Sometimes you live more life in an hour than in most weeks, and sometimes it is possible to live more in a few weeks than in all the rest of your life. This is how those days in 1944 are to me. And also I know what was said in that other language I already loved because, as I shall explain you, these events during the battle were later talked over with Jacob again and again.

Far from being difficult to remember, my problem is that it is impossible to forget.

When I heard them, I thought poor tortured Sam was uttering beautiful strange shell-shocked words. But Jacob knew they were a poem, which later he taught to me. As also one other, of which I shall tell you soon, that I have treasured throughout my life.

In the silence after Sam had spoken we heard a dry voice rasp, 'Hopkins.' We all turned to see it was Jacob who had spoken, propped up on an elbow, looking at us with gaunt sunken eyes, and smiling a smile like the smile of a starved dog. He had returned to consciousness while we were laughing. He told me later he had heard us as if he were buried a long way down beneath the earth, and our laughter had dug him up. Everyone turned to look. 'Gerard Manley Hopkins,' Jacob said. Hugh, a soldier sitting near him, moved so that he could give him support, saying, 'Look who's come back to the land of the living.' I went to him at once, and helped him drink some water and later to eat some biscuit. We had no bread by this time, and very little of anything else. The soldiers had eaten all our stored food, except some bottles of preserved fruit that Mother had kept in the cellar.

Naturally, as soon as he could speak properly Jacob wanted to know where he was and what had happened. He was confused at first and weak from lack of food and drink besides everything else he had endured. He could not believe he had been unconscious for so long and was worried because he could remember nothing about what he had been doing when the shell-burst knocked him out. The wound in his leg was hurting. He wanted to see it. We persuaded him to wait until we dressed it again. We knew how painful that would be. I gave him a painkiller. After a while, he recovered himself and was calmer. But he kept saying, 'They should be here by now,' meaning the main army. 'They'll come,' Hugh told him, 'they wouldn't let us down.' Even at that moment their big guns were shelling the German positions not far from us, making a terrible noise and shaking the earth where we sat.

While this was happening Jacob kept giving me intent looks, struggling, I guessed, to remember who I was. At last it dawned.

'The angel of mercy!' he suddenly said but quietly, only for me to hear.

'And you are Jacob Todd,' I replied.

He gave a little laugh that brought the melting look back in to his eyes. 'They call me Jacko,' he said.

'I like Jacob better,' I said.

'Me too. What's your name?'

I told him, he tried to say it but was no better at our Dutch pronunciation than most of his comrades, so now it was my turn to have a little laugh at him. 'Your friends call me Gertie,' I said.

'Not me,' he said.

'No?'

'It's no name for an angel. So what shall I call you? Have

you another name? One I can say.'

'Yes. But I never use it.'

'Why not?'

'I don't know. I never have.'

'What is it? Come on, you have to tell me. You know you can't refuse a wounded soldier. It isn't allowed.'

'Maria.' (It is really Marije, but I wanted to make it easy for him.)

'Maria,' he repeated. 'A good name for an angel. Can I call you Maria, Maria?'

His eyes persuaded me of course. Youth is my excuse!

I said, laughing, 'All right. But only you. No one else.'

The weather had become very cold and during that night *regende het pijpenstelen*, as we say in Dutch—which means, it was raining in sheets. I thought the sky as well as our house was falling on our heads. We were all feeling very miserable. Jacob began to shiver. During a lull in the fighting Father rescued from the wreckage upstairs a pair of his trousers and a pullover for Jacob to wear, for what was left of his army clothes was useless. 'Better not let Jerry catch you like that,' said Hugh, 'or he'll take you for a spy and shoot you.' He meant it as a joke, I'm sure, but it sent a tremor through me. I could see it also made Jacob think for a moment, but then he picked up his plum-red paratrooper's beret and put it on, took his paratrooper's scarf and tied it round my neck, and said, 'That'll fox him!' It was not a good joke, but we laughed anyway as we huddled against each other for warmth.

The next day an officer brought orders for the men to leave. Only then we learned that those at the bridge in Arnhem had had to give up on Thursday. Not for forty-eight hours, as planned, but for four days they held out against tanks and guns and mortars, and greatly outnumbered by the Germans. Only when they ran out of ammunition, and were almost all captured or injured or dead, had the few remaining given in. Now, eight days after the first paratroopers landed, the British soldiers trapped in Oosterbeek were surrounded by ever stronger German forces. It could not be long, a day or two at most, before they would be overrun. The only way to save them was by withdrawing across the river, from where they could reach the main army. But to have any chance of success, this would have to be done during that Monday night, with a barrage of heavy gunfire from the main army south of the river to cover their escape, confuse the Germans and make them keep their heads down.

Orders were given that the barrage was to begin at 8:50 p.m. that evening and the withdrawal at ten o'clock. Men defending the northern perimeter, which was furthest from the river, were to withdraw first, and so on, like an ebbing tide, down to those at the southern end on the river itself. As we were near the river end of the village, the soldiers in our house would be among the last to leave.

In preparation, the men were ordered to blacken their faces, to muffle the sound of their boots by wrapping them in strips torn from blankets, and to make sure their weapons did not rattle when they carried them. All other equipment was to be destroyed.

Of the wounded men, any who could walk were to leave. But those who could not or were too ill were to remain where they were, along with the medical officers and orderlies. They were to give themselves up and become prisoners of war when the Germans took over the village again.

In all the days of the battle till these orders came, everyone had tried to be cheerful and optimistic. Now a strange mood overcame us. That Monday the fighting was fierce, the worst of any so far. What remained of our house was often hit, even was burning in the upstairs rooms at one point, but Father and some of the lightly wounded men managed to put the flames out while the uninjured men went on firing at the enemy, who had occupied houses on the other side of the street. Twice German soldiers almost reached us, but were fought off, hand-to-hand sometimes, though not without cost. Ron, who had been with us throughout that terrible week and so often helped us, died in this defence of our home. His companion, Norman, brought the news to us in the cellar. Mother and I wept for this brave and kindly man who had done so much to try and make our lives bearable during the battle, never complaining, and who we knew left behind in his own country a young wife and baby daughter, whose photos he had often shown us. Norman sat silently with us, dazed by the loss of his friend, but before he could recover he was called for from above and had to run back up to face the enemy again.

I think this was the moment when I knew for sure that, after all, we had not been liberated but would soon once more be in the hands of the German invaders. And for the first time that week I was truly afraid. So afraid that my legs felt too weak to carry me and my hands trembled uncontrollably. I wanted to scream but could not utter a sound. My stomach tightened in a knot, yet I wanted to rush to the lavatory.

The wounded men with us in the cellar became silent and inward. It was as if they were ashamed. They did not want to look at us—Papa, Mama and me. Some of them said they felt that leaving us behind was a kind of betrayal. And, quite naturally, they suffered a punishing sense of failure. None of our privations together was as bad as this.

With resigned fortitude, for the rest of the day we helped them as best we could as they prepared for that night's danger. Even poor Sam would leave. He could walk, had recovered enough composure to understand what was going on and was calm enough for one of the others to lead him to the river. Also, I'm sure the thought of being left behind to become a prisoner had filtered through his addled brain and made him determined to keep control of himself somehow.

It struck me even then that his bravery in the face of his suffering was quite as great as the bravery of the men who went on battling to save us.

So all would be evacuated from our cellar. All except Jacob. He was too weak to stand unaided, never mind walk, which his injured calf made impossible. For a while he tried to persuade the others that he could make it if two of them would give him support. But the sergeant in charge said no, he would never do it. They might get him to the river bank, but what then? What if they had to swim across? They asked me what the river was like. I told them, about two hundred metres across and, I had to admit, the current was strong, especially after heavy rain such as we were having then. And very cold. 'It's too risky,' the sergeant told Jacob, 'you're not going.'

But this didn't satisfy him. When his officer visited, checking how things were going, Jacob tried to persuade him that he could go if he had help. But the officer refused and gave him a specific order to remain where he was.

After that he brooded for a while. Then announced with cheerful bravado that if he had to stay behind he might as well make himself useful. 'Carry me upstairs before you go,' he said to the others, 'and leave me with a gun and plenty of ammo. I'll keep Jerry's head down while you scoot out the back.'

I could not believe it when the others agreed.

'How can they let you do this?' I said.

He shrugged and smiled. 'It'll give me something to do. Take my mind off the pain in my leg.'

'You aren't strong enough,' I said. 'You'll certainly be killed.'

'Better than being taken prisoner,' he said. 'Can't stand being cooped up. I'd rather cop it, fighting. Honest.'

'No!' I said, quite beside myself by now. 'It's wrong!'

'Look,' he said, trying to take my hand to hold me still but I tugged it away. 'You don't understand. It'll help my pals get away safe and sound. In my place, any of the lads would do the same. We're trained for it. Honest. Just my rotten luck. I'm the one who's lumbered.'

'Rotten luck!' I shouted. 'How can you say that? This is not rotten luck! This is because of fighting. Because of war. Rotten war! I hate it! I hate all of it! I hate those who have done this! How dare they! How dare they!'

Everyone heard. Stopped what they were doing. Gave me sorrowful looks. I had not meant to make such an outburst. Fear and anger mixed with hunger and exhaustion cooked it up. And something to do with Jacob and myself of which I was still not conscious. This, I think, more than anything.

Mother came and put her arms round me.

'Remember your manners, my dear,' she whispered as she hugged me. 'Don't make things worse for these poor men. Think what it must be like for them. Soon they must risk everything to escape. Some will die. They know that.'

'If only we could do something to help,' I said, when I could speak calmly again.

Mama looked me steadily in the eyes. 'We've done all we can. I don't know what more we can do.'

It was not long before we found out.

POSTCARD
How long before my death
is the necessary question.
John Webster

By the time his tram arrived at the railway station the rain
had started again, heavily and with no sign of slackening.
For a few minutes Jacob sheltered in the crowded bustle of
the station concourse but soon began to fret that Daan van
Riet might tire of waiting and go out again. But he didn't
want to arrive soaking wet.

A flower stall occupied one corner of the concourse. His
grandmother had dinned in to him that it was a Dutch
custom for a guest to take flowers when visiting. He fingered Alma's guilders in his pocket. But it was not flowers he
had in mind.

'Hi,' he said to the man who was serving.

'Low,' the man said, without a grin.

He held out the coins and indicated the flowers. 'What
for four guilders?'

The man pulled a dubious face, but smiled, surveyed his
display with elaborate consideration for this big sale, and
selected one modest sunflower.

'And that bag,' Jacob said, pointing to a large brown
plastic bag discarded by some tubs of flowers.

'There goes the profit,' the man said, wrapping it neatly
round the sunflower before handing over the singular
bouquet with a mocking flourish. 'You must really love her
to spend like that. *Succes ermee!*'

Outside, Jacob held the flower in his teeth by the stem

while he tore the bag down one seam, then draped it over his head and shoulders like a hooded cowl. And thus protected set off at a brisk pace in the direction of the landmarks Alma had described.

Van Riet's address was not hard to find and looked like an old warehouse. A makeshift *stoep*, four steps of scuffed and weathered wood, led to an ancient heavy black-painted door. To the left of which Jacob found two insignificant bell buttons with faded nameplates. He pressed the one labelled *Wesseling en Van Riet*.

While he waited he surveyed the short street, which looked as if all of it had been ancient warehouses at one time. But now on one side of Van Riet's was a restaurant and a new-looking hotel, on the other a freshly renovated facade with big warehouse doors on each of its five floors converted into windows. Beside the narrow street ran an equally narrow murky-looking canal, out of the other side of which rose the back of the church, an oppressive bulk of dirty old red brick with arched, grimy and wire-netted windows. To the left of the church, a contrast and a challenge, was the back of a newish building with many regular modern windows: the rooms of a hotel, Jacob assumed. In the fogged greyness of the pouring rain the lowering church and the high flat-fronted buildings, narrowly separated by the sluggish canal and the cobbled street, appeared to him like a forbidden canyon. He shivered in his damp clothes, and tugged his plastic hood well over his face.

A bolt unlatched, the heavy door swung, surprisingly, outwards, and a tall young man with a shock of black hair, handsome triangular face, pale, with sharp bright blue eyes, long straight nose, wide thin-lipped mouth, and a slim body dressed in grey sweatshirt tucked in to black jeans, bare feet in thonged sandals, said, '*Mijn God!* Titus!'

'Jacob Todd.'

'Sorry, *hoor*.' Sounding like 'surrey whore', but couldn't

be. 'Daan.' Like darn. 'Come in.'

An ill-lit passage, wooden stairs painted rust red rising steeply at the end, rough bare old brick wall on one side, white-painted partition with a blue door in it on the other. Smell of damp dust and new paper.

'Smart hat.'

'Bit wet.'

'Want to take it off?'

'Thanks.' He presented the sunflower. 'For you.'

'Stolen for me. And before we'd even met! How gallant!'

'Stolen?'

'The woman who called said you lost all your money.'

'Oh, yes, but she gave me five guilders, just in case. I bought that for four. To be honest, what I wanted was this bag to keep the rain off and—'

'So I'm only an excuse. I'm devastated already.'

He held out a hand which Jacob shook, his own cold and rain-slicked in Daan's warm dry grip.

'Follow me. Are you used to our Dutch *trap* yet?'

'Stairs, you mean?'

'Stairs I mean and *trap* I mean. Your Dutch is brilliant, I see.'

'And,' said Jacob deciding he must match the challenge, 'your English is tricksy, I see.'

Daan let out what might have been a chuckle. 'I live at the top.'

The apartment was like none Jacob had ever seen before. He was all eyes. An expanse of shining exotic tiles in an intricate pattern of flower-like circles and rounded squares in olive green, pale and dark blue, triangulated on a white background, was repeated and repeated diagonally across the floor, which swept uninterrupted from front to rear and side to side of the building, until at the back a concertina Chinese screen, thin black frame and paper covering, cut off from view what could be glimpsed as a bedroom area.

The whole floor was immense, longer, he guessed, and as a wide as a tennis court. The walls were untreated old brick, hung here and there with a picture, some old oil paintings—a portait of a man who looked like an aged Daan, a landscape of old Holland—others modernist photos and coloured drawings. The ceiling was supported by thick wooden beams like the deck ribs of a sailing ship. Towards the front end of the room, the ceiling had been partly removed so that the floor above was visible and banistered like the upper deck of a ship, which was reached by a white-painted free-standing staircase like a ship's gangway. Looking up, he felt the floor beneath his feet swell and fall on the shift of the sea.

In the front wall a window made from large round-topped loading doors looked out on to the back of the church. A group of potted plants was arranged on either side. In this front part there was very little furniture: a large black leather sofa, two large leather armchairs set around a heavy wooden coffee table. An antique side-table against one wall carried an expensive TV and sound system, and further along a large glass-fronted sideboard full of nick-nacks and unfamiliar objects. Towards the rear of the room a kitchen occupied a recess formed by the enclosure of the main stairs and landing outside. Beyond the kitchen was the bedroom screen.

But what took his eye most of all was a floor-to-ceiling bank of books covering the wall between the front and the recess that contained the main stairs—about half the length of the whole room. He stared at it, stunned by this pano-rama of print among which, leaping out at him like the faces of friends among strangers, were a large number of books in English.

The whole apartment was such an attractive, odd mix-ture of old and new it made him reel with pleasure and envy. What a place to live! But how could Daan afford it?

After planting the sunflower in an empty wine bottle and

standing it on the coffee table, Daan had disappeared upstairs. Now he reappeared bearing a red sweatshirt and a
pair of jeans which he handed to Jacob saying, 'There's a
bathroom on the landing to the left of the stairs. Would you
like something to eat?'

'Thanks. I am a bit wet. And a bit hungry as well, to be
honest.'

'Go and change. I'll prepare something for us.'

They sat on high stools at either side of the work top that
separated the kitchen from the main room and talked while
they ate tinned vegetable soup zapped in the microwave,
Dutch farmhouse cheese, ham, tomatoes dressed with
garlic, fresh basil and olive oil, and a stick of French bread.

Daan wanted to know about the mugging. Jacob told the
story, now after practice on Alma nicely honed and enter-
taining, but playing down the meeting with Ton and
omitting the still too shying detail about Ton's crotch so
that he remained a she. Again he posed the question of Red
Cap's come-on behaviour.

Daan shrugged and said, 'Fancied you, I expect.'

'What,' Jacob said, 'you mean, she was making a pass?'

'Sure.'

'At me? Never! Just making a game of it. Having a bit of
fun. Don't you think?'

Daan smiled. 'If you like.'

'You remember when we visited you?' Daan said. 'You were
about five, I think. I was twelve.'

'No, I don't remember.'

'I played with you in a sandpit in your garden.'

'It's a fish pond now.' Jacob grinned and shrugged.
'Dad's mid-life crisis. He redesigned the garden.'

'You had a fight with your sister when she tried to join
in. You threw sand in her face.'

'Sounds likely.'

'Your father told you off.'

'He would.'

'You shouted at him. Fuck you, you said.'

'Never!'

'Yes.'

'I don't believe it.'

'There was a fuss.'

'I'll bet.'

'I hadn't heard that word in English before. Couldn't understand what all the upset was about. Your parents were embarrassed. Mine thought it was funny. They explained later, when they were laughing about it again.'

'And what happened?'

'You were sent to your room, screaming. But after a while your grandmother brought you down again. And you were grinning like—what is it you say?—the cat who drank the milk.'

'And my father was furious.'

'He didn't say much.'

'Not while you were there.'

'Only that your grandmother should not have done it, that she was spoiling you. I remember what she said, it was such a funny word.'

'Let me guess. Tosh.'

'Right.'

'Means nonsense. A favourite of hers.'

'You live with your grandmother now.'

'Yes.'

'Geertrui told me. She and your grandmother exchange letters now and then.'

'I know.'

'You and your grandmother are very close?'

'Very. Always have been.'

When they had finished eating and were tired of the stools,

they migrated with their coffee, Daan to the sofa, Jacob to an armchair with his back to the window so that he could view the room while they talked.

'The buildings in this street,' Jacob said, 'they look like they were old warehouses once.'

'They were. In the old days, the ships came right up to here. They would dock and discharge their cargo. At one time this house stored tea and another time perfume from Cologne. You saw that building like a tower at the end of the street?'

'The round one, with the little spiky spire on top?'

'It's called the Wailing Tower because the women used to wave their farewells from there when their men set sail.'

'It's a great apartment.'

'Used to belong to a man who loved sailing ships. And also Spanish tiles. Geertrui bought it from him. I've lived here since she went to the *verpleeghuis* . . . What do you call it?'

'I think you mean a nursing home. That explains it.'

'What?'

'The funny combination of furniture and stuff.'

'Funny?'

'Not funny funny. Just meant unusual, interesting.'

'How?'

He was beginning to wish he hadn't started on this. 'Well, the combination of old things and modern. The pictures on the wall, for instance.' He gave a nervous laugh.

'Most of it is Geertrui's, some is mine. I couldn't live here with only her stuff. But I don't like to make big changes. It's still her place, after all.'

'The books?'

'Geertrui's of course. Mine are in my room. I'm not the reader she is.'

'You're at university, aren't you?'

'Yes.'

'That was another reason I wondered about the apartment, to be honest.'

'How could a poor student afford it?'

'What are you studying?'

'Molecular biology. And the history of art on the side.'

'Wow!'

'Why wow?'

'Heavy stuff.'

'Oh, come on! Don't be such a snob.'

Jacob felt as if he had been slapped with a wet sock. Just when he thought he was getting on quite well. He always hated being wrong-footed, especially when he was only being sociable. And when it happened, he never knew what to say next. The right retort would only come later, too late, when he was on his own, inwardly squirming at the memory of being put down.

'More coffee?' Daan asked.

Jacob managed a nod and a subdued, 'Thanks.'

When he came back from the kitchen, Daan said, 'About Geertrui. What did Tessel—my mother—tell you?'

Jacob took a sip of coffee while he gathered himself. 'That your grandmother is in a nursing home because she's very ill. That your grandmother had invited Sarah to visit without consulting any of the family and that you didn't know I was coming till a few days ago. She also said your grandmother is a very stubborn sort of person and that her illness makes her behave very oddly sometimes.'

'That's true.'

'I was pretty embarrassed when she told me this yesterday. Felt I shouldn't be here, to be honest.'

'Mother's upset and worried about you.'

'I didn't know what to do. Still don't. Your father suggested I come to Amsterdam today and see Anne Frank's house. I like her diary, you see. He said we'd sort everything out this evening. He gave me your address. But he said not to mention it to your mother.'

68

'I know. He called me this morning from his office.'

'He didn't explain why. It all seems a bit weird, if you don't mind me saying so.' He hadn't intended the note of complaint he heard in his voice. But the wet sock was still stinging.

Daan said with cold patience, 'Geertrui has an incurable disease. She's in a lot of pain most of the time. They give her drugs to help which do make her behave, let's say strangely sometimes. But there's more to it than that.'

'I didn't know. And Sarah doesn't either. We knew your grandmother isn't too well, but not that she's that seriously ill. I wouldn't have come otherwise. I mean, in her letter your grandmother said there was going to be a party.'

'There is, but not the kind of party you mean, I think.'

'What kind then?'

Daan shifted in his seat and looked away.

'I'll tell you later. There's some other things I should explain. But I must talk to Tessel before I tell you. She's with Geertrui today.'

'I know. That's why your father suggested I come to Amsterdam.'

'I can't talk to her while she's with Geertrui. She'll be back home about five.'

Jacob couldn't decide which he felt most, weary or angry. 'Look, I'm sorry, but this is getting a bit much. I feel like I'm just a problem for everybody. Wouldn't it be best if I went back home?'

With serious emphasis and looking Jacob square in the eyes, Daan said, 'I really think you should wait till I can tell you everything. It's very important. Believe me. There are things you should know. It isn't just to do with us, with my family. It involves you too.'

Now anxiety ousted anger. 'Me! What? How?'

Daan held up his hands, palms towards Jacob, like a man warding off a blow. 'Later. When I've talked to Tessel. Trust me. Just for these few hours. After that, we'll decide

69

what to do next.'

'I don't know.'

'You can't go home right now, can you? One more night won't make any difference.'

'I'm not sure.'

Daan stood up and collected the coffee mugs.

'Listen, we'll do something to pass the time. There's something I'd like to show you. I think you'll be interested. Okay?'

'. . . All right.'

In the bathroom Jacob glowered at himself in the mirror. He hated it when people said they knew things they wouldn't tell him. But what could he do? Leave? And go where? Back to Haarlem, where his passport and air tickets were? But what with? Borrow from Daan? 'I'm pissed off and going back to your mother so can I have the price of the fare, please?' How berkish can you get! And then what, as there'd be no one in? Sit on the doorstep and wait, like a stray dog? Again! What would be the point?

He definitely was not enjoying himself.

But neither, to judge by his looks, was Daan.

Who, Jacob thought while he used the lavatory and changed in to his dried clothes, he rather liked. His midnight looks for sure: eye-locking. His self-confidence: enviable. His in-the-face directness: even when it stings, at least you know where you are, no faking. And something else. Something that tickled the blood. He couldn't quite put his finger on what it was. But he disliked him as well. For being so cock-sure, so *knowing*. Too clever by half, Sarah would say. He wanted you to submit to his superiority. To be the one in charge, the one on top. Well, let him, Jacob thought, why should I care? I only have to be with him for a few hours.

As he was leaving the bathroom he found Alma's napkin in

70

a pocket of his jeans and showed it to Daan, who smiled and said, 'An old Dutch saying. It means something like, If you have the will there is a way.'

Jacob laughed and said, 'We have one like that. But I prefer this one.' And he wrote under Alma's neat letters:

NOTHING VENTURED
NOTHING GAINED

GEERTRUI

Late that afternoon of the withdrawal my brother Henk and his friend Dirk came stumbling down the cellar steps. They were so dishevelled that in the dim light we hardly recognised them at first. Mother was greatly devoted to Henk. As soon as she realised who he was, she lost the composure she had so far maintained, and rushing to him, even in her haste treading on wounded men who lay in her path, she threw her arms around him saying, 'Henk! Henk! What are you doing here? Don't you know the British are leaving?' She was kissing him again and again, and stroking his face, as if to make sure he was not a ghost. Father, while this went on, was greeting Dirk, whom he liked very much, sometimes calling him his second son. 'What's happening?' he was saying. 'Are you all right? Why are you here?' Dirk was saying, 'Everything is okay. We're well. We've come to see that you are safe.'

As was always my instinct when such scenes were happening, I held back, waiting until the first excitement wore off. Then I could have my brother to myself. He looked at me over Mother's shoulder as she was hugging and petting him, and winked, smiling broadly, so I knew there was no trouble and that when he was ready he would explain, for Henk always took his time over everything, being one of the most calm and self-possessed people I have ever known. I loved him so much that once, before I was old enough to know better about saying such things, I told him I wished he were not my brother so I could have him for my husband!

72

When Mother at last remembered herself, she let go of Henk and turning to the soldiers who were watching with unconcealed amusement and a little envy too, I think (most of them were no older, some younger than Henk), she announced with her eyes full of tears, '*Mijn zoon, mijn zoon.*'

Understanding this was a family reunion, the men made room for us in the corner where Jacob lay so that we could sit together and talk as privately as possible in our crowded cellar. One of the soldiers, a youth called Andrew who had a wounded arm strapped in a sling, came over and gave us a bar of English chocolate saying, 'I was keeping this for something special. You've been special to us so I'd like you to have it.' I know from my own experience as well as from all our friends and neighbours told me after the war that such acts of kindness were not unusual during those ugly days, but I remember this one particularly because it happened at such an emotional moment for me and my family. And also because of the sadness I saw in that young man's eyes as he gave us his gift. It was not hard to guess he was thinking of his family at home in England and longing for the moment when he would be reunited with them, as Henk was with us. And I cannot help wondering if there was sadness in his eyes because some hint of intuition told him he would never see his home again. We learned later that he was killed that night, as he waited to be ferried across the river. I have many times paused at his grave in the soldiers' cemetery at Oosterbeek, and thanked him again.

As we ate our celebratory gift—and oh, my mouth still waters at the memory of the wonderful taste of it; no chocolate has ever tasted as delicious again, not even the best you can buy these days at Pompadour in Amsterdam—Henk told us his story. After I left them that Sunday afternoon, he and Dirk also saw the parachutes. They immediately made their way to where they were landing, and greeting the first English soldiers they met, offered their help. For the rest of the week, along with other Dutch volunteers, they acted as interpreters, guides, messengers, and gave whatever other assistance they could to the British officers. They asked for weapons so they could fight also, but this was not allowed. Since Wednesday they had been working at the British headquarters in the Hartenstein Hotel, where the museum of the battle now is.

There was much to tell us, Henk said, but it would have to wait. He and Dirk knew about the evacuation plan and had come to see that we were alive and safe while there was still time. But they could not stay. They would have to go back in to hiding at once.

'You know what the Germans are like,' he said. 'When the British have gone, they'll be ruthless with anyone who has helped them. And they'll be more determined than ever to send young men to forced labour.'

'He's right,' said Papa.

'But not just the men,' said Dirk. 'Young women won't be safe either, after this. There'll be reprisals.'

'We think Geertrui should come with us,' said Henk.

I was not surprised that this made Father agitated. 'Geertrui? No no, Henk. I don't like the Germans any more than you do, but they've behaved properly with the girls so far, you must admit. Why should they change now?'

'They won't like what has happened,' said Henk. 'The British have lost here, but it's only a matter of time before we're liberated. A few weeks. Maybe a few days. Their army is not far away, and the Allies are pushing up from Belgium. The Germans must know all is over for them. Who can say how they'll behave when they're desperate?'

'Henk is right,' said Dirk. 'And besides, the village is ruined. There's not a house fit to live in. How are you going to survive? Please let Geertrui come with us. She'll be safer in the country. And there's a better chance of food there.'

'Perhaps you and Mother should come too, Papa,' said Henk. 'There's nothing left for you here.'

Father took Mother's hand and they looked anxiously at each other for a moment before Mother said, 'There isn't much left, I know. But we've lived here, your father and I, all our married life. You and Geertrui were born in our bedroom. This is our home. It's where we belong. How can we abandon it? Why should we?'

Father said, 'You and Dirk go. You're right. It won't be safe for young men. But your mother and I must stay. We'll manage somehow. We always have till now. And Geertrui must stay with us. She'll be safe enough. Why should they harm us? We've done nothing wrong.'

'Nothing wrong!' said Henk. 'Father, you've harboured British soldiers. To the Germans that's giving succour to the enemy.'

'So have all our neighbours,' said Mother.

'But that will only make it worse,' said Dirk. 'Don't you see? They'll hate us for it.'

'You know we're right, Papa,' said Henk. 'If you won't come, at least let us take Geertrui.'

'Right or wrong, Henk,' said Papa, 'your mother and I are staying and so is Geertrui.'

I had listened to all this in silence. And with growing anger. One of our Dutch characteristics, so they say, is *overleg*, which means 'consultation'. Yet here a decision was being taken about my life—and possibly my death—without any consultation with me. My parents, my brother, and Dirk, who only a few weeks before had told me how much he loved me and how he would like to marry me if I would have him: all of them deciding for me at this dangerous time, and not one of them asking what I thought, what I wanted. Still today I feel the anger I felt at my family's denial of me at that moment.

With Father and Henk in disagreement there was an impasse in the conversation. Neither wanted to have a row. That would not be right! It would not be proper! We Dutch are embarrassed by such confrontations. I waited to see if, after all, anyone would refer to me. When they did not, I said, as self-righteous and pert as only a girl who is not yet a young woman can be, 'Would anyone care to know what I think and to hear my decision about my own fate? Or is that too much to ask?'

Instantly Dirk said, 'Surely you want to come with us?' Mother said, 'We didn't mean to leave you out. We only want what's best for you.' Father said, 'Of course you must stay with us. You know how much we love you.' But Henk said, 'I didn't think. Sorry, little sister.'

How perverse we human animals are! The apologetic attention the others lavished upon me only roused me more. And my dear brother Henk took the brunt of it, as so often those whom we love most do at such times.

I said, 'I am your sister, Henk, but I'm not so little any more. Or haven't you noticed? I'm quite old enough to make up my own mind, and I'm quite capable of looking after myself, thank you.'

Of course by now everyone was becoming upset, especially Mother, who could never abide such scenes.

'Geertrui,' she said in her school teacher's voice. 'Stop it! Behave! No arguments, please.'

There was an embarrassed silence. Father stared at his boots, Mother slowly cleaned her spectacles, Dirk inspected our cellar's shell-shocked walls. Only Henk could still look me in the eye, and at last broke the ice.

'All right, big sister,' he said with a smile he knew I could not resist, 'tell us your decision. We really do want to hear it. Truly!'

Still it was hard for me to swallow my ire and speak pleasantly, but with an effort I managed. 'I would like to go with you, Henk,' I said, 'because I think you're right about what will happen after the British have gone, and that it will be better in the country.' I paused, enjoying the drama, I'm afraid, before going on: 'But I shall stay here.' Another shameful pause for dramatic effect. 'Though not because you want me with you, Papa.'

'Then why?' Henk asked.

'Because of Jacob.'

'Jacob?' said Dirk. 'Jacob who?'

'The English soldier lying beside us,' said Father.

'Why? What does he mean to her?' said Dirk at the same time as Mother was saying, 'You can't be serious.'

'I don't understand,' said Papa.

I said, 'Letting him fight while the others leave. He isn't fit. He'll be killed for sure. How can we let him do this? I shall stay and help him. It isn't right to send him in to the woods.' (Do you have this expression? I can't remember. It means to let someone down or abandon them.)

Papa was appalled. 'What are you talking about? We, sending him in to the woods! It's nothing to do with us. He's a soldier. He volunteered. If he wishes to help his comrades in this way, it is not for us to interfere. That's his business.'

'I don't care, Papa. I'm going to do what I can to help him.'

'Geertrui, you're not being rational.'

'Rational!' I said. 'Father, is there anything rational about what's happening to us here? Did being rational prevent this war? Did being rational save us from being invaded? Will being rational liberate us?'

'You're going too far,' said Mother. 'You should not speak to your father like this.'

'I'm sorry, Mama. I thought at least you would understand.'

'Understand what? I certainly do not understand you at all. You're overwrought. Take hold of yourself!'

But I was so angry by now, I would not be silenced even by my mother at her most stern. 'Mama,' I said, with as much calmness as I could manage, 'two Sundays ago we welcomed this man to our home as our liberator. We gave him water. We danced for joy. Have you forgotten? Then he was brought to us all but dead. For five days now we've nursed him. We've dressed his wounds. We've washed him. We've clothed him. We've fed him like a child. We've even helped him to go to the lavatory. Looking after him, I've seen and touched parts of a man I've never seen or touched before. He and I have slept huddled to each other for warmth while the enemy has demolished our home. We've treated him as one of ourselves, one of our family. Together, Mama, you and Papa and I, we've saved him from death. Yet because he's decided for the sake of his comrades—and for our sake as well, let me remind you—to do something he's not strong enough to do, when he'll surely be killed, you tell me, Papa, it's nothing to do with us. That we must not interfere. That I am not rational for wanting to help him. All I can say is that if he were Henk we wouldn't think twice about it. Well, in these last few days I've done more for this man than I have ever done for my brother. Isn't it only right that I help him now? Isn't it the decent thing to do? That's what I think being rational means, Papa. And that, Mama, is what I thought at least you would understand.'

Never had I uttered such a speech before. Never had I thought myself capable of it. Never have I made such a speech again. Because, perhaps, never did such anger seize me as possessed me that day. Upstairs in the ruins of my home foreign soldiers were fighting for my country. Here in the cellar I was fighting for myself.

No one said anything for a while, but stared at me in astonishment. Even the soldiers huddled around us had fallen quiet, sensing from our behaviour, I suppose, that we were troubled. Jacob, propped up against the wall by my side, had watched me intently all the time. I tried to avoid looking at him because I was sure I would burst into tears if I did, and then I would lose all my dignity and with it the effect my speech had made.

78

Outside, the guns thumped and rattled, and rain fell in cold torrents, filling the air in the cellar with an icy dampness. I remember that I was sweating from nervous reaction after my speech and how clammy the air felt on my skin.

The paraffin lamp which had supplied our light for the last two days chose that moment to run out of fuel and douse us in darkness, so we had to return to the flickering uncertain light of candles stuck inside preserving jars hung by twine from beams in the ceiling. Thank goodness, this provided a diversion that distracted us.

When we had settled down again, Dirk said, 'I don't understand why this man means so much to you, Geertrui, but if your mind is made up, there's only one answer I can think of. We'll just have to take him with us.'

As you will guess, this set fire to the discussion again. Father said such an idea was madness, we'd all get killed. No madder, Dirk replied, than hiding a Jew or working for the Resistance, as some of our friends and neighbours were doing. Mother said it wasn't practical—how could three people carrying a wounded soldier hope to get past the German positions without being caught?

'Where there's a will there's a way,' said Dirk.

'You're talking like a hen with no head,' said Father. 'If you're determined to do this mad thing, at least plan it properly. And for God's sake leave Geertrui out of it.'

'No, Father,' I said. 'I'm going. Henk and Dirk will find a way, won't you, Henk?'

'It's a ditch of a card,' said Henk. 'He'll have more chance of staying alive with us than he will lying upstairs in the state he's in, on his own with a gun.'

'It's the only way,' I said. 'He's got to come with us.'

Henk chuckled at me. 'Now look who's talking for whom,' he said. 'How do you know your soldier wants to come with us? Have you asked him? Or are you deciding for him?'

He was right of course. I felt shamefaced. Hoist with my own petard, as one of the 'familiar sayings' put it. *Wie een kuil graaft voor een ander, valt er zelf in*, is what we say: He who digs a pit for someone else, falls in to it himself.

'I hate you sometimes!' I said to Henk and the others laughed, which at least relieved the tension a little.

I shifted so that I could talk quietly to Jacob. I explained who Henk and Dirk were and that they wanted to take me to Dirk's family farm, where they were hiding from the Germans, because they thought I would be safer there than in Oosterbeek after the battle, and where there would be food. Jacob shook hands with them and they said *hallo*. Then I told him I had refused to go with them because I was determined to remain with him. He tried at first to laugh this off, saying, 'You can't do that. Don't be silly! I'll be okay. But thanks anyway.' 'Well,' I said, 'I'm staying whether you think me silly or not. But,' I went on before he could interrupt, 'Dirk has made another proposal.' And I explained about how we could take him with us, pushing him on our garden trolley, and hide him at the farm till his army liberated us, which would surely not be long. 'This way,' I said, 'you will not die in our upstairs room, which is something I cannot bear to think of, and you will not become a prisoner of war if you don't get shot, which you say you cannot bear to think of.'

I could tell from the change on his face how much he liked the idea. His eyes came alive as I had not seen them since the first day we met. But still he made objections, though I'm sure only because he thought he should. It was very risky, he said. Having to look after him would only make it more likely we would be caught or shot. The trolley would slow us up. If we were caught the Germans would shoot Henk and Dirk and me for helping a British soldier to escape. On and on like this for some minutes. What a maze men make of it when they want to argue. In and out and round about! I had soon had quite enough.

'Jacob,' I said as firmly as my then still searching English would allow, 'this is not building a dyke. There is not time for all this talk. You must decide for yourself. But for me, my mind is made up. Go or not, I stay with you.'

'You make it sound,' he said, 'like it's only up to me.'

'It is.'

'No. There's you. If you won't leave me, Angel Maria, then what I decide also affects you, doesn't it?'

'*Ach*, what a Jesuit!' I said, and wanted to hit him.

'But I'm right. Yes?'

'Yes!'

'So you should tell me what you think is best and what you want to do.'

Having insisted that everyone attend to what I thought and what I wanted, when it came to making the final decision and taking the responsibility, I didn't want to do it. I longed instead for someone to decide for me. At one and the same, both a failure of love and a demand of love. How typical of me, as I know after years of learning this lesson.

'I'll do whatever you want,' I said, hardly able to speak the words. 'It is your life I am trying to save, after all.'

'And your life you're risking to do it,' said Jacob. 'So we're in it together and should decide together.'

Still I did not want to answer, and hung my head to avoid those dangerous eyes.

Jacob pushed himself up into a position where he could look closely into my face and smiling said, 'Here's a fine anger!'

'Because I am angry,' I said, not yet understanding his English irony.

Touching my cheek with a finger, he said, 'Are we to fight each other as well?'

I managed to mutter a throttled 'No.'

'Pax, then?'

How not to return his smile? Clearing my throat I said, 'I think it would be best to go with Henk and Dirk.'

'Good. Me too. And as the man said, "It'll be an awfully big adventure."'

'Man? Which man?' I said. 'I haven't heard this saying before. Are you being serious? I don't know.'

'Have we time for all this talk?' he said.

'No,' I said, aware again of the noise outside and of Henk and Dirk and my parents watching us. 'You must explain me later. I'll tell the others what we have decided.'

I cannot say that Mother and Father were happy, but they were resigned. There had been more than enough *overleg* to satisfy our Dutch desire for consultation. With nothing more to be said we set about our preparations.

What a relief it always is when a decision has been made and you can get on and do something! Like a heavy burden lifted from you. You feel so much better at once, charged with a new energy and with fresh hope. Never have I felt this more than that day, with death visiting all around us and the prospect of a life of misery and humiliation if I survived and stayed where I was. Whatever happened now, at least I was making an effort to take charge of my own life and not giving myself in to the hands of our enemy. I have never been as religious as my parents, but such times bring back the old words. As I rescued my little emergency suitcase from the clutter of our days confined to the cellar, I heard myself muttering:

> My time is in thy hand; deliver me from the hand
>   of mine enemies: and from them that persecute me.
> The Lord of hosts is with us: the God of Jacob is our
>   refuge.

Which made me smile and reminded me of another passage:

> He shall choose out our heritage for us: even the worship
>   of Jacob, whom he loved.

This made me laugh out loud and say to the God of Jacob, as I changed in to whatever clean, or at least unworn clothes I could find, in the uncertain privacy of our coal-hole lavatory, 'Please choose a heritage for us that includes a bath.' I dread to think of how *erg* we must have *gestonken* by then.

Meanwhile, Henk and Dirk made a sortie into the back garden to prepare the trolley. And Jacob was talking to two of the other soldiers, explaining what was happening. When I came out of the lavatory, they had dressed him in one of their combat jackets, which would help keep him as warm and as dry as possible. It would also mean he was in uniform if he was captured, and would not then be shot as a spy. They had also given him a gun and stuffed the big pockets of his jacket with ammunition. 'Must you take that?' I asked. 'Insurance,' he said, patting the weapon like it was a pet dog. I did not approve at all and tried to persuade Henk to leave it behind. But instead he was envious, wishing he had one himself. Men with their deathly toys. There is no end of it.

Henk and Dirk agreed that we should leave soon after the bombardment by the British guns from south of the river started at 20:50. Henk calculated that this would be the safest time to travel across the British-held area, from our house near the eastern perimeter to the western perimeter on the edge of the woods in to which we must escape.

Night fell. With it rain fell in wild torrents. And through both wind and rain fell a hail of shells when the storm of the bombardment began, silencing the Germans, exactly as planned.

Time to leave. A terrible moment, when it was necessary for everyone's sake to appear calm and cheerful. A pretence I would not have been able to sustain had I known this would be the last time I would see my father. He died during the Winter of the Hunger that was visited upon us after the failure of the Allies to liberate my unhappy country until the spring of 1945. It is as well that the future is ever an unread book, for had I known I would never see Papa again, I could not have left him. Such accidents of fate suffered in one's youth return to haunt one with irrational guilt in old age. If only I had been there, I might have helped him survive. If only. By the time one is old, one is rich in this currency.

You see why I would rather not dwell on our parting. We embraced and kissed and shook hands and exchanged declarations of love and confident faith in our future together. All with that robust good nature and restraint of passion which is the glory of our Dutch civility.

And after our family farewells, the turn of the soldiers who shared our cellar. Those young men from a foreign country had in a few awful days become more intimate friends than any of our Dutch neighbours who we had lived beside for years. Not knowing, perhaps, how else to show their feelings, they pressed upon me as I said goodbye to each one, small gifts of the few personal possessions they had left. Cigarettes, though I did not smoke, some sweets, a cap badge, shoulder flashes, a pen ('Maybe you'll be able to write us a letter one day'), matches, a paratrooper's scarf, even a wristwatch ('You'll need to know the time, Gertie, wherever you're off to'), and from poor shell-shocked Sam, only just hanging on to himself, a book of poems which lies by me today as I write ('Help you with your English!'). Norman, oldest of them in age and time spent with us, waited appropriately till last in this goodbye parade. He handed me a small black leather wallet, with a picture in it of his family and himself, saying, 'Cheerio, Gertie. You're a brave and lovely girl. I want you to have this. I hope we'll meet again.'

And then with jokes and teasing, which is, I think, as much the English fashion on these difficult occasions as is our Dutch robust civility for us, we were led and helped and followed up the cellar steps and through the rubble of our dear home and out in to the back garden, where, in the roar and shudder of the embattled night, we sat Jacob on the trolley, his gun held ready in his bandaged hands, my emergency suitcase and his backpack tucked one on each side of him, and with the icy rain threatening either to freeze us or to drown us before we could be shot dead or reach our destination, we set off, Dirk leading the way, Henk pushing the trolley, and me by his side, my heavy heart pounding, my throat lumpy and dry, and my thoughts torn in shreds.

Such a leaving I would never wish on anyone.

Nor the cold coming we had of it to our hiding place.

We become what we behold.
William Blake

'Open your eyes,' Daan said.

He was standing behind Jacob, holding him by the shoulders, in one of the smaller galleries of the Rijksmuseum. Before entering he had made Jacob promise not to cheat, then guided him through the drift of visitors to this spot.

On the wall in front of him Jacob saw a portrait of himself. In ancient oils. Head to waist. Angled towards his left. In rich and rusty browns. Except for the pale triangular familiar face. Life size. Which shone as if bathed in sunlight, framed within the shadowed enclosure of a monk's hood raised over the head. Eyes lowered and heavy-lidded. Wide mouth with fleshy bee-stung lower lip caught by the painter in a shy demure pleased-with-himself smile. And the feature which took most of Jacob's attention because he hated it so much, the long thick nose with its blunt and bulbous end. His father's nose. His grandfather's nose. The Todd nose. His sister Poppy and his brother Harry didn't have it. They had his mother's pretty, slim-line version.

How often with the aid of a couple of mirrors he had scowled from every possible angle at that offensive hooter, that hideous snout, that swollen trunk, that tumescent nasal evacuator. He would sometimes squeeze and manipulate the end of his embarrassing blower between finger and thumb, like a sculptor moulding clay, hoping to reshape it into at least a presentable, if not a handsome conk. He had

86

in mind something like the fetching schnozzle that, for example, graces Michelangelo's David, or the one belonging to devastating River Phoenix, which and whom he had studied closely while viewing recently for the fourth time a video of *My Own Private Idaho*. To no effect of course. His discomfiting snitch remained as baneful as ever.

Unable to take his eyes from this image of himself, he said, 'Who is he?'

'Titus. Titus van Rijn.'

'Never heard of him.'

'But of his father.'

'Don't think so.'

'Who painted the self-portraits of Rembrandt?'

'Eh?'

'Who painted the self-portraits of Rembrandt?'

'Rembrandt, of course!'

'Whose full name was Rembrandt van Rijn.'

'Ah! But this isn't one of his self-portraits, is it, because it's of someone called Titus. So it's a portrait by Rembrandt of . . .?'

'His son dressed as a monk. Painted in 1660 when Titus was nineteen.'

Thinking only now to do so, Jacob glanced at the caption on the wall by the side of the picture, confirming that Daan was not making it all up, and then, stepping as close as he dared, inspected, nose-to-nose you might say, the portrait of himself as Titus.

A watchful female guard of sumo proportions moved towards him.

Titus seemed so *there* that Jacob felt the painted boy might at any second lift his head and look straight back at him and speak. His fingers longed to touch that reflexive face. Unthinking, he raised his hand.

'Back,' the guard said. 'Move back.'

Jacob took a step or two away but could not take his eyes from the painting. It mesmerised him. Which he thought, even at the time, was strange, for the picture was not impressive. Had he been wandering on his own through the gallery he might easily have passed by without noticing it, just as other people were now. Most of the picture was so dark that you could hardly tell what was there: some foliage in autumnal colours behind Titus's back was clear; and the monk's brown habit, which was made of a thick coarse heavy-looking material and was much too large for the boy's body, at least to judge from the head, so that he seemed to be encased inside its barrel chest and voluminous arms, like armour, rather than wearing it. But shining out from the middle of all this swallowing darkness was Titus's glowing face, alive and vibrant, the skin pale gold, the lowered eyes deep and perhaps a little sad, the full lower lip, which he might just have licked, fresh red and sensuous, yet still innocently delicate. Untouched, was the word that came to Jacob's mind.

'You like it?' said Daan coming to his side.

No picture he had ever seen had so absorbed and fixated him. He did not want to say this but made himself say yes.

'Then you should see the portrait of Titus in a red cap when he is a little older. In that one he looks right at you, straight in to the eyes. And you see his hair, which you can't in this one. Unlike you, he has long curly brown hair. Very beautiful. You should try growing yours the same.'

'No thanks.'

'It would suit you. You could easily see the portrait. It's in the Wallace Collection in London. I like it better than this one. It's better painted, and this one is a bit, how do you say? . . . *nuffig* . . . prim. The Madonna pose.'

'Madonna!'

'Not *Madonna*. I mean, the Mother of Christ. *The* Madonna.'

They laughed.

'And how is Titus like her?'

'The pose. Head down in innocent resignation. Hands

clasped on his lap. The monk's dress. Very saintly, very pure. Very prim. Just like all those thousands of pictures of the holy virgin. And *bij God!*, Titus certainly looks virgin, don't you agree?'

His eyes still on the picture, Jacob said, 'You know all this from studying art history, I suppose.'

'No. I study art history because of Rembrandt.'

'How come?' He did not really want to know but at least while Daan was talking he could go on gazing at Titus.

'For me, he's the greatest painter who ever lived. He is at the end of the old world and the beginning of the modern. He's fascinated me ever since the first time I saw *The Nightwatch*. That huge picture we passed on the way here. My father brought me to see it when I was eight. I thought it so dramatic, so exciting, I wanted to climb on to the canvas. Really! Into the painting—and be part of the scene. Of course, I know now it's totally a piece of theatre, not at all realistic. The lighting is artificial, the grouping of the figures is operatic, their attitudes are false heroic poses. So stagey. High camp! But when I was eight, it seemed more real than the people who were crowded around me, looking at it. From that moment I've wanted to know everything there is to know about Rembrandt. I see every one of his pictures that I can. I study his work, his life. Everything. Every detail. And my thesis will be on Titus. The role of Titus in Rembrandt's life. It's never been done. Not as a subject on its own.'

Jacob was only half listening and now couldn't distract himself enough from Titus to keep the talk going.

There was a silence between them before he felt Daan's arm slip round his waist, drawing him away.

'Look here,' Daan said, guiding him to a slightly larger picture next but one along the wall.

An old man with a lumpy face, a white and yellow hat like rolled-up towelling wrapped round his head, madman's fly-away curly hair sticking out from under it, forehead creased with many wrinkles from his raised eyebrows, watery eyes staring out at Daan standing by Jacob's left shoulder, his hands holding open a large book as if he has this very second looked up from reading. And like the picture of Titus, all the light, all the emphasis on the face. And like Titus, the nose—large, lumpy, bulged at the end.

Jacob chuckled. 'Looks a bit gaga.'

'Rembrandt when he was fifty-five, eight years before his death.'

'Looks like he's already on his last legs.'

'A self-portrait dressed as the Apostle Paul. Painted a year after the picture of Titus as a monk. Come. Stand further away.' Daan's hand took Jacob's shoulder and pulled him back. 'From here you see both pictures. Side by side. Looking at each other. Yes? Father and son at just about the same time.'

Not to be outdone, Jacob added, 'And each pretending to be someone else.'

'But what comes through, what you see, is not the *acteerspel*—'

'The acting? . . . The pretence?'

'Yes, not the pretence . . . *Door de gezichten* . . .'

'You mean, the true person?'

'Exactly. The true person. Don't you agree?'

Jacob considered each picture. 'Yes. That's right.' And it was. He saw it was so. 'It's the faces, isn't it.'

'That's one reason why I love Rembrandt. His truthfulness. Always honest. Loves people and loves them just as they are. Never afraid of life as it is.'

Jacob thought: This isn't a game any more. He's talking differently. He's being serious. He means it. We're not the same together. We've changed.

Again he felt something about Daan he couldn't quite put his finger on. Something he liked but which also disturbed him.

'So why write about Titus? What's so interesting about

90

him? It's Rembrandt you admire.'

'Well, for one thing. When Rembrandt was forced into bankruptcy—'

'He was?'

'Yes. He earned a great deal, was very successful, worked very hard. Work, work, work, all the time. But he also spent a lot. Had a madness for collecting things. A museum amount of stuff. All sorts of objects. His house was full of them. In the end, he got into debt and couldn't pay. So all his belongings were taken away and sold at auction. Titus went to the auction and used his own money to buy back as much as he could. Things his father would need. Among them the beautiful mirror in an ebony frame that Rembrandt used when painting his self-portraits. But on the way home, somehow or other the mirror was broken.'

'Oh-o! Bad news.'

'Very bad. Can you imagine how he felt? And think of what it means that he did what he could to buy his father's things back. So that Rembrandt could continue to do the only thing that mattered to him: paint pictures. Many people, historians, critics, have said that Rembrandt stole from Titus. That he exploited his son, used the money Titus's mother, Saskia, left to him when she died. In other words, they are saying Rembrandt was a selfish abusive father who only cared about his own career and welfare. I don't believe that at all. And the story about Titus going to the sale and buying the mirror tells me that he loved his father and would do all he could to support and help him. In fact, if it was not for Titus, Rembrandt would have been prevented from painting, because in those days, if you were made bankrupt you were stopped from practising your trade. To save Rembrandt from that fate, Titus became his father's employer, hiring him to paint pictures.'

Jacob looked at the two portraits with different eyes. The son who employed the father was employed by the father as his model.

'A good story,' he said. 'What did Titus do?'

'For a living, you mean? They say he tried to be a painter but wasn't any good at it. I don't believe that's what he really wanted. What he did, what he was, was his father's model. I think what he loved was sitting for his father. He loved being closely observed by his father, receiving all his attention, and loved watching his father at work.'

'Father watching son watching father.'

'Right. While one painted the other and the other knew he was being painted. That's important to it.'

'How? I don't quite understand what you mean.'

'Put it this way. I asked Geertrui the other day what she thought love is—real love, true love. She said that for her real love is observing another person and being observed by another person with complete attention. If she's right, you only have to look at the pictures Rembrandt painted of Titus, and there are quite a lot, to see that they loved each other. Because that is what you're seeing. Complete attention, one of the other.'

Jacob swapped his gaze between father and son, and saw what Daan meant.

'But in that case,' he said, speaking the words as the thought came to him, 'all art is love, because all art is about looking closely, isn't it. Looking closely at what's being painted.'

'The artist looking closely while he paints, the viewer looking closely at what has been painted. I agree. All true art, yes. Painting. Writing—literature—also. I think it is. And bad art is a failure to observe with complete attention. So, you see why I like the history of art. It's the study of how to observe life with complete attention. It's the history of love.'

'What happened? To Titus, I mean.'

'He married the daughter of a silversmith. They were together for only seven months before Titus died of the plague.'

'The Black Death.'

'It killed many at that time. He was buried in the Westerkerk.'

'Near Anne Frank's house.'

'A year later Rembrandt died. But not of the plague. Of a broken heart, I would say. We know he was buried beside Titus in Westerkerk. But his grave has never been found.'

Not knowing what else to say, Jacob detached himself from Daan's arm and went to view Titus in close-up again. Daan followed. The guard eyed them from the door.

'So,' Daan said, 'am I right? Titus looks exactly like you.'

'Only I don't go round wearing monky gear.'

Daan ignored the feeble joke. 'How does it feel?'

'Weird. Even weirder now I know who he is.'

The guard took a step towards them.

'She must think we're going to steal him,' Jacob muttered.

'There was an incident recently.'

'An incident?'

'Someone kissed Titus.'

'You mean someone actually walked up to the picture and laid a juicy smacker on his mouth?'

'Yes.'

'Hoi yoi! What happened?'

'No one saw.'

'So how do they know?'

'Whoever did it left the print of their kiss in lipstick.'

'I don't believe it!'

'The problem was, the lipstick was very hard to remove without damaging the picture.'

'And nobody knows who did it?'

'Not for certain.'

Jacob glanced at Daan. 'But you think you know?'

'*Nee, nee!*'

'You do, you think you know. I can see you do!'

Daan grinned.

'Come on, confess. Who was it?'

'My lips are sealed. Isn't that what you say?'

'So were Titus's! *Swalk!*'

'Swalk?'

'S W A L K. In capitals. Sealed with a loving kiss. Kids write it on love letters.'

Daan pulled a scornful grin. 'We have nothing like that.'

They stood in silence, studying the painting. Other visitors floated past, few pausing to give Titus more than a glance.

After a while Jacob said, 'All the time I feel that if I wait just another minute, he'll get up and walk out of the picture and come and join us.'

Daan said nothing, but, again placing his hand on Jacob's shoulder, steered him through the crowd back the way they had come. At the museum shop he stopped and bought postcards of Titus dressed as a monk and Rembrandt dressed as the Apostle Paul.

'Here,' he said, giving them to Jacob, 'yourself as a young man and yourself as an old man.'

As they went down the marble staircase to the exit he began to sing a plaintive song in a gravelly voice:

'*Mijn hele leven zocht ik jou,*
om—eindelijk gevonden—
te weten wat eenzaam is.'

'And what's that all about?' Jacob asked.

'A song by a Dutch poet, Bram Vermeulen,' Daan said.

'Which, being interpreted, means?'

Stopping at the bottom of the stairs, Daan thought, then said, with mock gravity:

'I've spent my life looking for you,
only to learn, now I have found you at last,
the meaning of solitude.'

POSTCARD

Vladimir: To have lived is not enough for them.

Estragon: They have to talk about it.

Vladimir: To be dead is not enough for them.

Estragon: It is not sufficient.

Samuel Beckett: WAITING FOR GODOT

'That was a long one,' Jacob said.

The phone conversation between Daan and his mother had gone on for over half an hour. Jacob had heard his name mentioned too often for comfort.

'Tessel is upset,' Daan said. 'Geertrui was difficult all day. She kept asking where you were. She wants to see you.'

'Glad I'm so popular.' The joke fell flat. Mild panic returned. Their viewing of Titus had attached him for a while. Now he felt estranged again.

'I explained what happened.'

'Which must have improved the shining hour no end.'

'I told you. She feels responsible for you. But with Geertrui driving her crazy, she doesn't know what to do for the best.'

'I should go back home.'

'No, no. Tomorrow you must see Geertrui.'

'I *must*?. . . '

'If you don't mind. On Sunday Tessel will take you to the ceremony at Oosterbeek. I'll stay with Geertrui. To-night, you'll stay here. I persuaded Tessel that would be best.'

'Thanks for asking.'

'I thought you'd prefer it. It's nicer for you here, isn't it?

95

And it'll be easier for everyone.'

'All my stuff is at your parents'.'

'You can manage for one night. We'll pick your stuff up on the way from Geertrui tomorrow.'

'Wait! Hold on a minute! Sorry, but you're going a bit fast. Before we go any further—you said there was something you would explain after you'd spoken to your mother.'

'Yes.'

'It sounded pretty serious.'

'It is.'

'Well, I don't want to be difficult, but I'd like to hear what it is first, before we make any plans.'

'Everyone is so . . . what is it? . . . *ongerust* . . . anxious, let's say.'

'Sure, but—'

'I know, I know! I'm often told I'm *bazig*. Masterful.'

'Bossy,' Jacob said, laughing.

'*Ja*. Bossy. I don't mean to be. But if something needs to be done, I can't put up with indecision. Like my father. He's the same. At difficult times Tessel this-and-thats. Always *er om heen draaien* . . . *Christus!* What's the English? Kind of going round and round—'

'. . . Dithers?'

'Dithers? Really?'

'Dithers.'

'Okay. *Dank u*. Dithers! Anyway, I can't stand it.'

'All right. But still . . .'

'Yes. All right. I agree. The problem is, Tessel said she should explain. She insists. On the phone just now, again, she insisted.'

'But when? I'm not going . . . I mean, I don't want to see your grandmother before I know—'

'Exactly. So I must tell you. Only, you must pretend to Tessel that I haven't.'

'What?'

'That you don't know.'

'I can't do that.'

'It would be best. She's very upset already.'

'But I can't. It would be lying. I hate lying.'

'You don't have to say anything. When she tells you, just listen. That's not lying.'

'It isn't?'

'You want a discussion on moral philosophy?'

'Not just now, thanks. But anyway, it's no good. It'll show on my face. My face always gives me away. I'm always being told that.'

Daan laughed. 'An open book!'

'Wherein men may read strange matters.'

'Eh?'

'Shakespeare. Sorry. The Scottish play.'

'The which?'

'The one about the Scottish king. You know.'

'No, I don't know. Why should I know?'

'Can't say the name.'

'Why not?'

'Bad luck.'

'You're not superstitious?'

'No, not really. Just a theatrical tradition.'

'Is that any different?'

'If you name the play, you have to clap your hands and turn around three times to ward off bad luck.'

'*Klets!*'

'It's true. I've been in this play. We put it on at school. I played Malcolm, the murdered king's son. It's a very boring part. Most of it was cut. Which is just as well, as I'm not much good as an actor. Anyway, people kept saying the name and we had terrible trouble.'

'What kind of trouble?'

'A broken leg one night, and a stabbing during the fight scene another night. That kind of trouble.'

'Accidents.'

'Maybe. It's a pretty violent play, *Macbeth*, but still.'

'Ah—*Macbeth*.'

'Oh, shit!'

'Now you want us to do the stupid business of clapping hands and turning round, I suppose?'

''Fraid so.'

They stood up, facing each other.

'*Krankzinnig!*'

'Better safe than sorry.'

They clapped their hands and turned round three times before falling in to their seats again, giggling.

Daan said, 'I can't believe I did that.'

'A rationalist like you,' Jacob said. 'Ought to be ashamed of yourself.'

'Ridiculous.'

'Puerile,' Jacob added, rather because he liked the sound of the word than meaning it, and hoping Daan didn't know he was laughing more as relief from social panic than from amusement.

Daan went to the kitchen and opened a bottle of dry white. It was after six o'clock, the time every day, he said, when Geertrui had always done so and he had become accustomed. 'The hour of the evening glass,' he said she called it. 'But this is only *een goedkoop wijntje*—you know—cheap stuff.'

'Plonk.'

'So I add some tonic. Make a spritzer. What about you?'

'Whatever you're having.'

'Have you no mind of your own?'

'Not about plonk. Or any sort of wine, come to that. Unlike you, I'm not accustomed.'

'Then I'll educate you.'

'Corrupt me, you mean.'

'Sometimes they're the same, don't you think?'

'They are?'

'You learn something, you aren't innocent any more.'

'If you put it that way.'

'One way, another way, the result is the same.'

'Won't argue the point, if you don't mind. Afterwards, maybe.'

They settled themselves with their drinks. The room had darkened in the evening light. Daan switched on a side-light by the sofa, which islanded them in the gloaming. The heavy beams loomed overhead. It seemed to Jacob more than ever as if they were sitting between decks in an old sailing ship. A long way out from land and going where, he didn't know.

Their mood turned solemn again. Daan eyed Jacob with a calculating stare that propositioned the years between them. Feeling adrift again, Jacob stared back, the wine perhaps helping him to hold his own. Dutch courage, he thought unsmiling.

At last Daan began. 'This is it, then. Yes?'

'Okay.'

'You know Geertrui is ill.'

Jacob nodded.

'But more than just ill. She has cancer of the stomach.'

He paused, waiting for a response. Jacob could say nothing, only swallow, aware of his Adam's apple rising and falling like a sharp stone plugging his throat and his stomach tightening as if infected by the words.

'Incurable,' Daan went on. 'And very painful. Often more painful than is bearable. More and more often.'

Jacob forced himself to say, 'How awful.'

'They do their best with drugs. But by now, it isn't enough. Sometimes I think it's like the pain eats the drugs, and gets worse, gets stronger from feeding on them.'

Jacob had to put his glass down but managed to say, 'Surely there's something they can do?'

Daan shook his head. 'It's in the terminal stage.'

'You mean, she hasn't much longer?'

'A few weeks. But before the end the pain is—' Daan took a deep breath as though he had felt a sudden twinge himself. 'One of the doctors told me it's worse than the worst torture.'

Jacob tried to grasp what this meant, a pain beyond cruelty. But could find no clue to such horror in his own life. He said, for something had to be said, 'And there really is nothing they can do?'

'*Niets*. Nothing much.' Daan turned his face away before adding, 'Only one thing.'

Instantly, Jacob knew what it was he was about to hear. His body stiffened against it, yet at the same time his strength seemed to drain out of him, leaving only a sensation of flabby weakness trapped in his rigid frame.

Daan didn't pause but continued at the unforgiving pace of someone required to speak the inevitable.

'They can assist her death. And Geertrui wants it. Is to have it. It's decided. You understand?'

Jacob nodded. 'Euthanasia.' And added, 'We debated it at school,' thinking even as he spoke how banal it sounded.

'And what did you say?'

'Most people were against it. They said it was anti life. And that it would lead to people with power getting rid of anybody they didn't want.'

'Like Hitler and the Nazis in Germany.'

'Yes. And not just them. Stalin was just as bad in his own way. Pol Pot. Now we live longer and there are more and more very old people. We keep on hearing about how much they cost to keep. Well, if euthanasia were allowed—'

'We've had all those arguments here in Holland. And you, you agreed?'

'About that, yes. But . . .'

'But?'

'Some people argued that everybody should have the right to die decently. To make decisions about their own death. We didn't ask to be born, they said, but at least we should have some say in our own death. Especially when we can't, you know—function properly any more . . . It's a question of personal freedom.'

'And you? What do you think?'

'I agree with that. About dying decently and having a say in how you die.' He gave Daan a cold look. 'But it's easy to talk.'

Daan drained his wine. 'It's allowed here so long as everything is done properly. The illness must be in the terminal stage and causing extreme pain. Geertrui's is. Two doctors must agree. They have. An independent doctor must review the case on behalf of the authorities and agree. This has been done. The nearest relatives must be consulted and agree. We have. But it wasn't easy. My father and I accept it. But Tessel was completely against. Nothing to do with reason. Emotionally. She just hates it. She and I—we had bad rows about it. We said terrible things to each other. She accused me of wanting Geertrui out of the way so I could get my hands on the money from selling this apartment, which Geertrui has left me in her will. I accused her of liking to see Geertrui suffering because of . . . well, because of some family history. I suppose at such times people do say unforgivable things to each other. We've made it up. But it still hurts. I think that's why Tessel wanted to tell you all this herself. She wanted you to hear it her way. And also why she didn't give you my address yesterday.' He poured more wine and eased himself in his seat. 'Well, anyhow, Tessel is the one who's with Geertrui the most and has to cope with the suffering, which has worn her down. And Geertrui argued and pleaded and went on and on till in the end Tessel had to accept that whatever she feels it's what Geertrui wants that matters.'

Silence. Jacob's mouth was dry. Reaching for his drink, he had to steady the glass with both hands. The chill of the crisp liquid shocked his gullet and cut the heat of his stomach. He glanced at Daan, who was looking back at him from the sofa, watching. Piercing blue eyes, handsome, inquiring, probing. Time and again since they'd met Jacob had caught Daan observing him like this. Why? What was he searching for? Was there something he wanted?

Jacob rubbed his damp brow with fingers still cool from his glass.

'Nine days,' Daan said. 'The Monday after next.'

The announcement hit Jacob like a blow in the face. He could say nothing, not even that he did not know what to say.

Instead, tears, involuntary, unexpected, began to swamp his eyes till they brimmed over and trickled down his cheeks and dripped from his chin on to his chest. He made no effort to resist them or to wipe them away. He was not sobbing out loud or gasping for breath or snivelling or making any sound at all, and remained completely still in his chair, staring ahead in to the deep shadows that buried the other end of the long room. The familiar hated affliction—feeling awkward, foolish, inept, embarrassed—surged through him, but for once he did not care and paid it no attention. The mouse dream flitted through his mind. Then he thought of Anne Frank and of his visit to her house—no, not her house, her museum—that morning. And now this and these tears. All somehow connected.

After a while, Daan said with quiet hardness, 'Don't cry for Geertrui. She wouldn't want it.'

'I'm not,' Jacob said with a flash of insight that came as he spoke the words.

'Why, then?'

'Because I'm alive,' Jacob said.

GEERTRUI

I still regret that Dirk killed the German soldier. As we struggled in the dark through the village, from house to house, from street to street, and from tree to tree across the park behind the Hartenstein Hotel, buffeted all the time by the thunderous bombardment of the British guns shelling the German positions, and soaked by the icy rain, I prayed—for I still prayed in those days—that no one would be killed. Not my brother Henk, not our friend Dirk, not our British ally Jacob, not myself, but not a German soldier either. There had been enough killing. I hated so much the evil of it all. It was as if a poison had risen in us and was ravening our souls.

We had almost escaped when it happened. Henk and Dirk had been friends since they were small children. They had played everywhere in this area and had walked and bicycled to each other's houses many times by many different routes. They knew every millimetre of the ground between. That is why we felt so confident that we could find our way at night and in such dreadful weather, and avoid the Germans, who we knew were only sparsely dug in in the wooded area along the western perimeter between them and the British. We thought we had succeeded, were just beginning to relax, when there he was in front of us, suddenly rising out of the earth.

I do not think he had seen us. I think he stood up, perhaps only to ease his aching limbs or rearrange himself in his uncomfortable slit-trench. Whatever it was, I think he was more surprised by us than we were by him. And this is what saved us. For luckily he hesitated a moment. Jacob was holding his gun ready to fire, as he had since we set out. But an hour or more of sitting on our garden trolley in the cold and rain had stiffened his already weak body. He did manage to point the gun, but his fingers were so frozen that he fumbled when he tried to fire. As he did so, the German came to his senses and raised his weapon. At that moment Henk let go of the trolley and flung himself at me, pushing me to the ground and falling over me, meaning to protect me. So I did not see what happened next, only heard the shooting of Jacob's gun. When it was over I learned that as Henk flung himself upon me, Dirk grabbed the gun from Jacob, pointed it and pulled the trigger, hitting the German in the face and killing him at once. A farmer's son, Dirk was used to handling a shotgun, but he had never used anything like Jacob's British sub-machine gun. What he did, he did in the heat of the moment, by instinct. Just as it was Henk's brotherly instinct to push me to the ground and protect me with his own body. We were lucky that the German had not spotted us before he stood up, we were lucky that he hesitated, we were lucky that Dirk moved so quickly, we were lucky that Jacob's gun was ready to fire, and we were lucky that the gun's mechanism worked properly despite the conditions. As so often at such times, especially in war, the outcome depended on luck. Not on heroism, if heroism depends on rational thought, for there was no time for thought. Only on the irrational, arbitrary, unjust nature of luck.

To me it seemed that in the same instant that Henk pushed me to the ground he was pulling me to my feet again, and we were scurrying as fast as the trolley would allow through the trees and away from the gunfire and exploding shells and the dead German soldier and away from any of his comrades who might have been hugging the earth for dear life in their trenches nearby. As it was the shells of our allies which were making them keep their heads down, I suppose another piece of luck was that we were not killed by what military politicians nowadays so wittily call 'friendly fire'. (Will there never be an end to the cynical misuse of language by those who rule us.)

When at last we reached the farm at about three o'clock that morning, our reception by Mr and Mrs Wesseling was not as warmhearted as we might have hoped. Of course they were glad to see their son and to know that he was alive and unharmed. But they had not wanted him to run off and help the British in the first place and, I'm sorry to say, blamed Henk, because they believed he had persuaded Dirk to do it against their wishes. To be fair, I cannot blame them. Dirk was their only child. His mother was beside herself at the thought of losing him. Now he had returned from what his father called his 'pigheaded prank' in the middle of the night, bringing with him not only the friend who was in their bad books and the friend's sister, but also a wounded British soldier who could not look after himself and whose presence was a death warrant with all our names on it if the Germans found him with us. In the circumstances, we could not expect them to be overjoyed at our arrival.

Jacob was in a poor state, almost unconscious and in great pain. We got him inside and cleaned him up and changed his sodden clothes for some of Dirk's, which fitted him well because they were alike in size. After that, Henk and Dirk and I cleaned ourselves and changed in to dry things. Nothing much was said while this was going on. The Wesselings were good, practical country people who disliked upsets and displays of emotion and who responded to such a crisis with calm efficiency, doing what had to be done to restore life to everyday normality and order, whatever their thoughts and feelings about the difficulties we had inflicted upon them.

As soon as we were all ready, Mr and Mrs Wesseling

took Dirk and Henk with some food in to the parlour to discuss the situation, leaving me to tend to Jacob. Together we sat by the kitchen range eating wonderfully fresh bread, and pea soup which I fed to him because his hands were still not adept enough to handle a spoon. After the deprivations of the previous days this seemed like heaven. Heaven to be warm and dry again, heaven to feel well fed again, heaven to be out of danger and away from the noise of guns and bursting shells, heaven to be in a clean, well-ordered home with its comforting sights and sounds and smells. But not a heaven I could completely enjoy. For I thought of Mother and Father still trapped in the hell we had just escaped, with unknown perils still to face once the British retreat left them exposed to the Germans' wrath. I prayed for them as I sat back in my chair and stared in to the fire.

Which is the last thing I remember before being woken by Henk hours later. Heaven had proved too much for me. After days of weariness and anxiety which I had not allowed myself to give in to, food, warmth, safety, and the comforting silence had sent me to sleep, a sleep so sound and deep that I had not heard the Wesselings and Henk return to the kitchen, where they had found Jacob as well as myself dead to the world, and had decided it was best to leave us where we were till morning. Mr and Mrs Wesseling had retired to bed. Through the rest of the night first Dirk, and then Henk, had kept watch from upstairs windows for any sign of approaching Germans. Only when the family was getting ready for the day's work did Henk wake me with coffee, and quietly tell me what had been decided.

You will not know what a Dutch farmhouse was like in those days, so I must explain you, if you are to understand how we lived and what happened the next few weeks.

Like most of our farmhouses, the Wesselings' had a large cowhouse attached to it. Both buildings had their own entrances, but you could get from one in to the other on the inside by a connecting door in the dairy, which was convenient for bringing in the milk. The cowhouse was big enough for twenty or more cows, in two rows along the sides, each with its own standing-place, head to a manger, tail over a gutter for the manure, and an aisle between the rows wide enough for a hay cart, which entered the shed by big double doors in the end of the building. Above the cows, under the arch of the roof, a gallery ran all round, where hay and unused equipment were stored. The gallery was reached by a ladder, which, at the Wesselings', was tied by its top rung to one end of the gallery. From its lowest rung a rope went up through a pulley attached to a crossbeam in the roof, by which the ladder was swung up in to the roof, out of the way, when not in use.

During their time 'underground' before the British arrived Dirk and Henk had built a hiding place in one corner of the gallery. First they erected walls made of wood from old boxes. Then they stacked bales of hay in front of the walls and piled loose hay over the bales. In the other corners they made similar stacks of hay, so that all looked very much the same. To enter their hiding place you forked loose hay from the bales and had to know exactly which bales to pull away to reveal the gap in the wooden walls. If you knew what to do, getting in and out was quick and easy. Of course, the Germans expected people to hide in hay. But unless they were very suspicious or had been tipped off, they only poked about with a hay fork or a bayonet and rarely took the time to dismantle a whole stack. It was too much trouble—and hard work.

Inside the hiding place, there was enough space for a double bunk, a small table with a couple of milking stools beside it for seats, and storage space made of orange boxes stacked one on the other, their open ends facing out, where were kept food and drink, basic utensils like knives and forks, plates, mugs, spare clothing, books, a chess set—everything they needed to survive for a day or two without emerging. There was also a makeshift lavatory with a tight-closed lid. In the slope of the roof just above head height was a skylight, which provided fresh air, and from which, by standing on one of the stools, you could view the surrounding country on the front side of the house. A cosy little den, in fact. They liked it so much I think they even preferred it to being in the house. Do boys ever grow up?

Naturally, they were expected to work for their living. The Wesselings had lost all their labourers. There was far more to do than Mr Wesseling could manage on his own. So Dirk and Henk looked after the cows, milking them, feeding them, cleaning out the manure, which was inside work and did not expose them to any chance visitor. They worked the machine in the dairy that separated the cream from the milk for making butter. They fed and cleaned out the horses and pigs and hens. When it seemed safe to do so, they repaired broken drains and did whatever other odd jobs Mr Wesseling wanted done. Part of the farmhouse and outbuildings was protected by a row of trees, which helped break the wind blowing across the open fields. So it was fairly safe for them to work on that side of the farm, so long as one of them kept a look-out. A long track led from the main road, through the fields to the house. If anyone was seen approaching, there was enough time for Dirk and Henk to run in to the cowhouse and hide in their den. But just in case we were taken by surprise they had made a temporary bolt hole in each of the outbuildings. 'We're like rats,' Henk said to me once when I was visiting in the days before the British came. 'And we're just as hard to catch!' Dirk said. They were both grinning widely, as if they were enjoying themselves, which I think they were. Boys again, defying authority.

The danger was not only from squads of Germans coming with an official permit to search the place, but also from individual soldiers, or two or three together in their spare time on the hunt for food or delicacies they couldn't buy in the towns. They were not supposed to do this, it was strictly against orders. So they would behave with elaborate politeness and good humour, knowing that if the farmer complained to their officers, they would be in trouble. Especially they wanted Mrs Wesseling's homemade sausages and her young cheese, but eggs and butter too, and fruit. They would pay well or barter with wristwatches or other items they thought might tempt a farmer or his wife. Because they were not supposed to be there, these unwelcome visitors were easy to handle, but it was important they saw nothing suspicious which they might report to their superiors, who would then certainly arrive with an official search party. Or which, just as bad, they might use to blackmail the farmer into giving them whatever they wanted whenever they cared to turn up. For who knows, they might only be pretending to be ordinary off-duty soldiers hunting for food, while actually being on the hunt for clues to Resistance activity. Most suspicious of all would have been two fit young men hanging around the buildings or any sign of more people being present on the farm than could be accounted for.

It was not only German soldiers who came calling. Dutch people from the towns, where food and fuel were in short supply, would arrive begging for help. In the months after the battle, during the Winter of the Hunger when things became desperate and even the Germans were in difficulty, so many came trudging up the track we almost had to defend ourselves against them. And though these were our own people, we did not dare trust them. Any of them might have been members of the NSB (*Nationaal Socialistische Beweging*), the Dutch Nazi party—that shameful blot on our history, which we try to forget but should always remember, for it reminds us of what, without vigilance, any of us can become. Those people would have given us away out of fanatical ideology, that eternal scourge of the human race. But others, the majority of our nation, which we like to think is the most honest in all the world? When people are desperate they behave as they never would in better times. It is easy to condemn such behaviour, but only if you have never been in such circumstances yourself.

This is how it was the morning of Tuesday 26 September 1944, with a hiding place already prepared. In their *overleg* during the night, the Wesselings had decided that I could stay in the house with them. If anyone asked, it was easy enough to explain that I was a friend of the family who had been visiting when the battle with the British began, which prevented my returning home to Oosterbeek. My identification papers were in order. We all agreed it was a convincing story. Dirk and Henk would go on as they had before, working around the farm and sleeping in their den.

Jacob was the problem. Weak and ill and unable to stand, never mind walk, nursing him in the small confined space of the boys' den would be difficult for everyone. The important thing was to get him fit and well enough to move around as quickly as possible. This could best be done if he was looked after in a proper bed in the warmth and convenience of the house. Though Mr and Mrs Wesseling were not happy about it, because of the risk, they agreed that Jacob should be kept in one of their bedrooms for a few days. We must just hope that the Germans would be too busy dealing with the aftermath of the battle to bother searching or even visiting a farm well away from the area.

But Mrs Wesseling made it very clear to us and to me especially that she expected me to be in charge of Jacob, to do the nursing, the fetching and carrying necessary, as well as helping her with general work around the house. She had enough to do, she said, looking after us all without having to look after a wounded soldier as well. And besides, she added, she did not speak his language.

I did not object or argue. I had, I said, taken Jacob on at home, it had been my own decision to come here with him,

110

I knew he was my responsibility.

Mrs Wesseling was a firm, even you might say a stern woman, and she was determined the Germans should have no excuse to disturb her family and her home, to which I must say she devoted herself completely. But there was more to the demands she made on me than this.

We all knew of Dirk's feelings for me, he had made them plain enough to his parents as well as myself weeks before. His mind was set on marrying me. In this I had given him no encouragement. Not because I did not like him. No no. He was a handsome young man and one of the kindest, most considerate of people I have known. But I did not love him in the way, I thought then, you ought to love someone if you married him. I also knew that Mrs Wesseling did not think I would make the right wife for her only son. I knew because she had told me so quite directly one day when we were on our own. Dirk, she told me, was a farmer's son. One day he would inherit the farm, which had been in the family for generations. He needed a wife brought up to the farming life. She had nothing against me, she said, I was 'a nice enough girl', but I was of the town, and brought up to an easy, comfortable, bourgeois life. I did not know the ways of the country or the hard work of a farmer's wife. 'If you don't work a horse when it's young,' she said, 'it won't work when it's old. And,' she added, 'it's too late for you.' Even if I tried to adapt, she told me, I would never be happy. And if I wasn't happy as his wife, her son would not be happy as my husband. He was infatuated with me at the moment, she went on, but he was very young, it would wear off, and then he would see sense. 'So whatever you might think, young lady, I'll thank you to keep off.'

I did not argue. I had no intention of marrying Dirk. And like many who make it their business to 'speak my mind with no frills', as she put it, Mrs Wesseling never liked the compliment being returned. So even though I would have liked to say a few straight words on my own behalf, I kept silence rather than cause a breach between us that might harm Henk's friendship with Dirk, and my own too, for he was a friend and a good one. Nor did I blame Mrs Wesseling, for she was trying to protect her only son from making a life-long mistake. Perhaps, I thought, in her place I would have done the same. As would my own beloved mother. Mothers and their sons, is there any love more determined? I think not, unless it is fathers and their daughters. The difference, I have often noticed, is that a mother battles on behalf of her son against the world, whereas a father battles to possess his daughter for himself.

As the days passed during the week or two after our arrival I began to see that Mrs Wesseling might have something else in mind than merely keeping me away from Dirk. She knew that however careful an eye she kept on me and however hard she made me work in the house there would still be plenty of occasions when Dirk and I could be together and plenty of places around the farm where we could be out of sight, if we wanted to be alone. Perhaps she hoped that by working me hard and giving me plenty of drudgery and unpleasant jobs to do—like plucking and gutting chickens and cleaning out the family's outside dry lavatory—she would put me off her son by putting me off the life marrying her son would entail. Well, I did not mind that either. I prefer to be busy, was not afraid of *vuil werk* (dirty work), and had had a good training from my own mother in dutiful behaviour. Though I must admit, in Mother's hands it was a training sweetened with a large measure of witty humour and easy laughter, which, I'm sorry to say, was absent from Mrs Wesseling's dour recipe. At her conception I fear her Calvinistic god must have mislaid her funny bone, poor woman. A mistake which that particular deity too often made. But even this did not bother me. I was young. And when you are young, the world bounces.

By nightfall of our first day everything was as Mrs

Wesseling wanted it. Jacob was tucked up and sound asleep in bed in a room next to the stairs that led down to the back-door passage of the house where also was the door in to the dairy, which led in to the cowhouse. If Germans were spotted coming along the track we hoped there would be time to evacuate him to the hiding place before they reached us. Of course, Dirk and Henk had resettled themselves in their den. All signs of our arrival and of the presence of anyone other than Mr and Mrs Wesseling and myself had been carefully removed. With everything done and back to normal, or as normal as it could be in the circumstances, Mrs Wesseling and I cleared away the evening meal and washed the dishes before ironing the day's laundry, while the men disappeared to one of the outbuildings where they had a radio hidden, and listened to the news on Radio Oranje, our Dutch-language station broadcast from London by the BBC.

Here is memory. For me now there is only memory. Memory and pain. All life is memory. Pain is of now, forgotten as soon as gone. But memory lives. And grows. And changes too. Like the clouds I can see through my window. Bright and billowy sometimes. Blanketing the sky sometimes. Storm-tossed sometimes. Thin and long and high sometimes. Low and grey and brooding sometimes. And sometimes not there at all, only the cloudless blue, so peaceful, so endless. So longed for. But let us not talk of death. Only of clouds. Always the same and yet never the same. Uncertain. Unreliable, therefore. Unpredictable.

Would I had kept a diary all these years. There is no memory so good as that preserved in writing at the time of living it. Had I done so, how much more I could tell you of my days with Jacob. But now the clouds cross my mind according as an unseen wind wills them, and I am not always sure which came before which in the order of events. Unlike the days of the battle, which I seem to remember in turn as they happened, the period of our time together at the farm, until the time of the end, comes to me as a montage, never the same at each viewing. Always a few scenes, those I treasure the most. But some not remembered for years. And others often but at random. For me, this is a pleasure. Each viewing holds a surprise. But for you, for whom there will be only this one viewing—? Well, I do my best.

Waking Jacob each day while he was convalescent in the farmhouse became a little ritual begun the first morning. He was a great sleeper. He liked sleeping, he said, because he dreamed a lot and enjoyed his dreams. They were often like a wonderful film show. And he slept heavily. All his life, he said, he had hated getting up. And he certainly was always hard to awaken.

The first morning I did not know this, but was not surprised after all he had gone through that he slept so deeply. I took him a bowl of coffee (fake slop, ersatz, all we could obtain by that time in the war, but acceptable when hot and sweetened with honey from Mr Wesseling's bees). I stood by his bedside with his coffee, and said his name. But nothing, only heavy breathing. I shook his shoulder. But still no sign of waking. Sweat shone on his brow. I put down the bowl on the table by his bed and smoothed his hot brow with my hand a number of times. Still no movement. Even my cool hand did not stir him to consciousness. I sat on the edge of the bed and quietly spoke his name. 'Jacob. Jacob.' Nothing. Asleep, he looked like a small boy. So *kwetsbaar*—so vulnerable and innocent.

By instinct, that biological tic which controls our actions far more than we like to think, I began to sing as a mother might to her child.

Vader Jakob, vader Jakob,
Slaapt gij nog? Slaapt gij nog?
Alle klokken luiden. Alle klokken luiden.

Bim Bam Bom. Bim Bam Bom.

This worked no magic either. But then, while singing the canon again and smoothing his hot brow with my cool hand, at last he showed signs of life. His eyes flickered. His mouth spread in a satisfied smile. He moved in the bed. And finally his eyes opened, looking straight in to mine.

I finished the song and for a moment neither of us spoke. Until Jacob said,

'Comb me smooth, and stroke my head,

And thou shalt have some cockell bread.'

'What?' I said, as I did not understand a word.

But he only grinned and said quietly, 'Angel Maria, rescuing me again.'

'Only from sleep this time,' I said. 'Thank God.'

'If we had God to thank,' he said, 'we wouldn't be here.'

'You talk riddles again,' I said. 'What do you mean?'

'Nothing,' he said.

'Here,' I said, taking the bowl from the table and bringing it to his mouth. 'Drink this. If anything will, it will cure you of saying nothing.'

He laughed. I too.

Thus it became each morning a ritual. The waking song and my soothing hand, an exchange of nothings, before my helping him drink his coffee. Some mornings I knew that he was not sound asleep when I came to him, far from it, but pretended to be because he wanted me to perform the ritual. It gave him pleasure. And me too.

Until the morning that brought this happy time to an end.

POSTCARD
I see with an eye that feels
and feel with an eye that sees.
J. W. von Goethe

'Look,' Daan said, 'this has been a hard day for you. You
need some food. Me too. There's a café round the corner I
use a lot. Let's go.'

Daan bustled, clearing away the empty bottle and
glasses. Jacob wanted to say no, wanted to be on his own,
but suddenly felt so tired, so drained, he allowed himself to
be borne along on the wave of Daan's determination. There
was relief, even pleasure, in giving himself up to the other's
decisiveness.

The small café in a narrow side street full of bars and
cheap restaurants was already crowded with young, or anyway youngish, men and women, most of whom it seemed
were smoking, hazing the room with the tangy burn of
cigarette and pot that made Jacob's nose twitch. Daan led
the way, pausing two or three times to exchange greetings,
to a corner table with two vacant chairs by a window looking out on to the narrow street. Where he left Jacob, who
watched the tourists wandering by outside so as to avoid the
eyes of the people inside.

He tried to loll at ease, alone in this noisy bonhomie, but
catching sight of his reflection in the window saw the strain
on his face. Would he ever learn to relax and be natural on
his own in public? But then, what was his natural self? And
what did 'natural' mean? He wished he knew. Some people
(most people?) seemed right from the start, from birth, to

116

be at home in the world, seemed to know who they were, what they were, where they belonged. Daan, for instance. But he, me, this person other people called Jacob, did not. Now less than ever. As if (how many hours was it?) thirty hours—only thirty!—in this foreign country had begun to strip away from him, like peeling off a protective skin, the few certainties he thought he knew about himself, leaving him disorientated and displaced.

How to find his bearings?

Or was he just tired? Or maybe a little drunk?

Daan returned after an aeon, accompanied by a cheer-fully harassed busty bar girl, bearing between them plates of pasta and salad, a basket of bread, glasses of wine, and eating irons.

'Enjoy your meal,' the girl said after a no-nonsense distribution of the goods.

'How did she know I'm English?' Jacob asked.

'Because you look it,' Daan said.

'Am I such a stereotype?'

'Only when you're trying not to be.'

'Hey, Daan!' A big man, all black leather with a crimson scarf snaking round his neck, was breast-stroking his way through the crush to their table.

Daan stood to greet him. 'Koos!' They exchanged a bear hug and a rapid three-barrelled kiss—right cheek, left cheek, right cheek again—a national greeting between friends that Jacob had observed at first with some surprise but was now growing accustomed to. The English with their Judas kiss of a single moo; the French with their dual display; the Dutch with their triple smacker. And, he'd noticed, you could tell how trusty the participants were in their affections by how close the kisses came to the mouth. Routine greeting: the lips hardly touched the face and were aimed high and earwards on the cheek. Friends, platonic and enjoyed: the kisses placed lightly on the middle cheek. Good friends, family: the kisses gently planted close to the mouth. Close

117

close friends, lovers: the kisses delivered full-lipped, on the edge of the mouth. And when sensuous, the last of the three mouth-to-mouth: the life-saving seal of intimate complicity.

So far, thought Jacob as he began eating his pasta while Daan and his mid-cheek pal prockled Dutch above his head, so far no one had even brushed a threesome on the outer reaches of his cheeks, never mind pressed a pucker on his lips. He remembered Anne recording in her diary how she longed to be kissed (and him thinking how wet Peter van Daan must have been not to do it), and sympathised, kissing, in his opinion, being among the best of pleasures. But why, he wondered as the oil of his salad slicked his tongue, was such a comic action as melding your damp oral membranes with someone else's so desirable? Where did such an impulse come from? What on earth could it have to do with evolution and human survival in the Darwinian circus that it should be so widespread and wished for? Whyever, all he knew was he felt the miss of it. He'd not had a kissing friend for months. And truth to tell he fancied such a moment at the moment rather more than this salad and pasta, and wished there was someone who felt he deserved it. Then suddenly he remembered the singular fleeting touch of Ton's lips on his, and experienced a frisson of pleasure.

At which point, Daan and his friend gave each other a goodbye handshake and Daan sat down.

'Didn't introduce you,' Daan said. 'Koos was in a hurry. Wanted to tell me some news and go.'

'Funny name.'

'Funny?'

'Odd.'

'Not to us.'

'Ah—yes. Sorry. Didn't mean to be rude.'

'You think your own name is funny?'

'No.'

'Koos is short for Jacob.'

'It is?'

'Yes. And Todd seems funny to me.'

'Why?'

'Because in Dutch it means rag. You know—a torn piece of cloth. Which perhaps is why no one is called it.'

'Interesting. Because in olden times, the middle ages, sometime about then, in England a tod—only one d—was a weight of wool. About sixteen kilos by today's measure, I think.'

'How knowledgeable you are.'

'I like knowing about names. They're full of meanings and full of stories too.'

'So you'll know that in German tod means death.'

'Yes, I know that.'

'Put the Dutch and the German together and you're Koos the death rag.'

'Now who's being rude? In English, when we say "on your tod", we mean "on your own", which comes from rhyming slang for "alone". Like "apples and pears" means "stairs".'

'Tod rhymes with alone?'

'It's a bit complicated. There was a famous jockey called Tod Sloane. He was so good he was always coming first a long way ahead of all the others. So Tod Sloane, which rhymes with alone, got shortened to "on your tod".'

'And you think our Dutch names are odd.'

'What about Van Riet?'

'Of the reeds.'

'Reeds, as in reeds that grow by water?'

'Yes. Very appropriate name for a Dutchman, don't you agree?'

'We used to use them to thatch roofs.'

'We too once. But also it means cane and bamboo. So furniture and baskets. Very useful plant.'

'What about Daan?'

'Like Dan in English. Short for Daniel. Daniël in Dutch.

119

Which, come to think of it, we must get from the French.'

'The man who had the courage to go on his tod in to the lion's den.'

'Did he?'

'In the Bible.'

'Not my favourite novel.'

Jacob gave Daan the expected grin before saying, 'You're not religious, then?'

Daan sniffed and pushed his empty plate aside. He had eaten with breakneck speed. 'The only god to which I bend my thinking head is the unthinking god between our legs.'

Jacob glanced up from the remains of his salad, checking whether or not Daan was joking. There were no signs of it. Once more Jacob felt he was being probed, that Daan was seeking something from him. He thought, he's done it again, caught me out, just like he did when we were looking at Titus, and when he was telling me about his grandmother. Switched the mood. Come at me suddenly from another direction.

'Whose unthinking god between whose legs did you have in mind?' he asked trying to sound unimpressed.

'No one's right now,' Daan said. 'Unlike a friend of mine over there who hasn't taken his eyes off you for the last five minutes.'

Jacob turned to look and saw Ton standing at the bar gazing back at him with an undemanding smile. Jacob managed a nod of recognition before turning back, head down, hoping to prevent Daan observing the blush he felt blooming on his face. Ton a friend of Daan's? Dear lord, he thought, that's torn it.

And of course Daan had noticed. 'You know him?' he asked.

Jacob performed an unconvincing act with his paper napkin, cleaning his lips and fingers before tossing the screwed-up napkin aside.

'He's a friend of yours, did you say?'

'Right.'

Jacob shifted in his seat. Daan was bound to invite Ton over. Better come clean. He made himself look Daan in the eyes.

'Remember,' he said, 'I told you how I met a girl this morning who bought me a beer just before my stuff was stolen?'

'Yes.'

'Well, to tell the truth, I thought she was a girl, but then, just before she went, well, something happened, and I realised she wasn't a girl at all but a boy. And it was him.'

'Ton?'

'That's what he said his name was. Ton.'

'You thought Ton was a girl's name?'

Jacob shrugged. 'Isn't English. Hadn't heard it before.'

Daan regarded Jacob deadpan for a moment before his face cracked and he burst into a bout of what Jacob felt was indulgent laughter. Then he got up and went over to Ton. They exchanged a three-barrelled hello unquestionably of the very close-encounters kind. They talked a moment, laughing a lot, then both came back to the table. Ton held out his long-fingered hand; Jacob shook it with a tentative quickness, as if touching forbidden fruit. He could see why he had mistaken Ton for a girl: small, delicately slim, neatly built, and his face had the light fine features of a girl with a smooth skin that showed no sign of a razor.

'We meet again after all,' Ton said.

'Yes,' Jacob said, and heard himself add, 'I'm glad.'

They exchanged complicit smiles as they sat down, Daan giving his seat to Ton, to whom he said something in Dutch before going off to join a group of people standing by the bar. He did all this with the decisiveness Jacob now recognised was characteristic of him.

'Some people he knows,' Ton said. 'He thought we might like a chance to talk on our own.'

There was a pause before Jacob forced himself to say,

'This morning . . . I thought . . . Your name. I've never heard it before.'

'From Antonius. Antony. In English, I guess I'd be Tony.'

'Don't like Tony. So I'm glad you're not.'

As always when his self-consciousness was at its worst, he heard himself speak like a man listening to his own echo. Which is why he noticed the unintended pun that tickled his pedantic funnybone and made him chuckle.

Ton, smiling in sympathy, said, 'A good joke?'

'Sorry. Not really. Just that Ton spelt backwards is not, and I said I'm glad you're not—!' As usual the joke vanished in the explanation, and his laughter with it.

But after a blank moment Ton said, 'Not not but Ton, and when not Ton, not.'

And they could both laugh with relief.

'I thought you said your name was Jack.'

'I did.'

'But it's Jacob.'

'They call me Jack at home. Or my father does anyway.'

'That explains it.'

'Explains what?'

'Daan talked about you. But when we met this morning, well—I didn't think you were that person.'

'No. Why would you?'

Jacob hoped that Ton would go on talking so that he wouldn't have to think of something to say. There had been so much said today already and so much he had had to say that he was beginning to flag. He wasn't used to the company of strangers, never mind strangers who were foreigners in a foreign place. He would like to be on his own, to give his soul time to catch up with his body (as Sarah would have put it). But there didn't seem much chance of that for a while.

But Ton sat in silence, his eyes never leaving Jacob's face. It was the first time Jacob had ever met anyone of around his own age who possessed such stillness. It wasn't that Ton was laid back or merely lethargic, it wasn't a pose or anything negative. You couldn't help being aware of him, of his presence. Yet at the same time, he seemed to be as thin and as light as air. Like a wraith. Strangely beautiful. Ethereal. Which, Jacob realised, was why, along with his looks, he had found him so instantly attractive that morning. And why he had mistaken him for a girl. Or was this only an excuse? And an excuse for what? For his own confusion?

To stop himself probing that thought he said, 'Thanks for your little present.'

Ton smiled. 'Have you used it yet?'

'No such luck.'

'We should do something about that.'

'Thanks a bundle.'

'And,' Ton went on, not joking now, 'you understood what I wrote?'

'With a little help from a friend.'

'Daan?'

'No. An old woman who helped me after I was mugged.'

Ton reached over and laid a hand on Jacob's arm. 'You were mugged? When?'

'Just after you left. A kid in a red baseball cap. Ran off with my anorak.'

'Did you lose much?'

'Money. Train ticket. Everything really. Everything on me, I mean.'

'No!' Ton's other hand covered his mouth. 'My god, I remember! He was sitting behind you. Thin. Very bad—how do you call it?—spots.'

'Acne.'

'Acne. *Jeugdpuistjes* we say. Youth spots. Yes, I saw him. He was quite ugly. If I hadn't left you, it wouldn't have happened. I feel so guilty.'

'Why? I didn't lose anything important. Like, I mean,

my passport or credit card or anything. Didn't have them with me, luckily. Only some money, the map and stuff. Didn't Daan explain just now?'

'Only said you wanted to meet me.'

'He said that! That I wanted to meet you? I didn't say that!'

'So you didn't want to meet me again?'

Ton looked so abashed that Jacob was quick to say, 'Yes, yes, I did want to meet you. I do want to see you. I only meant I didn't actually say it to Daan. He made that up.'

'Oh, Daan!' Ton half rose, turning to look for him, but he was standing with his back to them. '*Typisch*!' he said, hitching his chair nearer to Jacob and sitting down again. The noise in the café was so strident now, it was hard to hear a conversational voice. 'He likes to arrange other people's minds for them.'

Jacob laughed. 'I've noticed.'

The bar girl pushed between them, picking up the empty plates and glasses, and speaking to Ton in Dutch.

He asked Jacob, 'You want something?'

'I've no money.'

'One drink for free. Two, and we must meet again. So I insist.'

Jacob smiled. 'All right. A coffee, thanks.'

The bar girl went.

Jacob said, 'I'm not used to so much wine. Daan really likes it.' He was aware of feeling mildly unstable and of dampness on his skin.

'But I thought you were staying with his parents.'

'After I was mugged, I remembered where he lived. His father told me. Which was lucky or I'd have been a bit stuck. Daan decided I should stay at his place tonight. My grandfather fought at Arnhem. He was badly wounded. Daan's grandmother and her family looked after him. But he died.'

'Yes, I know the story.'

'You do? You know Daan pretty well, then.'

Ton laughed. 'Yes, I know Daan pretty well.'

The bar girl arrived with Ton's beer and Jacob's coffee.

When she had gone, unable to quell his curiosity any longer, Jacob said, 'Could I ask you something?'

'Yes.'

'Something personal.'

'Isn't it always, when someone asks if they can ask you something?'

'Are you gay?'

Ton chuckled. 'As a flag in a high wind. Isn't it obvious?'

'And something else?'

'Be my guest.'

'This morning . . . were you trying to pick me up?'

'Not trying. I did.'

'You did?'

'But I dropped you.'

'Why?'

'Because I found out I made a mistake.'

'A mistake? How?'

'You thought I was a girl.'

'Daan told you.'

'No no. You did.'

'Me! When?'

'When we were looking at the map.'

'What did I say?'

'Nothing much. Enough. You told Daan what happened?'

'Yes.'

'That you thought I was a girl and discovered I wasn't?'

Jacob nodded.

'He must have liked that.'

'He did. You saw him, just before he came over to you. Laughing his head off.'

'You only told him then?'

'Yes. Well, he said you were a friend of his so I thought I'd better come clean.'

'Jacques, you're so naive.'

'Sorry, I'm sure.'

'No, it's nice. I like it. Makes a change. But—' He became serious. 'Sometimes, it can be dangerous too. This morning, for instance. Putting your coat over the back of your seat. Then showing you had your money in it. And doing that in the Leidseplein. Which isn't as bad as other places for pickpockets, like the Dam or the back of the railway station, but bad enough, if you don't take care.'

'You needn't go on. I've learned my lesson.'

'But that's why I blame myself for what happened. I should have looked after you better. Warned you about your coat. Taken you somewhere nicer.'

'Why? You didn't know me.'

'But I wanted to. I'm not a rent boy, you know. I don't cruise the streets. I wouldn't anyway, it's just not me. I'm too particular. How can I say? Easily disgusted, if you understand me.'

'Fastidious?'

'Is that the word? Well, when you sat down I was at a table a few rows away. I liked the look of you so much. And the waiter didn't come to you. And you looked so alone. And I thought you might be gay too. But not experienced. Like I say—naive. You were such a target for trouble. I wanted to help you. Felt protective, I suppose. Which was nice, because usually it's the other way round. People usually feel protective of me. Like Daan, he does. But this time it was my turn, and I liked that feeling, to tell the truth. I thought we might become friends and I could show you some of Amsterdam. I love Amsterdam so much, it's such a wonderful city. I like to share it. So I sat beside you and we started talking. And you were so nice, you took off that ugly anorak for me. I'm glad you've lost it because now you can get something better.'

'Was it that obvious? How could you tell?'

Ton thought for a moment. 'When you're an open gay, like me, you only survive, even in Amsterdam, where it's easier than in most places, if you learn pretty quick how people behave. What makes them do what they do. You have to be all eyes. Have to learn the danger signs. And to avoid trouble, you have to—let's say—be ahead of it.'

'Anticipate it?'

'Yes, anticipate it. Or else in this wonderful world of ours, where everyone believes in individuality, and being yourself, isn't that so?—'

'And being what you want to be.'

'Being what you *are*—'

'True to yourself.'

'And we are all so tolerant of each other, aren't we, and this and this and this, and well . . . Where was I? I've got lost in my English! . . . Oh yes—Or else, if being what you are is being like me, you soon get your head beaten in. Or worse. That's what I wanted to say.'

'I know,' Jacob said, 'I know.'

With surprising simplicity, Ton raised a hand and stroked the back of his fingers down Jacob's cheek, and, smiling, said, 'No, dear Jacques, I don't think you do. You've heard about it. You've read about it, I guess. But you don't know it. If you knew, you wouldn't ask about it.'

Jacob hung his head, smitten with embarrassment at Ton's caress, but also in a pique. To mask his feelings, he took a sip of coffee. It was almost cold and had a thick bitter taste.

On a sudden impulse he said, 'Then show me.'

'Show you!' Ton's face was as close now as it had been while they sat together reading the map of Amsterdam that morning. 'Show you what?' His breath feathered Jacob's brow. 'What it's like to be me? Or what it's like to have your head beat in? Or what it's like having sex with me?'

Jacob shrugged, sat back and ran a hand through his

127

hair. His stomach curdled; he felt sick.

'I don't know,' he said with difficulty. 'I don't know why I said that.'

'It doesn't matter. Another day, if you still want it,' Ton said, then, looking at him with a different care: 'Are you all right? You don't look well.'

'I'm okay,' Jacob lied.

'Maybe, I think, you've had enough. I'll get Daan. You should go home.'

He was gone before Jacob could stop him. The loud talk and laughter seemed to assault Jacob directly now as if Ton's presence had been a baffle, and the smoky air thickened his lungs. He withdrew into himself.

The word 'home' echoed in his head. Daan's apartment, 'home'! He wished he really was at home, and imagined his room at Sarah's. But then, for the first time, and with a shock which braced his nerves, realised that was not his home either, but a room in Sarah's house. And at his parents', where he used to live, the room that had always been his till he decided to stay with his grandmother had been taken over by his brother Harry because it was bigger and, as Harry had said, Jacob didn't live there any longer whereas Harry did. If he wanted to stay for a night or two, then Harry's room, the smallest in the house, would do. Jacob hadn't objected; how could he? He had chosen to leave, had preferred to live somewhere else—or rather, to be accurate, with someone else. At the time, because he was doing what he wanted, he didn't mind about his room being taken over. Indeed, he was secretly pleased. He had grown up there, it belonged to his childhood. He regarded leaving it as the end of his childhood. By giving it up he had taken the next step towards becoming adult, a person in charge of himself. And achieving that state was something he had always wanted for as long as he could remember. He had never really liked being a child, had always wanted to be grown up, independent, responsible for himself. Had always wanted to be as free as he could be to live life as he wanted to live it. Even though, he had to admit, he did not yet know exactly how he wanted to live.

But it was only now, here in this crammed, smoky, noisy café hidden in a back street of a strange city in a foreign country, a long way from anywhere he had ever called home, that the actuality of being independent, of being responsible for himself, informed his inflamed nerves and inhabited his disturbed mind.

As if his memory had been waiting for this moment, back to him came the poignant little tune of the song Daan had sung to him after they had visited Titus that afternoon, and along with it Daan's voice speaking the translated words. *I've spent my life looking for you, only to learn, now I have found you at last, the meaning of solitude.*

And, Jesus!, he thought, is that it? The long and the short of it, the be all and end all, the last word? Alone, alone, all all alone. On your tod, Todd. Is that what being grown up, being adult, *means*? Solitude?

He felt a hand laid on his shoulder and heard Ton say, 'Jacques?'

He stirred himself, looked up in to the boy-girl face, put his hand over Ton's, and smiled.

Ton said, 'He's coming. See you again soon, eh?'

Jacob nodded.

Ton smiled, and bending to him, placed a kiss at the corner of Jacob's mouth, left, then right, and a third, gently lingering, on his lips.

POSTCARD
'Begin at the beginning,'
the King said gravely,
'and go on till you come to the end.'
Lewis Carroll

Jacob stared out of the window of the mid-morning train
from Amsterdam to Bloemendaal on his way with Daan to
visit Geertrui. To take his mind off the coming ordeal he
concentrated on the view.

People had told him Holland was boring, a land of cosy
little red-roofed boxes arranged with Toytown predictability, and with not much of anything between one place
and another except unending flat fields and canals. But this
was not how it was, not for him that morning. The flatness
of the landscape with its wide low sky, softened with haze,
so that land and sky almost merged, he found soothing. The
trim cared-for appearance of the houses and gardens, farms
and fields, canals and dykes, even the factories and modern
office blocks they were passing at this moment appealed to
his liking for the clean and orderly. But as well: the colours.
Burnished reds of old brick and roof tiles. Fresh shining
greens and browns of the strips of field, each framed by
thick dark pencil-lines of ditches. Belts of sky-reflecting
water ruffled to silver by the passage of workhorse barges.
And something in the atmosphere of the people that he
liked, a sense of purpose, of getting on with life without any
fuss. He hadn't noticed any of this till now. For the first
time since he arrived he began to like the place. And why
now, in a train on his way to see a dying old woman? He

130

thought: How difficult it is sometimes to explain yourself to yourself. Sometimes there only *is*, and no knowing.

Daan was sitting in the opposite seat reading a newspaper, its title, *de Volkskrant*, in letters which looked old-fashionedly modern, spiky and stern. He was wearing specs, the first time Jacob had seen them: small oval lenses in thin black metal rims, also old-fashionedly modern and also making him look a bit spiky and stern. He had hardly exchanged a word with Jacob since last night. Briefly to show him where to find food for breakfast, a sentence or two about when they must leave the house, and how they would pick up Jacob's belongings on the way back. And an explanation: 'I'm no use in the morning. A night person. It means nothing if I don't talk.' Which Jacob didn't mind, for he wasn't in a talking mood either.

He had slept surprisingly well, heavily in fact, all things considered—yesterday's horrors, catastrophes, shocks, strange bed in strange house, but/and yes, now he thought about it, pleasures too (Ton, Titus, Alma). During the night he had surfaced only once, two thirty by his watch, when he heard voices and laughter in the big living room below, one Daan's, the other Ton's, but he had plunged back in to the depths again at once.

This morning he'd woken with a spongy head and lethargic limbs that had to be forced to get out of bed. Revived by a shower he could take his time over, luxuriate in, not worrying about anyone else needing it, because he had his own guest's bathroom, which hadn't been the case at Daan's parents' house, where there was only one. Daan had loaned him a change of underwear (blue boxer shorts, red T-shirt), and to go over the T-shirt instead of his tired sweater, an old black jacket in a loose baggy style Jacob decided he rather liked, even though it was a touch too large, because it made him feel different and more Dutch and therefore less conspicuously English, which amused him, because the designer label inside said *Vico Rinaldi*.

The station had been busy and the train was full of gadabout Saturday crowds, tourists with luggage, locals with shopping, a high proportion of younger people with their clutter of backpacks and sports bags, chattery but not loud. They had a robust up-front freshness of look and manner; not at all English, but not alien either; and not as he was himself, Jacob thought, but how he might wish he could be. Tried to pin it down, this quality that attracted, but had come up with nothing better than 'unaggressive confidence' before the train pulled in to Haarlem station and most people got off.

Daan folded his paper and leaned towards Jacob. 'One more stop. Tessel will be at the *verpleeghuis*. We won't stay long, it would tire Geertrui. The nurses know you're coming, so the doctor will have given Geertrui some extra help to keep the pain down while we're there. I'll let you know when it's time to leave. So it should be okay, nothing to upset you.'

Nothing to upset you felt like a rebuke, a judgement even, as if Daan were saying that Jacob was not up to the situation, not strong enough to witness the dying woman's pain and so must be protected from it. And that he was an outsider, not one of the family, a visitor who, good manners dictated, must not be troubled by family torments. He resented both judgement and fact. But, he wondered as the train moved on, should he react in this way to what was, after all, a passing remark, not meant as he had taken it? But, meaning it or not, Daan had touched a nerve.

Determination gathered in him, felt like a force-field round his spine, that he would not turn away from whatever he found or hold it off, but accept it. Enter in to it. And to do this for his own sake. For the sake of his self-respect.

This much of an answer he knew. It surprised and pleased him. Not such a wimp after all, then. Perhaps.

132

*

He had expected the nursing home to be a cosy little building where a handful of old people quietly spent their last days with the comforting help of dutiful nurses. Instead, the building Daan led him to was huge. Three storeys with several wings branching out from the central block in the middle of a well-tended park provided with plenty of trees and flowers and patches of garden no doubt meant to dress the place up to look like a well-to-do country house or a luxury health spa. But nothing could disguise the institutional bulk of the 'home' or the endless comings and goings of cars and vans and buses and bikes and various vehicles of a clinical type, and the people—patients, visitors, medical staff—who thus arrived and left. In fact, not a home in any honest sense of the word but a busy hospital for the treatment of the legion of ailments, failings, accidents and calamities, including the final requirement of death, that afflict the elderly, senior citizens, those in the autumn of their years.

And how, thought Jacob, the human race insists on conning itself with euphemisms. As in: passed away, lost, met his end, taken from us, breathed her last, called to God, departed, at rest. Not to mention the more comic coinings not advised for use in the presence of the newly bereaved, such as cocked his toes, gave up the ghost, croaked, kicked the bucket, pegged out, gone to meet her maker, dropped off the hook, snuffed it. All meaning nothing else than dead. The only word that said exactly what is meant. For which reason, it seemed, people preferred not to use it.

By now they were inside the main entrance, which Daan said was called (another euphemism) the village square. To Jacob it looked like it had been designed with the departure hall of a small domestic airport in mind. Appropriate in the circumstances, come to think of it. Not only check-in desk (*receptie, informatie*), but shops, library, flower stall, café, areas to sit and wait, even rooms for meetings. All set about with indoor trees and bushes growing in chunky plastic tubs. And as with passengers and their hangers-on something of the same pretence of calm and cheerfulness inadequately disguising boredom, anxiety, impatience, relief and a general desire not to be there at all, radiating like emotional sweat off the patients-to-be and those accompanying them, the ones seeing-off and those being-seen-off, the relatives and friends taking-away and the soon to be ex-patients being-taken-away. (The corpses of the dead ones, he supposed, would be carted off from some discreet exit at the back of the building so that none of the living, patients or guests, would be faced with the final reality of the reason for them being there.)

Jacob was relieved that Daan did not linger but took him quickly to the lift, which carried them up to the third floor, and then down a wide corridor with windows in bays where people sat overlooking the park. Very pleasant and civilised, Jacob thought, but still a hospital, with hospital sounds and hospital smells. And worst of all, that lukewarm hospital air, flavoured with disinfectant, that seems both clammy and too dry, and also as if it has been breathed and breathed again by fevered lungs and never ever been outside for refreshment. Everywhere, signs of thoughtfulness, of an attempt to make the place into what it was not—soothing modern colours on the walls, well-framed pictures, more real plants in companionable groups, comfortable chairs, cheerful curtains—all better than any hospital he had been in at home, even the newish place where Sarah recently had the hip operation that prevented her from coming to Holland.

Geertrui was in a room on her own, the only patient like that on the ward. The other rooms held six or four or two. A concession, Daan had explained, a last privilege.

While Daan approached his grandmother to say his hellos, Jacob observed from the door, hesitating between

134

out and in. Geertrui's white-haired head was propped up on a bank of white pillows in a white iron-frame bed shrouded (the only right word) with white coverings. The walls of the room were pink. On a white bedside cabinet, a still-life of colour: an earthenware bowl of oranges, apples, pears, bananas; a blue glass vase brimming with red roses; a bronze-framed triptych of photographs displaying pictures of two men and a woman. The woman Jacob recognised was Mrs van Riet, Daan's mother, younger than now. One of the men was Daan. The other man he didn't know. Not a hint of medical gear, no sign of sickness. But he guessed this was deliberate. Like a living room tidied up for a visitor. In the air, though, he sensed tension, an uneasy silence.

She's like a moth, Jacob thought, who has settled for the winter, prepared for hibernation. But her large sunken eyes were alert, and took him in, peering from either side of Daan's head as he stooped to give his grandmother, slowly, delicately, a three-barrelled kiss.

Mrs van Riet was sitting in the only arm chair at one side of the bed. She got up and came to Jacob.

'I'm sorry about the trouble you had,' she said in subdued tones. 'Are you comfortable at Daan's?'

'Yes, I'm fine, thanks.'

'Tomorrow I'll take you to the ceremony at Oosterbeek. I'll come for you at nine fifteen. Please be ready, we mustn't miss the train. We'll talk then.'

'Nine fifteen. Right.'

'Now I'll go and have coffee while you visit Mother. She insists it must be alone.'

Mrs van Riet went, leaving her unhappiness behind like a vapour trail.

Daan was standing by Geertrui's bed, waiting for Jacob to be ready. Geertrui lay unmoving, her eyes, a washed-out blue, fixed on him.

'Geertrui,' Daan said, '*dit is* Jacob.'

When he did not move, because he could not, Geertrui,

smiling, said, 'Please. Come.'

Daan placed a chair where Jacob could be seen by Geertrui without her having to lift her head.

The expression 'walking on eggs' made sense to him for the first time as Jacob crossed the room and perched on the edge of the chair. It was the intensity of Geertrui's scrutiny that unnerved him. This was not a woman you would wrangle with. Necessary to sit with a straight back. Yet there was hardly anything of her. So little sign of a body under the cover that she seemed like a disembodied head and a pair of arms lying on the counterpane that ended in fine small hands, almost a girl's except that they were mottled with the brown spots of old age.

'Hello, Mrs Wesseling,' Jacob said. 'Sarah sends you her greetings. She also sent a gift and a letter, but they're in my things at . . . Well, I expect you know.'

'I've explained,' Daan said. 'I'll leave you together. I'll just be along the corridor. Geertrui says she'll send you to me when it's time for us to leave. Okay?'

Jacob nodded. Daan gave him a look that meant 'Don't stay long.' Then spoke to his grandmother in Dutch and kissed her again. There was a tone in his voice Jacob had not heard before. Very soft, tender, precise. Like a lover to the beloved.

All the while Geertrui did not take her eyes off Jacob. Daan went, closing the door quietly behind him. There was a long silence before she spoke.

'You have your grandfather's eyes.'

Jacob smiled. 'That's what my grandmother says.'

'And his smile.'

'That too.'

'His . . . nature?'

'Some. Apparently, I'm not as practical as he was. With his hands, I mean. With tools. He liked making things.'

'I know.'

'Furniture, even. Sarah still uses some of it. And

136

gardening, he loved gardening, whereas I hate it. He was a big reader, and we share that. But I'm not as brave as he was, I'm sure.'

'Have you had cause?'

'To be brave? Does bravery need a cause?'

'There can be none without.'

For the first time since he entered the room her eyes left him. He could still not take his from her. But without her eyes on him he could relax enough to ease back in his seat.

After a silence Geertrui said, 'You live with your grandmother?'

'Yes.'

'Not with your parents.'

'No.'

He waited, knowing she wanted him to explain, but pretending innocence. Would she wheedle or come at it direct? A game he played with Sarah.

'Are you going to tell me why?'

Direct. Not a woman for pastime games. Not now anyway, with so little time left to pass.

'If you'd like me to.'

'Yes.'

He knew this mood also. Tell me a story, entertain me. Was that his job today, his reason for being here? Young children like to be told stories to help them go to sleep. Maybe old people like being told stories to help them die. Well, he thought, if that's why I'm here, I don't mind. As good a job as any. And a lot easier than conversation. Begin at the beginning, the King said, gravely, and go on till you come to the end.

'You know I have an older sister, Penelope, and a younger brother, Harry? Penny—our father calls her Poppy—is three years older. Harry is eighteen months younger, so he's fifteen and a half. My father dotes on Penny. Well actually, they dote on each other. I mean, just about verging on the obscene, in my opinion.' He laughed,

137

but there was no reaction. 'I know Freud is supposed to have said that sons are in love with their mothers and want to kill their fathers, but in our house, it's not like that at all. The problem is father loving daughter and vice versa. At least they don't want to kill Mum.' Still no reponse. 'By the way, the mother-son thing is called the Oedipus complex, isn't it. I wonder if the father-daughter affair has a name as well?'

'Electra,' said the head from the bed.

'Electra?'

'Electra complex. Daughter of Agamemnon and Cly-temnestra. You don't know?'

'No.'

'Electra convinced her brother Orestes to avenge their father's murder by their mother's lover Aegisthus. Go on with your story.'

'Okay. Thanks. Well, Penny's an assistant manager in a chain-store boutique. We don't get on at all. I think she's a fashion-crazed zombie and she thinks I'm a boring and pre-tentious snob. At least, that's her latest accusation. Harry is our mother's favourite. Not just because he's the youngest but because she had a hard time having him. He's good at sport, so our father quite likes him as well, and he plays the oboe in the local youth orchestra. He's also very handsome. In fact, he's so good at everything I ought to hate him, but I don't. I like him a lot, and am very proud of him. We get on fine. He wants to be an acoustical engineer.

'I'm not good at sport, play the piano well enough to annoy anyone who happens to listen, am not particularly handsome, and prefer to be on my own than in with the crowd. So you see, I'm piggy-in-the-middle in our family, and also the odd one out. But I don't mind because I've always had a special kind of feeling for my grandmother and she for me. Mother says that from the time I was born Sarah took me over. It was she who insisted I be called Jacob after my grandfather. Mother was happy with that, but Father was against it.'

'Why?'

'Dad never knew his father of course, because of Jacob dying before he was born. But you know all about that. Sarah told me Dad was conceived on Grandad's last weekend leave just a few days before he was sent to the battle. And besides, Dad has never been happy about the way Sarah idolises Jacob—that's what he calls it—and romanticises—his word again—their three years of marriage. He says it's unhealthy. No relationship, he says, is ever as perfect as Sarah makes out hers was with Grandfather, no matter how much the two people are in love. I wouldn't know. All I know is she never married again. She's had quite a few men friends, but she always says none of them ever matched up to Jacob. I think she feels that somehow his death didn't end their love but sealed it for ever. She's very determined, is Sarah. Once she's decided about something, that's it, no changing her mind. Pigheaded, Dad says.

'Not that Dad and Sarah have ever really got on. They're chalk and cheese, Mum says. Leave them on their own in a room together and after five minutes the third world war starts. And Dad certainly has a hang-up about not having had a father. Whenever I used to complain about anything to do with him, he would always say, "You should be grateful you've got a father to complain about." But that would only make me more annoyed. Once, it annoyed me so much, I shouted at him that he was the one who ought to be grateful, because I wished I didn't have a father, and certainly not him. I was about eleven at the time. I think I meant it as a sort of angry joke, you know how it is when you're having a family row. But that's not how Dad took it. It was the only time all through my childhood when I thought he was going to hit me. He didn't, he's very anti-violence. But he was more upset than I've ever seen him. He rushed out of the room and disappeared in to his

139

workshop—he's a big do-it-yourself addict—and didn't reappear for ages. Mum was furious with me. A mega telling-off ensued. Much to sister Penny's satisfaction, I might add.

'Dad and I got on all right while I was young, till I was about ten. And then I don't know what happened. Well, a number of things actually. Dad finally accepted that I didn't think football was a matter of major importance in life, and that I was never going to be a do-it-yourself fanatic either. I didn't like the way he and Penny started behaving with each other, he really did become obsessed with her, and still is. Anyhow, we started having serious rows.

'I know it must sound silly, but the turning point was one day when I was about thirteen and I suddenly realised I didn't think Dad's jokes were funny any more. And that was it. After that he was just this man who happened to be my father and was mostly an embarrassment, a sort of relic from the nineteen sixties. With his long straggly hair thinning on top. And his stupid granny glasses. And a permanent appearance round the eyes of having just got up after not having gone to bed. Then there's his roly-poly midriff hanging over his factory-distressed jeans that show off his slumpy bum. He looks like John Lennon gone to seed. John Lennon—*who else!*—being his personal idol and the music of the Beatles the height of his musical taste. Sarah always says he was badly infected by what she calls the sponge-brain flower-power toxins wafting over the Atlantic from America in the late sixties when Dad was in his twenties. By the way, he and Mum met at a Rolling Stones so-called concert. Pardon me while I chunder.'

Jacob paused, aware that he'd allowed himself to be carried away, the telling taking over the story. Had he overdone it? Geertrui's eyes were closed but he knew she was listening, and an amused smile encouraged him to continue.

'Anyway, that's how it was when I was fourteen and

Mum had to go in to hospital for a big operation, which was followed by weeks of convalescence. Father and Penny could manage the house between them, and because Harry was, well, *Harry*, he was all right. But not me. I was a problem. The first week Mum was away the rows between Dad and Penny and me got really bad. So Sarah suggested I go and live with her till Mum was home and well again. To ease the strain on us all, she said. And for once Dad agreed with her.

'Sarah's house is a cottage in a village about four miles from my parents', so I can easily cycle home if I need to but at the same time I'm far enough away for us all to be out of each other's hair. And, as I told you, Sarah and I get on really well. We like the same things—music, reading, going to the theatre and stuff like that. And we both like to be on our own quite a bit of the time.

'Eventually Mum got well again. It took about four months. But by then I was so happy at Sarah's I didn't want to go back. Which pleased everybody, I need hardly tell you. Except Mum. I haven't said, have I, that I love Mum a lot. She hasn't got stuck in the sixties the way Dad has, and she hasn't gone to seed either. Not that she tries to behave like someone young, I don't mean that. I suppose I mean she's kept up with her proper age but stayed young inside. Actually, Mum is the one Harry gets his good looks from. And he's very like Mum in his ways, which must be why I get along so well with him. I know Harry is her love child, as Sarah puts it, but I don't mind because I also know Mum and I are friends. Which I've come to think is the best thing anyone can say about a parent. I've always been able to tell her anything and talk anything over with her. So Mum and I talked it over and we decided I should stay on at Sarah's but that I was always welcome to go back if I want to to what I don't any longer think of as home.

'Which is how I came to live with my grandmother.'

*

Hospital noises filtered in from the corridor.

Geertrui's eyes opened.

For the first time her head moved.

They looked at each other, eye-to-eye.

At last Geertrui said, 'And have you forgiven him?'

'Forgiven who?'

'Your father.'

'Forgiven him? What for?'

'For being your father.'

The question tripped him. 'Do I . . .? Have I . . .?'

Geertrui waited a moment before asking, 'Are you glad you are alive?'

Jacob took a deep breath. His heart rate increased and he felt himself blush. For a fading moth this lady had the attack of a Rottweiler.

He managed to say, 'Yes. Well, mostly. Sometimes not. I get depressed now and then and wish . . . Sarah calls them my mouse moods and says I'll probably grow out of them.'

Geertrui gave a short dry chuckle that sounded like walking over gravel.

'Blame biology,' she said.

He wasn't sure whether or not she was being ironic. But he was glad of a chance to smile and say, 'Yes!'

Geertrui's head turned away and her eyes closed again.

After a silence she said, 'Daan has explained you what is to happen to me?'

He could only nod, even though she wasn't looking.

'Do you understand?'

Another deep breath before he could reply, 'I think so.'

'Do you approve?'

'I don't—'

'No.' Geertrui stopped him. 'Approve is not the word. It's not for you to approve or disapprove. Wait.'

Another silence. Then:

'Would you do such a thing yourself?'

Jacob struggled with the question, remembered his tears

yesterday, feared they might come again. This would not be the time. There was too much. And too little.

Time, time! Suddenly everything seemed to be about time. A life time. Time for this, time for that. The time of your life. A time to live. No time left. A time to die.

'I don't know,' he said with steady seriousness. 'I really don't. In theory I would. But in . . . reality. It seems so . . .'

Words failed him. A glottal stop in his gut.

Clearing her throat of gravel before speaking, Geertrui said, 'Then you are still glad to be alive.'

A statement not a question.

Jacob paused before saying, 'Yes. I suppose I am.'

'Even in your, what was it?'

'Mouse moods.'

'Yes, even in your mouse moods you only play with the idea of not being.' She cleared her throat again. 'Biology, you see. It's because of biology that we want to live and not to die. And it is because of biology that we come to a time when we want to die and not to live. What matters—'

A flash of pain crossed her face. She caught her breath and held it a few seconds. Sweat glazed her skin. Lying on the bed cover, her hands were clutched like claws.

Alarmed, Jacob said, 'Are you all right? Shall I call someone?'

Geertrui raised a fisted hand, indicating no.

It was a while before she relaxed again.

'You must go soon.' Her voice was strained. 'But before, I must ask you two questions.' She pursed her dry lips and rubbed them together. 'Tomorrow you go to Oosterbeek. Will you come and see me again on Monday? There's something I wish to give you.'

'Sure. Yes.'

'Now, the other question. Will you read something to me? A short poem.'

Who can refuse a dying woman? 'If you want me to. I don't know how well—'

143

'Your grandfather liked it. He read it to me. I read it over his grave. I should very much like to hear you read it.'

Jacob could only nod.

'The drawer of my cabinet. The book there. A slip of paper marks the page.'

A battered, dog-eared volume, its red and cream cover faded and grubby.

'The Ben Jonson?' he asked.

Geertrui's head turned and her eyes were on him again, intense, devouring.

He had never seen the poem before. He glanced through the few lines, rehearsing them in his head, fearing he might stumble over the unfamiliar Jacobean English.

Time. Time.

He took a breath while telling himself to be calm, to concentrate, to see only the words, follow the lines, trust the punctuation: just as he'd been taught while rehearsing the Scottish play.

He breathed in. And began.

> 'It is not growing like a tree
> In bulk, doth make Man better be;
> Or standing long an oak, three hundred year,
> To fall a log at last, dry, bald, and sere:
>> A lily of a day
>> Is fairer far in May,
> Although it fall and die that night;
> It was the plant and flower of Light.
> In small proportions we just beauties see;
> And in short measures life may perfect be.'

Clinical noises echoed outside.

In the room, hospital air embalmed the silence.

GEERTRUI

The innocent happy time came to an end early the next morning. Until then each day our rising habit was thus. Mr Wesseling got up first at five thirty. He revived the fire in the kitchen range before going off to his farm work and to make sure Dirk and Henk were awake, who then got up and milked the cows. At six Mrs Wesseling got up and cooked breakfast for seven o'clock. I got up after her and did some housework until breakfast was ready. After we had eaten I took Jacob his coffee and performed our wake-up ritual.

But that morning Mrs Wesseling and I were still in bed and Mr Wesseling was busy reviving the fire when Dirk rushed in from the cowhouse, shouting for us all to hear, 'Germans! Germans!' It was a word that, like a magic spell, conjured us instantly into most vigorous action. Dirk had been dressing in the hideout when by lucky chance he saw from the skylight a German army truck turn from the main road in to our track. As soon as we heard his warning shout, Mr Wesseling rushed out to intercept the soldiers and to prevent them from entering the house for as long as possible. Mrs Wesseling ran from her room to the stairhead, yelling at Dirk to go back to the hideout. As for me, my first thought was of Jacob. I flung myself out of bed and hurried to his room, calling his name, knowing he must be roused and moved quickly somehow. But where? By the time I had reached him and shaken him awake Mrs Wesseling joined us, like me still in her night dress, her sleep-tousled hair loose about her head, and Dirk, despite his mother's anxiety for him, was pounding up the back stairs in his bare feet.

'Where are they?' Mrs Wesseling was shouting to him. 'On our road in a truck,' Dirk called back. 'Father's gone to stall them.' At the same time I was explaining to Jacob what was happening, and was helping him out of bed. But his wounded leg still could not carry his weight or even move itself without causing great pain. He was sitting on the edge of the bed when Dirk joined us. 'Quick, quick,' Dirk said, 'I'll carry him on my back.' 'No, no,' Mrs Wesseling cried. 'No time. You'll never do it. They'll be everywhere. Go, go! We'll think of something.' Just as my first thought had been of Jacob, hers was of Dirk. No matter who else was caught, herself included, her only child must not be. Dirk made an attempt at protest, but his mother, quite frantic, took him by the arms and began to push him with all her weight out of the room, crying, 'Hide, Dirk, hide, hide!'

By now we could hear the Germans driving in to the farm yard. And I too was becoming distraught. 'What shall we do?' I could hear myself saying. 'Where shall we hide him?' Such awful panic. I think never so much in all my life. This while I was trying to help Jacob to stand, who was also spluttering, in English of course, words I could not (then!) understand. Later he told me he was cursing himself for allowing himself to relax during the last few days when we should have planned what to do in such an emergency. But they were days, he said, when he had felt suspended, out of time, out of place, with no past and no future, only an endless, self-contained, charmed, timeless time. But now the spell was broken.

Only when we heard orders shouted in German echoing round the yard, and the clatter of boots as soldiers spilled out of their truck did Dirk, realising there was no time left, obey his mother and stumble away down the stairs, through the dairy in to the cowhouse, where Henk was waiting, ready to swing the ladder up in to the roof when Dirk had climbed it and to close the entrance to their hiding place as soon as they were inside. They made it in the nick of time.

146

Mr Wesseling's attempt to delay the soldiers with questions about what they wanted and to inspect their permit were brushed aside by the officer in charge, and the soldiers were sent to search each building: two with their officer came in to the house by the kitchen door, two in to the cowhouse by the big end door. Mr Wesseling was ordered to remain by the truck guarded by the driver.

In the seconds after Dirk left us, Mrs Wesseling recovered her composure with a surety that astounded me. Whatever else I may say about her this I must: she possessed admirable self-discipline and remarkable courage. 'Calm,' she muttered as much to herself as to me. And then as if all emotion had been siphoned out of her, she glanced at me with Jacob leaning against me, his arm round my neck, looked round the room, and after a meditative pause that seemed like an eternity there came over her face an almost amused expression.

'Quick,' she said, going to the *bedstee* and opening the doors.

As I do not think you have such a thing as our *bedstee* in England I should explain you that it is a bed in a cupboard in the wall. Many of our old houses had them. Usually they were in the kitchen-living-room at the side of the fire. During the day the bed could be shut away from view by closing the doors or a curtain. At night it was a cosy bed. And thus the little space and few rooms of the old houses could be used to the maximum without a bed getting in the way or depressing the eye during the day. Like some of the better-off farms, the Wesselings' had a second floor and bedrooms up there. But still a *bedstee* provided an extra sleeping place when necessary. Luckily there was one in Jacob's room. I had not even thought of it till now, when Mrs Wesseling opened its doors.

'Get him in, get him in,' she said, and helped me almost carry Jacob to it and tumble him in, he hopping on one foot and me explaining to him what was happening.

147

'Now you,' said Mrs Wesseling as soon as Jacob was lying flat on his back on the mattress.

'What! Why?' I said, breathless though I was with the exertion and excitement.

'Just do it. On top of him. Quick!'

At such a moment there is no time for discussion or even explanation. Already we could hear the clatter of a soldier's boots on the stone tiles of the floor downstairs and the sharp commands of his officer. Besides, there was no resisting the force of Mrs Wesseling's will when she was in such a determined temper.

So in to the *bedstee* I clambered, and lay down flat on my back on top of Jacob. Only to find myself covered at once by the duvet, which Mrs Wesseling swept off Jacob's bed and flung over us.

'What are you doing?' Jacob whispered to me.

'Quiet,' I whispered back. 'Don't even breathe!'

Now we could hear the soldier's boots stamping up the stairs.

'Look ill,' Mrs Wesseling muttered to me before she made for the door, and surged out without a pause on to the landing, where she confronted the soldier as he reached the top of the stairs.

'What are you doing here? What do you want?' I heard her demand in angry German.

'Orders. Out of the way,' replied the soldier.

'How dare you! What orders? Show me your orders?'

'Officer. Downstairs. Out of the way.'

The soldier's hobnailed boots stomped along the landing to the furthest room, Mrs Wesseling's bare feet slapping along behind, and she harrying him all the time. 'What do you think we are doing here? Hiding an army? We are farmers, doing our best despite everything to grow food to feed people like you. How dare you come here like this?' And the soldier growling back at her, 'Quiet, woman. Go away,' as he searched the rooms.

148

He was not very diligent at his job, or perhaps he just wanted to get away from Mrs Wesseling as quickly as possible, but he did little more than look under the beds, inspect inside the wardrobes (knocking the backs with his rifle butt, for it was well known that people often constructed hiding places in the wall behind a wardrobe), a few taps on the ceilings and walls for any give-away hollow sound of a cavity.

Finally he arrived at Jacob's room. Mrs Wesseling made sure she preceded him and stood just inside the door, looking across at the *bedstee*. As he entered, she said quietly, 'A guest. She's sick.'

The soldier stopped in his tracks.

'Sick?' he said with alarm.

'Tuberculosis,' said Mrs Wesseling to him with a gesture of resignation, adding quietly, 'Very bad, poor girl. No hope.'

Peering over the duvet, I saw the soldier's nose twitch, as if he smelt the dread disease.

'My God!' he said, turning on his heel, and stomped out of the room and away down the stairs.

'Stay there,' Mrs Wesseling mouthed at me when he had gone, then followed after.

For some time I lay on top of Jacob in the *bedstee* before I heard the Germans driving away and Mrs Wesseling came panting up the stairs to tell me they had not discovered my brother and Dirk. How long this was—ten, fifteen minutes, more—I could not tell. Not because those were less time-tied days; clocks were not everywhere as they are today. But another reason kept from my mind any knowing of time or thought of the soldiers.

While the soldier was clattering about in the bedrooms I lay in the *bedstee* rigid with panic, trying to control my breathing, and fearful for my pounding heart. But when he gave up and went downstairs the relief was so great my bones turned to dough and I lay where I was, too weak to

149

move, and my nightshift soaked with sweat. It was only then I became aware of Jacob's body under mine, my weight pressing upon him, his head on its side under my left shoulder, his chest rising and falling as he breathed under my back, his angular hips beneath the swell of my buttocks, my legs stretched inside of his. I felt his warmth percolating through the clinging layers of our sweated nightwear, I felt the architecture of his bones, the cushioning of his muscles.

And because instinctively as I tumbled in upon him he had clasped his arms around my waist and held me firm, while I clutched the duvet close under my chin to ensure nothing of us was exposed but my face, we thus lay clamped together, at first conscious only of the danger stalking the rooms, then conscious only of our two bodies so closely pressed together. Never before had anyone held me like this, never before had I felt the intimate shape of a man's body against my own. This itself would have been enough to startle me. Not that I disliked it, not at all. Indeed, while before my heart was beating with dreadful fear, now it beat with excitement. But then something else occurred, something even more startling. I felt Jacob's sex swelling between my thighs. As if it were being inflated by a bicycle pump.

It would be wrong to say that I did not know what was happening, but it would also be wrong to say that I was entirely sure what it meant *for me*. What should I do? How should I respond?

This must seem to you inconceivable. Knowing, as young people, even children, now do, the sexual functions of the body, I can understand how it must seem to you impossible that a young woman of nineteen could be uncertain, if not ignorant, of a man's stiffening penis. But so it was, and I must ask you to accept that what I felt was such a confusing mixture of surprise, an unfamiliar kind of aroused sensation in my body, and uncertain emotions about what I wished and what I ought to do, that there came over me a shyness so complete that I could not move but was as if paralysed, unable to respond as part of me wished to do without knowing precisely how, but neither able to flee as part of me felt I ought to do. All I could do was remain as I was, every cell of my body tingling as never before, intensely sensitive to my own and to Jacob's body and to my own and his every smallest movement.

No more than this occurred. We lay moulded together in a suspended state of desire, me too shocked to remove myself and Jacob not daring to move lest he more embarrass himself and offend me, till Mrs Wesseling arrived and broke the spell, when I fled to my room, she calling after me the news of the others' safety, for I was afraid my face would betray my feelings, and needed to calm myself in private before I dared look anyone in the eye again.

As for Jacob, poor man, he had not intended such arousal. Nature overrode human discretion, biology was to blame. Consider: a virile young man, for weeks away from home and after enduring for many days the stress and strain, highs and lows, of a fierce battle that sent some men mad, after being wounded, escaping the carnage, and then days of cosseted recovery nursed by a young woman attractive enough in her modest way. Consider he then suddenly finds himself pinned down in a narrow bed by this same young woman while danger and its removal stretches and relaxes his nerves and flushes adrenaline through his veins. How else would anyone expect this young man's body to behave, except as a lion's to a lioness after the hunt or as a seedling thrusts through winter ice in spring?

We had escaped by the skin of our teeth. I need not tell you that we were all badly shaken by the sudden arrival of the Germans, and by how they were so quickly upon us that we were almost caught with our feet in the ditch. Because of this, we agreed it was too dangerous to keep Jacob in the house any longer. He was well enough to be moved to the cowhouse hiding place. But so cramped would it be at night for the three of them that Dirk and Henk decided to take turns sleeping in one of the emergency hide-outs in the other farm buildings.

This change was made that very morning after the raid. And during the next few days I discovered what an unwelcome and unexpected difference it made to my life. For three weeks, first in our cellar at home and then at the farm, tending Jacob had been the main object of my attention. In fact, he had become the centre of my life. Some of us forget as we grow old how consuming can be the power of a young woman's devotion. I have not. Perhaps because of what happened I have not been able to. Remembering those days I feel it still as keenly as I did then. Suddenly, no more than an hour after the few intense moments in the *bedstee* had brought to the surface thoughts, feelings, emotions, physical sensations that till then had moved, if they had stirred at all, only in the hidden depths of my being, suddenly he who had enlivened them, had fished them into view, was taken from me for the first time since he was brought to me unconscious in our cellar. What this abrupt separation meant to me I did not understand instantly during the next few hours, while we prepared the hiding place for him and carried him there, nor while I cleared up 'his' room in the house and laundered his bedclothes, nor during the rest of that day as I went about my routine chores, and carried his meals to him in the hiding place and sat with him while he ate. In that time there was too much to do, and the overhang of anxiety brought on by the raid numbed any thought of consequences. What I was most aware of then was relief that Jacob had not been captured and gladness that he was still with me.

But in the evening and especially while I lay in bed during the following night, I felt my deprivation. Felt his absence in the house, in the bedroom next to mine. He was not there for me to sit with after the day's work. He was not there during the night to listen for should he need help. He was not there in the morning, alone in his room for me to wake with our tender ritual. And it was only in the night, after I had visited him in the hiding place to say goodnight, where I had found Dirk and Henk with him, drinking farm-brewed beer and smoking foul-smelling wartime cigarettes, the atmosphere so alien and unwelcoming of me, a woman —it was only then as I lay in my bed that the tears came. And when they dried up there came the fantasies of a girl's first sexual longing. I felt again my body pressed down on his in the *bedstee*, felt his erection against my thigh, wished for the touch of his hands and the sound of his voice speaking softly in to my ear such words as those of the poem he had read to me from Sam's book only the evening before.

Shall I compare thee to a summer's day?
Thou art more lovely and more temperate:
Rough winds do shake the darling buds of May,
And summer's lease hath all too short a date:
Sometime too hot the eye of heaven shines,
And often is his gold complexion dimmed,
And every fair from fair sometime declines,
By chance or nature's changing course untrimmed:
But thy eternal summer shall not fade,
Nor lose possession of that fair thou ow'st,
Nor shall Death brag thou wand'rest in his shade,
When in eternal lines to time thou grow'st.
    So long as men can breathe or eyes can see,
    So long lives this, and this gives life to thee.

For time-stretched minutes I beamed all my wishes towards him in the hiding place, willing him to come to me, silently, secretly, to join me in my bed. I knew he could not even climb down the ladder without help, never mind hobble from there to me, yet told myself he would do it somehow, being sure in the flush of my desire he could do anything if he felt for me as I felt for him. For longer minutes still I lay on my back waiting, urging him to me, and listening to every click and sigh of the sleeping house, holding my breath at any scantest sound that might signal his arrival, only to deflate in an agony of disappointment when it proved not.

I had little idea of exactly what I hoped he would do when we were together. Ignorance of possibilities and lack of any experience limited my imagination to the most obvious pleasures. All I knew was that I longed to have him beside me, to kiss and caress me, to speak to me words more intimate than any I had so far ever heard, to be wrapped around by him, held and folded into him. I had no words other than such blurred figures as these, learned I expect from my reading of romantic fiction, to tell myself of what I sensed I desperately desired.

And so that night I suffered the adult awakening which is such painful pleasure, made difficult for me because there was no one to whom I could talk about it. Had I been at home and the times been normal, I would have told my mother and shared my adventure with my closest friends. But my mother was out of reach, and my bosom friends were scattered who knew where? On the farm who was there? Only Mrs Wesseling, and I knew I could not trust her to understand and support me. So I had to keep my turmoil to myself. And thus I learned: nothing festers like a passion concealed.

That Jacob was taken from me was hurt enough. What made it worse was the change his move to the hiding place wrought in Jacob himself. So much in the company of Dirk and Henk, three young men confined together, he quickly became, as you say, 'one of the boys'. A man brasher than the one I knew. Huddled all night in their bivouac of a den, they encouraged each other in bombast and bravado. Of course, this was inflamed by unspoken jealousy and competitiveness over me between Dirk and Jacob, which at the time I was blind to. Nor was it helped by the fact that Dirk could speak little English and Jacob no Dutch, so that Henk had to interpret for them both. Whenever I visited they teased me, as much to impress each other as to amuse me (as I pretended it did) or annoy me (which I pretended it did not). Oh, how boring is such boyness in grown men! My adored brother, my would-be suitor, my captivating soldier: I hated them all in this ugly reversive mood.

Four days went by, five, a week, two. Things got worse. The boy-men became boisterous, rowdy, impatient of their confinement.

One day towards the end of the second week there was an angry mood between Jacob and Dirk with Henk striving to keep the peace. They would not tell me what the matter was. Henk, who I asked about it when by ourselves, would only say that the trouble would pass. Perhaps, as I think was so, they had argued about me. Whatever the reason, Jacob began a regime of exercises to strengthen his wounded leg and to fitten him up again after his time in bed. But even this became a cause of competitiveness, and Dirk also started, as people say now, 'working out'. Anything you can do I can do better, and more of and more than. I tried to remonstrate, fearing that Jacob's wound might open up again, but he would not listen. He could not go on as he had been, he said; he must make his escape back to his own people.

I should explain you that the Allied advance in to Holland had not gone as quickly as we had expected and hoped. We heard news of the armies from our radio. But news of what was happening in the towns and villages around us we heard from people who called at the farm, begging for food, and from occasional letters from relatives and friends. This is how we learned that the Germans had completely evacuated Oosterbeek after the battle. Most of the village

155

had been destroyed. But no one was allowed to visit what was left without special permission from the German authorities. Early in October a letter finally reached me from Mother. She and Father were living with Father's cousins in Apeldoorn. She described how urgently the Germans were hunting for men aged between sixteen and fifty to work for them. Placards announced that they would be well paid and extra food rations would be given to their families. But few men turned up. Soon after, dead men were laid out at street corners, their bodies displaying the signs of torture, a notice pinned to their clothes on which was one word: Terrorist. This was intended to frighten everyone of course, and it did. Mother saw wagons full of men followed by long lines of men on foot guarded by a few soldiers. It was then that they took Father, though she did not tell me this at the time. He had given himself up to avoid reprisals against Mother or his cousins if he tried to hide and was found.

From others we heard that the same kind of thing had happened in Groningen, one of our most northerly cities, in Amersfoort in the heart of the country, west in the Hague, in Deventer near us here in the east. Everywhere. Now we understood what was meant when we heard on the English news that when the Allies liberated Maastricht, one of our southernmost cities, on the border with Belgium, there were hardly any men there at all. They had been taken not only as forced labour, but so that they could not help the British when they arrived.

As this news reached us in dribs and drabs, Dirk especially, but Henk too, became more and more angry, more and more frustrated because they were 'shut away', as they put it, doing nothing to help defeat the hated enemy who occupied our country and visited such suffering upon us. It was cowardly, they said, to remain so. Their boy-bluster soured to belligerence. While they went about their tasks on the farm, and at night in the stew-pot of their hideout, they concocted one plot after another by which to disrupt the Germans and kill them. They talked of home-made bombs designed to blow up German command posts, of lying in ambush for patrols, of stretching wires across country roads to disable soldiers on motorbikes or cycles. Anything at all, no matter how madcap it might be. Mr Wesseling urged them to be patient. The Allies would come soon, he said, and it was more important that young men like Dirk and Henk be there, ready to help rebuild our country after the liberation than that they gamble their lives in hazardous ventures of a kind better left to the experts in the Resistance. Mrs Wesseling pleaded with Dirk to listen to his father and to do nothing rash, and I with Henk, who I knew could influence Dirk if he felt strongly about some-thing, but knew just as surely that he could be influenced by Dirk. They were always from their first meeting as small boys such inseparable bosom friends that what one did the other would do out of loyalty. And Henk, though the more intelligent and calm-headed, was also the more easy-going, and thus usually the one who was led rather than the leader. With Dirk so hot for action I feared for Henk's welfare. While this was going on Jacob kept quiet, and wisely too, for had he taken my side he would only have inflamed Dirk the more.

All might have been well had we not been raided again, this time at dusk. It was a half-hearted affair. We saw them coming in good time for the boys to shut themselves away. The soldiers had their orders but we could tell they did not expect to find what they were looking for (men of an age to take away, we assumed). Instead, their officer hinted that they would give up without causing too much trouble if we handed over a few items of food of the scarcer sort. They left with a sack full of farmhouse cheese, eggs, a cake of butter, along with our unspoken but heartfelt scorn.

When Dirk heard of it he was furious, shouting at his

157

father that giving in like this ensured we would be raided again in a few days when more would be demanded. And on and on it would go, worse each time. And if ever we refused, the place would be torn apart on the pretext of searching for men, arms, illegal radios, whatever reason the officer felt like using. And if that happened, they would be certain to unload the hay from the cowhouse gallery, and the hiding place would be found.

'You know how it is with them,' he said. 'Make them obey the rules or they despise you and do whatever they like with you. It's against the rules for them to take food without official authorisation. They know that. Now we've broken the rules, we've given in to extortion and they'll be back for more. We aren't safe any longer.'

That night we went to bed despondent and worried.

Next morning Dirk and Henk had gone. They had taken Jacob's gun and ammunition with them. And each had left a hastily written letter, Dirk to his parents, Henk to me. I still have my brother's.

Dirk had scribbled a note at the end.

I never saw Henk again.

Beloved sister,

We cannot wait any longer. We must help rid our country of the invader. Dirk is right. The Germans will raid the farm more often now. Later, when the Allies are near, they will take it over as a command post or stronghold for a gun emplacement. If—no, when—that happens we would be caught. And then the Germans would treat us badly and you and the others too. Rats always behave worst when they are cornered. Better that Dirk and I go now while there is a chance of fighting rather than wait to be captured and killed or made to work for them. This is also the best thing for you. Less harm will come to you if we are not found here. For this reason also, help Jacob to leave as soon as he is fit enough. <u>Do not delay.</u>

We have decided to try and contact the Resistance, and, if they cannot use us, to make for the British army in the south. We should have done this months ago. Anyway, after the battle that destroyed our home.

I know you will be upset. I would have told you of our plan but I would not have been strong against your tears. What we are doing I must do. To keep faith with Dirk. But also for my own pride. I hope you understand.

Be sure Dirk and I will see you very soon, when we will bring freedom with us. Until then, dearest sister, whose life is more precious to me than my own, take good care of yourself <u>before all else</u>.

Your brother Henk.

I carry you in my heart. All my love, Dirk.

A bridge too far.
Lt-Gen. F.A.M. Browning
I still have nightmares so violent
that my wife gets bruised in bed.
I am not bitter; I've had nearly
fifty more years than those poor devils
who lie in the Oosterbeek cemetery.
It seemed a good idea at the time.
It was a gamble;
some you win, some you lose.
We lost that one.
Staff Sergeant Joe Kitchener,
Glider Pilot Regiment, the Battle of Arnhem

Sunday 17 September 1995.

08:00. Filtering through the haze of what will become a
bright, warm, late-summer day free of the rain that show-
ered the previous three days of his trip, the reflected light of
the morning sun woke Jacob in the guest room of Geertrui's
apartment on the Oudezijds Kolk in Amsterdam.

On his way down to the bathroom he neither saw nor
heard any sign of Daan, whom he assumed must still be
asleep behind the Chinese screens beyond the kitchen. After
a quick wash and use of the lavatory, he dressed in, at last,
his own clothes. Black sweatshirt, clean blue-green jeans,
red socks, light tan Ecco town boots. Feeling more himself
than he had since arriving in Holland, he ate a quick
breakfast of toast, honey and tea, prepared with as little
clatter as he could contrive in a kitchen still strange to him

so as not to disturb Daan, whose early-morning testiness he wished to avoid. Already there was too much occupying his mind for comfort. The feelings spun by Geertrui yesterday tangled with his anticipations about today.

After leaving Geertrui, Daan had taken him to the Van Riets', where they collected Jacob's belongings and ate a meal with Mr van Riet, during most of which Daan and his father discussed family business in Dutch, apologising for doing so, but which Jacob was glad of, being in no mood for polite chatter. The visit to Geertrui had disturbed him in ways he could not yet explain even to himself.

When they got back to Amsterdam Jacob took a long hot bath and spent the rest of the evening on his own, thankful that Daan had a date and would not be back till late. It was a relief after the constant company of strangers to be on his own, with the pleasures of the apartment to himself. He poked about among the books, played music on the super sound system, flicked through the numerous channels on television, and spied now and then from the front windows into the rooms in the hotel across the canal. (Surprising how many people left the curtains open, their rooms lit like little stages, while they performed private functions. Unpacking, undressing, sorting money, applying make-up, lying on the bed in their underwear. Daan had told him of seeing people having sex straight and gay, of a naked young woman dancing round her room and other similar entertainments. But, typical of his luck, Jacob thought, all he saw that was out of the ordinary was a middle-aged man of awkward obesity, dressed in singlet and boxer shorts, trying to cut his toenails, a project the man gave up after failing by various contortions to reach his toes with the clippers.)

But all the while and until he fell asleep sometime after twelve Jacob brooded on his hour with Geertrui, trying to reset his dislocated emotions. Now, this morning, the disturbance was just as aching.

After breakfast he padded his way from the kitchen,

across the cool expanse of Spanish tiles, to the ship's gangway that took him to the upper deck and to his room, where, in a plastic carrier bag with a logo and the word *Bijenkorf* printed on it [beehive: he'd looked it up last night], which he'd found in the kitchen, he packed his Olympia camera and a pvc jerkin Daan had loaned him in case of rain.

Ten minutes were left before Mrs van Riet would come for him. They would take the 09:32 to Utrecht, where, Daan's meticulous accountant father had told him, they would arrive at 10:00 on platform 12a and leave six minutes later from platform 4b on a train that would get them to Oosterbeek at 10:47, allowing only just enough time to walk to the battle cemetery by 11:00, when the main ceremony was due to begin.

Sunday 17 September 1944, Southern England.

By 09:45 on a day that began misty but soon became fine and sunny, 332 RAF and 143 American aircraft, along with 320 gliders hooked up for towing to their LZs [Landing Zones] by the other aircraft, altogether carrying approximately 5,700 men and their equipment, including such items as jeeps and light artillery guns, were ready to take off from eight British and 14 American airfields dotted across England from Lincolnshire to Dorset in the largest paratrooper operation ever undertaken.

The remainder of the total of 11,920 men who were to fight in the battle were to be flown to the battle in a second wave the next day, Monday, to the DZs [Dropping Zones] in fields near the village of Wolfheze, three miles west of Oosterbeek and seven miles from their objective, the now famous 'bridge too far' that spanned the Lower Rhine in the centre of Arnhem 20 kms from the German border.

Private James Sims, aged 19, of 'S' Company, 2nd Battalion The Parachute Regiment, 1st British Airborne Division, Battle of Arnhem:

162

On the Saturday night most of us relaxed; some played football, others darts. Some read and some wrote letters. I went over to the canteen and sat on a chair with my feet up on the unlit stove. The cat crept on to my lap and purred contentedly as I scratched its ear. One of the 'C' Company men showed me a religious tract he had just received in a parcel from home. On it was a picture of a windmill and the words 'Lost on the Zuider Zee'. He thought it was a bad omen; it was certainly a strange coincidence [because the coming operation was secret]. We eventually turned in and I slept surprisingly well.

Sunday started off just like any other day except for some butterflies in the stomach. 'Have a good breakfast,' they advised, 'as you don't know when you'll get your next meal' . . .

Young Geordie and myself were warned to get ready. As we had not been in the battalion long, we were designated as bomb carriers and were given the harness with six ten-pound [4.5 kgs] mortar bombs to cart into action. We were issued with Dutch occupation money, maps, escape saws, forty rounds of .303 rifle ammo, two .36 grenades, an anti-tank grenade, a phosphorus bomb, and a pick and shovel, as well as the rifles we already had. [*Sims, pp 50-1*]

Major Geoffrey Powell, officer commanding 'C' Company, 156 Parachute Battalion, 4th Parachute Brigade, went in the second wave:

Now came the familiar toil of struggling into jumping kit. Over my battle-dress and airborne smock, I was already wearing full equipment: the haversack containing maps, torch and other odds and ends; [gas-mask] respirator, waterbottle and compass; pistol holster and ammunition case; and on my chest the two pouches crammed with Sten [gun] magazines and hand grenades. Across my stomach I then tied my small pack, solid with two days' concentrated rations, mess tin, spare socks, washing kit, pullover, a tin mug, all topped off with a Hawking anti-tank grenade. Slung around my neck were binoculars, while a large shell dressing, a morphia syringe and red beret were tucked into my smock pockets. Next I wrapped myself in a denim jumping jacket to hold the bits and pieces in place and prevent the parachute cords snagging on the many protuberances. Over everything went a Mae West life-jacket, with a camouflage net scarfed around my neck and the parachutist's steel helmet, covered with scrim-decorated net, on my head. On my right leg I then tied a large bag, into which was packed a Sten gun, together with an oblong-shaped walkie-talkie radio, and a small entrenching tool: a quick release catch allowed this bag to be lowered in mid-air so that it would dangle below on a thin cord and hit the ground before I did. Next Private Harrison helped me into my parachute, and I did the same for him, after which we both tested each other's quick release boxes to make certain that they were working properly . . . After much thought, I had decided to take two luxuries, a red beret and an *Oxford Book of English Verse*. [*Powell, pp 19-21*]

Promptly at nine fifteen Mrs van Riet rang the bell at her mother's apartment. Jacob picked up the *Bijenkorf* bag, clumped in his town boots down the steep gangway to the main floor, checked his appearance in a mirror on the wall by the door to the main stairs, and was on the way out when he heard Daan call from his bed behind the screens.

'Have a good day.' He parodied the American cliché so heavily Jacob wondered whether Daan wasn't taking the piss. 'Say hello to Mother,' Daan added with no less slant.

To which a sleepy female voice unknown to Jacob tagged on, '*Tot ziens, Engels*man.'

In automatic reflex Jacob called back, 'See you.' All the way down the three flights to the street Daan's bedtime companion pricked his curiosity.

Mrs van Riet waited on the makeshift *stoep*, her cropped

greying hair matched by the grey of a hooded half-coat worn loose over a calf-length linen dress in an abstract pattern of greys and dark blues, a much-used light tan leather handbag, the tone of Jacob's town boots, hanging at her waist from a shoulder strap, sturdy dark brown walking shoes on her feet. She looked tired but smiled a welcome, putting on a good face in a way Jacob recognised from the times when his mother was ill before her operation. Getting through, Sarah called it. He instantly felt guilty and an impulse to do whatever he could to please her and make amends for being a chore.

They exchanged good-mornings with a hello handshake and a kind of semi-formality Jacob regarded as a touch old-fashioned but enjoyed nevertheless. He felt again, as he had each time he had met Mrs van Riet, that she was wary of him. Or, he decided now as they set off up the street, she was a shy person. Not, then, like her mother or her son, nor, come to that, her talkative husband. He warmed to her for that, as people are apt to do who find their own embarrassing weaknesses present in another.

'My son,' Mrs van Riet said, 'I know is not one who will look after you as he should. I would prefer you stayed with me.'

Shy maybe, but direct enough.

'I'm doing fine, thanks,' Jacob said. 'It's a lovely flat.'

'Yes, my mother's apartment is, let's say, unusual. But my son's way of life—. Well, so long as you are not completely neglected. I suppose being young you understand more than I approve. I'm very conservative, my son tells me.' And after a pause. 'You are very welcome to stay with us in Haarlem at any time.'

'Thanks, but really, I'm all right. Daan's been very good to me. I like him very much.'

'I feel responsibility for you to your family.'

'I'm seventeen, nearly eighteen, Mrs van Riet, I can manage, honestly I can. But I'm grateful to you for being

165

concerned.'

'It would be easier for you to call me Tessel, if you would like.'

'Yes. Thanks.'

They crossed Prins Hendrikkade at the junction into the station, too busy watching the lights and avoiding traffic, especially the higgledy-piggledy trams and buses and bicycles, as well as the streams of people, to hold any kind of conversation. The forecourt was even more crowded than yesterday. Blocking the middle, a thick circle surrounded a busking sextet dressed in national costume (Peruvians?) playing a jaunty tune on wooden Pan-pipes and podgy drums. Inside, the concourse was a scrimmage of Sunday trippers. Tessel led Jacob straight to their platform.

'I bought your ticket on the way,' she said, handing it to him. 'You should have it in case we are separated.' She glanced him a smile. 'Beware of pickpockets!' And at the thought clutched her handbag closer to her.

On the platform with a few minutes still to wait, Tessel said, 'You heard about the old soldiers parachuting yesterday?'

'No.'

'Several of the men who survived the battle. I read of it in the newspaper this morning. They parachuted yesterday on to the same fields where they landed in nineteen forty-four. Think of it! Most of them in their later seventies. They were going to do it last year for the fiftieth anniversary but the weather was too bad. So they did it yesterday instead. To be sure they were safe they were each attached to a young soldier.'

'Amazing!'

'I thought so too. I think it said that one of them was eighty.' She laughed. 'And one asked if he should take his false teeth out in case he swallowed them when he landed.'

Jacob laughed too. 'And did they make it in one piece, false teeth and all?'

166

'As far as I know. When I told Mother about it this morning on the telephone, she said she wished she had been there to see it.'

'Maybe she'd have liked to jump as well.'

'Oh yes. Already you understand my mother.'

'She reminds me of Sarah. It's what she would have said.'

'My mother saw them coming down on the day the battle started. Did she tell you?'

'No.'

'I'm surprised.'

Their train arrived.

Settled into seats side by side in a full carriage, Tessel went on as if their conversation hadn't been interrupted.

'She likes to tell the story. I've heard it so many times since I was a child.'

'We didn't really talk about the war.'

'I thought you would. After you left, Geertrui said very little. Nothing about your visit.'

The remark was all but a question.

'She—your mother—'

'Geertrui.'

'Well, Geertrui. Sorry, I'm not very good at pronouncing it.'

'Like your Gertrude.'

'Yes. Gertrude. Hamlet's mother.' He tried again and failed again, but failed better this time.

They smiled at each other over his incompetence with the Dutch gargled gee and the moo of *rui*.

The train started off.

When they were out of the station, Jacob said, 'She asked me why I live with my grandmother. I think I said too much about it. Used up too much time. I was a bit nervous of her, to be honest.'

'Mother has that effect on many people. Me too sometimes, I should confess. The nurses even. They like

167

her, but they are a little afraid of her also.'

'She asked me to go and see her tomorrow. She might tell me about the battle then.'

He felt Tessel stiffen beside him. Sitting packed together side by side, it was difficult to turn and check reactions on her face without seeming rude.

'This is a very difficult time for us,' she said. 'You understand?'

'Yes.'

'Geertrui is a very determined person.'

'Yes.'

'As I told you, she invited you here without consulting any of us. Me or my husband anyhow. Daan, I don't know. They are very close with each other. She only told me a few days before you arrived.'

Now Jacob did turn to face her.

'I feel very embarrassed about it.'

'No no. It isn't your fault. I shouldn't have mentioned it again. I only meant to say that Mother has always been a little full of secrets. And determined . . . stubborn, I should say, in her personality. Now it's even worse because the drugs they give to help her endure pain make her confused.' She shrugged. 'It's just how she is.'

Jacob looked beyond the passenger in front of him, a young woman whose knees he was having trouble not touching with his own, away down the carriage, but with unseeing eyes. He remembered Tessel meeting him at the airport, as arranged in a phone call with Sarah. She had seemed tense and brusque, even impatient with him. He had wondered if this was a typical Dutch way of going on or just the way she was. She had been nervous too, dropping the car keys, taking a wrong turning on the motorway, apologising for her poor English (which in fact struck him at the time as very good, especially as he hadn't bothered to learn a word of Dutch)—that kind of thing. In the house, she had shown him 'his' room (still teenaged Daan's to judge by the posters and clothes and other stuff that occupied it, everything as neat as a museum), had given him a few minutes to settle in, and then had sat him down with a cup of strong Dutch coffee and explained in a rather flustered manner that she would not be able to do much to entertain him during his stay. She would take him to Oosterbeek on Sunday. But until then he would have to occupy himself. Of course, Jacob had said, yes yes, that would be quite okay. And then the story about Geertrui and her invitation came tumbling out, as if she could keep it to herself no longer. By which time Jacob's insides were squirming, he felt he was an encumbrance, and wished he had not come.

It was Mr van Riet who suggested he should go on his own next day to visit the Anne Frank house and who then spent an hour and a half, first of all explaining the train system, then instructing him in the map of central Amsterdam, showing him where the Anne Frank house was located and how to get there by tram, which in turn led to a discourse on the city's trams, and the listing of various places Mr van Riet thought Jacob might like to visit—the Rijksmuseum to view the Rembrandts and Vermeers, the Historical Museum, where there was, he said, a fascinating exhibition showing the growth of Amsterdam over the centuries along with a model revealing how the old Amsterdam houses were built of stout wooden frames standing on platforms of logs sunk into the waterlogged sand which was and still is all there was to build on, thus proving, he said, laughing, the Bible is wrong when it says that a house built on sand cannot last. In Amsterdam whole streets of houses built on sand three hundred years ago are still standing and are as elegant and beautiful now as they were when they were new. In order to see these houses in a short time and from a good perspective, Mr van Riet advised, Jacob should take one of the tourist boats that cruise the canals. He marked on the map the places where the boats could be boarded and indicated how much the trip would cost. This reminded Mr van Riet to make sure Jacob understood Dutch money, including a ten-minute account of the meaning of the pictures and engravings on the notes and coins, which was, naturally, followed by a comparison with the British currency and its relative value. There was a side-track at this point on the importance of a common European currency coming into force as soon as possible, with one regret that the proposed designs were not at all as attractive or tasteful, in Mr van Riet's opinion, as the present Dutch money. But the trading and politico-economic advantages were more important than mere appearance. We must all remember what brought Hitler to power: economic instability and a weak currency. Well, yes, bigotry and racial prejudice. But economic stability and strong trade were the essential factors for a healthy nation.

It was after this postprandial tutorial (Jacob had said almost nothing except for required noises of understanding and the odd question or two to show willing) that Mr van Riet suggested Jacob accompany him and the family dog (a bouncy, slightly drooling and ageing, not to mention smelly Sealyham) on their nightly walk. And it was while they were out that Mr van Riet gave Jacob Daan's address, saying as he did so not to mention this to his wife. There were family problems between her and Daan at present, to do with his wife's mother. Mrs van Riet was in an upset condition. Nothing for Jacob to worry about. You know how women can be—he chuckled—especially women of a certain age. Daan would be glad to help Jacob if help were needed, and, Mr van Riet knew, would like to meet him anyway.

All this left Jacob feeling in an awkward position and wishing even the more that he had not come.

James Sims:
We clambered aboard the aircraft on the order 'Emplane'. The twin engines [of the Douglas Dakota C-47

'Skytrain'] burst into life with a shattering roar, the plane gave a shudder and rolled forward along the tarmac. The American pilots taxied in Vic formation. Our aircraft lurched over as it turned at the head of the runway and stopped. Staggered on either side of us were two other aircraft and behind us were three more.

The plane shook as the engine revolutions increased. We began to pick up speed and were soon thundering along the runway. The noise grew to a howling storm of sound as we bumped and bucketed along. We glued our faces to the small windows and waved to our comrades in the other aircraft. It seemed as though we would hurtle on until we smashed into the boundary fence but a subtle change in the motion of the aircraft told us we were airborne; Lieutenant Woods confirmed this by lifting his outstretched hands and smiling. It was approximately 11:30 a.m. and—a sobering thought—we would be in Holland before lunch was over. . .

We watched the friendly soil of England drop away as we rose ponderously heavenwards. The Dakota was a sluggish aircraft and completely unarmed. When our aerial armada reached the coast we fell in with our fighter escort, mostly RAF Hawkers, Tempests and Typhoons armed with cannons and rockets. We had been promised 'maximum fighter support', which meant a thousand aircraft and was very comforting.

The imposing airborne army swung out over the North Sea and we settled down for the journey. We sat eight-a-side down the ribbed fuselage on bench-type seats. We were a right British cocktail of mixed blood: English, Irish, Scots and Welsh; Geordies, Scouses, Cockneys, men like Brum from the Midlands, men from Cambridge, Kent and Sussex. There were three Brightonians in our platoon. Some of us had been shop assistants, others salesmen, farmers, and barrow boys; there was even a poacher.

Lieutenant Woods as Number One was seated next to the open doorway. I was Number Fifteen and the man

171

behind me, the last man out, was Maurice Kalikoff [a sergeant and a Russian Jew—'a first class soldier and one of the finest human beings I have ever met'] . . .

I tried to tell myself that this was what I had always wanted. It went with the red beret, wings and jump pay. We were flying at about four thousand feet [1220 metres] over masses of billowing cloud which reflected the sunshine and made me think I was already in heaven. It was one of those moments in life of sheer beauty. The Dakota droned on over the sea. Talking was impossible so we either dozed or read . . .

We were nearing the Dutch coast and were warned to brace ourselves as the aircraft dived down through the clouds to about two thousand feet [610 metres]. We were still over the North Sea when a German naval vessel opened fire on us. Fortunately it was a small boat and only had a machine gun. The American pilot took instant evasive action and we held on to one another, bracing our feet as we banked alarmingly. We watched fascinated as a stream of tracer bullets arched towards us, slowly at first but then finally whipping past the open doorway like angry hornets.

Now we were told that the Dutch coastline lay just ahead, and my stomach did another somersault. All that marked the coastline of flooded Holland [the Germans had flooded the coastal area to try and prevent Allied landings] was a long ridge of land, not unlike the spine of some extinct prehistoric animal. As we flew inland the water gradually gave way to ribbons of soil and then whole fields. [*Sims, pp 52-5*]

The change of trains at Utrecht was simple enough but the platforms and stairways were crowded. Again, they sat side by side, this time with Jacob next to the window the better to see the view. As they travelled east, the country became less flat, there were patches of wooded areas, not such a noticeable grid of canals.

'Do you know a lot about the battle?' Tessel asked.

'Wouldn't say a lot,' Jacob said. 'Read a couple of books on it, out of interest, you know, because of Grandad. And I've seen the film of course. Anthony Hopkins as a dashing officer. Pretty funny. Don't expect that's what it was really like.'

'Films never are, I would think. How can they be?'

'One of the books I read was a proper history. But the one I liked best is by an ordinary soldier who took part, not an officer, just a squaddy. The sort of man I suppose my grandfather must have been. It's not brilliantly written, but I like it because he tells you the sort of detail that doesn't get into books written by professional historians who are trying to cover the whole battle. He tells things you can only know if you were there. And being an ordinary guy, he sees everything differently from the way historians or officers do. And he's not gung-ho, you know. But he's proud to have been there and done that. So it makes a good story as well as being a history of the battle.'

'I've never read anything about it,' Tessel said. 'I heard so much from my mother it was enough. Besides, all war is horrible, dreadful, I don't like to hear about it. And that war, Hitler's war, is still so much talked about here in the Netherlands, on and on, almost as if it only ended yesterday. I wish people would stop. So much pain, why do we go on remembering it so much? It would be better if we forgot. But people say, no, we must always remember so that nothing like it ever happens again. To which I ask, when has the human race ever forgotten about their wars, and how much has that prevented another being fought?'

'I don't know. But I don't think I agree. You know Anne Frank's *Diary*?'

'Everyone must by now, surely?'

'And you know how she wanted to be a famous writer? Well, she started rewriting her diary not long before she was captured because she heard a broadcast by one of the

173

Dutch ministers. He said he wanted everyone to save letters and diaries and things like that, things they had written during the occupation, and after the war they would collect these together and put them into a national library so that in future people would be able to read what it was actually like for ordinary people during the war, and not just have to rely on books by professional historians.'

'It was done. It's our State Institute for War Documentation in Amsterdam.'

'Don't you think that was a great idea? Don't you think it's good to know how things were and what people were like in the past? I mean, know about it from what the actual people wrote at the time?'

'I suppose it is, yes. I just dislike going on and on about the days of the war as if that were all there was of the past.'

'Well, yes. But it's always boring if people go on and on about anything.' He had Mr van Riet in mind.

Tessel laughed. 'Yes, that's true.'

'Sometimes I wish there were some letters of Grandad's, or a diary maybe. It's not that I want to know about the battle, as a battle, but I would like to know what it was like for him, what he did, and what happened to him. Everything as *he* saw it. I'd really like that. He'd be more alive for me then. I mean, alive in the way Anne Frank is alive for me. Because when you can read what someone wrote, the way she did, you somehow feel you're living with them. Inside their head, if you know what I mean.'

'Yes, I know. Of course, Geertrui can tell you quite a lot, but that's not what you mean and anyway is only how she remembers it. And memory—. Well, memory is not to be trusted, in my experience. Memory tells what happened the way memory wants it to have been. This is my opinion anyway.'

'That's what my father says. He always accuses my grandmother of inventing my grandfather. He says the man she talks about isn't the one who existed, but the man she wishes he had been.'

'And what does Sarah say to that?'

Jacob laughed. 'She hits him with the frying pan.'

'What?'

'Sorry. Metaphorically . . . Figure of speech?'

'*Ach*, yes,' laughing, 'I see! Yes, I imagine she does. Oh, but now you must look, because we are passing the fields where the men landed.'

A broad flat area of ground, blond after harvest, trees along its far-off edges, and some, silver birches, here by the railway. Almost exactly as he remembered in photographs taken from the air during the landings and from the ground soon afterwards. For a weird moment what he'd read came together with what he was seeing and he felt he was there, not now but then, not nineteen ninety-five but nineteen forty-four. With his grandfather, a man then only a few years older than he, now. Daan's age in fact. He looked up at the sunny cloud-rising sky, and thought: Jumping together into the up there not knowing what danger lay waiting in the down here.

James Sims:

An American crewman came back and told us we were going down to seven hundred feet [214 metres] for the run-in. We put on our close-fitting helmets and adjusted our rubber chin guards. We hooked up and then heaved the kit-bags containing six mortar bombs, pick, shovel, rifle and small pack on to our legs, securing them with special web straps. As each of us had at least a hundred pounds [46 kgs] of equipment we would be sure of a rapid descent and little oscillation, and would be a difficult target for enemy machine gunners. We stood upright and closed up behind one another in single file. Our right hand held the kitbag grip and our left was on the shoulder of the man in front. Someone cracked, 'Pass right down the car, please!' Another joker plucked at my parachute and said, 'Blimey, cowboy, this isn't a chute, it's an old army blanket.'

It was essential that we followed the man in front out quickly as any hesitation could mean we would be hopelessly scattered on the DZ. Lieutenant Woods stood framed in the doorway, the slipstream plucking impatiently at the scrim netting on his helmet. The red light glowed steadily and then the green light winked on. 'Go!' The lieutenant vanished. We shuffled along the heaving deck of the Dakota . . . three . . . four . . . five . . . an American crewman had set up a cine camera and was filming our exit . . . six . . . seven . . . eight . . . a chap from Maidstone half turned and shouted something with a grin but it was lost in the roar of the engines . . . nine . . . ten . . . eleven . . . through the doorway I could see a huge Hamilcar glider on tow right alongside us; one wing of it was on fire but the glider pilot gave the thumbs-up sign . . . twelve . . . thirteen . . . fourteen . . . the man in front of me hunched over slightly as he went out. Almost before his helmet disappeared I jumped but the slipstream caught me and whirled me around, winding up my rigging lines. I was forced to let go of my kitbag grip in an effort to try and stop the winding up process, for if it reached the canopy I was finished. The roar of the aircraft engines had been cut off and for the first time since leaving England I could distinguish other sounds. All around me parachutists were disgorging from Dakotas and I found myself in the middle of a blizzard of silk. The parachutes were all the colours of the rainbow; and it was an unforgettable sight. I was conscious of taking part in one of the greatest airborne descents in the history of warfare but this exhilaration was tempered by the trouble I was in. Luckily the twisting rigging lines had reversed their motion and I spun beneath them as they unwound. I did not feel much like an eagle as I fell—the experience was more like being hanged. Although my canopy was now fully developed I faced another problem. My right leg hung straight down with the kitbag on it and I was quite unable to reach the grip to pull it up again.

Down below was a scene of orderly confusion as myriads of ant-like figures scurried over the DZ towards the different coloured flares marking battalion rendezvous areas. The sounds of shouts and shots drifted up, punctuated by bursts of machine-gun fire. The Americans had dropped us right on target and I had no difficulty locating the yellow flare, which showed where the 2nd Battalion was forming up. Everywhere order was developing out of seeming chaos as the airborne soldiers quickly organised themselves. The ground, which a moment before had seemed so far beneath me, came spinning up at an alarming rate. I was not looking forward to the landing, as my leg still dangled helplessly below me, weighted down with the kitbag. We had been told that to land in this way would almost certainly result in a broken leg, and any second I was going to find out.

Wham! I hit the deck with a terrific jolt, but all in one piece, and immediately struggled out of my parachute harness, slicing through the cords that held my kitbag to pull out my rifle. That was the first priority. In the distance time-bombs exploded, sending up great fountains of earth. They had been dropped twenty-four hours previously in an effort to persuade the Germans that this was just another bombing raid. Some hopes! [*Sims pp 55-7*]

Moments later they arrived at Oosterbeek, the station no more than a suburban halt in the bottom of a deep cutting, the platform newish looking, no buildings, only a shelter. A few people got off with them, some carrying flowers, but not the crowd Jacob had expected. Weren't there to be many at the ceremony? Last year the BBC news had shown a thick mass of people crammed in to the cemetery, but that had been for the fiftieth anniversary.

They climbed the steps to the road. Here more people were on the move, across the bridge over the railway and right, in to a road marked by a discreet signpost, 'Arnhem Oosterbeek War Cemetery'. Well-heeled detached houses, very like an English middle-class private estate: ample well-treed gardens, some with tall clipped hedges, some with fences, the bourgeois battlements of privacy, neatly cut grass verges by the road, trees lining the side where the railway ran in its cutting. The same railway along which the paratroopers had tried to make their way into Arnhem, only to be stopped by the Germans and surrounded in the village. But these houses would not have been built then; it would have been wooded country with the village starting on the other side of the tracks.

After two or three hundred metres the road turned sharp left. Up ahead, cars and coaches were parked among trees that formed a forecourt. Two square brick towers with arched doors in each side stood at the entrance to the cemetery. To his left, over a chain-link fence that struck him as somehow inappropriate, and a border of low bushes on the other side, Jacob could see the expanse of the cemetery, the regimented lines of regulation-shaped white gravestones almost obscured by a packed crowd of spectators. Only when he and Tessel were inside and had found themselves a place on the fringe could he also see that the centre of the graveyard, a wide grass cross formed by the layout of the graves, was completely filled with old people seated in rows and facing a canopied platform at the centre of the cross, the men mostly in blue blazers and many in red or blue berets. For a moment he felt it was as if they had just got up out of the graves to attend a concert. And, he thought, in a peculiar sense they had, for these must be the survivors, their wives and, no doubt, the wives of some of those who had not survived.

He was astonished at the thousands of people (six, ten?) who were gathered in this parade ground of the dead. 1,757 graves, he learned, 253 of them belonging to unknown soldiers whose remains could not be identified. And these still being added to as more remains were found in forgotten burial plots intended during the battle as temporary graves.

Tessel took his arm and edged them down the line, squeezing apologetically past people who blocked her view.

'We should get as close as we can to your grandfather's grave,' she muttered. And then she stopped and pointed. 'There, you see, in the third row, with the red rose bush almost as high as the gravestone.'

'Yes, yes. I see.'

'Your grandmother and Geertrui planted the rose the last time they were here together. Daan comes to prune it and feed it twice each year.'

The sight put a silence on him. He had seen photographs. (This is your grandfather as a little boy. You used to stand just like that when you were his age. This is your grandfather as a young man with his motorbike. He was a terror then. This is your grandfather just before we got married. He was so handsome. Here we are on our last holiday together at Weston. This is your grandfather in his uniform.) And he had liked that. Used to pore over them, wishing he had known the man whose name he bore and who he was supposed to resemble in so many ways. But this—standing here near his grandfather's grave bearing the bones of a young man not much older than himself—this was not the same. Photographs were no more than a trace of shadow, not the thing itself, not the person.

There in front of him, two body-lengths away and his own height below, was a reality. The body. Or what was left of it by now. The body but not the man. In some way he had never faced before, never thought of before, he knew at once that what was left of the man, what was essential of him, was not under the ground with the physical remains. What there was of his grandfather was standing right here in his grandson's town boots peering at the dead man's grave.

The thought was unnerving, as if a ghost had materialised inside him. He took a deep breath and looked away, up into the sky. By now the sun was fully out, in a dome of cloudless blue arching above the carpet of seated survivors fringed with a border of people standing five or six deep, from babes in arms to old men with walking-sticks. Nearby, a squad of young paratroopers in their red berets and camouflage jackets, a pair of middle-aged women in bright Sunday best, a troop of boys in their Nikes, a bevy of girls in white T-shirts and jeans, three men in grey suits, their jackets over their arms and their sleeves rolled up. All quiet. Not entirely silent. Not hushed as in church, not subdued as at a funeral, not reverential or passive, not even still, for there was movement here and there, comings and goings, and a constant trickle of new arrivals joining the throng. But no bustling officials, no fussing, no hint of pomp and circumstance. They were waiting, and yet they were not waiting. Rather as if what they were waiting for was already with them. There and not there, he thought. Being and not being. Absent presence.

James Sims:

[Colonel Frost] gave the order for the advance on Arnhem and the rifle companies began to move off. We were to bring up the rear with our 3-inch [7.62 cm] mortars as their supporting artillery. A number of Germans had already been captured. Dressed in their best Sunday uniforms, they were, at that moment, probably the most embarrassed soldiers in the German army. They had been caught in the fields, snogging with their Dutch girl friends, and their faces went redder and redder by the minute as they caught the drift of some of the remarks the grinning paratroopers flung at them.

'Right, on your feet!' came a shout, and we moved off in single-file sections on either side of the road in what was called 'ack-ack' formation. The Dutch countryside was very neat and well kept for wartime, the roads being overhung with trees and the fields fenced off with wire. Houses were scattered here and there and the inhabitants came out with their children to wave to us and watch us pass. Jugs of milk, apples, tomatoes and marigolds were passed to us. They stuck the flowers in the scrim of our helmets and decorated our barrows with them. 'We have waited for you for four years,' seemed to be the limit of their English but the phrase was repeated over and over again by these smiling friendly people, who seemed to consider the war as good as finished now that we had arrived.

We pushed on south of the Wolfheze district where we had landed, in the direction of Heelsum. The bracken-covered heath on each side of the road rendered our exposed thrust very liable to ambush, and indeed not far ahead there was a burst of small-arms fire which sent us scurrying for cover. Leading elements of the battalion had made contact with the enemy, but the firing soon stopped and we passed on. When we reached the scene of the skirmish the smoke and smell of cordite still lingered in the air. By the side of the road lay a tall fair-haired sergeant from the rifle companies; I recognised him as an ex-Guardsman who had been on the anti-tank gun course at Street when I was there. Now his face was blanched with pain and shock. He had caught a burst of machine-gun fire down one side of his leg and his comrades had bandaged him up before leaving him. As we passed we murmured words of encouragement and threw him boiled sweets and cigarettes. The next time I saw him was in Stalag XIB [prisoner-of-war camp in Germany], minus that leg.

Yet another burst of fire sent us diving for cover again but this time it was our lads who had done the firing. A German staff car was stopped on the road, the windscreen shattered and the tyres shot to pieces. A German officer lay dead in one of the front seats. Beside him, hunched over the steering-wheel, was the driver. In the back was the body of another German officer slumped forward with his hand still on the shoulder of the dead driver. He had clearly been in the act of warning him when the British paratroopers had stepped out into the road in front of them and opened fire. The officer in the front seat appeared to be some sort of general, so this must have been a severe blow to the enemy. I approached the staff car filled with curiosity, for not only had I never seen a German officer before but I had never seen a corpse . . .

My mother had told me as a child that if I traced the shape of a cross on the forehead of a corpse I would not dream about it. Gingerly I touched the stone-cold forehead of one of the German officers. 'What the hell are you doing?' yelled a sergeant. 'Get mobile, you'll see plenty more like him before you're much older!' [*Sims, pp 60-2*]

An English and a Dutch clergyman came to the platform. A hymn was sung accompanied by a band Jacob could not see. O God, our help in ages past, Our hope for years to come, / *O God, die droeg ons voorgeslacht, in nacht en stormgebruis.* The sound of those thousands singing was swallowed up in the empty sky. Empty but for a solitary jet, high high up, its white vapour trail so straight and thin it might have been drawn with a ruler on the blue. Feeling its peculiar aptness, Jacob raised his camera and shot the view. A baseline of grass and graves and people, bordered by a line of frothy trees, above which the soaring blue with a diagonal white line stretching from the blue at top left to the green tree tops at bottom right.

All around people had copies of the Order of Service with the words of the hymns. Where had they got them? He hadn't seen anyone handing them out. He looked at Tessel. She smiled, turned to a couple of men standing on her other side, spoke to them in Dutch, and was handed the copy of the man next to her. The words were in English on the left and Dutch on the right. Be thou our guard while troubles last, And our eternal home. / *wees ons een gids in*

182

storm en nacht en eeuwig ons tehuis!

A colonel came to the microphone to read the lesson. Psalm 121 vv 1-8. I will lift up mine eyes to the hills : from whence cometh my strength. / My help cometh from the Lord : who hath made heaven and earth. Words, Jacob knew, as old as Shakespeare. Their plain beauty, winging out of the cornucopia of the amplifiers, decorated the trees and sparkled in the air. Suddenly, he felt proud of them, of the language that for the first time in his life he consciously claimed to himself as his own.

Prayers were said. A second hymn was sung. Abide with me, fast falls the eventide: The darkness deepens; Lord with me abide: / *Blijf mij nabij, wanneer het duister daalt, De nacht valt in, waarin geen licht meer straalt.* A hymn Jacob had never liked. The heavy moan of its words and its cloying tune irritated him. Were it anything material he would want to kick it. Far from encouraging hope or giving relief, it seemed to him to wallow in the prospect of death with smothering sentimentality. Yet it was one of the most popular of popular hymns. Again the thousands of bilingual voices melded in the air and were lost in sky, some people, as is the way on such occasions, singing heartily, others hardly more than mouthing the words.

The inevitable sermon followed, though called an Address on the programme. Or rather, not one but two. The mere thought made Jacob want to sit down, but that would mean subjecting himself to the infant view of feet and knees and overhanging bums, so he remained standing. Perhaps the clerics would have the decency to be brief. The English reverend spoke first. He had been with the 10th Battalion at the battle. At least he'd been there and done that. The strange contrast inclined Jacob's attention to this ageing minister, so typical in sound and look, often mocked, of a Church of England country parson, soft spoken, mild mannered, studiously amenable, and the brutal mayhem he must have lived through fifty years ago. The Revd spoke of the men who had made their delayed anniversary jump yesterday. Talked about their training for it, each in tandem with a young soldier on whose knees the older man was instructed to sit. It wasn't like that in my day, the Revd quipped, and Jacob thought of Ton and their conversation in the café the other night. Even here sexual phobia spreads its elbows in the nudge of a joke. Here where bodies lay side by side, buddied in death, as they were buddied in the life that made their deaths. He thought of James Sims and the ten thousand like him, some of them sitting here now, whose best memory of their time in a kind of hell was of what they called comradeship. That was what brought them here. And who would return year after year for fifty years to remember those who died and not call it love?

With the predictability of sermons, the story of the gallant old men making their jump had to be conjured into a moral lesson. The magic words for this lesson were said by one of the young soldiers who had told his old partner, 'Put yourself in my hands, relax, enjoy yourself, and trust me to land you safely on the ground.' This, the Revd suggested, was just like life and just like God. What we had to learn to do was put ourselves in to God's hands, sit back, enjoy life, and trust God to bring us safely to our destination. Or something like that. It was hard to be sure, for the Revd's words seemed to vanish into the air just as the singing had. But at least the Revd had been mercifully brief. He was followed at once by a Dutch Roman Catholic priest, who read out in his own language what he had to say. During which Tessel leaned to Jacob and said quietly, smiling, 'This is so like us Dutch. The English priest spoke as if without preparation and was amusing. The Dutch priest reads out what he wants to say and is very serious.' But again was considerately brief.

A final hymn. Praise, my soul, the King of heaven, To his feet thy tribute bring; / *Loof de Koning, heel mijn wezen, licht in het duister, wijs de weg omhoog.* More cheerful, more a

184

goer. They swung through its robust verses at a welcome lick, ready now for an end to the formalities.

However, Jacob's attention was elsewhere. While the hymn was being sung school children, both sexes, and between about eleven and sixteen years of age, all carrying bunches of flowers, came from the entrance, processing to the sides of the cemetery, from where they found their way, each to a grave, in front of which they stood at the ready. There was nothing stiffly formal about this, their clothing was colourful, casual and variously fashionable, they were well behaved and quiet but not regimented, purposeful but not po-faced, and only one or two showing signs of shyness. By the time the hymn was done, each had reached what must have been an appointed place. Here and there an adult, with teacherly authority or parental care, sorted out the ones who seemed uncertain or mistaken. While the Lord's Prayer was recited, they stood before their graves like guardian angels, some hands in pockets, some heads bent, some looking around, some smiling at spectators on the fringe, but all aware of their role in this play of memory.

James Sims:

The now familiar smell of spent ammunition lingered in the air and a pall of smoke hung over the scene of what had clearly been a short sharp engagement. The riflemen had hurried on to the next objective . . . but they had left one of their number behind. He lay propped up against a wooden seat in a clearing overlooking the river. It was a pleasant spot, shaded by trees, with a beautiful view over the Lower Rhine, the sort of place where lovers plan their future and old men dream of the past. But today there were neither lovers nor old men, only a boy from a rifle company, his legs buckled under him and his helmet removed. The front of his battle-dress was soaked with blood, and someone with rough well-meaning had stuffed a white towel inside the front of his shirt in a vain attempt to staunch the

185

wound. Out of a waxen face his eyes stared past us into
eternity and we crept by as quietly as possible as though
afraid of waking him from that dread sleep. [*Sims, p 65*]

Lieutenant Jack Hellingoe, No 11 Platoon, 1st Parachute
Battalion:
. . . we just burst in through the doors of the nearest
house and went upstairs, right into the loft. The Germans
were spraying the houses; bullets were coming through the
roof and windows, whizzing around the rooms inside and
hitting the walls behind us. They were really brassing those
two houses up.

Private Terrett, the Bren gunner, bashed some slates off
with the Bren and put the gun down on the rafters pointing
through the hole. We could see straight away where the
firing was coming from, from the houses and gardens up on
the higher ground, only 150 to 200 yards away [137 to 183
meters]. You could easily see the Germans moving about
there. Most of the fighting in Arnhem was at very short
ranges. I told Terrett to get firing and I think he got a
couple of mags off at least before the Germans got on to
him and a burst hit him. It took the foresight off the gun,
took the whole of his cheek and eye away, and we both fell
back through the rafters, crashing down into the bedroom
below. I wasn't hit, but Terrett wasn't moving at all. Someone slapped a dressing on him, and he was dragged away. I
thought he was dead, but I found out many years after the
war that he was still alive—a great surprise. He had lost an
eye, but they made a good job of his face. [*Middlebrook, pp*
178-9]

The moment was coming that Jacob knew about because
Sarah had often told him of it, when children from local
schools laid flowers on the graves in a ritual that had been
enacted every year since the first memorial service the year
after the battle, in 1945. Fifty years. The children who laid

the first bouquets would now be sixty, sixty-five, Jacob calculated, old enough to be grandparents themselves; and their children who laid flowers, old enough to be parents of those laying them today. A floral family tree.

He had watched to see who would stand by Jacob's grave. A slim boy, perhaps thirteen, with close-cropped auburn hair that showed off a fine round head and oval, boy's-still-girlish face, wearing a lovat green zip-up jerkin, rust-red shirt, light grey jeans, and Hush Puppy boots. He was carrying in his arms as if it were a baby a bunch of wild flowers. Jacob recognised blue harebells, rose mallow, some pink flowers Sarah called Laveterea, lavender-purple fire-weed, even some tall-stalked buttercups, and reeds with dark-brown cigar-like ends, all set off with ivy. No one else had such an unusual armful. When he arrived at his place, the boy inspected the gravestone's earthy surround, bent and removed some fallen leaves, which, not knowing where else to get rid of them, he stuffed into a pocket of his jeans. Then he waited, head bent and still.

Another Dutch minister said a few words about the children and thanked them for being there.

And the high point of the ceremony arrived. The children stooped and laid their flowers at the feet of the gravestones. The silence as they did this was more tense with emotion than at any time so far. The air shimmered with it. Jacob could not take his eyes from the boy by his grandfather's grave, who laid his flare of blooms just as everyone else did, but then with careful delicacy spread them in a fan of colour as if arranging them in a vase. When he had finished, he leant back on his haunches and surveyed the effect, bending forward two or three times to improve the show by adjusting some of the blooms. He did this with such patient concentration, as if entirely on his own, that Jacob felt he was watching someone absorbed in a private act, and should turn his eyes away.

The boy was still on his haunches, the other children by

this time standing in their places, when the English Revd recited the traditional poem to the war dead by Laurence Binyon. They shall not grow old, as we that are left grow old . . . We will remember them. / *Zij zullen niet oud worden, zoals wij, die het wel overleefd hebben . . . wij zullen aan hen denken.* A bugler sounded the Last Post and Reveille, the notes so tangible and plangent they were written on the staves of the trees. Then the band played the British National Anthem. And it was over.

A brief suspended pause, a typically English hiatus when no one wanted to be first to move lest they be thought pushy and forward, or worse, might embarrass themselves by doing the wrong thing. But then came an audible collective sigh as the strain of all their best behaviour was exhaled, before people started talking, laughing, walking about, greeting each other, introducing one to another, peering at the inscriptions on gravestones, stooping to give solemn attention to particular memorials, taking photos. A kind of party got going that reminded Jacob of summer fêtes Sarah made him go to in her village, though the general mood was still modestly polite, this being the place and the occasion it was. The kids who had laid the flowers were quickly surrounded by adults, parents, relatives, friends their own age, and the British visitors: the focus of everyone's pleasure and attention now, as if this was after all their occasion, like a vast communal birthday party with a surplus of foreign grandparents. Foreign but not foreign. Another strange note that gave the day its tune: the Brits were the guests here, yet occupied the place as if it were their own front garden, while the Dutch, whose land it was, behaved as if they were visitors from next door sharing a neighbours' family party. And so they behaved one to another as both hosts and guests, owners and visitors, with the graves as background and the children as diversion.

Hendrika van der Vlist, 23-year-old daughter of the proprietor of

Hotel Schoonoord, Oosterbeek:

Someone is calling: some Englishmen want to see us. A jeep with a doctor and an N.C.O. orderly is standing in the front garden.

We are asked to get the hotel ready to be used as a hospital within an hour's time.

'We'd love to do so, but it is a terrible mess inside and we are without staff.'

'Ask the people in the street for help,' the doctor says.

'All right, we shall do our best.'

Then suddenly we remember that there is no longer any electric light in the house. Last night [Sunday] the Germans destroyed the connection.

Perhaps light was shining from some windows. They may have thought this the way to stop it.

But it does not matter.

The pudding is left on the table, untouched. We have other things to do. First I run to our neighbours across the road for help, then to our other neighbours. On crossing Utrechtseweg I see, in front of Dennenkamp estate, English soldiers lying flat on the road. They are aiming at Germans who have entrenched themselves in the manor-house.

Explosions are also heard from Pietersbergseweg [the hotel was on the corner of Utrechtseweg and Pietersberg-seweg]. Here Germans are in the house called Overzicht. War is close upon us.

But there is no time for reflection.

Provided with a broom, a pail and a mop, everyone comes running in readily, glad to be able to help. If the Germans against whom we malingered and sabotaged for four and a half years, could have seen us.

Men and women, young and old, are working hard. An hour is so short! Mother takes the lead downstairs, I try to settle things upstairs. 'Would you be so kind as to sweep the floor. Then you could mop it up.'

'Kaja, a big job for you. All that rubbish has to be taken

189

to the dustbin. What shall we do with that beautiful portrait of Hitler? [The Germans had used the hotel as a billet for their soldiers.] Well, if you want you may keep it—don't you think it is a nice souvenir! Alternatively you might smash it.'

'Hadn't we better roll up those dirty carpets and take them to the garret? Better no carpets than dirty ones, and now we can swab it all.'

'You are ready? All right, go and dust room number 11.'

'Would you please sweep room 14? Presently I'll ask someone also to mop it.'

'Look Kaja, here is some more rubbish.'

'Would you mind cleaning all the washbasins in this floor? There's a brush.'

When I come downstairs I see Mother looking around, gleaming with satisfaction. It all looks quite different now! All those ready hands have been able to tidy it up in so short a time.

Straw is carried in and it is put on the floor of the small drawing-room. In the big lounge rows of beds have been placed. The veranda and the dining-hall have been left untended. They have terrazzo floors. We think them too cold for the patients.

And then—we have not finished—there is a flow of wounded men coming in.

They are carried in on stretchers. Others are walking cases. Some are walking with difficulty, to others it is not difficult, it is their arms or hands that have been wounded.

And it all happens so quietly. Not much is spoken. The helpers who have been cleaning stop their work. They are almost ready.

Quickly we take the pails and the brooms out of the way, we don't want anyone to be tripped up by them.

And all the time more and more patients are coming in.
[*Van der Vlist, pp 11-12*]

*

'I want to photograph the boy who laid the flowers on my grandfather's grave,' Jacob said to Tessel, and set off through the crowd to catch him before he disappeared. Tessel followed. The boy had produced a camera from his jerkin pocket and was aiming a shot at his flowers and the gravestone when Jacob reached him.

When the boy had taken the picture Jacob said, 'Excuse me.'

The boy gave him a clear green-eyed look.

'Can you speak English?'

The boy nodded. 'Some.'

'Would you mind if I took a photo of you beside this grave?'

Tessel spoke in Dutch. The boy smiled and said to Jacob, 'This man your grandfather?'

'That's right.'

The boy said, 'Wait, please,' and turned, looking here and there for someone he finally spotted among a gaggle of people about Jacob's age three rows of graves away.

'Hille,' he called and waved to a girl, who, as she came over to them, Jacob saw was the mirror image of the boy. The same round head with close-cropped auburn hair, wide-set large eyes, wide mouth with full lips, clear oval face, as boyish as the boy's was still girlish. She was in a loose white long-sleeved polo shirt tucked into blue jeans, a purple sweater tied round her waist by the arms, the rest hanging over her backside.

The boy spoke to her in Dutch. She too gave Jacob a broad smile. 'My brother says this is your grandfather's grave.'

'Yes.'

They turned their gaze to the gravestone, as if deferring to a mutual friend.

Of course, Jacob had seen Sarah's photos of the stone, but now, confronted by it in tangible reality, he felt for the first time the strangeness of seeing his own name memorialised. J. TODD. And knowing he was standing on what remained of his grandfather made his feet tingle. A weird image came to him of his grandfather reaching up through the earth, grabbing him by the ankles, and pulling him down on top of him into the bed of the grave. Ever been kissed by a corpse? He was appalled at the image and felt guilty for even thinking it.

'What means J?' the boy asked.

'Jacob. My name as well.'

They looked at each other again.

'I'm Hille,' the girl said. 'This is my brother Wilfred.'

'And I am Tessel,' Mrs van Riet said.

'Oh, yes, sorry,' Jacob said, latching to his adult manners. 'This is Mrs van Riet.'

At which they all performed the required handshakes, Wilfred with serious formality, Hille and Jacob exchanging wry smiles at the displacement.

Jacob said, 'I wanted to take a photo of your brother and his flowers. I know my grandmother would like it.'

'I laid flowers on it one year when I was Wilfred's age,' Hille said. 'Maybe you'd like me in the picture as well?'

She might have been joshing him, but he said, 'Okay.'

'Our mother as well,' Wilfred said. 'She laid flowers on this grave.'

'When she was in school. Many years ago of course!' Hille said. 'But she isn't here today. We're moving house tomorrow so she's busy.'

Hille and Wilfred arranged themselves either side of the gravestone, each with a hand resting on it. Jacob stood back, squatted so as to include all the stone and the flowers as well as the two people, took the shot and, as usual, another just in case.

'Yes, yes. That was nice,' Tessel said. 'Jacob, would you like me to take one of you?'

So now Jacob replaced Hille and Wilfred and both Tessel and Wilfred took a shot of him. At which Hille said she would like to be taken with Jacob, and this was done by each of the other two. Then Wilfred wanted to be taken with Hille and Jacob, so Tessel took one with each of their cameras so that both families would have the picture. This left Tessel out, which Hille said couldn't be allowed, so pictures were taken of Tessel with Jacob, and then of Tessel with Hille and Wilfred.

They formed a quartet again on the grass over dead Jacob, looking one to another, laughing, thinking of what to say now.

'You haven't been here before?' Hille asked Jacob.

'No.'

'Want to walk around?'

'Sure.'

They set off through the crowd, Wilfred and Tessel walking behind, talking together in Dutch.

'It's their ages,' Hille said. 'Nineteen, twenty-two, twenty.'

'I know it must sound stupid, and I don't really understand it, but there's part of me that wishes I'd been here. In the battle, I mean.'

'Men!' Hille said with a snort. 'That's why there's wars.'

'I hate wars. Hate violence any time actually.'

'It's the man part of you who wants to have been here. Testosterone. You can't help it, poor thing.'

'Well, if I had been, in the battle I mean, I'm pretty sure I'd be in one of these graves and not a survivor. I'm no hero, that's for sure.'

'There's no such thing,' Hille said. 'No one's a hero.'

'Don't you think some people show more courage than everybody else, and are braver and all that?'

'Do you?'

'Well, yes, I think so. When you read about what some of the men did in this battle, for instance. Not just fighting, but saving other soldiers at the risk of their own lives. They did amazing things other people didn't dare do.'

'And what did they do when they went home?'

'What?'

'What did they do back home? How did they treat their wives or lovers? How did they behave to their work colleagues?'

'I've no idea.'

'Does it matter? If they are a hero.'

He pondered the question and Hille.

'Yes, I suppose so. To me it would. What are you geting at?'

'You're not stupid—'

'Thank you, ma'am!'

'—You know what I'm getting at. It's not that I don't believe in bravery or courage or those things. Just, I think most people are brave and courageous but in different ways and different—how do you say? *gelegenheden*—occasions.'

'But no one is especially brave?'

'Women giving birth, our famous Anne Frank says.'

Jacob stopped in his tracks.

'You know *Anne Frank*? I mean, you like it?'

'Yes, why?'

'So do I! My favourite book.'

'Yes?'

They eyed each other with sharpened interest.

'But,' Jacob said, 'I thought I knew the *Diary* pretty well. By heart some of it. But I don't remember anything about courage and women giving birth.'

'It's not in the old book.'

'What d'you mean, the old book?'

'The one we've always had.'

'There's another?'

'Yes, now. Don't you have it? In Dutch it's called *De Dagboeken van Anne Frank*. In English I guess that would be "The Daybook—the Diary—of Anne Frank".'

'But that's what my copy is called.'

'Is it? In Dutch the one we always had is called *Het*

194

Achterhuis, which means "The Back of the House".'

'So what is this other book?'

'It's all of the diary, everything she wrote, not the text Anne's father made. You know about that?'

'About Otto cutting some parts out of the diary before he published it? Yes, I know that. But I didn't know all of the diary had been printed.'

'It's a very large book. You'd like it. There are chapters about the history of the diary, how it was saved, and about the scientific tests our government did to prove it was not a fake like the disgusting neo-Nazis try to say it is. Oh, how I hate those people! And all kinds of other things. It's a wonderful book. My mother gave it me for my birthday.'

'I haven't heard about it.' Jacob said. An angry anxiety came over him as if he had been denied some life-sustaining information.

'Is something wrong?' Tessel asked as she and Wilfred joined them. Hille and Tessel spoke to each other in Dutch while Jacob stood there and fretted.

'I really need this book,' Jacob said. 'Have to have it.'

'Perhaps it isn't in English yet,' Tessel said. 'Perhaps only in Dutch.'

'There's an English bookshop in Amsterdam,' Hille said. 'On the Spui. They should be able to tell you. Try there.'

'I will, I will, by god I will!' Jacob said with such vehemence that the two women laughed, while Wilfred looked on as serious as ever, not knowing what the joke was.

They started walking again.

Jacob said, 'She talks about women giving birth being more courageous than men?'

'It's a wonderful part.' She glanced at Jacob. 'And her father cut it out.'

They reached the focal point of the cemetery at the opposite end from the entrance. A tall white cross set on a plinth. It was surrounded by a crowd of people, many of whom were laying wreaths and bunches of flowers at its foot, piling them up in a pyramid there were so many. Across the floral mound from where Jacob and Hille joined the crowd stood a party of three old men in their uniform of blue blazers and grey slacks, one wearing a red paratrooper's beret, the others in blue berets, and each with rows of medals paraded on his chest. The man in the middle held a banner, its flag furled in his white-gloved hand. They stood at attention in silent solemn state as people milled about beside them. On impulse Jacob raised his camera and took a snap.

And instantly felt disapproval of himself, as if he had stolen something.

'For my grandmother,' he said to Hille as if it were to her he must apologise.

But she wasn't listening. Instead was looking up at the slim white cross towering above them. Inlaid into the stone was an outsize bronze sword, handle, blade and guard matching the stone cross itself.

'The sword of Christus and the cross of *oorlogskruis*,' she said.

'*Oorlog*?' Jacob repeated as best he could.

'War. Sad, don't you agree?'

'Sad?'

'The cross. The sword. Stuck together,' she said. 'Done. Finished.'

And she ambled away.

An anonymous officer:

I am very bitter about Arnhem; I lost too many friends. When I got married at the end of the war, I realised that my best man was the ninth on a mental list of who I would have liked; the first eight were all dead or incapacitated. For years I could not talk about or read about Arnhem. When I did start reading, I came to the conclusion that it was all due to the flag-waving attitude of people like [Field Marshal B.L.] Montgomery who wanted to show how much cleverer they were than the others. [*Middlebrook, p 452*]

Lance-Corporal Harry Smith, South Staffordshire Regiment:

Even today it is hard to explain the feeling, but something seems to come over me. I go withdrawn and want to be by myself and keep quiet for days. Then my mind—or should I say myself—all of a sudden goes back to Arnhem. Then, after thinking things out as to what might have happened, or if this should have happened or that should have happened, I seem to worry something terrible for a while before I slowly return to myself. [*Middlebrook, p 452*]

Ms Ans Kremer, who lived at No. 8 Stationsweg, Oosterbeek:

The fighting made a very great impression on me. I was not afraid, but I had a feeling about the wounded and the dead just lying around and the dying—a feeling I cannot put a name to. Like the one we saw being hit, who shouted, 'Goodbye' three times, then died. Because of that, I now use 'Goodbye' very rarely; there is a kind of finality about it for me.

Those events have always stayed with me, not all the time, and certainly not consciously, but now and then a face, a smell, a noise or situation brings up a vague memory or a vivid picture, with the sad feeling that goes with it. Those men are, for me, friends. Somehow there is a bond, and when we meet I want to give them a good time and make them comfortable. They came to help us be free again, and I feel grateful but also indebted to them because of all the suffering and dying of so many, known and unknown to us. 'Grateful' is too small a word. There are feelings you cannot really put into words properly. [*Middlebrook, pp 452-3*]

They arrived at the entrance.

'I'd really like to know about your grandfather,' Hille said. 'We've always wondered who he was, what he was like, this man whose grave we laid flowers on. But the years my mother did it, and I did it, no one came up and said it was their relative's grave. So we could never ask. Until today. What about a coffee? We could go to a café and talk.'

Jacob would have liked nothing better. Everything about this girl appealed to him. Her looks. The things she said. The funny, slightly aggressive way she said them sometimes. And Anne Frank. As always when someone specially attracted him, he wanted to touch her; but he wanted more than to touch this girl.

He pushed the thought from his mind lest he gave himself away, and to allow himself time to answer he looked for Tessel, who was lagging behind somewhere with Wilfred.

'I'd like to,' he said. 'But I'm with Mrs van Riet, with Tessel, and—'

'I don't mind,' Hille said in her matter-of-fact style, 'she seems very nice, but it wouldn't be the same, would it?'

He glanced at her, and she smiled the same complicit smile she had given him when they all shook hands.

'No,' he said, 'it wouldn't.'

'If I asked, would she mind?'

'I expect you'd get your way. I expect you usually do.'

'I'm quite good at it, you're quite right.'

'But I'm not sure. It would be a bit rude to desert her when she's looked after me and brought me here.' He shrugged. 'And there are complications.'

'You're not going to go polite on me, are you, *Engels-man*?'

He laughed. 'Can't help it. It's my nature. As the scorpion said to the frog.'

'Oh dear, we must do something about that!'

'*We* must?'

'Why not? Be fun, don't you agree?'

'Quite like being polite, as a matter of fact.'

'I can see that.'

'Makes life easier. Oils the works, my grandmother says.'

'I've heard of mothers' boys. But not of grandmothers' boys. You're not a grandmother's boy, are you?'

He chuckled nervously. 'A bit. Can't help it. I live with her, you see.'

'Your soldier-grandfather's wife?'

'The same.'

'And you're a Jacob as well.'

'Incestuous, isn't it.'

'My god!'

She gave him a knowing look.

'What about you?' Jacob said. 'Are you a daddy's girl, like my sister?'

Now Hille chuckled, an echo of his. 'A bit. Can't help it. I live with him, you see.'

They laughed.

She added, as if winning a point, 'So was Anne.'

'Yes,' Jacob conceded, 'true. But not like my sister. She's not just a bit of a daddy's girl. She's more of an obscene daddy's girl, if you ask me.'

'You don't like her.'

'Not much.'

'What a pity. My brother Wilfred and I, we get on well. I like him a lot, to tell the truth. He's *so* serious! It's funny how serious he takes everything. Perhaps he could lighten up a bit. But I love him just the way he is.'

'You look a lot like each other.'

'Everybody says so, which is a good joke.'

'Why?'

'He's adopted. Mother couldn't have any more children after me, and they wanted a son, so they adopted Wilfred, and I was so pleased. I picked him out.'

'Really!'

'Really! That's what Mother says anyway. I was only four, but she says I took to him right away. So they decided it had to be Wilfred.'

'But you do, you look so alike.'

'Yes, I know. I see it too. And I don't mind, because I think he's beautiful.'

Jacob wanted to say she was right but that would give away too much of what he was feeling about her.

Even before Tessel had quite reached them, Hille was speaking to her in rapid Dutch, during which Tessel smiled and nodded and replied and glanced now and then at Jacob, who couldn't pick out much except his own name and the words Amsterdam and *koffie*.

'Of course you must stay and talk to Hille, if you wish,' Tessel said to him when the conversation was done. 'I don't mind at all. It will be easier for me. I can go straight to Geertrui. But will you be all right, getting back to Daan?'

'No problem,' Hille said, grinned and, mimicking with shocking accuracy, intoned to Jacob, 'Put yourself in my hands. Relax. Enjoy yourself. Trust me to land you safely in Amsterdam.'

GEERTRUI

Mrs Wesseling was so deranged by her son's action that she would not leave her room for days. It was as if Dirk had died. She kept repeating, like a mantra, that she would never see him again. In her grief she blamed Henk, saying he persuaded Dirk to leave. She blamed me for coming to the farm and unsettling her son. She blamed me too for bringing Jacob with me and putting her family in even more danger than they were before. She blamed her husband for not being more firm with their son. Worst of all in its vehemence, she blamed herself for allowing this to happen. She should have sent Henk away the first day he and Dirk decided to go into hiding; she should have sent all three of us away the night we arrived; she even said she should have let the Germans find Jacob instead of hiding him in the *bedstee*, because at least that would have saved her son.

Her torment was painful to behold. And nothing Mr Wesseling or I could do soothed her anguish. It was a shock to see an adult who I had known only as a strong woman, controlled in every way, indomitable, so suddenly crumble, becoming almost infantile in her distress. Another lesson, one of the most affecting of my life, in how fragile is human nature. In the moment it took to read her son's letter this mature, experienced, dominant woman disintegrated as if the yarn that held the garment of her self together had been pulled out and she had unravelled into a tangle of twisted thread. And though Dirk did eventually return, she never completely recovered her former self, never became the confident, imposing person she had been, but for the rest of her life was a nervous, uncertain woman, withdrawn, hard to amuse, always expecting the worst. Her one constant pleasure, and I often thought her only consolation, was playing the harmonium, an instrument she had learned as a child, but had given up in her teenage years, and now took up again as if she had never left off. She played it only for herself, sometimes for hours on end, never liking anyone else to listen, and invested in her playing all of herself that before she had poured into her son. It was as if, while playing the harmonium, she lived another life, an alternative life that did not fail her as her other everyday life had failed her. Until in the end, before she died, playing the harmonium and listening to records of other people playing it, became her world, and there was nothing besides. All else had vanished, her husband, her son, her previous life forgotten. She remembered only music and the logic of the keyboard. She died of cancer in her early sixties while fingering on the counterpane of her bed the notes of some composition only she could hear.

But I have reached ahead of myself. Let us go back to the days after Dirk and Henk disappeared.

Mr Wesseling was of course upset, but took it better than his wife and with optimism. They'll return, he said, probably in a few days, when the anger is out of their system and they find it is not so easy as they think to fight like a guerrilla. As for his wife, at first he regarded her withdrawal with the same down-to-earth acceptance. He was not an imaginative man, but phlegmatic and fatalistic. For him always, things were as they were, that was life, and you did well to make the best of it. There was an expression he frequently used: It's God's way with us that we deserve what we get. Besides, women were a mystery to him, their peculiarities beyond explanation. Their domain was the house and the domestic animals, with which he did not interfere. So when his wife took to her room, he shrugged it off as merely a woman's reaction to bad news, and left her care to me along with the rest of the 'woman's work', paying me no attention, except to say, 'You'll be worried about your brother. He'll be all right. They're resourceful boys.' And that was that. Back to work. The unremitting toil of a farm, where animals and crops never take a holiday nor allow those who tend them any time off. The land is a cruel master. And the best I can say of Mr Wesseling is that he loved it and tended it with complete devotion. It was his redeeming quality, and, I must say, I always liked him and got along well with him.

However, Mrs Wesseling was right: I was not born to the farming life and was not the type for it either. I do not know how I would have survived the next few days had it not been for Jacob. But for him my guess is that I would have given up and abandoned the Wesselings as abruptly as had my brother and Dirk, no matter what pangs of guilt I would have felt at such desertion. But Jacob was entirely my responsibility. I had taken him on against everyone's advice, and to forsake him now would have been to forsake myself. I would never have been able to live with myself ever after. Because of Jacob I had to stay with the Wesselings, had to do whatever work fell to me, however weary and distressed I felt. And must do all I could to help him become fit enough to survive. I do not say escape, because already, though only half-consciously acknowledged to myself, I dreaded the day when he would leave me.

So Mrs Wesseling withdrew to her room, Mr Wesseling buried himself in his work, and I fled from the burden of the housework whenever I could to be with Jacob.

Most of these times with him were in the evenings after our meal. Mr Wesseling would go off to listen to Radio Oranje from England, and I would go to Jacob, with the extra excuse that the skylight in the roof of the hiding place gave the best view of the main road and the track to the house, so I could keep watch for unwanted visitors while

Mr Wesseling listened to the broadcast. He would come to us afterwards, tell us the latest news of the war, check on Jacob's progress, then leave us together while he went to sit with his wife. His English was very poor so he never stayed with us for long.

Now, after Jacob being so dependent on me for his physical needs, I became dependent on him for emotional support. He was my only confidant. Few men are good listeners. (At least, it was so in my young days. Is it different now?) But Jacob was. And for a day or two after Henk's departure he had a lot of listening to do as I poured out my distress at the loss of my brother, my anxieties about my parents, my complaints about Mrs Wesseling, my lonely plight, and my fears for each one of us. Everything which till then I had so carefully guarded and kept from him because I had been so determined to keep up my spirits and not depress Jacob lest I hinder his recovery. I suppose I had thought of myself as his rescuer, his nurse, even, as he called me, his guardian angel. His Maria. Now, in a day, this changed. The dyke was breached, my emotions flooded out in a deluge, and Jacob became my refuge, my protector, my companion.

And it was such a relief! Not to have to be strong all the time, not to have to appear cheerful and optimistic, not to have to be decisive, not to have to be always undaunted. Not to have to pretend so much. But just to *be*. I think I wallowed in the luxury. For a day or two at least. And Jacob did not discourage me. What a release! Like a prisoner unchained.

One evening, as we sat either side of the little makeshift table in the hiding place, the sound and smell of the cows in their stalls below filtering to us through the walls of hay, I cried as I talked. Cooped up as we were, yet it was like walking out in to the rain after a long dusty time inside.

And as if we were friends walking in the rain, Jacob reached out, and we held hands across the table. This was

204

the first time we made such intimate contact. As I have told you, I had washed this man, including his most private parts, many times. I had cradled him while he slept in our cellar during the worst of his suffering. I had fed him mouthful by mouthful as one feeds a baby. I had changed the dressings on his wounds. I had even assisted him as he used the lavatory. There was nothing of his body I did not know and had not touched. But that was the touch of his dutiful nurse, his angel Maria.

There had, of course, been the moment in the *bedstee*, and the desires and fantasies that had aroused. But I had tried to suppress them, had tried not to let myself think of them. In those old-fashioned words no one uses seriously any more, I had remained chaste. What had happened, I told myself, had been no more than an accident and must not be dwelt on. Even though at night I could not get it out of my mind or, worse, out of my dreams.

But now it was not Angel Maria who touched him, it was he who touched me, Geertrui, reaching across the table to take my hand as I talked and wept. I did not resist. At that moment nothing could have given me more comfort, nor more pleasure, than my hand held in his. Yet what confusion of emotions it stirred in me, as my distress and fears blended with the desires and longings that had kept me awake at nights and which now at last found a response, an outlet, a reply, a physical confirmation in the caress of his fingers on mine.

Instantly, in the second his hand took mine, I no longer thought of him as a wounded soldier, an escapee, a foreigner. Nor, honesty requires that I add, as a married man either. But only as mine and myself as his. In that uncompromising second I gave myself completely to him. And did so consciously, wilfully (not, please note, *willingly*, but *wilfully*). And have never thought of him or of myself in any other way from that day to this.

I want to be clear. Not for a part of a second did I hold

back, resist, demur. I propose no explanation, make no excuse. Nor do I offer the slightest regret. Quite the opposite. I cling to this moment, this decision. And endure its consequences. Of nothing in my life am I as certain as I am of my love for Jacob. Had he lived, I would have done everything in my power to keep him.

That evening we talked, held hands, gazed in to one another's eyes, as lovers have done forever in that delicious time when they first acknowledge one another. No more than this. We did not even kiss. Yet it seemed to us that all our lives were there with us in that makeshift secret room. As that favourite poem I mentioned earlier puts it: 'in short measures life may perfect be'. There is no more. There can be nothing better. The two hours or so which Jacob and I spent together that night were a measure of perfection. Brought to an end by Mr Wesseling calling to me from below, on the excuse of reminding me how late it was, and waiting for me to join him at the bottom of the ladder after I had said a hasty goodnight to Jacob.

I did not resent Mr Wesseling's intrusion, but liked him for it. He added to the excitement of the evening and gave me a sense of security, of my welfare being watched over by a fatherly eye. And by then, after so many stressful days away from my parents (the first time in my life I had been away from them for so long), I needed such reassuring papa-love as much as I was ready and longing for the unsettling passion of falling-in-love for the first time.

You will rightly guess that I slept very little that night. And that my mind was lively with new hope. Hope for what the future with Jacob might be like, where we would live and how. New love has tunnel vision, its retina is a movie screen, it views the world remade in its own amotopian image.

Next day the unremade world was just as it had been the day before, only worse. Colder, muddier, dustier, bleaker.

And my predicament—servant to Mrs Wesseling, farmgirl-housekeeper to Mr Wesseling—more of a burden than ever. All I wanted, all I pined for was to be alone with Jacob. But thank my genes, I am blessed with an active nature. The lower my spirits plunge the greater my impulse to be up and doing. An inheritance from my mother. So I threw myself into my chores with a frenzy forged of frustrated desire.

Yet so perverse is human nature, each time I saw Jacob during that day, to take him his breakfast and mid-day meal, hot water to wash in, return laundered clothes, I was overcome with such chronic shyness that I could hardly look him in the eyes. I tried to behave as matter-of-factly as possible, tried to bustle about as if too busy to stop and talk, tried to pretend that nothing had changed between us, that I was still only his friendly nurse Maria. But of course it was useless. Everything had changed. Harder than looking at him was touching him, and hardest of all, being touched by him. Usually, I changed the dressing on Jacob's wounded leg after breakfast. But this morning his leg was no longer merely a wounded limb, it was a part of the desired body of the loved one, which I craved to kiss and caress. So I muttered something about an urgent problem with Mrs Wesseling to put off changing his dressing till later, when, I hoped, I had prepared myself.

'Later' came after the mid-day meal. We had always spent half an hour together then, relaxing before the afternoon's work. That morning Mr Wesseling had cleared out dung and used straw from the cowhouse. Jacob had helped by hobbling about on the gallery, forking fresh hay and straw down to Mr Wesseling. By mid-day he was dusty and sweaty, his bandage was grubby, had worked loose and was annoying him. If I did not want to change it, he said irritably when I took him his meal, he would do it himself. But this I could not allow. No hands but mine, not even Jacob's, must tend my patient, my beloved. Such jealousy! I had never felt a hint of it before. Till then, I thought of jealousy as an ugly weakness, which I viewed with scorn. Now it seized me in an unmistakable spasm of emotional cramp that took me by surprise and flustered me all the more.

Without a word I scampered off to collect a pitcher of hot water and fresh dressings. When I returned Jacob was sitting on the bed in his underwear, having given himself as good a wash as he could manage in cold water. I had seen my patient like that often, but not since our changeful time together the night before. I wanted to throw myself in to his arms. Instead, tried to act my former self. But bustled too clumsily. Into the basin I poured water from the pitcher, but sloppily. Onto one knee at his feet I went down with a painful bump. With trembling hands I took the end of bandage that had come loose above his knee and began to unwind it from his leg. But because my fingers were all thumbs I fumbled as I rolled the unwinding ribbon, which fell into the basin of water by my side. As if the basin were a reservoir piped to my eyes, this ineptitude produced a flow of tears. Which I forced myself to ignore, keeping my head down so that Jacob should not see them, while I reached into the basin with slow-motion control, retrieved the drowned bandage, and with studied care went on unwinding the remainder from his leg, after which I laid the roll of soiled cloth aside. Stood. Discarded the contaminated water. Rubbed the basin clean. Placed it on the floor again. Poured more, now only tepid water in to it from the pitcher. Bent over Jacob's leg and was about to start removing the dressing that covered the wound—always the worst part of the process because congealed blood glued the dressing to the sore, making it painful to strip off—when Jacob's hands took me by the shoulders and, using me to support himself, got to his feet, and still holding me, waited until I could no longer keep my head bowed, could not help but look him in the face, and look at last in to his eyes. Those eyes that from first sight had bewitched my heart.

Such a moment, such *stasis*, is not to be endured for long. There can only be advance or retreat, acceptance or rejection, acknowledgement or denial. What else could there be from me then but advance, acceptance, acknowledgement? With the clarity of unthinking instinct I raised a hand and drew his face with my fingers, from brow and temple to lips and chin. The stubble of his unshaven cheek sent a tingle down my thighs. As my fingers cupped his chin, he leaned towards me and kissed my lips with lingering delicacy. Grasping his head with both hands, and rising on my toes, I kissed the lids of his closing eyes, first right then left. Wrapped my arms around his neck. Pressed myself close, all of myself, firmly to him. And for the second time felt his sex swell, but now against my belly, and with trembling pleasure at the fact of it, the sign of his desire for me, and the longing to know the power that it stirred in me.

Not a word was spoken, only the exhaling of sighs and crooning of pleasure that is the glossolalia of love.

(What a foolish old woman I am to tell you all this! What can the detail of it matter to you? Am I not merely embarrassing you? Besides, love-making is so universally the same that there is never anything to tell of it that is not a cliché. But like those tedious holiday-making travellers who turn up to coffee armed with their snapshots, I am impelled to spell it out by some irresistible compulsion. To relive it myself, perhaps? To memorialise something that fixed the rest of my life? To confirm its reality? No matter.)

We clung to each other, kissing deeply, for some long while, the brevity of which was agonising. No more that day than this. At last reluctantly breaking apart when we heard the sound of Mr Wesseling returning to work among the cows.

After quickly redressing Jacob's wound, I hurried back to my chores with a bursting urgency, my blood singing, my thoughts in confusion, and longing longing longing for more.

Other signs of my condition I won't dwell upon, such as the flush of my skin, the perking of my breasts with the imprint of Jacob's chest upon them, the almost painful ache in my womb, the wetness under my arms and between my legs. Thank heaven there was no one in the house to observe my fluster and bliss. By the time of the evening meal I had collected myself, but knew that if I took Jacob his food I would return in disarray again, even if I could tear myself away from him. So I asked Mr Wesseling to take it to him, with a message that I would visit later.

But I did not go later. Or, I mean, not later that evening. A great nervousness gripped me. I could not trust myself. How would I behave? How *should* I behave? How would Jacob behave? And how should I respond to him? Would I know how? There was fear as well as longing in my passion.

What is more, suddenly I felt unfit for him. My body dirty, my clothes dowdy and faded, shapeless and unlovely. Of what did I smell? That evening's cooking? The dust of the house? The hen coop where I had just been to lock the hens up for the night? The cheesy smell of the dairy, where I'd spent half an hour working the machine that separated the cream from the day's milk? Or my own body sweat and sex odour? The thought appalled me. I could not bear myself a moment longer. It was as if my outer self was a repulsive carapace, a hardened shell, old and outworn, imprisoning a new self that strained to break free. I wanted to discard it like a snake sheds its skin or a butterfly its chrysalis as it emerges from the husk. Wanted to? No, no. *Had* to! Not a possibility. Not something wished for. But an imperative. A necessity. A biological requirement.

I had not bathed for some days. This was not unusual. We did not take baths so much then as we do now. And showers, at least where I lived, were unheard of. People were less fastidious about their bodies. But our house in Oosterbeek had a bathroom, whereas the farm still did not. So I noticed the difference. The inconvenience, if nothing else. On the farm there was all the trouble of boiling up enough water, preparing a portable bath, which was always placed in front of the kitchen range, both for the warmth and to make it as easy as possible to transfer water from the boiler to the bathtub. Afterwards there was the trouble of emptying the bath and clearing up. And there was the question of propriety and modesty. While the women were bathing the men would keep out of the way and vice versa. In the Wesseling household, the men bathed on Friday nights, the women on Saturdays. Any change in this ritual was remarkable. After an illness, perhaps, or for some special occasion—a birthday, for example, or before a journey away from home. But never simply on a whim. Never just because you felt like having a bath.

This was a Thursday. What reason could I find that would satisfy Mr Wesseling's surprise at my taking a bath that evening? I could think of only one that he would not question, for I knew even mention of it would so embarrass him that he would not want to discuss it. It would also quite genuinely embarrass me, for women were not given to discussing womanly conditions with men in those days, even if the men had heard of them, which it is almost unbelievable now to say that many, even married men, had not. The particular functions of the female body were treated between men and women as if they did not exist. Open talk of them, at least in respectable religious families, was regarded as at best bad manners and at worst as a social sin worthy of severe punishment. My excuse also had the advantage of being a fact. My period had finished the day before. The only untruth I would have to tell would be the smallest hint that my period had been in some unspecified way unpleasant, and Mr Wesseling would leave the house without a second question. Which he did, saying he would go and listen to the news, then call on Jacob, and be back in an hour or so, if that would be long enough. Yes yes, I said, and away he went.

211

It was while I was bathing that the thought finally surfaced that I was doing this not for myself but for Jacob. In preparation for receiving him into myself, like a bride.

'I mean to go to him,' I said out loud, 'because I want him inside me.'

The shock of my shamelessness made me gasp. I would never have believed myself so forward! Yet at once with almost cold rationality, I began to plan how I would do it. I would finish my bath, clear up, dry my hair in front of the fire, then go to my room. There I would pare my nails, oil my hands and legs, inspect and tend to every nook and cranny of my body, scent myself with lavender, arrange my hair, and dress as becomingly as my few spare clothes kept for 'best' would allow. I would take my time, enjoy myself, wash from my mind the strain and stress of the last weeks, fill it only with thoughts of Jacob. I would wait until Mr Wesseling had retired to bed and I heard his volcanic snores (a regular feature of his sleep). Then I would steal away to Jacob.

Not until I was in my room, the warmth from my bath quickly chilled by the cold damp air of the autumn night, did it occur to me with as cold a chill that the romantic encounter for which I was so eager might produce unwanted consequences.

About the practicalities of sex (need I tell you?) I knew next to nothing. Even about what went where and how it got there I knew only the rudiments, and these from the uncertain authority of friends, not from parents or teachers or books. Among the things I had been told about under the desk, so to speak, at school, was the so-called 'safe period' method of contraception. It was all right to have sex seven days before your period started, for the three or four days of the flow, and for six or seven days following. Otherwise you had better make sure that the man left the church before the last hymn was sung. (How we giggled, we girls, as we uttered that ridiculous code we thought so secret for *coitus interruptus*. And how confident and proud we were of our possession of these adult 'facts'.)

Well, as I told you, the flow of my period had finished the day before. But, I thought now, how could I be sure my school friends were any more accurately informed about the 'safe period'? And even if they were, how safe was 'safe'? One hundred per cent? Doubt invaded my romantic amotopian fantasy and kept me brooding for some time after Mr Wesseling's volcanic eruptions commenced. Long enough for me to decide in calmness of mind that love cannot be love without risk. It seemed obvious to me, though I do not know how or when I had learned it, that love that is real is always dangerous. And more dangerous to the one who gives it than to the one who receives it.

Even then I had few illusions about the behaviour of the human body, just as by then the war had left me with few illusions about human behaviour. The body, I was sure, could be just as errant as human behaviour, just as untrustworthy, just as prone to fluctuations from some supposed norm. Any rule, any law, whether enshrined in nature or made by human beings, implied exceptions and provoked deviation. I knew I was about to break several human laws —religious (fornication, connivance in adultery, coveting another woman's husband), legal (having sex before the age of consent), and social (betraying the trust of my parents and of people who had taken me in at risk of their own lives and cared for me at their own cost). Why should my body not be just as vagrant and break the natural law? If I were caught, there were heavy punishments for all these transgressions. Was I prepared to accept the consequences, I asked myself as I examined my body in the mirror in the candle-lit coldness of the night. And replied to myself aloud, with the brave arrogance of untried youth, 'Yes. Yes, I am.'

So, with my mind made up, I gave myself to Jacob.

Growing up is, after all,
only the understanding that one's
unique and incredible experience
is what everyone shares.
Doris Lessing, THE GOLDEN NOTEBOOK

'Have a *pannenkoek*,' Hille said.

'What's that?' Jacob asked.

'A pancake.'

'Eggs and flour and stuff beaten into a batter and cooked in a frying pan?'

'I think so. I'm not great on cooking. The French call them *crêpes*? We love them in Holland.' She smiled across the menu and shrugged. 'You can have things in it. *Spek*, for instance, which is, er, bacon. Or apple and—*kaneel*?'

'Sorry, no idea.'

'Taking you out is hard work.'

'Sorry again.'

'No, it's okay. I like practising my English.'

'Are you?'

'I'm talking English, aren't I?'

'Taking me out.'

'I invited you.'

'Didn't Wilfred want to come?'

'Had to finish packing his things.'

'The bacon will do, thanks.'

'I'll have the apple and *kaneel*. Then you can try it and tell me what *kaneel* is. What to drink?'

'White wine?' Daan had given him a liking for it.

214

'Okay.'

'We could go Dutch, if you like.'

'What?'

'Go Dutch. Don't you know that expression?'

'No.'

'Means we'll each pay for own meal rather than one of us paying for both.'

'Why is that Dutch?'

Jacob laughed. 'No idea. Why ask me?'

'It's your language.'

'So? Can you explain all the expressions you use in Dutch?'

'No. But I wish I could.'

'We have lots of Dutch sayings.'

'Like?'

'Dutch uncle. A man who isn't really your uncle but treats you like he is. Dutch courage. The kind of courage people get from drinking a lot of booze to help them do something they don't want to do . . .What else? Let's see. . . . Dutch oven, which means your mouth. Lots of hot air, I suppose.'

'Charming.'

'Dutch auction. An auction where the price starts high and comes down step by step till someone buys, instead of starting low and going up.'

'I know that one. And double Dutch.'

'Talking nonsense.'

'But why?'

'Probably because to us Dutch sounds very difficult to understand, so something double it must be gibberish.'

'Thanks a lot! It's no more difficult than Swedish. And what about Chinese? Why not double Chinese? Are there more?'

'A few, but I don't know all of them.'

'Are they all rude about us?'

'Rude? I suppose mostly they are. Wonder why?'

'I'd guess history, wouldn't you?'

'You mean the time when we fought each other.'

'Like the Danes are rude about the Swedes.'

'Yes?'

'People always make up jokes and say nasty things about people they've fought, don't they? Like we do about the Germans. Or my grandparents do anyway.'

'Hate has a long memory.'

'Is that an English expression as well?'

'It is now. I just made it up. Or at least as far as I remember.'

That Hille laughed out loud made him feel good. He was liking her more and more. Couldn't take his eyes off her. Especially her wide mouth with its lilting curl-over lower lip. And the pearly lustre of her skin that stirred in him a longing to caress it.

The waitress came and they ordered.

When she had gone, Hille said, 'You know where you are? This restaurant, I mean.'

The place (to his English eyes, a cross between a pub, a café and a restaurant, all three at once) was full of old soldiers (red berets or blue berets still on their heads, medals still lining their chests) packed round the tables, eating and drinking with their friends and talking English ten to the dozen. Jacob and Hille had taken the last two seats at a little table squashed into a corner. Apart from the waitresses, they were the youngest people there by many years. Jacob had been so occupied by Hille that he hadn't noticed anything else. Now he looked around and saw there were pictures (real paintings or reproductions, he couldn't see from where he sat) high up on the walls, which depicted scenes from the battle. He'd seen some of the same pictures in books.

'I don't know much about the battle,' Hille said, 'battles not being, like you say, my cup of tea. But this place is quite famous.'

'What's it called? I didn't notice.'

'The Hotel Schoonoord.'

'Rings a bell. Wasn't it used as a hospital?'

'This isn't the same building. What was left of that one was pulled down because it was so badly damaged. This one was put up on the same place after the war. I know about it because the daughter of the owner wrote a diary of what happened during the battle and it was published. Hendrika van der Vlist. She was twenty-two or -three at the time. It's really good. Not as great as Anne's. But you'd like it. And I know you can get it in English because I've seen it at the museum about the battle, just along the road from here. We could buy it for you.'

'Sure.'

'The museum was the English headquarters, so you might want to see it anyway.'

'Oh, you mean, the hotel, the Heart something—?'

'Hartenstein. They show you a film about the battle, and in the cellars they've made kind of scenes of how the place was during the battle using real things from those days. And with wax models for the people, you know? Like Madame Tussaud's. It's *spookachtig*, I think. But interesting. There's a nice park behind it with lots of trees. We could have a walk if you want to, it's really nice.'

'Great. But listen, we could go Dutch, you know. You really don't have to pay for me.'

Hille said as the waitress arrived with their food, 'You've told me about your grandfather. You can pay for your meal by telling about you.'

'Thought there'd be a catch somewhere.'

'Of course! I'm Dutch, after all. From us, you get nothing for nothing.'

'Okay, okay! *Pax*!'

With sudden seriousness, lifting her glass in a toast, and looking Jacob square in the eyes, Hille said, '*Vrede* forever.'

Just as she did this one of those unaccountable silences

fell of the kind that sometimes occur in a crowd of people, a simultaneous gap in all the conversations. The two words of Hille's toast filled the silence, as if addressed to the entire room. There was only a second's hesitation while the words sank in before everybody raised a glass, as if it had been rehearsed, and called out, '*Vrede* forever!' The following silence while the toast hung in the air was broken by one of the old soldiers shouting out, 'It was for you we did it!' At which glasses were set down and everybody laughed and clapped or banged the table and cheered.

Hille pulled a what-have-I-done face at Jacob and they both had to suppress giggles of embarrassment.

When it was over Hille said, 'Give me your plate. There's something I want to show you. You have mine and taste the *kaneel* and tell me what it is. Do you like *stroop*? A sort of . . . syrup, I think you call it.'

'Expect so,' Jacob said, handing over his plate and taking Hille's from her. 'Not something I've had.'

'Lovely and sweet, but not sugary, you know? We have it on our *pannenkoeken*.'

Jacob was sniffing at Hille's. 'I can tell you what *kaneel* is just from the smell. Cinnamon.'

'That's it, yes. Cinnamon. Try it.'

He cut a sliver. 'Very tasty.'

'Would you like it? We can order another.'

'No, they're huge. One will do for me.'

Hille had taken a dispenser, turned it upside down and quickly poured a stream of thin treaclish syrup from its nozzle on to Jacob's pancake, moving the dispenser about as if she were writing with a fat pen. Which, Jacob saw when she held up his plate to show him, she had been. On his pancake in syrup letters expertly shaped, no dribbles or blotches, was his name, but spelt: JAKOB.

'Smart,' he said, 'and clever.'

'You try on mine.'

She handed him the dispenser. Jacob tried using it as

Hille had. But of course the gummy liquid poured out much faster than he expected. What he achieved was a hardly readable squiggle, a wobbly approximation of his attempt at HILLA.

'All you need is practice,' Hille said, as they swapped plates again. 'I prescribe a *pannenkoek* every day. And if this is an *a*, it should be an *e*.'

'Well, if it comes to that,' Jacob said, echoing her mock-tetchy tone, 'this *k* you've given me should be a *c*.'

'I know, but I liked *k* better. If you don't, then eat it and it'll be gone.'

'I will. Ditto you with your *a*. I'll start with the offending *k* right here in the middle of this giant flapjack and work my way out.'

'Good idea . . . Flapjack?'

'American for pancake.'

Hille said, chopping out the *a* with a circular swirl of her knife, 'Maybe we should always start everything from the inside and work to the outside, and not from the outside to the inside. Maybe life would be better that way. What d'you think?'

'Don't tell me you're a philosopher as well as a pancake fanatic.'

'But I am. I like to think about the meaning of things. Don't you?'

'Yes, I do. And this is really good pancake.'

'I think everything has a meaning. Especially things that doesn't seem to have.'

'Don't seem to have.'

'Don't, don't. Yes, sorry. Jakob Todd is a good name for a philosopher. A bit—*ouderwets*. What's that in English? . . . Sort of ancient—?'

'Old-fashioned?'

'Right. Old-fashioned.'

'Am I old-fashioned? Maybe I am.'

Hille looked up from devouring her pancake, which was

219

disappearing at about three times the rate of Jacob's, and considered him with only half-mocking seriousness. 'Yes, I think that's true. I agree, you are *ouderwets*. Not out of date or anything. I don't mean that. Just old-fashioned.'

Jacob put his head down because he wasn't quite sure what game was in play now. Was she only joking, or actually telling him something she wanted him to know?

'Is that bad news?' he asked.

'Good news,' Hille said, tucking into her pancake again. 'I'm getting very pissed off with the way everything has to be new-fashioned. How everything has to be the latest thing. Like, what you're supposed to wear, and music. All that stuff? I used to think it mattered. Now I think it sucks.'

'Really?'

'Yes, I do,' she said.

He laughed with relief.

'I mean it!' Hille said with vehemence.

'I know. Me too!'

'Then why,' said Hille starting to laugh with him, 'why are you laughing?'

'Because! . . Why are you laughing?'

'I don't know! . . . Because you're laughing!'

'So we're laughing because we're laughing!'

Their laughter subsided into smiles.

Jacob shrugged.

All at once there was nothing he could say because there was too much to say. And because there were disturbing feelings milling inside him that he had never had before. He didn't dare put a name to what they meant.

Hille finished her pancake and sat, elbows on the table, chin on her knuckles, staring at him.

After a while she said, 'I don't know anything about you really. But it's like I've always known you.'

Jacob was glad he still had some food to finish, though he didn't want it any longer, as an excuse to avoid her gaze.

When it was obvious he wasn't going to say anything

Hille said, 'Have you ever felt like that about anybody?'

There was a different tone in her voice, the edge had gone, the self-assurance.

He waited for a moment while he worked out what he wanted to say, sensing he could either keep things going between them as they had been so far or make something else happen. But he also sensed this something else he didn't dare name would open his most secret self to another person in a way he had never risked before. Nor had ever wanted to. All those parts of him that his shyness had kept locked up; parts he had never really examined carefully even for himself. As his intuition told him this, for he could not say he thought it in words, he was aware that his heart rate had increased and his temperature had risen with it.

Keeping a grip on himself, he decided that whatever he said, he wanted it to be true. Or at least, as true as words could be for an experience he hardly understood.

Having forced himself to take his time finishing his pancake, putting his knife and fork down, lifting his head and at last looking Hille straight in the eyes, he spoke quietly and with deliberate care.

'No, I haven't felt like that about anybody. But today I have felt . . . I don't know quite how to put this . . . That I've met someone who I've been waiting to meet for . . . Well, forever is a big word, so let's say . . . For a long time.'

Hille didn't blink. But her pale face blushed as he was sure his own had as well.

'Dunno why I feel like that,' he added. 'Dunno how it can happen so suddenly. Dunno what to say about it.'

Hille nodded.

And just when the intensity of the moment was about to become unbearable Hille unfolded her fingers and with a movement that could not be mistaken for accident laid her right hand, palm up, on the edge of the table half way between them. As if it were a magnet to his metal, Jacob laid his left hand, fingers to palm, on hers.

221

Another silence while they gave all their attention to the flow of current. Cheerful noise from another world went on around them.

'Where to begin?' Jacob said at last. 'There's so much.'

'Inside out?' Hille said.

'I feel like I'm inside out already!'

She chuckled. 'Me too!'

'Outside in? For a breather.'

'The park? Behind the museum.'

'Yes.'

'Some nice places.'

'Yes?'

'Among the trees.'

'Yes.'

'And the sun. Beautiful today.'

'Yes.'

'Let's go.'

After looking round the Hartenstein Museum, where they bought an English copy of Hendrika van der Vlist's diary, *Oosterbeek 1944*, and a Parachute Regiment T-shirt as a souvenir for Sarah, they wandered in to the park and found a hide-away spot under some trees.

'Remember Anne's first kiss from Peter van Daan?' Jacob said.

'Through her hair,' Hille said, 'half on her ear and half on her cheek.'

'She was nearly fifteen.'

'Made me laugh the first time I read it. I must have been about thirteen then, and already knew I liked kissing *a lot*!'

'How old were you when you had your first serious kiss?'

'Eleven. A boy called Karel Rood. He was fourteen. Everybody wanted him for a boyfriend. We thought he was very beautiful. Now he's a *domkop* and as attractive to kiss as a *slak*. And don't ask me the English for it because I don't know. Slides along the ground, sticky and wet?'

'A slug?'

'Anyway, not nice to kiss. He was good at it then, though. What about you?'

'Oh, a couple of girlfriends. But I'm not as good at it as you are, I think. Expect you've had more practice, like writing with syrup.'

'You're not so bad. You have very kissable lips as well. We can have some more practice now if you like.'

'Good idea.'

'After Anne has her first kiss,' Jacob said, 'she goes on and on about whether she should tell her father what she and Peter are getting up to. Remember?'

'Sitting in the attic with their arms round each other,' Hille said. 'And taking turns to lay their heads on each other's shoulders.'

'And that's before they have a real mouth-to-mouth smacker. Which doesn't happen for eleven more days. Imagine waiting all that long! No wonder she's trembling when it happens.'

'Thought I knew the *Diary* but I don't know it as well as you do.'

'I remember about her first kiss because I was kind of fixated on Peter for a while. You know I told you how I used to highlight passages in orange. Well, when I had this thing about Peter I highlighted all the passages that had anything to do with him in green. Then I read them at one go, all the green passages, so that I could concentrate only on what Anne did with him, what she thought about him, and all that.'

'Why? Why do that?'

'Because I kept thinking what I'd have done if I'd been him, and how I would have behaved. The two longest green passages are about her first and second kisses. I kept thinking: Why is Peter hanging about? Why doesn't he get on with it? I know I would have.'

'I wonder if you would have done, if you really had been him. Well, not him, but yourself, like you are now, but then. Because you can only ever be yourself, can't you? Poor Peter. In nineteen forty-four, when life was different from the way it is now, sex especially, locked up in a few rooms for two years with all those adults watching him all the time. Would you have done any better?'

'I know. You're right. But I was only fourteen, fifteen, when I was thinking like that.'

'I'll forgive you, then.'

'I'm relieved! And will you tell your father what you've been up to with an Englishman in the park, like Anne tells her father about what she was up to with Peter?'

'Might. Might not. Does it matter?'

'What would he say if you did?'

'Hope you enjoyed yourself.'

'And?'

'I'll need to try some more to find out.'

'Good idea.'

'Do you have a kissing boyfriend at the moment?' Jacob said.

'No,' Hille said. 'I had one till about three weeks ago. But at the moment I'm boyfriendless.'

'Why did you split up?'

'Oh dear! Well, he was handsome and everything like that, you know. Good at sex. And funny. And always very nice to me. Gave me flowers. Brought me presents when he didn't have to. Wrote me love letters. Many of them. Which I liked very much . . . More than I liked him, I think now. Anyway, I really had it bad for him, for six months, about. He was, let's say, my first real boyfriend.'

'But?'

'This will sound awful, but honestly, I started to feel *teleurgesteld* . . . What's that in English? . . . Disappointed.'

'Disappointed?'

'Difficult to put into words. Especially for me English words . . . It was like for Anne with Peter. She says the same. I remember exactly her words, because she doesn't use ordinary Dutch and I liked it so much the first time I read it that I said it over and over. She says: *dat hij geen vriend voor mijn begrip kon zijn.* Which means something like . . . he was not a friend for my understanding.'

'You mean: Not a friend who understands me.'

'No, not only that. Not really that at all. More like: Not one who is of my same mental and spiritual level . . . Not a friend of what I am . . . who I am . . . It's difficult!'

'Not a soul mate.'

'Perhaps that. It's kind of poetic how she puts it.'

'Not someone you've been waiting to meet all your life.'

'Ha! No! And besides, he—Willem, I mean—was getting very serious. *Very* serious. Even talking about marriage. I mean! I know he was three years older than me, but *marriage*! At my age? Not me, thanks. So I said goodbye.'

'And there's no one else?'

'Oh, poor me! How will I get along! No, no one.'

'Can I apply for the vacancy?'

'Are you available?'

'Entirely unemployed.'

'You'll have to pass a big test.'

'To check my qualifications?'

'And if you pass the test, there'll be a long trial period before you're offered a contract.'

'I could say the same to you.'

'Sure. Okay. I'd expect that. It's a two-way contract.'

'Let's start right now with more of the practical exam in kissing and cuddling. Just to find out if the job is worth applying for.'

'Good idea.'

'Don't you think life is very iffy?' Jacob said.

'What does that mean? Iffy,' Hille said.

'Well, look: If I hadn't fallen out with my father, and if my mother hadn't got ill when she did, and if she hadn't been kept in hospital as long as she was, and if my sister wasn't such a—what did you call that boy who gave you your first kiss? *Dom* something?'

'*Domkop.*'

'Sounds just right for my sister, whatever it means. So, to continue: If my mother hadn't had to stay in hospital, and if my sister wasn't such a *domkop*, I wouldn't have gone to stay with my grandmother. And if my grandmother hadn't given me *The Diary of Anne Frank*, and if I hadn't fallen in love with Anne, and if my grandmother hadn't broken her thigh, which kept her from coming to Holland, and if she hadn't sent me instead to visit the woman who took care of my grandfather, and if my grandfather hadn't been in the Paras, and if he hadn't fought in the Battle of Arnhem, and if he hadn't been wounded, and if he hadn't been rescued by the Dutch family, and if he hadn't died while they were looking after him—if none of all that had happened I wouldn't have met you and we wouldn't be sitting here engaging in a bit of wanton nooky—'

'What!'

'Billing and cooing.'

'Again!'

'Amorous philandering.'

'Talk English, *domkop!*'

'I *am* talking English. You mean, talk Dutch, I think.'

'Well, why not? Why should I do all the hard work?'

'Anyway, as I was saying, if all these ifs hadn't happened, I wouldn't be here with you. And I would be very very sorry about that.'

'How could you be sorry about it, if it hadn't happened? If it hadn't happened you wouldn't know about it. So you couldn't be sorry about it not happening.'

'Ah, clever clogs, but it *will* have happened in one of my

alternative lives. You know—the lives hot-shot scientists tell us we are living at the same time as this one we know about. Which being so, how do you know that what happens in one of your alternative lives doesn't sometimes leak through into your consciousness in this life, and make you sad that you aren't living that particular alternative life instead of this one? Don't you sometimes feel depressed for no reason you can think of? I do. And maybe that's why. We've had a leak from an alternative life and want that life now. Like wanting an ice cream when you were little, which you knew was in the freezer, but your mum wouldn't let you have it.'

'You do talk a lot when you get going.'

'Only to the right person. With the right person I do like talking, I admit. D'you mind? Should I shut up?'

'No, I like it. Usually, I'm the one who talks a lot. And I like watching the funny way this thing, your *Adamsappel*, goes up and down when you talk.'

'Only, the point I was making—if you don't mind taking your finger off my Adam's apple because it's nearly making me gag up my *pannenkoeken*—is how iffy life is. Makes you wonder what life would be like if there weren't any ifs at all.'

'Dead.'

'What?'

'Dead. Life would be dead. If there weren't any ifs we wouldn't be here. Nobody would be. We would not *be*. So we'd be the same as dead.'

'You mean, all life is just one big if?'

'Isn't that obvious?'

'It is now, thanks. And, now you come to mention it, have you noticed that life has an if in it? I mean the word. L, *i*, *f*, e. So the iffyness of life was there all the time. I just hadn't noticed. What a *domkop*!'

'Not in Dutch it isn't.'

'Why? What's life in Dutch?'

'*Leven.*'

227

'Spelt like how?'

'I get the English letters wrong sometimes. I'll write it on your hand with my finger.'

'L . . . e . . . v . . . e . . . n.'

'Yes. *Leven.*'

'Okay. Hm, that felt nice. And it really gives the game away, doesn't it. E, v, e in the middle. You Dutch don't have an if in your life, you have an Eve. The English are all ifs and the Dutch are all Adam and Eve.'

'And don't you like the Dutch kind of life more than the *Engels*? So let's get rid of your *domkop* English ifs and get back to the nice Dutch Adam and Eve stuff.'

'Good idea.'

'Talking of dead,' Jacob said.

'At the moment I like the kissing best,' Hille said.

'Seriously.'

'I am serious.'

'But seriously serious. There's something I want to ask you.'

'Okay, ask.'

'I told you about the old lady, Geertrui, and seeing her in hospital yesterday.'

'And?'

'What I didn't tell you is she's going to have an assisted death in a few days.'

'*Ja* . . . So?'

'Well . . . I wondered what you think about it. About assisted death itself, I mean, not just hers in particular.'

'There's been so much talk about it here, I'm almost tired of hearing about it. A friend of mine at school, Thea, a relative of hers, an aunt, had an assisted death. Her aunt was in bad pain, and couldn't do anything for herself any more. All she wanted was to die. And everybody agreed that would be best. The right thing to do. Thea as well, who loved her aunt very much. Afterwards, Thea had a really bad time. I mean so bad she was ill, away from school for days. She felt so guilty and so sorry. She kept thinking there must have been more they could have done. Or that they'd been selfish, wanting her aunt dead so that they wouldn't have to suffer her pain with her and look after her. But still, even when Thea was ill, she said she knew they really had done the best thing. But that didn't stop the bad feelings. She still has them sometimes, when she's feeling low. But Thea herself also says she knows that people often do feel bad when someone they love has died. Doesn't matter how the person died, they still feel guilty. And that's true. I know myself. When my grandmother died last year, I felt bad, even though she died all of a sudden of a heart attack. I felt guilty, as if I'd killed her. Or I hadn't done all I could to make her happier. Or tell her how much I loved her. So maybe it's always going to be bad for the friends and the family, however a person dies. My opinion is that we should be allowed to die . . . *fatsoenlijk* . . . What's that in English? Properly? . . . No . . . decently . . .?'

'With dignity?'

'That's it. With dignity. But more. With *integriteit.*'

'With integrity.'

'Yes, with dignity and integrity. I think everyone should have such a right. People who are against it say evil people, like Hitler, would use a euthanasia law to kill people they don't like or want removed. But it seems to me that evil people don't need a law to do it, they do it anyway. Hitler did, and Stalin as well. And, you know—serial killers. That's why they're evil. And I also think that if there aren't proper euthanasia laws and proper rules and, what do you call them?—safety guards—'

'Safe guards.'

'—about how it can be done and when, and such things, assisted deaths will still happen, because people want them. But without laws people have to do it in awful ways and against the law, making everybody who knows the person feel like a criminal. And it shouldn't be like that. Here in the Netherlands the doctors and the government made an agreement about it, but there isn't a proper law yet, but I hope there will be soon.'

'The thing is, though, it seems to me, people should take part in making the decision about their death, and some people can't because they aren't capable any longer. Like very sick people, or people with serious head injuries.'

'That's why we should make up our minds about what we want while we're still young and capable. And we should sign a proper legal document that's a record of what we've decided. I have one.'

'You mean, you've already decided when you want to die?'

'Not when. More like when I don't want to be kept alive. If I'm knocked down in the street, for instance, and never become conscious again, or get ill from some disease that makes me not able to think, or something like that. I have a *Euthanasiepas*, which I carry around with me. And my family and our doctor and our lawyer all know what's on it and have a copy of what I want.'

'You've got it with you?'

'Of course. In case anything would happen and the police or hospital doctors need to know.'

'Can I see it?'

'Sure.' . . .

'It's just like a passport. With your photo like a passport photo.'

'Don't look at it. It makes me look stupid.'

'Okay, okay, I won't. What's all this?'

'Addresses. *Naaste relatie*, my nearest relative. *Huisarts*, our family doctor. *Gevolmachtigde*, our attorney. So that the police or whoever can contact them quickly.'

'And this here?'

'The list of my conditions.'

'Like what?'

230

'Oh—that I'm not to be kept alive by artificial methods if my brain is too damaged to repair. Or if I will never be able to feed myself again or look after myself. Things like that.'

'And your parents let you do this?'

'Why not? Aren't I old enough to make up my own mind about my life and my future? We talked about it, naturally, because it's important. At first they weren't very positive. But I persuaded them. Now they agree completely, and each of them, my mother and father, has their own *Euthanasiepas*. I'm really proud of them for that, because they were against it at first, for themselves, even though they wouldn't have stopped me doing it. It was harder for them. They belong to an older generation, you know? They were born after the war, but not so long after, and my grandparents were still very prejudiced by it, the occupation and Hitler and the death camps and what happened in the Winter of the Hunger. My father's family hid a Jew, like many Dutch families did. They remembered all that and any talk of putting people to death upset them very much. And this influenced my parents. I understand all that. But we don't have to be held back because of it, do we? Yes, it's a difficult problem to solve, but that doesn't mean we should refuse to try, does it? In my opinion it's one of the most important problems our generation will have to face, because of how many people are living longer and science can keep us alive so long, even when we aren't functioning properly. So I think we have to give people the right to decide about their death. And I'm proud of my parents because they faced it, and listened to me, and changed their minds. I think that was brave of them.'

'The kind of bravery you meant this morning?'

'Yes. Ordinary people's bravery. To me that's real bravery. But you don't get medals for it or monuments put up for it. And now, *Engels*man Jakob, with all this talk, I'm thirsty. Would you want coffee or something? We could get some before we go for your train.'

231

'Good idea.'

They arrived at the station with five minutes to wait. Jacob bought a ticket for Hille from a self-service machine.

The flow of talk dried up. They stood in silence side by side, holding hands, and staring down the empty track. No one else was waiting. A lone blackbird sang from the top of a tree on the bank opposite. A car crossed the bridge. Clouds hung above them tinged by the late afternoon sun. There was a touch of autumn chill in the fading summer air.

Jacob's energy suddenly drained out of him. He was overcome by the strangeness of the day: of being in a foreign land, holding hands with a foreign girl he had met only six hours before while he was standing on his grand-father's grave in a corner of a foreign field. He needed time to take it in. The thought of the journey back to Amster-dam with Hille made his head feel heavy and his body weak. Not that he wanted to leave her. No one had made him this happy for a long time. Every part of him felt better for being with her. But he also felt talked out. And what would they do in Amsterdam? Hille couldn't just get on the next train back, could she? Should he take her to the apart-ment? Would Daan mind him turning up with a girl? He wished they could part now while everything was going good. But then what? Could they meet again? Would they want to after a day or two, when they'd cooled down and the excitement had worn off? Would Hille think she had made a mistake? Would he?

His shyness had not interfered for a second from the moment he set eyes on Hille. But now it flushed through him like an overdose of some foul narcotic, a downer that paralysed his confidence and induced moody doubt. All afternoon he had felt liberated, free to be himself in a new way. A self that had been suppressed, hidden, not allowed out, had been released. He liked this new self, and told himself that he was not going to let it be shut away again.

With an effort of will he said, 'I'm very glad we met.'

'Me too,' Hille said, not turning to look at him.

'We've had a great time.'

Hille nodded.

'I'd hate it to be spoilt.'

'Why would it be?'

'A lot's happened. Between us, I mean.'

'Yes.'

'And seeing my grandfather's grave . . . It's affected me more than I thought it would.'

Hille let go of his hand and turned to face him.

'You need some time.'

He looked at her. The green eyes. The lips he was already more familiar with than with anyone else's.

'It's like part of me—you know—the part that thinks—needs to catch up with the part that does things.'

She smiled. 'Yes, I know what you mean.'

'I could get back to Amsterdam okay on my own.'

'Would you prefer that?'

'I don't want to leave you. Really.'

'Should I come to Utrecht? Make sure you change on to the right train? Would you like that?'

'What I'd like best . . .'

'Yes?'

'Is to say goodbye now, and meet again another day. If you can. If you want to. If you would like to, I mean.'

'I'd like to.'

'And I'd like to.'

'And I want to!'

'Great! . . . Only . . . When?'

The train came into view.

'I've school all this week. And there's moving our house. But I could come to Amsterdam one evening. Or you could come here. Meet me out of school.'

'Okay. Should I phone?'

The train was pulling in to the platform.

'You don't have my number.'

'Shit! No, I don't.'

'Get in. I'll come as far as Wolfheze. It's the next station. Not far. I'll walk home.'

They stood in the space by the door. The train started off. Hille found a pen.

'Where shall I write it?'

Jacob took *Oosterbeek 1944* from the Hartenstein bag.

'On here. Your address as well, just in case.'

Hille took the book and wrote inside the back cover. While she did this Jacob found the card on which he'd written Daan's address and phone number.

'Here, have this. Everything is a bit, well, fluid let's say. Don't know where I'll be staying or for how long. But with Daan for the next few days I think. And he'll know where I am, if I'm not there. I'll phone. But I'd like to hear from you. If you want to.'

Hille smiled. 'Yes, *domkop,* I do do want to. Okay?'

'Sorry! It's travelling. Always hypes me a bit.'

'Sure you don't want me to come with you? At least to Utrecht?'

'I'll be fine. It's just . . . you've got me in such a state—'

'Oh, *I've* got *you* in such a state, have I! All Eve's fault, is it, *meneer Adamsappel!* Again!' She was laughing. 'We're almost at Wolfheze. Are you in too much of a state to give me a last kiss?'

'Not a last last kiss, I hope.'

'No,' Hille said, taking his face in her hands. 'Only a last kiss for now. How about that?'

'Good idea.'

GEERTRUI

I will not say that days—or rather, nights—of bliss followed,
only that this is the time of my life I hold most dear. Six
weeks. Blink and it is gone. Yet it is longer in memory and
fuller with memories than many of the years between then
and now. It is the time I shall die thinking of. Of him then.
Of Jacob, my beloved Jacob.

After ten days confined to her room, Mrs Wesseling appeared on Sunday morning dressed ready for church. Without a
word to her husband or myself as we sat eating breakfast,
she cycled off. When she returned, she put on her house
clothes and set about her work as if nothing out of the
ordinary had happened. And that afternoon she began playing the harmonium. Not then or ever afterwards was her
withdrawal mentioned or even hinted at. But the change in
her was complete. The old Mrs Wesseling had vanished as
if she had never been; the new was the opposite of the old.
It was as if nothing mattered to her any more. No more did
she criticise or bustle me. No more inspect what I had done.
No more advise how I should behave or instruct me in my
work. No more give me orders each morning. Rather than
being glad of this, I felt sorry for her. The old Mrs
Wesseling may have been difficult, angering me sometimes,
but she was alive and vital. Whereas the new Mrs Wesseling
was like an automaton, a robot, a creature without a will or
even a mind of its own, doing what she did only because
she was programmed to do it. Machines are all very well,

but not when they were once human beings.

In one way only was this good for me. Mrs Wesseling no
longer took any notice of the time I spent with Jacob—when
I was with him and for how long, and what I was doing. If
she was aware of me leaving my room to go to him at night
and returning in the morning just before it was time to get
up, she never said a word about it. And so I did as I pleased
when I pleased, though always discreetly enough not to call
attention or give offence.

I think of this as the time when Jacob and I lived together, husband and wife in all but name. We did not talk
much about the future. There was little to be said except
that we wanted to spend our lives together and must do
whatever had to be done to make it possible. Our first con-
cern was to get Jacob fit and well again, and our second was
to survive the war.

Jacob no longer thought of escaping. We decided he
should remain in hiding until the liberators arrived, then see
what could be done to make it possible for us to stay
together. If this was not allowed, if Jacob was ordered to
return to England or to join the fighting forces again, then
we would have to accept it, and wait until the war was over,
when he would come back to me. We had not the smallest
doubt that this would happen.

New love is like a star, it radiates energy. Young love
shared is a firmament. Doubt is not available. And shut
away on the farm we were living in a kind of cocoon, iso-
lated from other people. In ordinary times we would have
mixed with friends and family, telling our closest confidants
of our love, of our hopes and plans, and they would have
encouraged or dissuaded us, reminding us of everyday realities and helping keep our feet on the ground. As it was, we
lived in a bubble of paradise we made for ourselves. With
that ability common to all lovers in their first passion, we

shut our minds to every thought that in the smallest measure might spoil our time together or interfere with the fantasy of our future life. Love is blind, they say, and there is none so blind as those who will not see. So the world was as we wished it to be; and if by some mischance it were not, why then, we would make it so.

But bubbles are easily burst. We were very lucky ours remained intact for as long as it did.

Though we tried to ignore it, the war came closer every day. The winter set in cold and wet. More and more people came trudging along the lane, begging for food, often bartering with valuables that twisted the heart: heirlooms, gold lockets for keeping a snippet of a lover's hair, silver frames that once held treasured family photographs, stamp albums containing collections begun in childhood, even gold wedding bands were offered by the desperate.

From these saddening visitors we heard news from the towns. Of the Germans constantly hunting for men to work for them. Of bombing raids on the Faber works in Apeldoorn. Of Arnhem being evacuated and pillaged by the SS in retribution for the help given to the British during the battle. Of Allied paratroopers dropping near Bennekom and of fighting going on around there. Someone had heard from a friend in the Hague that a sack of potatoes cost 180 guilders (a ridiculously large sum). In Rotterdam 40-60,000 men had been taken away by the Germans. Everywhere schools were closed. The trains were not running because the railway workers had gone on strike against the Germans. No one could get shoes repaired because there was nothing to repair them with (had we anything, our visitors asked, that might be made into new soles?). In places where there were large numbers of evacuees came tension, arguments, fights even, between the evacuees and the locals because of the shortage of food and accommodation. And everywhere people were on the move, migrating from one place where life had become too difficult to another place where they had heard things were easier, safer, better. In the north, Friesland, Groningen, Drente, food was said to be plentiful. And so on the word of rumour only, people set off, their few possessions on a cart or strapped to a bicycle, in search of relief. But parts of the south had been liberated, so some progress was being made. 'But when will they reach us?' people asked. 'When will we be free of these barbarians?' 'Will it never end?' 'How long, O Lord, how long?'

And they would set off back down the lane with rueful glances at us because we had not sold them more of what they were convinced was our hoard of good things: butter, cheese, fruit, bread, meat, flour, milk. The most pathetic were the women with little babies in their arms, prepared to do anything, anything at all, for a little food for their children.

As the Winter of the Hunger wore on farmers got a bad name because so many people came to their doors pleading for help that they could not satisfy them all. Some of the visitors were violent in their desperation. In the end, fearful for their own welfare and even for their lives, many farmers turned everybody away with a hardness of heart that would have astonished and shamed them in the years before the war.

Often too, and more and more often as the days went by, we heard fighter planes—Spitfires and Hurricanes, Jacob said—roaring low overhead. If they spotted a German vehicle, or indeed anything that might belong to the enemy, they strafed it with gunfire. We saw this happen to vehicles on the main road three or four times, wrecking the vehicle and spilling its occupants, dead or wounded, onto the road. Each time we went out and waved and cheered as if the carnage were points scored in a game. And each time we left the wreckage and its dead or wounded occupants where they were. 'Let them rot in their own filth,' Mr Wesseling said, and spat, before he returned to work. If the Germans had not come along and cleared things away before nightfall, the Resistance would be there in the dark, picking over the remains for anything useful.

It was the strangest of strange times. During the day, the endless hard work of the house and farm, the worries about the war, the effort to keep my relationship with Mr and Mrs Wesseling happy. In the evening and at night in the hiding place with Jacob, the passion and tenderness of our lovemaking, the fun of our private talk and jokes, the consolation, the fantasy of our future together, the refreshment of the things we read and recited to each other from Sam's book (the only one we had in English).

Mostly while Jacob read to me or while we talked I would sew. Sewing! How much of it we did, we women, in those days. Darning the men's socks, making underwear and our dresses, turning sheets sides to middle to prolong their life, making and remaking cushions and curtains, tablecloths and chair covers, repairing tears in the men's work clothes, making new collars for their shirts from the shirt tails. On and on, an endless task. No one does this now. It was a chore, but in those long evenings with no such diversions as television or videos or CD music or computer games or even radio during the war, sewing was a restful, relaxing activity. While the hands and eyes were busy with gentle skill and a routine task the mind and tongue could wander freely. And, we were always told, the devil finds work for idle hands (another familiar saying). Not to be busy with such necessary work was regarded as all but a sin, and sewing was the least tedious task for the quiet hours. Besides, it encouraged the *gezelligheid*.

Gezellig. I do not know how to put this in English. It is such a particularly Dutch quality, something deep in our culture and our national consciousness. My dictionary offers words like 'cosy, companionable, sociable, together-

239

ness'. But *gezellig* means very much more to us than these suggest. Less nowadays, perhaps, than in my youth. Then it was almost sacred. Anyone who disturbed the *gezellig* had committed a social crime. For sure, these times with Jacob possessed for me a special kind of *gezellig*.

When he was not reading to me, we talked of books we loved. Jacob told me of English writers and books I had never heard of but which, after the war, I found and read for myself. And I told him of our Dutch writers I admired most. We sang to each other the popular songs we knew. He told me of his life in England, of his job as an electrician, of his liking for cricket, a game I had never seen and which he tried to explain without any success; it still baffles me. I told him how I thought of becoming a teacher, like my mother. And about my friends, and stories of my growing up. And so the hours went by. Though best of all I loved the hours in bed together.

Away from him, outside the hiding place, it was hard to avoid the realities. The endless grind of house- and farmwork, the stress of dealing with begging visitors, the brutality of the war, and the nagging fear that we might be raided, Jacob found and all of us arrested. The exhaustion of it! The clash of emotions warring inside me. The worries and feelings of guilt that I pushed down in to the deepest recesses of my being, hiding them from myself.

The only way I got through, the only way I survived, was by living moment to moment, second by second of the day and the night. There was only now. This instant. Allowing nothing else. No memories. No thoughts of tomorrow. Away from Jacob, I locked myself inside myself, threw myself into the work to be done so that the time away from him would pass as quickly as possible and whatever happened would affect me as little as possible. Then, back with him in the hiding place, I unlocked myself, opened to him, concentrated only on him, poured myself into him. There is no other way I know how to put it than to say: He was the whole world to me.

The strangest time, the most intense I have ever known. How could my time with Jacob ever be surpassed? Ever equalled? And life being what it is, how could it last?

Of course, it did not.

The end came on the first bright sunny day for two or three weeks. One of those nostalgic days in winter that are a memory of summer gone and a foretaste of summer to come. It reminded me of the Sunday morning in September when I saw parachutes filling the sky as I cycled home from the farm. How long ago it seemed, how different a person I was now from the girl who raced home calling out to herself, 'Free, free!'

It was such a lovely day, calm and mild, that in the morning I hung out some bed sheets to dry in the garden. It would be so nice to smell fresh air in them when we went to bed, instead of the heavy hay-smell of the barn where we usually dried them in winter time. Just before sunset, I went to take them in. Mrs Wesseling was playing the harmonium in the room which looked out onto the garden. She had opened the window, as we had opened all the windows of the house that day to air the rooms. She was still at the stage of teaching herself again, after the intervening years when she had not played, by using the lessons she had learned as a child. I cannot forget the little piece she was practising that afternoon, a simple waltz by Becucci. The music spilled around me as I took in the sheets and folded them. I had been with Jacob after the mid-day meal. He was urgent that day, full of desire, and I was still hot from the pleasure of it. He had worked so hard at getting himself fit, his wound was healing well, he was walking almost normally again, and he was becoming very strong. I remember feeling weak with happiness and impatient for night to come so that we could be together again.

241

Occupied with myself, I did not hear him come up behind me. Only knew he was there when he put his arms round my waist and hugged me to him. I let out a little scream of surprise and dropped the sheet I was folding.

'What are you doing!' I said. 'You shouldn't be out here like this. It's dangerous.' He was kissing the back of my neck and chuckling. 'What if Mrs Wesseling should see?'

But it was no use. I did not even try to break away.

'She won't see,' he said in to my ear, 'she's too busy looking at the music.'

He turned me to him, his arms round my waist, his hands on my bottom, pressing me to him, my arms round his neck, my hands holding his head. I felt him growing against me.

'You are insatiable!' I said, laughing. A word he had taught me, joking at me.

'Let's do it now,' he said, 'in the open air, right here in the garden on your clean sheets. Wouldn't that be just dandy?'

'Wonderful,' I said. 'One day.'

He said nothing for a little while. His eyes gazed at me, those dark eyes that were the first of him I ever saw and fell in love with at once. He was not laughing or joking any more.

Then he said, 'Let's dance.'

And we did. In small steps to the slow time of Mrs Wesseling's rusty fingers. Hardly moving, in fact, our feet were so clogged in the winter earth. But the rhythm of our bodies loving each other.

We circled on the spot like this. Slowly. So slowly! I remember the sun twice blinding his head in its halo. We had not turned full circle again when Jacob suddenly stopped and took a step back. An awful rigid robot step. This I felt. What I saw was his eyes. I had not taken mine from his since he had turned me to face him. Now, in the instant of his sudden stop, the life left them. He had gone from them. I heard myself say, 'Jacob?' But he gave no answer. And then he collapsed. Fell to the ground as if struck by a blow.

I have always consoled myself with the thought that at least his death was quick, and that if he suffered at all it was for the briefest moment. I cannot wish better for anyone.

Of myself, I can only say that part of me died that day too. My cries brought Mrs Wesseling running from the house and Mr Wesseling soon after. They tried to revive Jacob, but only because of the human instinct to keep life going at any cost and to prove to each other that we did everything we could before giving up. It was obvious at once to each of us that he was dead.

When that was done we covered Jacob with a sheet, and carried him in to the house. Inside, we laid him on the kitchen table. To struggle up to a bedroom with him was unthinkable. We stood round the table staring at his shrouded body.

'What can have happened?' said Mrs Wesseling.

'It must have been a heart attack,' said Mr Wesseling. 'What do we do now?'

I could say nothing. But suddenly began to tremble as if my body was shaking itself to pieces. Mrs Wesseling took me to a chair and sat me down by the fire, then brought a shawl and draped it round me.

'Hot coffee,' she said to Mr Wesseling, 'with plenty of honey. For the three of us.'

When it came I could not hold the cup. Mrs Wesseling had to feed the coffee to me with a spoon.

'We should fetch the doctor,' Mr Wesseling said.

'Why?' said Mrs Wesseling. 'What can he do?'

'A priest then. To bury him.'

'We don't know his religion,' Mrs Wesseling said. 'And

who dare we trust?'

'Then what are we to do?'

'Bury him. What else can we do?'

'Where?'

'I don't know. A corner of the garden.'

I heard all this, but as meaningless noise, like people talking in a foreign language. Nor was I thinking anything. My mind had shut off. I was conscious only of Jacob's shrouded body from which I could not take my eyes.

The Wesselings fell silent. Mrs Wesseling fed me the coffee spoonful by spoonful. I remember the tick of the *staande klok*, so loud it seemed to fill the room.

After a while, when the shakes had subsided, Mrs Wesseling said to me, 'You can't sit here like this. It isn't good. Come to your room. We'll see to everything.'

It was as if she had injected some fortifying drug, for instantly all of me seemed to come into focus, so to speak.

'No, no,' I said, straightening in the chair. 'No. We've been together through everything. I've looked after him since they brought him in to our cellar. I must look after him now.'

'But, Geertrui,' Mr Wesseling said, 'Jacob is dead.' He said this as if he thought it would be news to me.

I remember smiling at him and saying with a calmness that pleased me, 'Yes. I know. And I know we must bury him. And I know we must do it ourselves. I'll prepare him. Would you be kind enough to dig a grave? We should do it as soon as we can, don't you agree?'

When I think of it now, I'm surprised that the Wesselings accepted what this nineteen-year-old suggested without any discussion. During the next few hours Mr Wesseling made a coffin. It was no more than an oblong box, constructed of planks of wood nailed together, which he lined with tarpaulin.

While he was busy Mrs Wesseling helped me prepare

Jacob's body. We undressed and washed him. Then dressed him again in underwear, a white shirt, black trousers and a pair of black socks, everything as new as Mrs Wesseling could find. When we had done this we tidied the room, draped the table on which he lay with red velvet, and placed six white candles in tall freshly polished brass holders, three on each side of Jacob's body. We extinguished the other lights and stopped the *staande klok* precisely at midnight.

After that I collected Jacob's few personal belongings, along with his soldier's identity disk, and put them in a flour tin, which we hid in the bottom of Mrs Wesseling's linen cupboard, hoping it would survive any visits from raiding Germans so that I could send Jacob's possessions to his family after the war. Which is what I did. For myself, I kept only the paratroopers' insignia from his battle dress and a keepsake which I will tell about later.

When nothing more could be done, I persuaded the Wesselings to go to bed. For the rest of the night I kept vigil at Jacob's side. In that time I read aloud our favourite poems from Sam's book. And wept.

As soon as there was enough light to work by, Mr Wesseling went straight out in to the vegetable garden, where he began to dig a grave in the furthest corner. It took him three hours to dig deep enough to be safe. All the time Mrs Wesseling kept watch for anyone approaching the house.

When the grave was ready, Mr Wesseling brought the coffin on a handcart to the door. He and I carried it in to the room and placed it on the floor by the table. Mrs Wesseling and her husband lifted my love, my lover in to the coffin. I put one of Mr Wesseling's air-tight tobacco tins by his side. In it was a piece of card on which I had written Jacob's name, his date of death, and a brief summary of the circumstances. A precaution, in case something should happen to the three of us before we were liberated and one day someone found the grave.

Mr Wesseling had made sure that enough of the tarpaulin was left to cover Jacob's body.

Then came the most wrenching moment. Mr Wesseling closed the coffin and nailed the lid down.

That done, we stood in silence, the others feeling, I'm sure, as I did, that there was something more we should do, something we should say. How could this bleak moment be the end? After surviving the battle and his wounds and the journey to the farm and the raids by the Germans, after working so hard to get him well again, after our loving time together, how could it end as it did? How could life be so unfair?

'We must get on,' Mr Wesseling said quietly. 'There's no time.'

We carried the coffin to the handcart, Mr Wesseling at the head, his wife and I at the foot. And then a short procession from the house to the corner of the garden, Mr Wesseling pushing the bier. I did not care whether we were raided now or not. Let them come. Let them take me. Let them do what they liked. Let them kill me. What did I care about life now that Jacob was gone. Dead. I made myself say the word to myself. Dead. As we walked to the grave I wanted to be dead with him.

After the recent rain, the ground was waterlogged. Already the bottom of the grave was flooded. I closed my mind to it, shut out what we were doing. I do not even remember how we lowered the coffin in to the grave. Only taking the spade and insisting that I be the one to cover the coffin with soil. And I went on shovelling with greater and greater speed, with a growing anger that gave me strength, until Mr Wesseling took my arm and said, 'Enough. Don't exhaust yourself. I'll finish it.' At which the anger seemed to seep away, leaving me almost too weak to stand.

Mrs Wesseling put her arm round my waist and together we watched as Mr Wesseling finished filling in the grave, and then scattered the remaining soil.

'I'll lay some flagstones on it later,' Mr Wesseling said when he had finished.

'God rest him,' Mrs Wesseling said. 'This is a sad business.'

'After the liberation, we'll see he's properly laid to rest,' Mr Wesseling said. 'There's nothing more we can do for him now. And there are the animals to see to.'

He turned and went off with the pushcart to his work. And Mrs Wesseling led me back in to the house.

All day it bothered me that we had said nothing over the grave. It may seem an odd small thing to be concerned about, but the mind finds many ways to protect itself in times of grief. And so at dusk I went out alone, and stood by Jacob's grave, and recited one of his favourite poems from Sam's book, an ode by Ben Jonson. He liked especially the last two lines, which he said summed up life better than any other words he knew.

> It is not growing like a tree
> In bulk, doth make Man better be;
> Or standing long an oak, three hundred year,
> To fall a log at last, dry, bald, and sere:
>> A lily of a day
>> Is fairer far in May,
> Although it fall and die that night;
> It was the plant and flower of Light.
> In small proportions we just beauties see;
> And in short measures life may perfect be.

POSTCARD
The great object of life is sensation –
to feel that we exist.
Lord Byron

He woke late next day, ten thirty, having slept the sleep of
the dead. Only the need to pee got him up. He meant to go
back to bed, but on the way to the bathroom his kiss-and-
tell with Hille in the park came back to him so vividly that,
by the time he had relieved himself, the remembered sensations were so current on his skin, the desire for it all again
was so straining, that he couldn't help but relieve himself of
this other call of nature with a hand job that produced more
satisfaction than any for a long time. Because, he told himself, it was inspired by somebody real—yes, some *body*, and
yes, some *mind* too—not a fantasy, not a virtual reality he
couldn't lay his hands on (or lay in any way) but an actual
reality he could actually lay his actual hands on.

When he had done the make-do deed, he looked at his
sleep-rustled frig-sweated self in the mirror, smiled, winked,
and said out loud, 'Skin, skin, I do loooove skin.'

He felt happy for the first time since arriving in Holland.
He must have been happy yesterday with Hille, but he
hadn't thought whether he was or wasn't because happiness
was happening then. Do you only know you're happy when
the happiness itself is in the past? Is the cause of happiness
an active state and the knowledge of happiness a reflective
state? The kind of questions Sarah would like to discuss.
Would Hille? He knew with pleasure that the answer was
yes. After breakfast he must write to her. Not *must*. Wanted

to. A twinge of guilt at that thought. And to Sarah too, not so much *wanting to*, but must. She'd feel hurt and neglected if he didn't send her something soon, even just a postcard. Apart from a brief phone call the day he arrived to let her know he was safe, he hadn't been in touch. Sarah affected not to mind such things but he knew she did. And knew she preferred written messages to phone calls.

Anyway, he repeated to himself as he happily brushed his teeth, he felt happy. He happily stood under the shower, happily washed his hair, happily soaped himself all over, happily played the detachable showerhead down and over and up and under and round himself, happily got out of the shower and happily towelled himself, happily clipped his toe- and fingernails with the dinky scissors happily included in the compact traveller's toilet bag his mother had given him as a going-away present, happily brushed his hair, which he was happy he had had cut severely short for this trip, and happily viewed his sluiced, spruced and glowing body in the mirror.

Mirror, mirror on the wall
who is the fairest of us all? —
And you'd better say me
or I'll smash your face in.

For once he was moderately pleased by what he saw. Especially he was pleased with his dinger, which, now roused, was game for more attention. But he decided no, it must wait. His stomach needed attention even more. (Yesterday, when he arrived back from Oosterbeek, he had felt so shattered and had so much to brood on he had gone straight to bed without eating, as much to be on his own and not to have to talk to Daan as because he was tired. He had meant to get up later and eat but had fallen flat-out asleep almost as soon as he lay down.)

While dressing, he went on thinking about Hille. He had not felt like this for a girl before. For some girls he'd felt randy, yes, and there were girls who were friends but who didn't turn him on. But no girl had ever *unsettled* him, mind and body, the way Hille did. Not to mention make him feel as happy as he felt this morning. *Scareee*, he said to himself as he went down to the kitchen, and wondered how she was feeling about him today.

In the kitchen he found a note from Daan written on a large sheet of yellow paper, which was hanging like a banner from the lampshade above the counter.

> *Jacob:*
> *Change of plan.*
> *Geertrui:*
> *Asks you see her*
> *tomorrow, 11:00,*
> *not today.*
> *Me:*
> *Am with her.*
> *Back 18:00 approx.*
> *Then want to hear*
> *all about yesterday.*
> *You:*
> *Make yourself at home.*
> *Do as you wish.*
> *Need company?*
> *Ton would like it for sure*
> *that you call him.*
> *Be happy.*
> *Daan*

He said hooray, and set about making breakfast. In the fridge he found half a Galia melon wrapped in clingfilm. He ate it straight from the husk, scooping the flesh out with a spoon. A cold refreshing juicy start. Next: in Dutchland do as the Dutch do. For breakfast the Dutch do thin slices of cheese and thin slices of ham. Plenty of that in the fridge. And grainy bread in the bread bin, not quite fresh but okay to toast. Butter. And for after the cheese and ham, because there was no marmalade and anyhow he'd gone Dutch, these chocolate whatsnames, *hagelslag*, look like mouse droppings, which he'd seen Mrs van Riet scatter on her bread at breakfast the first morning and thought at the time how odd, associating such stuff with topping for cakes at teatime. Tea? He'd been surprised at how much tea the Dutch drank till, mentioning it yesterday, Hille made the history connection between the Dutch and their once but no longer colonies, now Indonesia was it?, where they must have picked up the char habit as the English picked it up during their (our, but he didn't feel it had anything to do with him or that he wanted to have anything to do with it) time ruling India. But he could only find Earl Grey, which he didn't like: too scented. Never mind. Be not daunted. Dutch coffee, why not, Douwe Egberts, in a pleasantly ominous black bag, ho ho ho and a bottle of rum. Make it in the nice dinky two-cup silver cafetière standing on the draining board. But why don't the Dutch, or this Daan Dutchman anyway, use an electric kettle instead of always boiling water for tea the slow way on the stove? (That's what he could give as a thank-you present when he left, Sarah having dinned into him that he must do such a thing as a sign of gratitude. But would it be a bit domesticky dull? More the sort of thing you'd give to someone getting married. He'd never been much good at thinking what to give people for presents. Now now, no mouse mood today: avaunt and quit my mind. Maybe Hille would help him choose something better.)

For the attention of Ms Hille Babbe:

In reply to your recent advertisement for the post of kissing-boyfriend, I hope my interview and test yesterday gave satisfaction. If you require a second interview and further tests of my qualifications, may I be so bold as to suggest that we arrange as early a date as possible as my stay in the Netherlands is an all-too-short one. I assure you of my eagerness to prove myself worthy of the vacant position.

Dear Ms Babbe:

I am pleased to inform you that you successfully completed the first test for the post we discussed yesterday and that you did so with higher marks than any other applicant has ever scored. In fact, your score was so high it is off the scale. On the basis of this achievement I would like to offer you a contract immediately. However, if you still have any reservations about taking the post, I am only too ready to cooperate in further explorations of the employment benefits I can offer. I look forward to hearing from you about another meeting as soon as is convenient to you.

Hille:

By the time you read this we will probably have talked on the phone. But there are things I want to say now which I can't say on the phone because you will be at school. (It's 11:00, and I've just got up.) Anyway, apart from that, there are some things I can say on the phone, some things I can't, and some things I can only say in writing. Not that this letter is about things I can only say in writing. I'm only writing it because I can't be with you. That is what I would like the most. Not necessarily saying anything at all. Being with you would be enough.

Since yesterday I haven't stopped thinking about yesterday. Well, that's not completely true. Can't be, can it? Was I thinking about it while I was asleep, for instance? (Don't know, can't remember. Do we think while we sleep? Is that what dreams are? Sleep thinking. Last night I slept like a log—did you?—and can't remember dreaming anything. Can you, and if 'Yes', what?) Also, I thought about what to have for breakfast (what did you have and what's your favourite breakfast?) and how to spend the day without you. (How was your day without me? Don't reply if the answer is 'Better than it would have been with you'.) But still: underneath (on top of, alongside, parallel with, whatever) those sorts of thoughts, everyday thoughts, all the time

252

in another part of my mind I was also thinking about yesterday. No, let's be accurate, not about yesterday. About you. I know, because ever since I woke up I've felt what I believe people mean by the word 'happy'.

You, yesterday, made me feel happy today.

By the way, talking of happy. I've just looked it up in an English Dictionary I found on the bookshelves in this apartment, and I discover that happy comes from an Old Norse word, happ, meaning good luck, related to Old English gehaeplic, meaning convenient, and Old Slavonic kobû, meaning fate. So, as just thinking about you makes me happ-y like never before, do you think it might be my convenient good luck that you are my fate?

There are a zillion and one things I want to ask you, from easy questions like 'How are you planning to spend the rest of your life?' to really important ones such as: 'Is it better to go with the flow or to let the flow go?', 'Whose films are funniest, Laurel and Hardy's or Charlie Chaplin's (or neither)?', and 'Will eternity be long enough to do all I want to do with you?'

I better stop before this letter gets any stupider. I could rewrite it so you wouldn't know how stupid I can be. But I'm not going to, because if we are going to get to know each other and become friends, which I hope we are, and which, to be honest, is what this letter is really trying to say, then I reckon you might as well know from the start how stupid I can be.

I'll make a guess: you like poetry. Me too. So I've written one specially for you.

> *Hille:*
>
> > *for you*
> > *earth plays*
> > *sky tunes*
> > *water sings*
> > *stones rock*
> > *time burns*
> > *fire quenches*
> > > *in me:*
> > > > *Jacob*

253

'Ton? Hi, this is Jacob.'

'Jacques! Hey, hallo!'

'Did I wake you up?'

'No no. It's okay.'

'I was wondering . . .'

'Yes?'

'I'm on my own today.'

'You're not to visit Geertrui?'

'No. Change of plan. And Daan is with her. The thing is, I need to post a letter, and I haven't done that before, in Holland I mean, and I thought you might . . . and, well, like you said, remember? . . . show me a bit of Amsterdam.'

'What time is it?'

'About twelve thirty. If it's a problem—'

'No, no problem. Good idea. Just thinking. Can you be outside Daan's place at two o'clock?'

'Two o'clock. Yes.'

'If it isn't raining. Wait in the apartment if it is.'

'Two o'clock outside Daan's place if it isn't raining. It isn't now. A nice day, actually. Sun's out.'

'Is it? Good. Okay. I'll be there. With a surprise.'

'A surprise? What sort of surprise?'

'A surprise without legs. And, Jacques . . .'

'Yes?'

'I'm very glad you called. *Tot ziens.*'

Dear Sarahgran,

Lordy but don't time fly! How's the hip? Wish you were here? I'm glad I am. As Kilgore Trout is wont to utter: Life goes on. I've seen AF's house (not <u>anything like</u> what I expected, but more of this as of the rest later), bits of Haarlem, bits of Amsterdam, also some Rembrandts (great), the Van Riets, and assorted Dutchjongvolk.

Best of all was yesterday. The ceremony was wonderful. There were times I wanted to cry. Thousands of people, lots of them young locals. But you know, you've seen it. Beautiful weather.

254

None of the embarrassing naff stuff I'd expected. No gung-ho
stuff. No flag waving stuff. No hero stuff either. And even the
religious stuff was all right. And you know how much I hate all
that holy guff stuff. Even sang the hymns, can you believe. I
mean <u>hymns</u>! They usually bring me out in spots. This time they
brought me out in smiles. But in a sad-happy kind of way. It was
more like a big family party than a dirge for the dead. There
must have been men there who knew grandad. Now it's all over,
I wish I'd had the gump to find one and talk to him. Why do I
<u>always</u> not think of the best things till <u>afterwards</u>?!

Stood on grandad's grave. That's when I wanted to cry the
most. Met two Dutch people who laid flowers on his grave, a girl
and her brother, Hille and Wilfred Babbe. Took photos for you.
Had a meal with Hille (she's 17) afterwards. Hope to meet her
again. Don't jump to conclusions. But she's pretty terrific. Yes,
I'll be careful. I know, I know, don't say it: Don't be too
impulsive, don't wear your heart on your sleeve. Your face, my
thane, is as a book wherein men may read strange matters. I
always do try to listen to what you tell me for my own good. But
I'm not so sure you're right about this. Or maybe you are right
and I don't care any more. Don't know why. Something to do
with this trip. Meeting Geertrui. The ceremony yesterday. I don't
mean I think it's okay to show your deepest feelings to everyone
all the time. But I am beginning to think you can hide them too
much and too often. Isn't it better sometimes to take a risk and
show what you feel, when the feelings and the other person are
important to you? Hiding them, holding them in, pretending to
feel something else than what you do feel—that can't be good.
Maybe I'm confused about it, but at least, you have to agree, I
am <u>trying</u>, which is another of the things you keep on telling me I
have to do! (No megamouse moods so far, by the way. Just one
brief flash of a retreating tail.)

This afternoon, a gay guy I met who knows Daan van Riet,
whose apartment (Geertrui's actually, it's very nice) I'm staying
in for reasons I'll explain later, too interesting-complicated for a
letter now, is going to show me some of Amsterdam. You see how

well looked after I am.

I'll send a card to the folks this afternoon. (Are you sending mine as usual? I'll miss it if you don't. Can't break the flow after all these years. You'll have sent this week's to the Van Riets', I guess.)

Got to go and enjoy myself some more. You know how it is with us tourists, one endless round of revelry. This is just to let you know I'm okay, thriving, enjoying myself. Lots of traveller's tales to tell you when I get back.

Your loving grandson,
Jacob.

As the clocks of Amsterdam chimed two in their tuneful jingle, Jacob stood on the wooden steps outside the apartment. A light cool sunny day with a gentle breeze puffing down the narrow street. His kind of weather, warm enough to feel comfortable, cool enough to freshen. A few people about, mostly locals by the look, but some tourists, wandering like lost souls in this street where there were no shops or attractions of the kind that make tourists feel easy.

He heard Ton calling his name. It seemed to come from below Jacob's feet. As indeed it did, for then he saw Ton climbing out of the canal.

'What are you doing there?' Jacob said, as Ton took him by the shoulders and gave him the usual three-barrelled greeting, the third kiss brushing his lips and throwing Jacob into a small confusion of pleasure.

'Picking you up,' Ton said when that was over, 'with your surprise without legs.'

A boat of course, a commodious dinghy with a smart outboard motor clipped to its stern, a pretty little craft, spotlessly maintained, its wooden hull the colour of fresh chestnut gleaming with varnish, bright brass fittings, deep blue waterproof cushions making a sofa of the bench fitted across the waist, a triangular pennant fluttering from its bow with the crest of Amsterdam on it: a blood-red ground with a black stripe through the middle on which three white 'x's in a row, a cross for each of the disasters that afflicted the city in the long ago: fire, black death and flood. The name was painted black on white on the prow: *Tedje*.

'Wow!' Jacob said. 'Very swish. Yours?'

'I wish! A rich friend's. The best way to see Mokum.'

'Mokum?'

'Amsterdammers' *bijnaam* for the city. Byname?'

'Nickname? Like Londoners used to call London the smoke.'

'Ah! I've just thought. You can swim?'

'Could probably make it across the canal.'

'That's okay. Let's go.'

Ton had brought a map so that Jacob could follow their route. They began by phutt-phutting out of the narrow water of the Oudezijds Kolk, past the Weepers' Tower and under the bridge that carried Prins Hendrikkade, turning left in to the broad water that took them past the cathedral front of the Central station, where trams and buses, bicycles and people swarmed, and (Jacob feeling smug in their private superiority) past the sleek glass-roofed tourist boats waiting for customers, before turning left in to the first of the spider-web canals, the Singel, but then immediately right under the bridge in to Brouwersgracht, which Jacob could see from the map connected the tops of all the canals of the western part of the old city, on past the start of Herengracht and Keizersgracht, before turning left in to Prinsengracht.

'My favourite,' Ton said. 'The most friendly. More for ordinary people. Lots of houseboats at this end, and over there, you see, to our right, the streets of the Jordaan, where the working people, servants and people like that, used to live, and where I live. I have two rooms in a friend's house. And you see the tower of the church ahead on the left?'

'Yes.'

257

'The Westerkerk.'

'Near Anne Frank's house.'

'Daan told me how you're mad about her. I thought you might like to see her house from the water.'

When they chugged by, the usual queue, on this now warm afternoon, three or four deep, lined up along the street for a hundred and fifty metres or so, reaching almost beyond the church to the square beside Raadhuisstraat, the busy main road to the Dam which Jacob remembered stumbling across as he fled Anne's house only four days before. A year seemed to separate then from now.

'And opposite, over there,' Ton was saying and pointing, 'there's a little shop, the best place to buy fresh coffee. A lot of good little shops around here. For only cheese or only wine or only anything. One of the things I like so much about Amsterdam, the little shops everywhere, selling all sorts of things. One shop near here sells only olive oil. They treat it like the best wines, which you must taste before buying. And also, everything is mixed up. An expensive art shop next to an old clothes shop, and a cycle repair shop next to a porno bookshop, a hand-made shoe shop next to a shop that sells only special kinds of metal things. All of Amsterdam, I mean this part, the spider's web, is like a big village where you can get anything you want and where ordinary people still live, not just rich people or tourists in hotels or no one at all, like in the centre of many cities.

'In fact, I don't think Amsterdam is a city. It is and it isn't, which is like everything here. And it isn't modern. I mean the buildings aren't. Look at them. Most of them were built hundreds of years ago. But it *is* a modern city too, in the way people live and what you can do.'

By now Jacob was settled comfortably on the blue-cushioned sofa-bench, where he had a clear view ahead and wasn't bothered by the sound of the engine phuttering behind them, Ton to his right steering with little shining brass levers for the engine and a miniature brass ship's wheel for the rudder attached to the hull. He lolled and began to luxuriate in the way you can only in a small open boat as it noses gently through calm water on a sunny day. But when he had done this before it had been through countryside during holidays with his family on the Norfolk Broads or in a longboat on English waterways. He had never floated, lolling and luxuriating, through city streets. Through countryside it seemed natural, part of the surroundings. But here it was like Ton said, not one thing nor the other. Not country but not city. Water but not a river. A way through the city but not a road. Not á river, not a road, and yet both. He lolling and loafing, while on either side cars and trucks and cycles and people on foot careered. It was as if two surfaces of life, two ways of living, rubbed together: water rubbing against brick (the sides of the canal were brick, most of the buildings were brick, and even the canal-side roads were brick cobbles); he and Ton in waterborne idleness and to either side of them the roadborne hustle of people busyness. Other boats passed them: sightseeing launches with passengers gawking, ugly little white plastic pedal boats, usually propelled by pairs of laddish tourists who must always shout hello and gaggle, a patrolling waterpolice boat, hunky work boats of one sort and another. Their bow waves set *Tedje* rocking.

By now, well down the length of Prinsengracht, along a straight stretch where there were few houseboats, the canal seemed wider, more open, and glistened. Perhaps it was the angle of the sun and the bright blue of the sky above and the breeze fribbling the leaves in their early stages of turning to autumn, or his viewpoint on the water, looking up at the valley of buildings on either side, but for the first time Jacob *saw*, actually took notice of the trees that lined the edges of the canals. They clothed the water on both sides, some tall and full-bodied, some small and tender and young, some in stages of middle-age, an extended family, lacing with greens the reds and browns and greys of the buildings with their upright oblong windows, their frames painted white. The trees softened the flat-faced facades which rose never more than four or five storeys, topped with decorative peaks and gables, often painted white or cream, which at first Jacob thought were much alike, but now he began to notice were varied in a multitude of flutters and curlicues and steps and scrolls and sheer slides. They finished off the buildings like wigs and hats and cowls on eighteenth-century gentlemen. And these shoulder-to-shoulder, cheek-by-jowl parades of buildings were, he thought, like books stacked tightly on a shelf, various thicknesses, various but not greatly different heights. A library of houses. And so beautiful. It was like suddenly looking at someone you hadn't taken much notice of before, hadn't even liked, and seeing that he, she, was very attractive. (He or she—which? Strong upstanding bricky maleness and curving flowing liquidy femaleness. Ton's neither, both, everything, and Amsterdam not being what it seemed.)

'I'm beginning to see what you mean about this place,' Jacob said. 'It's lovely.' He laughed. 'I could fall for it. Maybe I *am* falling for it.'

'I'm pleased. Join the club! I told you this was the best way to see Mokum.'

'You've always lived here?'

'No no. But wanted to from the day I first saw it when I was little, about five or six. I was born in a small town in the south.'

'Your parents still live there?'

'And my two sisters and four brothers.'

'Seven of you?'

'A good Catholic family.'

'Where do you come?'

'The youngest.'

'What does your father do?'

'As well as breed, you mean? He's a *tandarts*, a dentist.

And also a professional homophobe.' Ton chuckled and added, '*Doe maar gewoon, dan doe je al gek genoeg.*'

'Meaning?'

'Something like: Act normal, because that is crazy enough. Don't be any different to anyone else. Everybody must be the same. The worst side of us Dutch. My father's favourite motto.'

'And you aren't normal?'

'Not in my father's eyes. Never forgiven himself for breeding a queer. Keeps asking my mother what they did so wrong that they produced me. Was as happy when I left home as I was to leave. Can't handle that his friends might meet me. The way he behaves, you'd think it would mean the end of him. He even pays me to stay away.'

'You mean, he pays you not to go home?'

'Home? Where is home? This is the only place where I've ever belonged. Amsterdam is my home. These few streets and canals are my home. And yes, my wonderful father pays much money to keep me here. Well, he can afford it. There's a price for everything, isn't that right? And the price for being a homo-hater should be as high as anyone can pay.'

'Your mother. What about her?'

'She visits me. Every three or four weeks we spend a weekend together. Have a great time. Shops. Nightclubs. Films. Music. We get on well. We always did. She was the first person I came out to.'

'How old?'

'Fourteen.'

'What did she say?'

'Enjoy.'

'She didn't!'

'Why not?'

'Can't imagine most mothers saying that. Not from families like yours, anyway.'

'My mother is not most mothers.'

'But your father—'

'She loves him. Don't ask me why.'

'Hard to understand why some people marry the people they do.'

'Marriage!'

'You don't like it?'

'Do you?'

'Why not? With the right person.'

'Don't you think it's strange? Two people swearing to stay together for the rest of their lives and not to love anybody else—'

'Not in that way—'

'Whatever *that* way is!'

'Don't ask me.'

'I don't believe there is a *that way*. Do you? Friends. Can't do without them. Lovers. For sure, yes please. Someone to live with while it's right, while it works. Okay. But for ever? Never. Nothing is for ever.'

At that moment they were passing under a bridge, which the map told Jacob he should remember, and that in the reach of canal beyond it they would pass the house where he sheltered from the rain and where Alma rescued him.

'Could you pull over and stop for a minute?' he said, and explained about Alma.

It was easy to spot the house across the canal. It and its next-door neighbour were the only ones with the steps up to their front doors recessed in to the building. All the others had them outside, sideways on. And the profusion of plants around Alma's ground-level windows.

'Nice to live at this end of the canal,' Ton said. 'Also expensive.'

'I suppose I should have returned the money Alma gave me and thanked her for her help.'

'So? Do it now. And you should take her something.'

'Yes.'

'How about some chocolates?'

'Sounds good.'

'Come with me.'

They tied up the boat and walked in to Vijzelgracht, passing the café where Alma had taken him.

'Panini,' Ton said. 'Everybody knows it.'

And a paper shop with postcards on a spinner outside.

'Hang on,' Jacob said. 'I need to buy a card for my parents and post it with some letters.'

It was easy. Mostly the cards were the expected views of the city. But one took Jacob's eye. A back view of two Amsterdam police in their shirt sleeves on a sunny day. One was a podgy woman, her girth emphasised by her belt, hung about with holster gun and phone and bits and pieces of cop gear. Her colleague was goosing her bum.

He could buy stamps there too. He wrote a quick message on the card. *Well. Happy. Looked after. Hope you're all okay. With love, Jacob.* By which time Ton had discovered a postbox nearby on Prinsengracht.

Then a cake and chocolate shop, Holtkamp's, the sort of place Sarah would have liked. A little old-fashioned, women assistants in black dresses with white trim, very polite. Hardly room for more than four or five customers. Ton ordered in Dutch. A fancy little box with flowery decorations and ribbons. An assortment of scrumptious chocs, some very dark brown, some light brown and milky, some white, square, triangular, one a little ball, one with a sliver of glazed fruit on top, one lime green, one sharp orange, one bright lemon. Fifteen in all. And a price that would have paid for a meal at Panini, which, when he saw it flick up on the till, made Jacob catch his breath.

'Too much?' Ton asked, grinning.

Jacob shook his head. 'What the hell. She deserves it.'

They returned to the boat and took it across the canal to a mooring close to Alma's place. The day was humid by now, the sky veiled with haze.

'I'll wait here,' Ton said. 'The Dutch don't call without arrangement. Well, older people anyway. But she'll be happy to see you, I'm sure.'

She was. Jacob reached through the protective grille and tapped on the window-door of her apartment. When Alma opened up her face broke into a wide smile.

'Ach! It's you. Have you been robbed again?'

He laughed. Some people make you feel good the instant you see them.

'Just passing,' he said handing her the box of chocolates, 'and brought you this to thank you for helping me.'

'There was no need.' She took the box with obvious pleasure. 'You've been to Holtkamp's. Come in, come in.'

'No, I won't, thanks. I'm with a friend. In his boat. He's waiting. He's showing me the canals.'

'You've made a friend. Good. And you've recovered from your ordeal?'

'I'm fine. Staying with Daan. You remember? You phoned him for me.'

'I remember. Wait a moment before you go.'

She disappeared in to the depths of her cave. Jacob stooped to see what he could of the apartment. A small square room with a blond polished wood floor, bookshelves on the walls, a large black television and sound system, a round antique dining table in rich dark wood, a comfortable armchair by a mock black-metal pot-bellied stove. A neat, tidy, cosy nest.

When Alma returned she handed him a paper bag with four of the chocolates in it.

'For you and your friend so that you can share with me.'

'But they're for you.'

'I couldn't eat them all myself. It would be greedy. I like it that you have some too.'

'Oh, and I nearly forgot,' Jacob said, digging into his jeans pocket. 'The money you loaned me.'

'No. It was nothing. If you don't need it, give it to someone else who does. The boy in the red cap perhaps.'

They smiled at each other.

'And,' she said, 'before you return to England, come and have coffee. I'd like to hear of your adventures. I'll write my telephone number so you may call before.'

He felt honoured.

'Thanks,' he said. 'I'd better go.'

'Goodbye. Enjoy yourself.'

On impulse, he leaned down towards her, Alma presented her cheek after only the slightest hesitation, and he gave her the regulation three-barrelled kiss as formally as he could manage from his awkward position, bent almost double and supporting himself on the window frame. But he managed without mishap and was pleased with himself for doing it.

With Ton again, they chugged along at the engine's slowest pace, mused and brooded, joked and flirted, added new anecdotes to their growing anthology of each other's history. And now and then sat in silence, Ton gazing at Jacob and Jacob taking in the view.

From Prinsengracht they floated through the warm afternoon via Reguliersgracht in to Keizersgracht, from Keizersgracht via Bouwersgracht again in to Herengracht, down Herengracht in to the Amstel, and toured the river before returning to Singel, and so back to Daan's.

'We've been threading the maze,' Jacob said as they re-entered the Oudezijds Kolk.

'Cruising the spider's web,' Ton said.

They laughed together.

Was there, Jacob thought, anything better than getting to know someone who you felt all the time you already knew, as if, in some alternative life, you had always been the closest and best of friends.

GEERTRUI

Two months after Jacob's death I knew for certain that I was pregnant with our child. I told no one. To have done so would have made my life unbearable. Certainly, Mrs Wesseling would have turned me out of the house. And the child would have been taken from me when it was born.

You cannot know nowadays, perhaps cannot even imagine, what a disgrace it was then for a woman to become pregnant outside marriage. It was regarded as a sin of the worst kind. If a Catholic, the woman was usually sent to an institution run by nuns. There she was made to suffer for her sin and the baby was removed from her immediately after the birth. For the next few days, it was brought to her for breast feeding. Sometimes she was even blindfolded so that she could not see her child, and her hands were strapped to the bed so that she could not hold it. Then a nun put the baby to her breast while it suckled. Only a mother can truly know what cruelty this was. As soon as possible, the child was given away for adoption or sent to an orphanage, where its life would never be anything but vile. It would bear the damnation, the stigma, of illegitimacy, of bastardy, for the rest of its life. The men, the fathers, suffered none of this opprobrium, of course. Never was it more truly said that the sins of the fathers were visited on the children. Only we should add: and on their mothers.

Protestant women suffered a less brutal but no less cruel fate. Often they were sent to relatives or friends far enough away from home to be out of sight of gossiping neighbours. After the birth, if the child was not adopted or sent to an orphanage, it would be brought up as her own by one of the mother's relatives. I have known people who found out only when they were grown up that those they thought were their parents were in fact their grandparents, or that someone they thought was an aunt or older sister was in fact their mother.

The alternative, which was tried by many more women than we ever hear about, was either self-induced miscarriage or the humiliating obscenity of an illegal abortion with all the life-threatening horrors, physical, emotional, mental, yes and spiritual too, that went with it. Those who survived the ordeal carried with them like an incurable disease for the rest of their lives the feelings of guilt and wounded self-respect that fate and the people among whom they lived had inflicted on them.

I cannot help thinking that no society, no nation, no religion of any kind anywhere that enshrines such a moral code and imposes it on its people can be called civilised or, except it change, deserves allegiance.

Even in ordinary peacetime I would never have allowed myself to be treated in this way. But as things were, trapped in the ever-increasing chaos of the weeks before our liberation, with my parents out of reach, no doctor I could trust, no friends nearby who might help me, and the grief of Jacob's death still pulling me down in to the grave, I felt the despair and panic of those who are lost, abandoned, helpless. And because it was Jacob's baby, I knew I would never give it to others or to an unborn death. It was all I could ever have of him now. And at the times of my deepest despair it was only for this child who was part of him that I kept myself alive, walking the earth, and did not bury myself with Jacob's body.

In my grief after Jacob's death I could not bear to clear up the hiding place where we had spent our 'married' time, and pleaded with Mr Wesseling to leave it alone till I was strong enough to do it myself. He agreed, fearful of worsen-

267

ing my unhappiness, I think. And there I would sit, for hours sometimes, in a kind of waking coma, holding little items Jacob had used, his drinking mug, his knife and fork, his shaving brush, and reading the poems we had loved. Also writing him long long letters, as if he had only gone away to some unknown destination and would return one day, when he would want to know what I had done and what I had thought about while we were apart, and I would give him my letters to read.

In this way, by the time I knew I was pregnant the hiding place had become a sanctuary. A refuge, a place of safety and, yes, a holy place, a shrine to my lost love, where I prayed for help and comfort to the God who by then I knew is not God but is the unnameable unknowable source of all our frail being.

Besides my grief, which because of my nature I could express only in private (I detest displays of personal emotion in public), I had to hide what I knew of my condition from the only two people I saw every day and on whom I depended for food and shelter, for all my needs. And the hiding place was the only part of the house where I could be myself, could relax and let my feelings show, where I could weep and wail or brood or curl up on the bed, Jacob's bed, in which the smell of him lingered, *our* bed, and be sure no one would observe me or unexpectedly intrude. So precious did it become that when I think of all the rooms where I have lived in my life, that is the one I remember with most affection and the only one I regret I cannot see again—that roughly made, cold, barely furnished, hay-scented, cow-horned hiding place.

Another of the English sayings father and I learned: The darkest hour comes before the dawn. So it was for me.

I was in the hiding place one dreary evening in March 1945, brooding on the impossibility of my plight, when I heard someone climbing the ladder. My instant foolish wishfulling thought was that it was Jacob. But as instantly I knew it could not be and wondered who it was, for Mrs Wesseling never even came in to the cowhouse now and if Mr Wesseling wanted me, he called from below. By the time I had stirred myself to go and see, Dirk was there, standing in the doorway, darkly glowing in the light from a single candle burning in a jar on the table, his face so welcome and familiar and yet also the face of a stranger. Events separate people quite as much as time and distance. What has happened to one in the absence of the other makes foreigners of them. In the few weeks since we had last seen each other Dirk and I had lived through experiences that changed us. Neither was a youth any longer. We had entered into a new, adult phase. We both recognised this as soon as we looked in to the other's eyes before a word was said. And so our greeting was quieter than it would have been before, a little wary, but more tender too.

As we embraced, I remember saying with genuine relief, for here was a friend in need, 'You're home!' and Dirk saying, 'Yes, I'm home.' (What obvious things we say at such times!) And, as I released him and stood back, saying, 'Is Henk with you?', Dirk replying, 'No. I thought he would be here.'

They had been doing something for the Resistance about which Dirk said he would tell me later. It had gone wrong. They had run for their lives, had decided they should split up, and agreed to meet again at the farm. It was months before we heard that Henk had been caught and shot. But the night Dirk returned and until we heard the truth, we kept hope alive by telling each other that he was sure to be hiding somewhere, that Henk was a survivor, and that once the war was over he would come back to us. I never really believed it. But at such times one pretends, even to oneself, or life would not be possible. As one of your poets says, 'Human kind cannot bear very much reality.'

We sat down at the table then, just as Jacob and I had

sat so often. Dirk explained he had seen his parents before coming to me. 'But, Geertrui,' he said, 'what has happened to Mama?' Far from the joyful welcome he had expected, her coddling him, her treating him as if he were still a boy, she had been cool, almost bitter. 'Ah, so you've decided to come back, have you!' she had said. 'You walk out on us when we need you most and now you come back, you're in trouble or you want something, is that it?' He had tried to explain but she wouldn't listen. Even while he was still talking she had gone to her harmonium and started to play. And then Dirk used the words I had often said to myself when I watched her playing: 'It was as if she was not with us any longer but living in another world.'

It had always been obvious to me that Dirk was his mother's boy. That was one reason why I had been uneasy about accepting him as a serious boyfriend. I do not think he had ever understood this about himself. But the distress he now felt at his mother's withdrawal made everything clear. I tried to comfort him by saying that I thought his mother was suffering a nervous breakdown. Awful things were happening. His mother's way of coping was to withdraw inside herself. She had been under great stress all through the occupation. Our arrival had made it worse. Then her son, the most precious part of her life, had suddenly disappeared. That she might never see him again was more than she could bear. So she had shut herself up to protect herself. Now she behaved towards him as she did because she could not face the hurt of losing him again. As for the harmonium, perhaps when she played she really was living in another world, the happy world she had known as a child when she first learned to play, where none of these terrible things existed. When the war was over she would recover and he would have his mama back again.

When Dirk had pulled himself together, he asked about Jacob. His father had told him what had happened, but only briefly. He wanted me to tell him more. The tears came almost as soon as Dirk spoke Jacob's name. I had told no one about us or about Jacob's death because there had been no one to talk to. It was bottled up inside, and as soon as the bottle was opened everything that had happened between us came pouring out like champagne when the bottle has been shaken before the cork is popped.

What a need we humans have for confession. To a priest, to a friend, to a psychoanalyst, to a relative, to an enemy, even to a torturer when there is no one else, it doesn't matter so long as we speak out what moves within us. Even the most secretive of us do it, if no more than writing in a private diary. And I have often thought as I read stories and novels and poems, especially poems, that they are no more than the authors' confessions transformed by their art into something that confesses for us all. Indeed, looking back on my lifelong passion for reading, the one activity that has kept me going and given me the most and only lasting pleasure, I think this is the reason that explains why it means so much to me. The books, the authors who matter the most are those who speak to me and speak for me all those things about life I most need to hear as the confession of myself.

But that is an aside. I meant only to explain you that I told everything to Dirk that night, not omitting how I was pregnant with Jacob's child. He listened without interruption, without moving, without any display of emotion. You must remember that this was the man who only a few weeks before had declared his love for me and had asked me to marry him. My story must have given him terrible pain. I shall always be grateful to him for listening with a sympathy rare even from a friend who had not his reason to feel hurt by it.

When I was finished there was silence. I remember a cow coughing below us. The thump of a large gun in the not so far distance. The blink and sizzle as a little bubble of water leaked from the impure wartime wax in to the flame of the candle on the table beside us. It would be a cliché to say that the world stood still, or that my heart stopped. It takes one of those best authors I was talking about to find words that are fresh and renewing for such a moment. Well, I am a reader, not an author, so you must put up with what words I can come by in these, my weary last days. Perhaps the word I need, for us is *gaping,* for you is 'hiatus'. (And— a silly pun! your grandfather loved puns—I do assure you this hiatus did gape at us!) All I can say is that something hung in the air for a while and that we, Dirk and myself, were suspended with it, hovering, waiting, trying to catch the meaning of it, its <u>significance</u>, as we dangled in the void.

It was Dirk, my dear dear always reliable Dirk, who broke the silence.

'Will you marry me?' he said.

And now, truly, I did gape at him.

'Please,' I said, 'don't joke with me. Not today. And never about this.'

He reached across the table, brushed the tears from my face, took my hand from my mouth, held it in his, and said again, 'Will you marry me?'

I said, 'You cannot mean it.'

'I do,' he said.

'Why?' I said. 'After what has happened.'

'I must make two conditions,' he said, as he always was: businesslike, to the point. No wonder his building company did so well. 'First, that you tell no one that the child is Jacob's. We will always say it is mine. And the second is that we begin our life together tonight.'

I looked at him in the eyes, this man I had known since childhood, with his straight Dutch honesty, this man who was my beloved brother's closest friend, and as I stared at him learned something about myself I had not known till then, something I would rather were not so. I can be calculating. Behind my emotions, let's say—whatever they were, however strongly felt—there was a part of me that remained dispassionate, detached, and which assessed like a mathematician manipulating figures, what was best for me to do next in the circumstances I found myself. This was the first time I was conscious of doing it. And what my inner calculator told me was that here was my best chance. Perhaps my only chance. I even calculated something else: that Dirk needed me as much as I needed him. Because of his mother's possessive treatment, he learned this about himself that night just as I learned how calculating I can be. He needed to break free, and I could help him do it. So there it is: I was fond of him, I enjoyed his company, he was competent and strong, he loved me deeply, far more than I could ever love him.

However, that part of me I came to think of in future years as mevrouwtje Uitgekookt held me back from saying yes at once. (*Uitgekookt* means 'shrewd' or even 'cunning', and when we add the suffix *tje* to a word we make a diminutive of it, which means I called my calculating self Little Mrs Shrewd. Or little mevrouw Smartass, as my grandson Daan puts it, he having watched too many American television programmes for his own good or for his use of the English language.) You must give an appearance of hesitation, mevrouwtje Uitgekookt told me. It isn't wise to give yourself away so quickly or so easily. This man will appreciate you all the better if you show some respect for your dignity and require the same of him. And so I thanked Dirk, and told him how astonished I was by his offer and how happy it made me (both were true and not pretence), but that I could not make up my mind right there and then (which was not true, I knew I would say yes). Would he agree that we should both think it over for twenty-four hours? After all, it would be a very big step for both of us. For him especially, as he would be taking on a child who was not his, as well as a wife for whom he knew he had not been her first choice.

Dirk agreed. And I could see he was pleased by what I had said. It was only after we had been married for a while that I found out that Dirk had always known about mevrouwtje Uitgekookt, just as I had always known that he was a big businesslike mama's boy. He said it was one of the things he liked most about me. 'I would not have married a woman who wasn't *scherpzinnig*.' (Sharp-witted—you would say smart, I think.) From him, this was the best compliment my Dirk could pay me. I hope, dear Jacob, you begin to see why we were such good companions for all our married life until Dirk died two years ago. For forty-eight years we always tried to be honest with each other, and anyhow, saw through each other so completely that there could be no pretence.

The following night we met in the hiding place. Little mevrouw Smartass had been working overtime. Yes, I told Dirk, I would marry him, do so gladly and with gratitude. But that I too had some conditions.

My first was that he remain here on the farm until the end of the war and not go off again to fight or work with the Resistance. After everything that had happened, after the separations, after the deaths, with the many dangers that still surrounded us, enough was enough. If he was to be my husband, he must stay with me.

My second condition was that, whatever he did after the liberation, he would not ask me to live on the farm. I knew I could never be a farmer's wife.

The third condition. I could understand, I said, why he wanted to sleep with me. Because then we could always honestly say we had slept together. We would not have to say exactly when. People would assume the child was his. We would not have to say anything about it. Well, I would go to bed with him, I would sleep with him in the literal sense. But nothing more. To do more until after the baby was born would be impossible, an offence against what I felt for Jacob and our child. And, it seemed to me, an offence against Dirk also. Nor, I added, could I go to bed with him here in the hiding place because for me this would always be the place where I lived with Jacob. So my third condition was that he must now help me pack away everything I associated with Jacob, and then we must dismantle the hiding place completely. This part of my life must be cleared up by both of us working together before I could begin my life with him.

I knew, I said, that I was in no position to impose any conditions on him, but only if he could accept these three would I agree to marry him, because unless he could accept them I knew we would never respect each other or be happy together.

We talked for a long time after that, three or four hours I think. Not because Dirk had reservations or could not accept what I asked. He accepted at once. We talked for so long because there were many questions about ourselves and our future that had to be discussed. And both of us being talkers, how could we do otherwise! I won't tell you of this, it has nothing to do with what I must tell you about myself and your grandfather. But I'm sure you can imagine it. And we could have gone on through the night, but if we were to fulfil Dirk's condition that we sleep together at once and my condition that the hiding place be cleared away, we had to leave off and set to work. It took us another two or three hours to complete the task. (How much quicker it always is to destroy something than it is to build it. Dirk and Henk had spent two whole days constructing the hiding place, not to mention the time spent making it as comfortable as possible.)

That done, we went in to the house to prepare ourselves. Mrs Wesseling had already gone to bed: Mr Wesseling was sitting by the fire, though it was well past his usual bedtime, pretending to doze but really, I could tell, waiting to see Dirk again. I went to my room. The two men sat talking for

275

an hour (I listened impatiently to the old grandfather clock striking). Then their footsteps on the stairs. Their final whispered goodnights. Their bedroom doors. And more waiting as the clock struck two more quarters.

I was lying in bed all this time in order, of course, to keep warm. It was a dreadfully cold night. And as so often when you are waiting anxiously for someone, I was on edge, annoyed at being kept waiting. Until you begin to think they will never come, and you drift off to sleep. As I did that night. The next thing I knew, Dirk was gently shaking my shoulder. I jumped, startled out of my sleep. The bed creaked loud enough to waken the whole house. We had to stifle our giggles. And so our life together began as I am glad to say it continued, with laughter.

Dirk and I were married in secret by the local mayor, a man we knew we could trust, two weeks later. It had to be in secret or Dirk would have been taken by the Germans and sent to forced labour. Our part of the Netherlands was liberated soon afterwards, in April. Jacob's child, my daughter Tessel, was born the following August. You know her as mevrouw van Riet, Daan's mother. You might say that she is your Dutch mother. And that Daan is therefore your Dutch brother. Jacob's body was exhumed and buried in the battle cemetery at Oosterbeek later that year.

I kept my word to my husband Dirk, and, while he was alive, never told anyone who Tessel's father really was. But when he died two years ago, I thought it right that Tessel should know. This was not an easy thing for her. But I have always believed it is best to know the truth, though it may be hard and hurts. I wanted my daughter to know the truth of her history. It matters where you come from and who began your journey, even though someone else fathered you along the way. Just as it matters that you know your place in the world. Besides, as I say, there is that urge to confession, the desire to tell our most secret stories. And a lie, even if it

is a lie only by silence, by omission as our Catholic neighbours would say, can consume your soul like a cancer.
Having a cancer of the body is enough for me. I wanted the
cancer of an unspoken truth lifted from my conscience
before I died.

There was someone else to whom I had to make
confession. Your grandmother, Sarah. I knew, of course,
that I had offended against her. It is no excuse to say that
your grandfather Jacob and I were young, nor that the
strains and conditions of the war were to blame, nor that we
both intended to be as forthright and careful as we could be
with Sarah when the war was over. These things were so.
But they did not acquit us, were not a vindication, were no
justification.

When I invited your grandmother to visit me, I had it in
mind to tell her. I said nothing of what you, Jacob, now
know about my illness and my coming death. Then she
wrote back to say she could not come but asked that I invite
you instead. Now that you were grown up enough to understand, she wanted you to visit Jacob's grave and meet me so
that you could hear the story of your grandfather's last days
'from the horse's mouth', as she put it (another of those
familiar sayings my father and I learned).

I was upset that I would not be able to make my
confession to Sarah face to face. I could have written it for
her. But to confess to someone in writing is not the same.
To speak face to face is to share the blunt emotion without
protection. Its rawness cannot be evaded. There is no
hiding place. The guilty teller must endure the wrath or
sadness, sorrow or reprisal, tears or scorn of the offended
listener. Must endure also, if they are offered, the humiliation of receiving the listener's understanding and forgiveness. Nothing is more cauterising than those two worst of
penances. Rage from the other somehow accepts that we are
as we are, no need for change, leaves us feeling virtuous,
vindicated, proves we have done the right thing. But calm

forgiveness and quiet, tolerant understanding confirm our mistake, reflect back in to us our wrong, provide no escape, and carry expectation of amendment. All this we avoid when we write our story and send it off to be read, at arm's length so to speak, and out of harm's way.

It was Daan's suggestion that I make my confession to you. You cannot tell Sarah, he said, so tell it to her grandson. Visit the sins of the fathers on him, it's his inheritance, as yours is mine. Let him do what he wants with it. He'll manage, just as I have. (You will know by now about Daan's kind of jokes.)

And that at first is what I planned to do. I began writing what I wanted to say only to help me get it right in my English, which was a little rusty at first, for though I have gone on reading much, I have not written much in English these later years. But as I went on the telling became the tale. And I began to think that you would like to have your grandfather's story written properly, as a document you can keep and perhaps one day give to your own children in their turn, so that they can read from the horse's mouth this part of their history. (Of course to them, it will seem very ancient history!)

So here it is.

And along with it, three things I want to give you.

One is the paratroopers' insignia I took from your grandfather's tattered uniform those first of our days in the cellar and kept for myself when I sent his other belongings to Sarah after the war. A memory of him and of the day I saw the parachutes descending from the bottomless blue sky.

The second is the book of poetry which poor Sam gave me, the only English-language book we had, from which your grandfather and I read to each other every day in our time together.

The third is the keepsake which I said I would tell you about. When Jacob and I declared our love, we wanted to exchange tokens, as people do at such a time. Jacob wanted

278

us to exchange rings. But I would not allow it. However we regarded ourselves, we were not married. Jacob's solution was to make two exactly similar little talismans. He got the idea from an old decoration used on the farms, a kind of magic charm made of wood or straw or perhaps metal which is fixed to the gable ends of barns or the peaks of haystacks to ward off evil and encourage good. Jacob cut ours with his soldier's pocket knife out of a little piece of tin he found in the hay loft. He smoothed the edges with my nail file and polished them with the cream we used to clean the household silver. And when he cut them he made sure there was a little ring at the top so that we could thread the charms on to necklaces and wear them under our clothes.

These *geveltekens*, facade-signs, are in many shapes, each having its own meaning. The design Jacob chose for our love token includes signs meaning it is a broom to brush away thunder, a tree of life, a sun-wheel, and a chalice or cup. 'Let this sign of my love for you and yours for me,' he said in a little ceremony when we exchanged our tokens, 'ward off the thunderous wrath to come for loving me, feed you from the glorious tree of life, ever cause the golden sun to shine upon you, and always fill you to the brim with pleasure in being my beloved Geertrui.' (And by this time, he could almost say my name correctly.)

The charm Jacob gave to me I have given to Daan. The charm I gave to Jacob I now give to you.

So here they are. Your grandfather's war. The words we spoke to each other. And the charm of his love for me. They are more precious to me than I can ever find words to say, whether in your language or my own.

They come to you from
Your Dutch grandmother
Geertrui

POSTCARD
That which hath been is now,
and that which is to be hath already been,
and God requireth that which is past.
The Book of Ecclesiastes

'Has Daan explained you why I wanted to see you today?'
Geertrui said.

Sitting in the same hospital seat as before, feeling just as
awkward and uncomfortable, with Geertrui propped up in
the crisp bed, her startling eyes fixed on the ceiling just as
before, Jacob said, 'No. Nothing.'

Silence. The air would twang if you fingered it.

'I have something to give you.' Geertrui snatched at her
breath. Waited another moment. Turned her eyes on him.
'Then we must say goodbye.'

Jacob's throat was cracked, he couldn't speak.

'The drawer of my cabinet.'

He managed to open it, though his joints were locked
and his muscles fused.

'The package.'

A parcel the size of a laptop wrapped in shiny blood-red
paper tied length-and-width with a sky-blue ribbon.

'Take it.'

He laid it on the bed at Geertrui's side.

'For you.'

He could still say nothing.

'Open it at the apartment. Not before. You promise?'

He nodded.

'All I can say to you is there.'

He stared at the parcel as if it might begin to talk.

Another silence. The air would splinter.

Geertrui said, 'Let us not prolong the pain.'

There was a movement on the bed.

Jacob looked up.

Geertrui was holding out her mouse's hand.

He stood.

Her fingers were so frail he feared he would snap them, so brought his other hand to cup hers between both of his.

'*Vaarwel*,' she said. 'Goodbye.'

He tried to speak but nothing came.

Instead, obeying his instinct, he bent to her, and with deliberate care lest his body betray him, kissed Geertrui on the cheek, one to the right, a second to the left, and a third, most gentle, on her narrow lips.

Her hand fluttered in his.

It fell from him as he straightened.

Unable to look at her, he took the parcel from the bed, held it tightly to his chest, and somehow made his way to the door.

As he reached it he only just heard her say, 'Jacob.'

Her eyes were glazed with tears, and she was smiling.

He looked back at her, wishing to say something.

But all he could do was nod and return her smile.

POSTCARD
xxxxxxxxxxx X xxxxxxxxxxx
xxxxxxxxx X xxxxxxxxxx
xxxxxx X xxxxxxx

'Yes,' Daan said. 'I helped her with it.'

They were sitting in Geertrui's apartment, the usual seats, Daan on the sofa, Jacob in the armchair, his back to the window overlooking the canal. Geertrui's story, 125 A4 pages bound in an orange ring file, lay on the coffee table between them.

'Helped her?'

'Typed it in for her. You'd never have read her writing. And anyway, she was often too ill to write, so she dictated it. She's always studied English, reads it all the time. Watches BBC a lot. So she's good at it. But still, sometimes she needed help. Finding phrases. Looking words up in the dictionary. And there were some passages, well . . . the medication.' He shrugged. 'I was her editor, I guess you could say.'

'But it's all hers? I mean it all really happened?'

'Did you think she made it up?'

'Just seems so amazing. Your grandmother and my grandfather.'

'One part I did write for her. It upset her too much. She couldn't even dictate it.'

'Which?'

'After Jacob died.'

'So you made it up?'

'No no. Geertrui told me what happened in Dutch. I

282

don't know why, but it's always easier to talk about very upsetting things in your own language.'

'So she told you—?'

'Yes. And then I wrote it in English, as much like hers as I could. Then I read it to her. And she changed some things.'

'Like what?'

'Let's see . . . Like the clock. The clock ticking. And stopping it at midnight. She hadn't mentioned it. Only remembered when I read her what I'd written. As if she was seeing it again while she listened. You wouldn't think it possible, but she's still grieving for him after all these years.'

As soon as he got back from seeing Geertrui, Jacob had gone to his room, opened her parcel, examined the contents, and at once read her story all through. Three hours later he surfaced, gasping for air. Unable to sit still, confused in his feelings and not knowing what to think, he needed to talk.

Jacob said, 'She makes a joke about you being my Dutch brother. But your mother really is my aunt. Which makes us first cousins.'

'You mind?'

'No. I like it.'

'Me too.'

Jacob's stomach cramped.

'Oh God!'

'What?'

'Sarah.'

'Yes?'

'She doesn't know.'

'No one knows, except you and me and my parents.'

'But—'

'Forget it.'

'She idolises him.'

283

'*Idolises?*'

'Well, almost. He's everything to her. Her whole life. She even made my parents give me his name, for God's sake! I'm supposed to be him reincarnate.'

'Then you've got trouble.'

'You talk about Geertrui still grieving. Well, Sarah never married again. No other man matched up. She believes she and Grandfather had a perfect marriage.'

'There is no such thing.'

'Sarah thinks there is.'

'Okay. All right. Perhaps she did for—how long were they together?'

'Three years.'

'But then our *grootvader* comes here to slay the German dragon and the first Dutch girl he sees falls for him so hard that she still has the hots for him fifty years later. Some *Mensch* this *mens* must have been, our grandfather, eh? Let's hope we pack his genes.'

'And maybe his genes include a heart attack in our twenties.'

Daan shrugged. 'When you go you go.'

'Don't joke about it.'

'I'm joking?'

'I'm serious.'

'I can see, I can see! You're serious, cousin-brother, you're serious! Lighten up.'

'Don't tell me to lighten up. I hate that phrase, it's so gormless. I don't know what it will do to Sarah when she hears what happened.'

'Hey hey! Wait, wait! You're not going to tell her?'

'But I have to.'

'No no. It would be wrong.'

'Wrong! Wrong not to tell her, you mean.'

'You can't be serious. What good would it do? Would it change anything for the better? No, only for the worse. She's an old woman. Leave her alone.'

'Geertrui was going to tell her. She thought it was the right thing to do.'

'Geertrui is also an old woman. And it's time you learned to say her name properly. She's also a very ill old woman who is going to die soon. Half the time she hardly knows where she is or what she's saying.'

'But when she did know what she was saying, she wanted Sarah to know.'

'Right. But she wanted to tell her herself. Face to face. Yes?'

'Yes.'

'Look, all that is their business. Hers and Sarah's. Old women's business. The business of people who are equals. People from another time. Another age, even. Another generation anyway. Things have changed. It isn't our business. Yours and mine. And it isn't our business to make their old age worse for them than it is. Old age is bad enough even at the best, in my opinion.'

'Well, what about what Geertrui says about lies poisoning the soul? Even just by hiding the truth. D'you want your soul to be poisoned?'

'Souls! Who knows about souls? And she was talking about when the lie is your own, not when it's someone else's. We'd all be poisoned from birth if that were the case. For her the lie is inside her. She has lived it. It's part of her life. So yes, if you want to say so, it could poison her. But for you and me, it's outside. We've only heard about it. For us, it's only information. It can't harm us. Not unless we allow it to.'

'It can. If I worry about it.'

'That's exactly what I mean! So don't let it worry you.'

'I can't help it. I'm a worrier by nature.'

There were loud boy shouts and girl screams from the canal. Jacob got up and went to the window. A gang of tourists, twenty-somethings, in joky hats and rabid holiday clothes were playing silly fools with pedal boats. As he

285

watched their hair-down mayhem a heron flew by at his eye level, following the line of the canal towards the railway station and the river, lazy beat of wings, legs like streamers, long neck doubled up, Concorde beak spearing the air. How lovely it must be, he thought, to see this old new everything-to-everybody city from a bird's-eye three-storey height, as it had been to see it from a fish's-eye boat level yesterday. Which reminded him of Ton. He wondered what Ton would say about Geertrui and Sarah. And what Hille too would say. He wished they were here now. But no, not both together. Too much to handle.

The *domkoppen* had started a race, pedalling like naughty children towards the sex district beyond the next bridge. Crying seagulls circled. In the old days there would have been sailing ships moored outside, their masts taller than the building. A two-engined KLM jet flew over on the approach to Schiphol. He would be flying back to England on Thursday. Two more days.

And suddenly he thought for the first time, surprising himself: I don't want to go back. I want to stay here. There's more for me here than there. And I can be more me here than I can be there.

He turned and glanced at Daan lounging on the sofa.

'Meneer Smartass,' he said.

Daan laughed. '*Ja ja!* But listen to your big brother, my worrier English cousin.'

'You old men, you do like giving advice to us young ones.'

'Hoi yoi! But, you want to be responsible for spoiling the last years of your grandmother's life? Then go ahead, tell her the terrible secret. But no, you won't. Not you. You aren't a spoiler.'

'Is that an insult or a compliment?'

'As you want.'

He sat down again.

'What does Tessel think?'

'She doesn't like any of this. She wishes Geertrui had kept it to herself. It's upset her. She loved her father—I mean Dirk. She's a Wesseling, not a Todd, she says. She knew nothing of Jacob. Dirk brought her up, and did it well. I liked him very much too. She's his daughter, she says, not Jacob's. She tries to put the whole thing out of her mind. But she can't, of course. When Geertrui has gone . . . perhaps then.'

'So she thinks I shouldn't have been told.'

'She thinks it's a mistake. And she wants nothing to do with any of this. She hates that we will talk about it. And now she fears what it might do to you. She didn't want you to come here. But on Sunday, she got to like you. She keeps talking about you.' He smiled. 'I think perhaps she sees in you the son she wishes I was.'

'Don't talk rubbish.'

'As you want.'

Now he did not know what to say. There was too much, and none of it was getting through to the front of his head, where he always felt the words for his thoughts were formed. His stomach was in a tight knot.

After a long silence Daan said, 'I want to make a call,' and went to the phone in the kitchen.

Jacob didn't move. His body still dwelt on his last minutes with Geertrui. While episodes from her story played in his head like scenes in a film. Making it more disturbing, young Geertrui was Hille, her Jacob was himself.

He knew there was danger of a mouse mood if this went on, but did not know how to stop it.

Daan came back.

'We could talk about this all night, it won't take us anywhere. What we both need right now is to take our minds off the subject.'

Daan's energy gave Jacob a jolt. He knew Daan was right.

'Sorry, I'm being a bore.'

'No. It's okay. I understand. We need some food. I've called Ton. He's coming over for a meal. We might go to a movie later. Why don't you play some music or something while I prepare some stuff.'

'I've a better idea. You and Ton have been buying me food and drinks and doing things for me all the time. My turn now. I'll make the meal.'

'You can cook?'

'Don't sound so surprised. You like veal?'

'Does a Dutchman like veal! Come on!'

'Okay, then I need escalopes of veal, prosciutto, the crudo kind, fresh sage, tomatoes, good olive oil, white wine vinegar, garlic, lots of fresh basil. Let's see, what else? Oh yes, stuff for a green salad, pasta, and fresh bread sticks.'

'Italian. Good. Some I have, some we must buy.'

'Not *we*. *I* must buy. And what about ice cream for afters?'

'You'll be in big with Ton. He looooves ice cream.'

'I'm already in big with Ton without the ice cream. Lead the way, MacDuff.'

'*Mijn hele leven zocht ik jou,*' Daan sang with exaggerated *lacrimoso* as they made for the stairs, '*om—eindelijk gevonden —te weten wat eenzaam is.*'

'All right, all right, don't rub it in.'

Spaghetti, the thin capellini kind, dressed with a salsa of chopped tomatoes mixed with lashings of fresh basil, olive oil, a dribble of wine vinegar, crushed garlic, a dash of salt and pepper and a sprinkling of sugar, all returned to the pot when the spaghetti was cooked to make sure everything was hot.

Flushed with the success of his cooking so far and from the wine, which he was drinking too quickly, Jacob felt mischievous.

He said to Ton with mock innocence, 'Daan took me to

288

see the painting of Titus the other day.'

Ton and Daan exchanged grins across the table.

'Daan told me,' Ton said. 'You liked it?'

'Quite nice. A bit brown though.'

'But he's so pretty, don't you think?'

'Daan said Titus looks like me.'

'Didn't you think so too?'

'I wouldn't say I'm pretty.'

'Wouldn't you?'

'Daan also told me that they'd found lipstick on Titus's mouth, like someone had kissed him.'

Daan was chuckling in to his pasta. Ton returned Jacob's innocent stare.

'Yes,' he said, 'I heard that.'

'But they haven't caught the culprit?'

'Haven't they?'

'They have no idea who did it. So Daan says. But, it's odd, I think he knows.'

'Daan!' Ton said. 'You never told me.'

'No no!' Daan said, grinning in to his wine. 'I know nothing about it.'

'What a vandal,' Jacob said. 'Why would anybody do such a thing?'

'It's a mystery, I agree,' Ton said.

'Maybe she—'

'Or he, who knows?' Ton said.

'Or he—Really?'

'Why not?'

'Okay. Well, maybe he or she was mad. Off his noddle. D'you think? I mean, kissing a painting!'

Daan said, 'Catholics kiss crucifixes sometimes. Orthodox people kiss their icons. I've seen people kissing flags—patriots, football fans. And sportsmen kiss trophies they've won.'

'Like at Wimbledon,' Ton said.

'Are they all mad?'

'You mean,' Jacob said, 'that someone admired the painting so much, or something, she—or he—kissed it like it was a holy relic or a trophy or something?'

Ton said, 'Well, it is quite a compliment, don't you agree, for a picture to be kissed? If someone loves it so much, why not? Instead of the poor picture hanging there, night and day on the wall of a museum, so neat and clean and shiny with its new varnish. No one allowed to touch it. People . . . what's the word?—[to Daan] *schuifelend*—you know, like this.'

He got up and demonstrated.

'Shuffling?' Jacob said.

'Shuffling,' Ton said, sitting down again. 'Shuffling by, most of them not giving poor Titus even one quick glance. Not one. The poor boy hanging there, his head down, with his pretty, sad smile, pretending not to mind. Think how lonely he must feel. So someone took pity. Someone showed he—'

'Or she,' Jacob said.

'Ach yes! Or she! Showed he cared.'

'And,' Daan said, aping Ton's tone, 'they dared the risk of being caught. If they had been, imagine the fuss. *Mijn god, het Rijksmuseum!* Hoi yoi yoi! Such courage!'

'There!' Ton said, raising his hands in supplication. 'Not mad at all.'

'I get it,' Jacob said. 'A lover's protest.'

'Could be,' Ton said. 'Against the, how shall we say?— the mausoleumisation—is there such a word?'

'There is now,' Jacob said.

'Okay, a protest against the mausoleumisation of art.'

'I hope he enjoyed himself,' Jacob said.

'Or herself,' Ton said.

'Sure,' Jacob said. 'I forgot. Him or—'

'*And*,' Ton said.

'And?' Jacob said.

Daan couldn't help laughing out loud.

'Him *and* her,' Ton said. 'Could be . . .?'

'Oh, I see what you mean,' Jacob said. 'Two of them did it.'

Ton shrugged.

Daan said, 'Enough, enough! Call the chef. I want my veal.'

Escalopes of veal, each dressed with a leaf or two of fresh sage and a slice of prosciutto crudo skewered on top, gently and briefly fried, taken from the pan while still tender and juicy. Served with a green salad, which Daan had dressed while Jacob looked after the veal. And, of course, more of the wine, an Orvieto Daan had chosen.

'Who taught you to cook like this?' Ton asked, tucking in with relish.

Daan said, 'Let me guess. Your grandmother Sarah.'

'Right,' Jacob said.

'Now how would I know that!' Daan teased.

'Which reminds me,' Jacob said. 'When I was out with Ton yesterday, we had this talk about marriage, and he said I should ask you about your view of love and sex and stuff.'

Daan said something in Dutch to Ton, who laughed and gave an apologetic shrug.

'Come on,' Jacob said, 'spill the beans.'

'Spill the what!' Daan said.

'Beans.'

'Beans? Why beans?'

'I don't know. It's just what we say.'

'*Honger maakt rauwe bonen zoet*,' Ton said.

'Not the same,' Daan said.

'Except the beans.'

Jacob said, 'What did he say?'

Ton said, 'Hunger makes raw beans taste sweet.'

'Well anyway,' Jacob said, 'spilt or sweet, Daan, don't avoid the subject.'

'It's too boring,' Daan said.

291

'Boring!' Jacob said. 'Love and sex *boring!* It might be boring to an old man like you, who's almost past it, but to a young man like me, who's hardly got started yet, it's anything but boring.'

Ton said, 'For Daan marriage is finished.'

'Finished? Didn't know he'd started.'

'Meaningless. For many years now,' Daan said.

'Not where I come from,' Jacob said. 'They're always banging on about it. Politicians and people. The importance of family life. The dreadful divorce rate. Tut tut.'

'And here,' Ton said.

'The last struggles of a drowning man,' Daan said.

'So?' Jacob said.

Daan put his fork down. 'You want the lecture?' He took a drink of wine. 'Okay, here's the lecture. Then it's enough maybe. Yes? Agreed?'

Jacob said, 'Dunno what I'm going to hear yet.'

'No. But it will be enough. Then the ice cream. That's the bargain.'

'What a dictator you are. Thank heaven you're not a politician.'

'Or a husband,' Ton said.

'You want it or not?' Daan said.

'Okay, yes,' Jacob said.

Daan wiped his mouth with his napkin. 'You've heard all the arguments. You'd have to be brain dead not to. Marriage belongs to an out-of-date social system, a different way of life from now. There's nothing *absoluut* about it. It's only a way of controlling the population. It's about property and land rights. [To Ton] *Overerving*—?'

'Inheritance,' Ton said.

'Inheritance. The purity of the . . . shit!—[to Ton] *geslacht?*'

'Let me think . . . [to Jacob] Lineage?'

'Line,' Jacob said. 'The family line.'

'Yes,' Daan said, 'the family line. Only if the woman was

292

pure when the man married her and she became his possession was he sure his children were his. And only if he was the only one who fucked her could he still call her his. Marriage is about the protection of the genes and about ownership. You've heard all this before. Yes? Well, it doesn't matter now. It's of no importance. Except to a few dinosaurs, like royal families and monomaniacal multi-millionaires, and to people with a vested interest, like priests and lawyers and politicians.'

'And not to them any more, to judge by their actions,' Ton said. 'Look at your British royals. What a mess, eh? What a hypocrisy!'

They laughed.

Daan went on, 'As for eternal love, loving the same person for ever, living with the same person for ever. Can you think of anything which is more obviously untrue? It's an illusion.'

'Sarah and Geertrui don't think so,' Jacob said.

'Ha!' Daan mocked. 'And look at them. What are they in love with, our two *grootmoeders*? Not *who*. *What*. You think our English grandfather was so wonderful as they both say? You think he was so perfect? You think he was this big romantic hero Geertrui makes him? No no. Of course not. Come real, *Jakob*.'

'Get real is what you mean. Another gormless phrase.'

'Gormless?' Ton said.

'I dunno,' Jacob said irritably. 'Stupid, naff, silly.'

'Come real, get real, who cares!' Daan said. 'Geertrui's Jacob is an illusion. *Verbeelding*. Fantasy.'

Jacob was rattled. 'I don't believe you. Maybe she sees him through rosy spectacles now, after all these years. Sarah too. But something big happened between them then. Something true. Something existed which wasn't a fantasy. They haven't made it up. You can't deny that.'

'Yes. *Then*. For how long. A few weeks? But if he had lived?'

'That's an if. Nobody can know.'

'Great! Okay! That's how it was. For both of them, a big love. And Jacob a great guy. Well, he must have been. We're his grandsons and we're great guys, yes?'

They laughed.

Daan went on, 'And yes, nobody knows how it would be between them now. That's my point. You're agreeing with me. Nobody knows, because what we know is that it was more likely not to be a big thing between them any longer after all these years. There's no *absoluut*. No for ever. So don't pretend there is. Don't make rules about it. Or laws based on it. If people want to say for ever to each other, okay, let them. It's up to them. But for me, no. Just like there are no rules about love. Who you love. How many people you can love. Like love is some kind of commodity in . . . [to Ton] *eindig?*'

'*Eindig, eindig . . .*'

'Shit! This is so boring to do in English. Why don't you speak Dutch, little brother?'

Ton had got up and gone to the bookshelves. Daan poured more wine. Ton came back, flipping the pages of a Dutch/English dictionary.

'*Eindig,*' he said, reading. 'Finite.'

'Finite?' Daan said. 'Okay, finite . . . What the hell was I saying?'

Jacob said, 'Love is not finite.'

'Right. Yes. Love is not finite. It is not that we each have a limited supply of it that we can only give to one person at a time. Or that we have one kind of love that can only be given to one person in the whole of our lives. It's a ridiculous thing to think so. I love Ton. I sleep with him when we both want it. Or when one of us needs it, even if the other doesn't want it then. I love Simone—'

'Simone?' Jacob said.

'She was here the other morning when you left. She called out to you. She lives two streets away. Ton and

294

Simone know each other. They were friends before I met them. We've talked about it. Ton never sleeps with women. That's the way he is. Simone only sleeps with me. That's the way she is. I sleep with them both. That's the way I am. They both want to sleep with me. That's how we are. That's how we want it. If we didn't, or if any one of us didn't, then, okay, that's it. All the stuff about gender. Male, female, queer, bi, feminist, new man, whatever—it's meaningless. As out of date as marriage for ever. I'm tired of hearing about it. We're beyond that now.'

'You are, maybe,' Jacob said. 'Not all of us, though. Not most of us probably. Not where I come from anyway.'

'No, well, nothing ever changes completely all at once, does it. That's why revolutions always fail. You can't do anything big with people all at once. But that doesn't mean you have to stay with the ones who belong to the old ways. Nothing would ever change if people did that. And me, like I say, I'm tired of discussing it. Let people go on the way they want to in the old way if they can't live up to the new way. But I'm not going to be stopped. I'm not going to be held back. I'm not going to live the kind of lie that keeps the old system going.'

Jacob said, 'I dunno. Doesn't seem to me to be as clear cut as you make out.'

'Yes it is,' Daan said. 'I love who I love. I sleep with who I love if we both want it. Nothing to do with male or female. Nothing is secret. If it ends between us, it ends. That's life. The pain is part of it. Without it, we'd be dead. All that really matters to me is the people I love. How we live together. How we keep each other alive.'

Daan sat back in his seat and rapped the table with his knuckles.

'There,' he said, grinning. 'Over. Finished. Ice cream now. Yes?'

There was silence round the table until Jacob said, 'Just because you say so.'

Daan stood up. 'We agreed. Tonight, enough.'

Jacob didn't move. Ton had watched him closely throughout Daan's diatribe. Now he reached out and gave Jacob's arm a consoling rub.

Jacob said, 'I see what Tessel meant on Sunday.'

Daan said, 'What did she say?'

'Something about hoping I was all right, staying here with you. Something about your way of life, but she didn't explain.'

Daan chuckled. 'She's afraid I'll corrupt you. She's not, let's say, comfortable with the way I live.'

Jacob looked up at Daan with a grin. 'And will you?'

'What?'

'Corrupt me?'

Daan pulled a sour face and, making for the kitchen, said, 'I hate missionaries.'

Three kinds of ice cream: vanilla, lemon, chocolate. And a bowl of cherries to pick from. More wine.

'If you love Ton so much,' Jacob said, refusing to give up, 'and you love Simone so much, and they love you, why don't you all live together?'

Daan went on eating his ice cream and gave Ton a weary look.

'Because we like to have our own places to go to,' Ton said. 'We like to be independent.'

'And so,' Daan said with heavy tolerance, 'when we see each other, it's always fresh. Never gets dull.'

'We're each other's guests every time. If we don't want to meet we don't meet.'

'So we never—how d'you put it?—*vinden die ander vanzelfsprekend.*'

'Granted,' Ton said, 'take each other for granted.'

'Right. We never take each other for granted.'

'We're there for each other. But we only meet when we want to. Except in emergencies.'

'Anyway,' Daan said, 'Ton's place is too small for more than one. This is still Geertrui's. Simone is a loner, she never wants to be with anyone for long. One day, we might change.'

'Why not? We're young.'

'But right now we like it the way it is.'

'Good,' Ton said, 'don't you think?'

'Brilliant,' Jacob said, meaning it, aware that he envied them.

'You should come and join us,' Ton said, laughing.

'Maybe I will,' Jacob said, and felt himself blushing because his tone gave away that he wished it.

One of those sudden silences intruded, an angel walking by, the old folk used to say.

Daan got up and went to the bathroom. Ton finished off the ice cream, his third helping. Jacob brooded.

It was as if what he had heard had started the insides of his body shifting about, not his organs, not his heart and stomach and liver, not his offal, but the parts of his inner self that inhabited his body. It was as if his self were a sort of three-dimensional jigsaw made of pliable bits which could be combined in to a number of different beings, different Jacobs, rather than just one. Now the bits were moving around, shaping a self who startled him. Not because this newly forming self was a stranger. Just the opposite. He had caught glimpses of him more and more often since he was about fifteen. A he that had been the leading actor, Jacob's other self, in day-time imaginings and night-time dreams, playing out inside his head secret wishes and unspoken desires. What was startling was that now this other he was revealing himself completely, like someone stepping out of dark shadow in to bright light.

But as usual, he, the Jacob sitting at the table, couldn't think what it meant. Except that it felt serious. He needed time on his own to work it out. Whatever, it was mixed up with what he had learned from Geertrui's story, and what he had felt, when he left her that day. And there was Ton and there was Hille. He just had not had enough time to take everything in. And he would have to leave for (he had trouble even thinking the word) home on Thursday. If only he had time to sort it out. Here.

Daan came back to the table and poured more wine.

'I've been thinking,' Jacob said, though he was thinking it only as he spoke, 'I'd like to stay on till, well, after Monday . . .' He couldn't bring himself to say 'Geertrui's death'. 'I'd like to be here then. And for the funeral.'

'No,' Daan said.

Before he could stop himself, Jacob said, 'Why not?' He heard the voice of a petulant kid.

'You would not be welcome.'

'Oh, thanks!'

'It's nothing to do with you.'

'Nothing—! After what's happened? How can you say that!'

'It's not allowed. It's all arranged. It's to be private.'

'So I'm the public?'

'We don't want it.'

'We? Who's we?'

'Geertrui. Tessel. Me.'

'How d'you know? Have you asked them?'

'I know.'

'No you don't. I'll ask them myself. I want to be here. I should be here. Geertrui will want me to be here. I've a right—'

Daan stood up. The table shook.

Ton, pushing his chair back, said, 'Daan!' and spoke rapid Dutch.

There was a sharp exchange. Which ended with Daan striding out of the room. His footsteps cascaded down the stairs.

Jacob was sweating and trembling. Too shaken to stand. And too embarrassed by himself to look at Ton.

When the static had settled Ton began clearing the table and preparing to wash up.

Jacob knew he should help, but a heaviness came on him, as if his body had been pumped full of air the weight of stone.

'Come for a walk,' Ton said.

Jacob couldn't move.

'There's a place I want to show you. Not a tourist place. And not far. You could scream and no one would hear you. Or whistle in the wind. You know how to do that, don't you, Jacques? Just put your lips together and blow.'

Which produced a smile. He knew Ton was quoting something, couldn't remember or didn't know what, but it was funny anyway.

He stood, felt queasy, held the table for a moment while he found his balance, then followed Ton out of the room.

It was late dusk and a bright three-quarter moon dodging scattered clouds. A brisk light breeze sharpened the senses.

Ton led Jacob to the railway station, and through the long central concourse under the platforms with its shops and milling crowds, and out on to a road that ran along the river. The little ferry that shuttled people across to the housing estates on the other side was just leaving.

Ton turned left. Past workaday iron-hulled boats, small tugs perhaps, moored at short piers. Beyond, a stretch that looked unused, abandoned, a few unattractive boxy buildings, scrub grass growing through broken concrete.

The road swung away from the railway, following the line of the river. Cars slurred by now and then. The street lights seemed to make the road even gloomier. No one else was walking.

Twenty minutes. The strip of land between road and river bulged. Edged with a high chain-link fence. From which hung a battered sign, *Verboden toegang*, needing no translation. Near the sign a gap had been forced by cutting links and folding back the loose flap of galvanised lace to make a hole big enough to stoop through. In the gloaming it was hard to see anything on the other side except humpy ground and wilderness bushes. Illegal entrance to the garden of Limbo.

Ton did not pause but bent down and shuffled through. A swirl of dust sent up by a passing car scarfed Jacob's face and in to his mouth. Mud's thirsty sister. As he went through the gap his sleeve caught on a ragged end of wire.

Ton took his hand. They made their way across the little wilderness and down an incline, careful where they put their feet. At the bottom, the remains of a wall about a metre wide stretched out in to the river. And, Jacob could see, it was one side of an oblong, forming an enclosure perhaps the size of two tennis courts. There was water inside, like a swimming pool, out of which here and there poked five or six stumps of decayed concrete.

'Where are we?'

'It's called Stenenhoofd. Stonehead.'

'What was it? Some kind of building?'

'A warehouse, I think. In the old days when ships would unload here.'

'It sticks right out in to the river.'

'Dare you go to the end? The wall isn't very wide.'

'I'd like to.'

Jacob stepped on to the catwalk through the water. The river was a metre or two below to his left. The further out from the bank they went, the stronger the breeze, reaching them now in an unhindered blow. He looked down once, almost lost his balance. His feet tingled. Knew then to keep his head and eyes up. Across the broad expanse of dark water were lights in buildings on the other side. They seemed a world away but could not have been more than half a mile.

He stopped on the farthest corner. Ahead, the river

widened so much it might have been the sea. And he on the prow of a ship cutting its way through wind and water.

Ton took his arm in a nervous grasp. 'I'd never have done this on my own!'

'Scared?' Jacob said, not taking his eyes from the expanse.

'A bit. Aren't you?'

Allowing the impulse, Jacob put his arm round Ton's shoulders.

'It's terrific. Like a ship at sea.'

'Thought you'd like it.'

Night now. But the moon lighting them. Its image slipping and sliding on the water.

Ton's arm came round Jacob's waist and held him tight. They snuggled to each other against the brisk air.

'Bracing,' Jacob said.

A small sturdy cabin cruiser ghosted by, its navigation lights marking its passage. A little bit of red port left in the bottom of the bottle.

'Woudn't it be wonderful to have a boat like that?'

'One day we shall. And sail the IJsselmeer. You and me together. Why not?'

'Okay. You're on. What would we call it?'

'Titus,' Ton said without hesitation. 'What about that? A boat called Titus.'

Jacob laughed.

As if a door had been closed, the breeze suddenly fell to nothing. They were becalmed.

'Want to sit?' Ton said.

They released each other and sat with their legs dangling over the river, and were listening to the new silence for a time before Ton said, 'Don't be upset with Daan. There's been a lot of stress over Geertrui. Family arguments. He feels it more than he likes to show. He's suffering a lot. And it's getting harder the nearer the day comes.'

Jacob said with regret, not complaint, 'I only said I'd like to stay on.'

'It was more than that. He's jealous. A bit.'

'Jealous?'

'Of you.'

'Of me! Why of me?'

'He and Geertrui are very close. He's devoted to her. He'd do anything for her, I think. Now you come along. She wrote her memoir for you. Daan spent hours helping with it. She had told him about your grandfather. But she didn't write it down for him like she has for you.'

'So he resents me?'

'Not resents, no. He likes you. Wouldn't have let you stay with him if he didn't. But that makes it worse. He's very competitive. Tries to pretend he's not. But he is.'

'Well, I'm not the competitive kind and I'm not competing with him for anything.'

'He knows that. He would have been with Geertrui tonight, but he decided to stay with you. You knew that, did you?'

'No.'

'He was worried about you.'

'Worried?'

'After reading Geertrui's memoir. He thought it had upset you.'

'It did.'

'He didn't want you to be alone.'

'Did he tell you that?'

'When he called. I said I would look after you, but he wanted to. He asked me to come round because he thought I might help.' Ton nudged Jacob with an elbow. 'He knows I fancy you!'

'So why did he get so angry and stomp out the way he did?'

'Daan has a temper. If he's upset and lets go, he can be violent. I've only seen it once. Very frightening. He doesn't like that about himself. Hates violence. If he feels it coming

on, he goes. Leaves the situation till he's calmed down.
Simone knows how to handle him when he's like that. He'll
have gone to her.'

'So he wasn't really angry with me?'

'Not with you. With himself. Daan is the most generous
person I know.'

Jacob took in a deep breath. There was a faint smell of
engine oil coming off the water that made his nose run.

He sniffed and said, 'You're telling me something, aren't
you?'

Ton hooked his arm through Jacob's and said, 'I want to
see you again. I want to know you. And I want you to know
me. Whatever way you want it to be. There's something
between us. I don't have to tell you that. Be nice to find out
what it is, wouldn't it? But now isn't the time. Daan is
going to need everything Simone and I can give him in the
next few weeks. I've known people who had relatives and
friends who were helped with their deaths. It's very hard.
They suffered afterwards. More than before, sometimes.
Being as close to Geertrui as he is, it's going to be really bad
for Daan. I just know it. He'll be wrecked. I really don't
know how it will be. Come back when it's over and Daan
has had time to recover. If you still want to. It'll be good for
us all then. You'll give us a fresh start.'

Jacob stared at the moonlit river. He was glad the darkness veiled them. And that he wasn't looking in to Ton's
face but at the slip and slide of the water.

After a while Ton said, 'Let's remember. Here. How it
looks tonight. And come and see it again next time . . .
Begin from where we left off . . .' He let go of Jacob's arm
and turned to face him. 'Yes?'

'Yes,' Jacob said with difficulty. He wasn't so sure now
that it was the smell of oil that was making his nose run.
'But . . . There's . . . just so much. I'm not sure I'm—I
dunno—strong enough. Brave enough. Not like you and
Daan.'

Ton gave a little huffing laugh. 'Bravery, it isn't! It's just how we believe life should be. Not for everyone. But for us. And people who think like us. We're learning how to live it while we live it. What else is worth doing?'

'After the last few days, I feel I've just been blindly following my nose till now.'

'Well, it's a nose worth following,' Ton said. Then added, serious again, 'One of the reasons I love Daan so much is that we think things together we never would have thought by ourselves. Or with anyone else. And for us, the sex is part of how it happens.'

'I know,' Jacob said. 'About the thinking, I mean. It was like that for me when he took me to the Rijksmuseum the other day.'

'He's obsessed with Rembrandt. I think he'd like to be the world expert.'

'What about Simone? What does she do?'

'An art student. She's obsessed too.'

'What with?'

'Her art. And with Daan. She has a project going. She's drawing and photographing him in every pose you can think of. All nudes. She plans to do one thousand and eighty pictures.'

'Why that number?'

'A full circle is three hundred and sixty degrees?'

'Yes.'

'But that's for a flat surface. One dimension. Simone says she wants to do Daan in three dimensions, and from every degree. So that makes three hundred and sixty times three, which is one thousand and eighty drawings. And the same number of photos.'

Jacob laughed. 'What an idea! Has anyone ever done such a thing before?'

'Not that I know of.'

'It'll take years.'

'Two, she says. She's into the second year. When they're

finished, she's going to exhibit them, and then she's going to start on twenty-six oil paintings based on the drawings she likes the best.'

'Twenty-six?'

'Because that will be Daan's age by then.'

'That's complete attention, for sure.'

'Geertrui's real love?'

Jacob nodded.

He stood up.

'D'you mind if we go. I'm getting cold.'

Ton took Jacob's hand to keep him steady while he got up. But did not release it when he was on his feet.

'I want us to say goodbye here. Looking at the night-time river. Remembering it and us together.'

'Won't I see you tomorrow?'

'My mother's monthly visit. I must be with her.'

'I see. Okay. Well . . .'

Ton reached up, put his hand round Jacob's head, and kissed him once, lingering, on the lips.

'Goodbye, Jacques. Till here next time.'

Jacob put a hand on Ton's head, just as Ton's held his, and returned the kiss.

'Goodbye, Ton. Till next time.'

Ton hugged him close for a moment before they set off along the catwalk and across the wilderness back to the road.

POSTCARD
One does not always sing
out of happiness.
Pierre Bonnard

Noise from downstairs woke him. Eight thirty, a grey and cloudy Wednesday.

He got up to go to the bathroom and found Daan ready to leave.

'Was going to write a note to you,' Daan said. 'Must be with Geertrui most of today. And Tessel. Business to settle. A lawyer. And doctors. I'll be back this evening. About seven. Will you be okay?'

'I'll be fine.'

'I'm sorry but—'

'I understand. Don't worry. And look, about last night.'

'No need.'

'Wasn't thinking. Too much wine. Anyway, whatever, didn't mean, well, you know—to make things worse. I'm sorry.'

'Nothing to be sorry about.'

'There's something I want to say.'

'Quick. I've only a few minutes before my train.'

'Only, well, I know it's hard for you just now. And I know you've put yourself out to look after me, and all that. And well, I just want to thank you and tell you that these last few days, you and Geertrui and Ton—'

'We'll talk later. Okay?'

'Sure. Right.'

They surveyed each other. Jacob in a white T-shirt and

blue boxer shorts, feeling crumpled and musty from his night's sleep. Daan crisp and clean in fresh black jeans and a blue denim jacket over a white buttoned-up shirt. But his eyes were blood-shot and weary.

'Got to go,' he said and taking Jacob by the shoulders, delivered a three-barrelled kiss, the last on the lips. The rough male kiss of blankets. 'You know where everything is. Help yourself. Your last day. Have a good time.'

Jacob thought to say as Daan went out, 'Tell Geertrui I'm really grateful for her gift, will you? I mean, that's putting it mildly.'

Daan's feet tattooed down the stairs.

'I'll tell her.'

He was finishing breakfast when Tessel arrived. She had come to find something Geertrui needed, she said, and went upstairs to a closed room at the back in to which Jacob hadn't been but which he presumed must be Geertrui's bedroom. She was there only a short time, returning with a small leather bag to the kitchen, where Jacob was washing up the remains of last night's dinner and this morning's breakfast.

'Would you mind,' Tessel said, 'if I had coffee with you? But I mustn't stay long.'

'I'd like that,' Jacob said. 'But you'd better make it. Mine's pretty unreliable.'

While Tessel was preparing the coffee she said, a nervous note in her voice, 'I hope Geertrui's memoir hasn't upset you. Made you unhappy.'

Is this really why she has come? Jacob wondered. 'Not unhappy, no. Not sure what I feel yet. But not that anyway.'

'Daan told you I did not want Geertrui to tell you what happened between her and your grandfather?'

Jacob nodded, not wanting to give Daan away but not able to lie either.

'It's true, I didn't,' Tessel said, pouring hot water on to the coffee. 'Not because I didn't want you to know, but because it seemed to me, after all this time—. What good does it do, knowing such a thing?'

'Don't know if it does any good or not. But I do like knowing Daan is my cousin and you're my aunt.'

Tessel turned and looked squarely at him for the first time since she arrived.

'Yes?' she said. 'I'm happy about that.' She smiled. 'And I have to admit I'm happy to be your aunt.' She turned away and added, while pouring coffee in to cups for them, 'There has not been much happiness in my family these last months.'

She carried their coffee to the front of the room, put the cups on to the table, and sat in the chair facing the window. Jacob followed her, and sat on the sofa. He could not help thinking that in doing so he had taken Daan's place.

'Your last day with us,' Tessel said.

He took a drink of coffee, then said, 'I know it must sound odd when you think what's happened, but I've really enjoyed being here and meeting you and, well—'

'We haven't looked after you as we should.'

'Honestly, it doesn't seem like that to me.'

Tessel looked at him. 'Really it wasn't only you who I was thinking that Geertrui might upset.'

'Sarah?'

Tessel nodded. He thought how much older she appeared today than on Sunday. Her face was drawn and tired. She sipped her coffee and put the cup down again before saying, 'You'll give her the memoir to read?'

'You think I shouldn't?'

'It's yours. You'll do as you wish with it.'

'Daan thinks I shouldn't as well.'

'But you'll find it difficult not to.'

'It isn't just that. I want to do what's right.'

Tessel sniffed. 'Ah yes!' She took another sip. 'It isn't

always so easy to know what's right.'

'Not always so easy to do what's right either.'

He meant it only as an observation, but it came out sounding like a criticism.

Tessel gave him a sharp look. 'You think I'm evading it. Or saying you shouldn't do what's right.'

A little flustered, Jacob said, 'No no. Didn't mean that. Only, I'm not looking forward to telling Sarah, and I'm worried how she'll take it.'

'So not telling her would be a kind of cowardice.'

'Is it?'

'And not to be a coward you'll tell her.'

'Hadn't thought of it like that. Is that what I'll do?'

'Or is it a greater cowardice to tell her?'

'How?'

'Then you have got rid of the burden.'

'What burden?'

'The responsibility.'

'What responsibility?'

'Of knowing something that might hurt someone very much. Someone you love and who has given you a great deal of love and care, a great deal of her life, in fact. The responsibility of knowing and of not telling her, to save her from a deep hurt.'

'You mean, it's harder not to tell than to tell, and might be more good—sorry!—better not to?'

'More good is right. A greater good not to tell than to tell. This is how I think, I must admit.'

Jacob kept quiet for a while, trying to settle the question for himself, but could think of nothing but the awkwardness of the situation. Tessel was making little picking movements with her hands, teasing at the arm of the chair, smoothing her skirt, touching her face, lifting her coffee cup and setting it down without drinking.

At last he said, 'I don't know. I'm still a bit surprised, I suppose. Need to read her memoir again. Hasn't properly

sunk in yet. And I'm always a bit slow, to be honest, thinking out how I feel, what things mean to me.'

Tessel took a deep breath. 'That isn't a fault in my eyes.
Act in haste, repent at leisure. Isn't that one of your sayings?'

Jacob gave her a smile and a grateful nod. 'Something
like that, yes.'

Tessel finished her coffee, and sitting on the edge of her
chair, said, looking at her hands overlapped on her knees, 'I
really came to say goodbye. Tomorrow, I won't be able to
take you to the airport. Daan says you're quite capable of
getting there on you own but—'

'I can. It's no problem. In fact, I'd prefer it.'

'But I still feel one of us should be with you.'

'There is no need. Honestly.'

'Also, I want to say how much I would like you to come
and visit us again. When . . . after—'

'I will. I'd like to. Very much.'

'Daan would like it too.'

'Promise. As soon as I can.'

She tried a light-hearted smile. 'After all, we're your
Dutch family. You're one of us. You belong to us.'

He laughed with genuine pleasure.

'You should come for a long stay. And learn to speak
Dutch.'

'That's what Daan says. He already calls me little
brother, which I hate as much as any little brother would.'

Tessel stood.

'I must go.'

She collected her coat and bags. Then stood by the door
facing Jacob.

'Goodbye,' she said. 'Don't let an anxious aunt confuse
you. When the time comes, you'll know what is the right
thing to do. Do it, whatever anyone says. Now, may your
Dutch aunt kiss you as a Dutch aunt should?'

She leaned to him and touched his cheeks with a three-times kiss he only just felt.

'Give my greetings to Sarah. Please let me know what you do. If you tell her, I should like to write to her about it. Will you do that?'

'Sure.'

'Thank you. Goodbye again. Next time I'll be a proper aunt. We shall have some fun together. There are places in the country, on the polder, I know you'll like to see. The real Holland. Not like Amsterdam.'

'I like Amsterdam a lot. More every day.'

'You do, you young ones.'

He watched Tessel make her way carefully down the stairs, and was glad she had come. There was something in her he recognised in himself. A kind of reserve. An anxiousness about the other person. And an impulse for what Sarah called good manners. Their Jacob-genes or accident, coincidence or inheritance? Did it matter? It was just how they were and he was glad.

Tessel's visit left him restless. He could settle to nothing. Couldn't read. Music irritated him, writing was impossible, might even, he felt, make him spew. Even though he wanted to write to Geertrui, felt he ought to, and say whatever he could while there was still time, now that he knew. But say what? There was too much to say. And too little of it that he could say. What did you say to a woman, to anyone, who was to die by her own decision in five days' time?

In the end, to escape his fidgetiness, he went out. At first he thought of going back to Stonehead, to see what it was like in daylight and because it was out of the way of people. But by the time he had walked to the station he'd thought again and didn't feel like sitting alone on a narrow wall in the middle of a river.

He watched the buskers for a while on the station forecourt. The band of Peruvians or whatever they were. A couple juggling bottles. Every so often he heard above the

311

noise a tram tringaling its bell before setting off on another round of its route. He liked the look of the Amsterdam trams, pencil bodies with bullnose ends, and liked their noises, their bells, hiss of pneumatic doors and brakes, whine and whirr of their engines, metallic grind of their wheels on the rails. They were old-fashioned and sturdy in appearance, yet modern and cheeky in feeling. Like the city they travelled. Why not, he thought, take a ride on one all the way to the end of its route and back again? A tram's-eye-view of a thread of the city.

He wandered over to a display board that showed a map of the city, the tram routes marked in red. He decided on the 25. It ended at a place with names he could say, Martin Luther King Park and President Kennedylaan, on a sharp bend of the river Amstel. Bound to be a café there where you could sit and watch what was happening on the river before coming back.

Off they went, tringaling, out of the station plein, tringaling, across the water, tringaling, on to Damrak lined with its tatty tourist-trap shops and bars—Sex Museum, Torture Museum—past the Beurs van Berlage, which used to be the stock exchange and was now an exhibition and lecture centre, down to de Bijenkorf, the posh department store facing in to Dam square and the royal palace with its grim grey heavy stone walls looking more like a prison than a palace (why didn't they clean it and brighten it up?), people everywhere, tringaling, Madame Tussaud's with a queue, tringaling, on to Rokin, smarter shops on one side—antiques, clothes, restaurants, an optician's where Daan bought his reading specs and said was a beautiful old shop inside run by the same family for generations—on the other side a canal with waiting tourist boats, and at the end of the street, tringaling, round a busy bend in to Vijzelstraat.

At which point he remembered riding this route in the opposite direction last Thursday after Alma had rescued him on his first day in the city and the last day of his previous life. So he would soon pass the café where they talked and the shop where Ton helped him buy the chocolates on Monday, the day (smiling, to himself) he fell in love with the city. For I have, he thought, haven't I? It's just like falling for a person. Not wanting to be parted from it, wanting to know everything about it, liking it as it is, the bad as well as the good, the not so pretty as well as the beautiful, its noises and smells and colours and shapes and oddities. Liking its difference from everywhere else. And its history as well as its present. And its mystery, for there was so much he did not understand. And the people who had begun to show him how to see it, Daan and Ton. And of course, its funniness. He had never thought of a city being funny. But Amsterdam was. He had not realised until this minute that it made him smile just to look at. Never mind what he saw on its streets. That man now, for instance, walking at a fast rate through the crowd, everyone making way for him, a very tall slim well-muscled bronzed black man with endless legs, wearing nothing but a black leather thong and posing pouch, a black leather halter round his shoulders, and a kind of black cap made of strips of leather. And not just walking but parading, showing himself off. An artwork. As beautiful as anything in a museum. A living mobile sculpture.

Keizersgracht was coming up. Prinsengracht next. He knew the order of the canals now and took pleasure in his growing confidence. Prinsengracht, where Alma lived. He had promised he would tell her about his 'adventures' before he left.

Over Prinsengracht to the stop in the middle of the road outside Panini. A promise. And, anyway, why not? On impulse, he got up just in time to slip out before the doors hissed closed. As he crossed to the pavement he saw the flower stall on the bridge. He bought a bunch of red tea roses, in deference to Sarah's instructions about visiting the Dutch, but also as placation for not having phoned to arrange a visit, as Alma had asked. And what if she were out? Leave the flowers tucked into the window grille and tringaling tramborne as previous.

But Alma was in, and greeted him warmly enough for him to feel unashamedly welcome. The guard-grille was opened to him and he climbed through the garlanded window-door, down three steeply raked steps, like the steps to a little ship's cabin, and in to the neat square cave of her living room. With the window-door closed, it was warm and cosy, the light filtering through the foliage soft and tinged with green, a globe standing on a shelf in the corner pooling a yellow glow round the chair where Alma had left a book open on the seat to answer his knock. The room was as unpretentiously elegant as anyone could wish.

Coffee and *kaneel*-flavoured biscuits, the smell reminding him of Hille, were conjured from a kitchen that was somewhere beyond the door through which Jacob could see part of a single bed covered with a daffodil yellow duvet in a room half the size of this one. Alma sat in her chair facing Jacob, who was perched on a squashy black linen sofa set against the street wall, above which was the window that made a pair with the entrance.

He had apologised while coffee was on the way for turning up unexpectedly. The roses had been exclaimed over and vased and set on the round antique dining table, where their blooms shone like a spray of blood against the deep aged chestnut of the table. His leaving next day had been discussed—his time of departure, which train to catch for Schiphol in order to allow enough time to check in, how long the flight would be (an hour and twenty minutes), who would meet him (his mother), and how long to get back home from Bristol airport (an hour's drive).

Then Alma said, 'Now, you visited Anne Frank's house? What did you think?'

Story time again.

'To tell the truth, I'd already been there when we met

the other day.'

'Oh? You didn't say.'

'No. I wasn't exactly in the right mood to start with. I don't mean because of being mugged. Before that. You see, I'd just got here, to Daan's parents, the day before. I think I told you that. And his mother, Tessel, who's very nice actually, I like her a lot, but then, well, she told me there was family trouble, she didn't say what, only that her mother, Geertrui, needed a lot of attention, and, well, anyway, I didn't feel too welcome, just the opposite.'

'You didn't mention any of this last week.'

'No. I'd been sent to Amsterdam for the day just for something to do and to get me out of the way, or at least that's how it felt. So I wasn't in a good mood.'

'I can understand why you wouldn't be.'

'And I'm never too happy on my own in a strange place. I'm not a city person at all, in fact. Except, I've really got to like Amsterdam. But that's another story. So here I was, in a bad mood, and went to Anne Frank's house because it was the only place I knew about and wanted to go to.'

'Because of the diary of course.'

'There was a queue.'

'As usual.'

'Quite a long one, which didn't help my bad mood one bit. I'm not very patient when it comes to queues. But I joined it and it seemed like waiting to see the two-headed man or the bearded lady at a fun fair. And when I got inside, people ahead of me, people behind me, all of us tramping up the stairs in to the rooms. In to her rooms. Which were crowded with people already, everyone kind of gawping and shuffling along. They weren't behaving badly. Just the opposite. Quite reverential really, quite silent, not talking, just whispering, and pointing and peering. I don't know. It just came over me that we were invading Anne's privacy. Treading all over her. But apart from that, the really stupid thing . . .'

315

'Yes?'

'Seems ridiculous. But, seeing all those people, and most of them about my age, all of us like pilgrims visiting a shrine, well, suddenly Anne wasn't mine any more.'

'Not yours?'

'No. Here were these other people who wanted to be where she had lived. Where she had written her diary. And I said to myself, "They think she's theirs too".'

'But, Jacob, you must have known how famous she is.'

'Of course I did. But that was different. I mean, there's knowing and *knowing*, isn't there. I knew it in my head, like a statistic, like a *fact*. But I didn't *know* it inside me. She was famous—*so*? So what? I read the diary all the time. Highlighted passages, like I told you. I don't think I'd ever thought about it. It was as if she were my best friend and I just, I don't know, assumed, believed, took it for granted, that Anne had written her diary for me. Only for me.'

'Then you saw those people in the secret annexe—'

'Especially in the room where she slept. You know how small it is and how the pictures she stuck up on the wall, the postcards and clippings from magazines—'

'I know.'

'—are still on the wall. No furniture. Stupid again, I suppose, but I'd expected to see the rooms just like they were when she was there. But they aren't. Nothing there. Just empty. Except for the model in a case, like a doll's house, showing how they used to be. That upset me a lot. I mean, I realised afterwards that the rooms couldn't be the same. I knew the Germans cleared everything out after the arrests. But it hadn't kind of seeped in to my mind what that meant. Except for the pictures Anne had stuck on the wall by her bed. That's what did it, I think. When I saw them, it was like she was still there. Or not her, but her ghost. And I started to go to pieces. All those times I'd read the diary. Everything it meant to me. Especially those parts I'd marked because they were so important. Anne talking to me. Saying what was in my head. Speaking my own thoughts and feelings. And then, these bare rooms, and all these people coming between me and Anne. And they thinking about her just like I was thinking about her. And why not? That's what she wanted. She wanted to be a famous writer, that's all she wanted, and that's what she was. What she is.'

'So you ran out?'

'No. Not straightaway. I tried to keep a grip on myself. I knew I'd been ridiculous to think the way I did. I knew I should be happy, should be pleased. Happy that so many people loved her the way I did. I managed to work my way in to the corner by the window and stand right up against the wall, trying to recover. I was shaking like a leaf and sweating cold sweat. I remember there was a man standing next to me, looking out of the window. He was English, middle-aged, a bit like my dad. There was a woman with him, he called her Joke, so I guess she was Dutch. While I was standing there, trying to pull myself together, I heard him say, "You see those houses across the garden?" And the woman said, "They are on Keizersgracht." And he said, "Did you know that Descartes lived in one of them?" "I think, therefore I am," the woman said. And the man said, "I think, therefore I am. I am, therefore I am observed." And then they laughed, and she kissed him.'

He looked at Alma.

'I think, therefore I am,' she repeated. 'And then?'

'I am, therefore I am observed.'

'Never heard that before,' she said.

'Nor me,' Jacob said.

'Not Descartes.'

'And don't you think it's strange that I remember it, every word?'

'Perhaps. And when you'd pulled yourself together, what did you do?'

'Followed the crowd. And you know how you go down

from the hiding place in to the museum part.'

'Where her story is told in pictures.'

'And where there's the glass cases with things in them belonging to Anne.'

'The real diary.'

'Yes, the diary itself. Well, I saw the diary and I could hardly bear it any more. The pictures in her room were bad enough. But they weren't her. Not Anne herself. But the diary—! When you come to think of it, that's what she was. That's what she *is*! Her diary is Anne. The book she wrote. Her handwriting. Her words that she wrote with her pen. I looked at it and looked at it. Couldn't take my eyes off it. I wanted to smash the glass so I could pick it up. I wanted to hold it. Wanted to smell it. Wanted to kiss it. Wanted to steal it! I really did! And people were jostling around me and trying to get as close as they could. Just like I was. I wanted to shout at them, "Go away! Leave her alone! You've no right here! Get out!" But I didn't, of course. Just got out myself. Don't remember doing that. Not at all. Next thing I remember is coming to when a tram nearly knocked me down. That was when I reached Leidsestraat, though I didn't know what street it was at the time. And ended up in the plein where I got mugged.'

'And then I found you,' Alma said, breathing out a sigh as people do at the end of a story. 'No wonder you were so upset. Perhaps more from your visit to Anne's house than from being mugged.'

'That's right.'

'The thief only took your money. What you lost at Anne's house was something much more precious.'

'I know. That's what I feel. But I still don't understand what it was, even though I've thought a lot about it.'

'Perhaps you lost some of your childhood innocence. Every time we learn an important lesson about life we suffer a sense of loss. That's my experience. We gain. But there's a cost.'

As Alma was speaking, Jacob knew quite clearly why he had come to see her. Without introduction or permission, he told her about Geertrui's memoir. Said how worried he was about how Sarah would take the news. Did not say that Daan and Ton and Tessel all thought he should keep it to himself. And ended without a pause by asking what Alma thought he should do. Tell Sarah or not?

She was silent. He could feel the weight of the question hanging in the air above their heads.

At last, when he was beginning to think he had asked something so offensive to her that she was not going to reply, Alma said, 'Are you sure your grandmother does not already know what happened?'

Her question took his breath away. The possibility had never occurred to him, not even for a hint of a second.

'She'd have told me,' he said when he could.

'And what makes you so sure of that?'

'We talk about everything. Wouldn't she?'

'You talk about everything. She sent you to see your grandfather's grave?'

'Yes.'

'Why not until now?'

'She said I was old enough to understand.'

'Understand what?'

'How he died, I suppose.'

'And how did he die?'

'Well, there was his wound. But from a heart attack, I think.'

'Yes, a heart attack. So she sent you to see his grave. Or did she really send you to Geertrui?'

'Geertrui invited Sarah, but she couldn't come.'

'You saw the letter?'

'No.'

'Then how do you know what Geertrui said?'

'I don't. It's just what Sarah told me.'

There was a silence before Alma spoke again.

'Why is it that young people so often think that old people cannot deal with life as well as they? Or that they cannot bear the truth any longer?'

Jacob regarded her for a moment, trying to assess what he was being told, what she was really saying. But her eyes were steady and her face gave nothing away.

'You mean, if Sarah doesn't know, she'll be able to take it?'

'I don't know your grandmother. It's for you to decide.'

'And if she knows, she'll be waiting to hear what I say.'

'Quite a dilemma,' Alma said, smiling.

She got up with a push on her knees like old people with arthritis do, and took the coffee cups to the kitchen.

When she came back she said in her cheery sociable voice, 'Your flowers are lovely.'

Time to leave. Jacob got up.

'I'd better go.'

'You'll come to Amsterdam again?'

'Yes. I'll be coming back, I'm sure.'

'I thought so. I hope you'll visit me and tell me what you decided.'

'Yes. Promise.'

Alma held out her hand. He shook it and gave her three of the most restrained and polite of up-cheek kisses.

'You're learning our ways very quickly,' Alma said, laughing.

Jacob.

Daan told me you asked to be here at my end.

I must say no.

It will be difficult, most for Tessel and Daan. They must live afterwards. They must not have anyone else to think of.

I have planned.

Only Tessel and Daan with me. The doctor also.

But you will think of me.

It will be noon, Monday.

Tessel and Daan will be here all the time from Friday.

We say our final goodbyes.

The doctor gives me an injection. When I sleep, he will give the injection to end my life.

There will be no pain. It will be the end of the most terrible pain.

From the time of our goodbyes until the end they will read words I love. One poem will be in English.

There will be no fuss.

After the funeral my body will be cremated.

Tessel and Daan spread my ashes in the Hartenstein Park at Oosterbeek.

Dirk's ashes are there. Where we grew up and spent the days of our childhood with Henk.

The grave of your grandfather is not far away.

It is beautiful.

Our family can come there to remember us.

I hope you will also.

May your life be blessed.

Liefs,

Geertrui.

'Hille?'

'Jacob.'

'Okay?'

'Okay. You?'

'Need to see you.'

'But you leave tomorrow, yes?'

'In the afternoon.'

'I was going to write.'

'You got my letter?'

'Yes.'

'I need your help.'

'Help?'

'Some stuff I've found out. And I need to see you.'

'There's chaos here. The move and everything.'

'I really need to see you.'

'But when?'

'Tomorrow. I'll come to Oosterbeek and go on to Schiphol from there.'

'I'm in school.'

'Just the morning.'

'I'm looking at what we've got.'

'You'd be back for the afternoon.'

'Maybe I could.'

'It's important.'

'Okay. But I'll come to you.'

'Okay. When?'

'About ten. Something like that.'

'I'll wait in the apartment. You know where it is?'

'Yes.'

'Thanks. See you then.'

'*Tot ziens.*'

The gift of pleasure
is the first mystery.
John Berger

'You wondered about my grandfather,' Jacob said. 'Now you know.'

Hille laid Geertrui's story on the coffee table between them.

'Glad I'm alive now and not then,' she said.

'But what d'you think? About my grandfather and her, I mean.'

'Things like that happened a lot. Especially at the end of the war. This year, we even had a day for it.'

'For what?'

'For people who were children of soldiers who helped liberate us. It was called Reconciliation Day. Some people, many people, who had children by soldiers and kept it secret, told their children for the first time.'

'In public?'

'Yes, if they wanted to. And the people who had always known helped them.'

'Amazing.'

'Why? I thought it was good. I liked it.'

'Can't imagine a day like that happening in England.'

'You didn't need it. You were never occupied and so you were never liberated.'

'Wouldn't happen even if we had been.'

'Maybe it is a bit Dutch.'

'Finding out my grandfather had a Dutch lover and a

323

Dutch daughter and grandson was bad enough. God knows what it must be like to find out your father wasn't who you always thought he was, and that your mother let you believe a lie all your life.'

'Some people went in pieces. Others took it very well. Some didn't seem to mind. It's always like that, don't you think? You never know how people will behave when they hear big news. You never really know how you will yourself till it happens. I don't anyway. Like I told you about when my grandmother died. Before, I wouldn't have thought I would feel guilty. I mean, why should I? I'd done nothing wrong to her, she was an old person and ill. Sick old people die. It's natural. It wasn't my fault she was sick and old. But I still felt guilty.'

'That's odd, because—one of the things I want to talk to you about. Since yesterday, when I had time to think about it, I've been feeling guilty. About Grandad.'

'Why? Because he and Geertrui were lovers?'

'Not that so much.'

'Because Geertrui had a child?'

'I can understand how it happened. Why it happened. The way things were for them. I might have been the same, probably.'

'Then why?'

'Because I know about it.'

'But it happened a long time ago. And it's not awful for you, is it? That you've got yourself a nice Dutch family.'

'No, that's all right. I like it.'

'What then?'

'I'm not so sure my grandmother will be that pleased.'

Hille slapped her thigh. 'She doesn't know! *Domkop*! I was only thinking of you.'

'Thanks. But that's why I feel guilty. Because I know and she doesn't. Almost as if I were my grandfather and she were my wife. Stupid, eh?'

The anxiety made him restless. He stood up, wondering

as he did why he always chose to sit in this chair, and went to the window. A family of coots was paddling along the canal, that spring's young ones looking quite grown up. No one in view in the hotel except a chambermaid making a bed. The grimy church windows blank and blind and wire-netted as always.

He heard Hille get out of the sofa, her shoes clicking on the tiles as she came up behind him and put her arms round his waist. He could feel through his shirt the squash of her breasts against his back, and the hardness of her hips against his buttocks.

'Will she be very upset?'

Her breath tickled the nape of his neck. He waited a moment before replying.

'You think I should tell her?'

Now she waited.

'Won't you?'

'Daan says I shouldn't. Tessel as well.' He didn't mention Ton or Alma, so as not to complicate it, and because he wanted to hear what she decided if she thought everyone else said no.

There was a longer pause before she spoke again. He didn't mind. He liked her hugging him this way. It was comforting as well as sexy. Kept very still, wanting it to go on.

'Like I said just now. You never know how people will behave. Especially with bad news.'

'I was hoping you'd help me decide.'

She stood back. He turned to face her. She took his hands, holding them between hers. Before she spoke she pursed her lips and scowled.

'If I were you, I would tell her. But I'm not you, and I don't know your grandmother.'

He gave a rueful smile and said, 'In other words, it's your problem, Jacob.'

She smiled and nodded. 'Don't mean it like you say it.

But it is, isn't it, you have to agree.'

He let out a long breath.

'I learned to read for myself when I was six. To congratulate me, my grandmother—Sarah—sent me a picture postcard. The picture was of a rabbit reading a book. On the back she wrote, "Well done! Now you can find out all the secrets of the world." When I saw her next time, she asked if I liked it. I said, "I like it so much, Gran, I wish I had a postcard every week." And since then she's sent me a picture postcard every week. Never misses. Doesn't matter if she's ill. Or away on holiday. Whatever. Every week she sends me a card. Even though I live with her now, she still sends them. By post. When there's no post, like when there was a postal strike once, she puts that week's card through the letterbox herself. The picture is always something she wants me to know, like a famous painting or a building or a person or a landscape. Anything. And on the back, if there's nothing she wants to write, she copies out a quotation from something she's reading, or she's heard on television, or she sticks on a clipping out of a paper or a magazine. Not always serious. Jokes sometimes, cartoons. I've kept them all from the very first. There are seven hundred and eleven so far.'

Hille studied him for a while. Then let go of his hands and went back to the sofa.

'That's one serious grandmother,' she said as she sat down.

Jacob followed and sat beside her.

'And my grandfather was the love of her life. She never married again. Now I've got to tell her this man she thinks is so wonderful and who she's still in love with—. It could kill her.'

'So don't tell her.'

'Then I'll feel bad about it for the rest of my life. I just know I will. Besides, she always tells me I wear my feelings on my face.'

'She's right. You do.'

'Thanks a lot! That really gives me confidence. So, she'll want to know about what happened while I was here. I've always told her everything. Never hid anything from her. She's bound to know I'm hiding something.'

'Then you've got a problem.'

'Sure. I've got a problem! Thanks for telling me what I know.'

Again the rising anxiety made him fidgety.

'I need to go to the bathroom,' he said. 'All that coffee while you were reading Geertrui's story.'

When he came back Hille was looking at the wall of books. The view of her back affected him as strongly as her front, the fall of her shoulders, the curve of her bum in her jeans, the proportion of her body on her legs. He looked at his watch. The morning was almost gone. He came up behind her and put his arms round her waist, just as she had to him a few minutes before.

'You'll not make it back for school this afternoon,' he said, 'if you don't go pretty soon.'

'Too late already.'

'You're not going?' He tried to keep the excitement out of his voice but didn't succeed. She'd feel it in his body anyway.

'About telling people difficult news.'

'Let's forget it. Just enjoy ourselves till I have to go.'

'When?'

'From here, about four.'

'There's something I want to say to you. Come and sit down.'

She unhooked herself from his arms and went to the sofa. Something in her manner told him to sit in one of the chairs. He deliberately chose the one he never sat in, facing the window.

Hille was leaning forward, elbows on knees, a fist held to

her mouth.

'About the position of kissing boyfriend.'

'Ah!' He could see the blow coming. 'You've given it to someone else.'

'No.'

'What, then?'

'There was a qualification I forgot.'

'Which is?'

'He must live close enough to do the kissing.'

'And I don't.'

'No.'

'So I don't get the job?'

'I can't be a girlfriend of an absent boyfriend. I wouldn't be able to keep it up.'

He said nothing.

'You understand?'

'Sure. You don't need to explain. Is that what you were going to write to me about?'

'Yes. And to say I'd like to be friends. If you want to.'

'I want to. But everything else? If we lived near to each other?'

'You'd get the job.'

'I would?'

'You would.'

'Can I have a kiss to prove it.'

She laughed. 'Good idea.'

'Look,' he said. 'Let's go somewhere. See some of the town together. Are you hungry?'

'I'm hungry.'

'Like a pancake?'

'If you say it in Dutch.'

'*Zal . . . het zijn . . . er . . . lijken . . . een pannenkoek?*'

Which gave her the giggles.

'Glad I'm good for a laugh, anyway.'

'Sorry! You did try. I know a good place near the Anne

Frank house. Even has an English name, The Pancake Bakery, so at least you'll be able to say it.'

'But won't give you such a good laugh.'

'I'll take the risk.'

'Before we go, I'll get my stuff together, then I'll be ready to leave.'

He picked up Geertrui's story.

Hille said, 'Can I see the things she gave you? The book and necklet your grandfather gave her.'

'Okay. Come up. You can look at them while I pack.'

She followed him to his room. The gatherings from his trip were in the Bijenkorf bag. He took out his grandfather's badge, Sam's book and the pendant, and laid them on the bed. Hille sat beside them and at once picked up the pendant, smoothing it between her fingers in a way so sensuous that it unsettled him.

He turned away and began packing his spare clothes in his carryall. Went down to the bathroom to collect his toilet gear. When he got back Hille was flicking through Sam's book.

He finished packing, all but his bag of gatherings, and went to the bed to get it.

'What else have you got?' Hille said. 'Can I see?'

'If you want.'

He tipped out the rest of the contents. Hille sorted through them.

'What's this? *Teach Yourself Dutch in Three Months*.' She laughed.

'Daan gave it to me last night. His going-away present. More of a come-back-soon present he said.'

'And will you?'

'You bet.'

'Learn Dutch in three months I meant.'

'Going to have a bash, yes. Seriously, I've been thinking. There's nothing to stop me studying here, is there? At university, I mean. Daan says a lot of their lectures are in

329

English. They have to be so as to attract foreign students. And he says I can stay here with him. So accommodation would be no problem. My home-from-home, he says.'

'Told you it was good to have a nice Dutch family.'

She put the book down and pushed away the used roll of film Jacob had taken in the Oosterbeek cemetery, and the Order of Service, to uncover the postcards of Titus and Rembrandt.

'Why these?'

'Daan thinks I look like Titus.'

She held the one of Titus against Jacob's face.

'A bit maybe.'

'You need to see the painting.'

'D'you like Rembrandt?'

'Quite a lot, yes.'

'I think Vermeer is better.'

'Is he?'

'Well, he's not better. Silly to say. But he's my favourite of the old painters. Maybe we should go and look at him now.'

'If you like.'

Then Alma's Panini napkin.

'What's this?'

He explained.

'But why did she write such a message?'

'Well, before I was mugged, this guy came and sat next to me and we got talking. It turned out he was a friend of Daan's but I didn't know it then of course. Anyway, he said if I'd like to meet him again he'd give me his phone number, and he wrote it in this.'

He picked up Ton's book of matches.

'But he didn't just write his number, he wrote a message as well. Which I showed to Alma so she could translate it, and she thought it was funny, so when we said goodbye, she gave me this napkin with the Dutch saying she'd written on it.'

Hille took the book of matches from him and flipped it open. When she had taken in what it was, and laughed, she said, 'So he's gay.'

'Yes, he's gay.'

'And he fancies you'

'And yes he fancies me.'

She dangled the open book in front of him between finger and thumb. 'But you haven't used it.'

He shook his head, smiling.

'Don't you think you should?'

'Really?'

'Don't want to take it home, do you?'

'But who with?'

'What about me?'

'If this is another test for a kissing boyfriend—'

'That's right.'

'Not sure I'll pass with high marks.'

'Let's find out.'

'Not too good at it. Might disappoint you. Haven't had enough experience.'

As she started undoing the belt of his jeans she said, 'You can learn on the job.'

'Why are you doing this?'

'Because you want it.'

'What about you?'

'I want it also.'

'Not sure we have enough time. Wouldn't want to miss my flight.'

Hille chuckled, and with wicked mimicry said, 'Put yourself in my hands. Relax. Enjoy yourself. Trust me to get you to the plane on time.'

ACKNOWLEDGEMENTS

The author and publisher gratefully acknowledge use of extracts from the following books:

Anne Frank, *The Diary of Anne Frank*, translated by B.M. Mooyaart-Doubleday, copyright 1947 by Otto Frank and 1982 by Anne Frank-Fonds, Basel, Switzerland, the edition used here published in England by Pan Books, 1954. Anne Frank, *The Diary of a Young Girl*, The Definitive Edition, edited by Otto H. Frank and Mirjam Pressler, translated by Susan Massotty, copyright 1991 by The Anne Frank-Fonds, Basel, Switzerland. English translation, copyright 1995 Doubtleday, New York.

Martin Middlebrook, *Arnhem 1944: The Airborne Battle, 17 - 26 September*, copyright 1994 by Martin Middlebrook, published by Viking, 1994.

Geoffrey Powell, *Men at Arnhem*, copyright 'Tom Angus' 1976, Geoffrey Powell 1986, first published by Leo Cooper Ltd, 1976, the edition used here being the revised edition published by Buchan and Enright Ltd, 1986.

James Sims, *Arnhem Spearhead: A Private Soldier's Story*, copyright James Sims 1978, first published by Imperial War Museum; the edition used, Arrow Books Ltd, 1989.

Hendrika van der Vlist, *Oosterbeek 1944*, translated by the author, copyright and published by the Society of Friends of the Airborne Museum, Oosterbeek, 1992.

Bram Vermeulen, 'Mijn hele leven zocht ik jou', from *Drie stenen op elkaar*, p 70, copyright Bram Vermeulen, published by Hadewijch, Antwerp, 1992.

References in square brackets at the end of quotations refer to pages in the books listed above. Every effort has been made to contact copyright holders. Any omissions are regretted and will be corrected in future editions.

The author thanks many Dutch and Flemish friends and colleagues for help and information during the writing of this novel.

Postcards from No Man's Land is a book that was saved by readers. If writing a short story is like sprinting the hundred metres, writing a long novel is like running the marathon. You have to train up for it, and during the race you have to pace yourself carefully or you'll be out of puff before you're half way there. It's easy to get it wrong and lose confidence. That's what happened in the middle of writing *Postcards*. I got it wrong and lost confidence so completely that I packed the half-written book away and gave up.

A few weeks later, while I was visiting Sweden, I met a group of fifteen-year-old girls who were keen readers of my other books. They asked me what I was writing next. I said I had given up. They were appalled, made me tell them about the unfinished novel, and argued and cajoled until I promised I'd try again. Every so often, for months afterwards, one of them sent me a postcard, asking, How long is our book now? When will it be finished? Books need readers, or there is no point in publishing them; and writers need readers too, sometimes, to keep them going.

Postcards is the fifth novel in a sequence of six. Each tells a love story of one kind or another. One of the stories in *Postcards* is about love of a place, in this case Amsterdam. Another is about the love you can feel for a character in a book – Anne Frank, who was a real person, of course, but you can only know her by reading her book, in which she is the main character. So Jacob is a fictional character who loves a real person, who he only knows because she is like a fictional character in a novel. Which is an example of the way *Postcards* weaves everyday reality with fiction, actual people and events with invented characters and events. Both are 'true' in their own way.

Because the others in the sequence are linked in various ways (which I describe in the Afterword to the last in the sequence, *This Is All*) I knew by the time I came to write it that *Postcards* had to be set in a city in a foreign land, where there had been a battle during the Second World War. None of the other novels had dealt with modern life in a city, the displacement you feel in a strange land where you do not speak the language, the horror of war, and the influence of history on our lives. Amsterdam and the

Netherlands provided all these.

Jacob's story is rather like the traditional folktale about the innocent abroad. An inexperienced young man goes off to a foreign land to seek a treasure. During his journey he meets strangers, some good, some bad, some who help and some who hinder, and all of whom give him something or take something from him, offer advice, and tell stories about themselves that are also stories about him. By the time his journey is over, he has learned many things about himself and about life. He may or may not have found the treasure he was seeking, but he has found treasure of the intangible kind that helps you to grow and become more consciously aware of life and more truly yourself, rather than the person other people want you to be. 'Every time we learn something,' wrote the playwright George Bernard Shaw, 'we suffer a sense of loss.' What Jacob has lost because of what he has learned is his innocence. But he is wiser for it.

Postcards is the only one of the five novels in which the main character's story is told only in the third person. The others are either all in the first person or mix first and third. The third person helps to keep the main character distanced from the reader, who observes him/her and what happens, rather than living it with him/her, as you do when a story is in the first person. But of course, there is Geertrui's contrasting story, a novel within the novel, told in the first person, which brings us closer to her than we are to Jacob. We live intimately with Geertrui, whereas we only travel alongside Jacob as a witnessing companion. And I suppose that's why so many readers have told me how much more moved they are by Geertrui's story than they are by Jacob's. They say they *think* about Jacob but they *feel* with Geertrui. And that was my intention. I chose to write the novel in this way, interleaving Jacob and Geertrui's stories, so that you enjoy their different textures, their different flavours, and your different relations with them, turn and turn about, one playing off against the other.

And I wonder if that is why *Postcards* has brought me more awards and prizes than any of the other novels, as well as a great many appreciative letters and emails. Or is it because it is the most conventionally told, the least demanding, and the easiest to read of all six books? Whatever the reasons, I'm pleased it is so much admired and enjoyed.